ALSO BY TAMARA JERÉE

A Wolf Steps in Blood

THE FALL THAT SAVED US

Tamara Jerée

WATER SIGN BOOKS

Published by Water Sign Books
Chicago, Illinois

ISBN 979-8-9878847-2-0 (ebook)
ISBN 979-8-9878847-1-3 (paperback)
ISBN 979-8-9878847-0-6 (hardcover)

Library of Congress Control Number: 2023909320

Edited by Maggie Morris, The Indie Editor
Illustration by Syd Mills
Cover design by Fay Lane

AUTHOR'S NOTE

While Cassiel's story is focused on healing, heavier themes of trauma and shame are explored to give context to the protagonist's journey. Please consider the major content notes: cutting scars, brief self-harm ideation, discussion of an eating disorder, family emotional abuse, and an abusive mother. This book contains sexual content and is only intended for adult readers.

ONE

I TRY NOT TO speak to the angels, but sometimes, I still hear their songs—when my mind is empty in the white noise of the shower, when I clumsily bloody my hands with the kitchen knife, when I stir sugar into my tea. These incidental joys and pains and nothings are the only times in my new life when I've been able to cry, compelled to do so as if by divine command. Their words course through me like molten gold, precious and searing. The world flashes white, then settles anew, unchanged but briefly brighter. Here's the proof that they still turn their eyes to me. I wonder whether they see a wayward child.

The first time I heard their voices, I'd regained consciousness on the cold cellar floor of my childhood home, my face tear damp. It's not so incapacitating as that anymore, but neither familiarity nor my angelic inheritance can fully diminish an encounter with the divine. I'm still human despite what my mother would like to believe about us.

Their songs are louder today, more frequent, as if the angels, too, have been keeping count.

Today marks the third anniversary of my leaving. I don't know what the angel song means on this day, whether the chorus is passing judgment or merely observing with me. They sang the night I left, bright and clear. I took it as a sign.

Three years ago, at midnight, when my sister Zuriel caught me descending the stairs of our family estate, I begged her one more time to come with me out into the world. It'd been our secret for months that I planned to leave, to live in

"

the city among regular people. I'd needed to tell someone, and she was the only one I could tell. My truth turned our relationship tense. We tried to be each other's shelter as we always had, but it couldn't last when I was trying at every turn to convince her to leave while she tried to convince me to stay.

"We can survive this if we have each other," she'd say to me—when she braided my hair, when we traced protective sigils into each other's skin. We sparred harder at the end as if winning meant the loser would have no choice but to adopt our perspective. I knew that as long as she would fight with me, she would fight for me.

But on those stairs, she'd stared too long at our clasped hands, and I doubted her. I couldn't breathe. Two stairs separated us, she above, framed by the darkened stained-glass window on the landing. I, below, looking up. A terrible look crossed her face, as if this final meeting was a test of her devotion.

I'd wanted her to say something about us. Instead, she invoked duty and legacy.

"Don't be like Gabriel," I said.

We rarely called her *mother*. To us, she has always been Gabriel. For some, she's a beacon.

Our records of all the angels and their nephilim are inconsistent, but the one most thoroughly documented through history is Gabriel. For the generation before my mother's, there was no Gabriel born, no nephilim namesake of the great archangel. The reappearance seemed a sign for some. Other archangels, too, had claimed nephilim in our family. We'd clearly been blessed. When I was young, pilgrimages to our home were common—and also how our mother spread her philosophy of denial and restraint as the way. She was a beacon, and I should've been grateful to be her daughter. Our Aunt Raphael might've become a black sheep, but in Gabriel's eyes, my siblings could make up for her lack. Because of their namesakes, Michael and Zuriel were burdened with more expectations, but Zuriel internalized the pressure the most. And suffered from it the most.

My sister gave me a tight smile. "You'll come back," she said, withdrawing her hand from mine to weave a familiar blessing in the air. For good fortune and protection, the one we drew before a hunt we knew would be especially dangerous. She pushed its energy toward me, and it settled into my skin with a light shimmer.

I wanted to tell her she had it wrong. I wasn't the one entering a dangerous world. It was a wasted blessing, and we didn't waste blessings.

I wanted her to say she'd miss me. I wanted an affirmation that we'd made this life less terrible for each other.

She retreated silently up the stairs, and I fought to breathe in her absence. Alone on the dark stairs, my bag cutting an ache into my shoulder, I considered scrambling after her, making one last bid for us. Together. As we'd always been.

But that had never been the way our family handled emotion. Big displays were anathema to us. For the last time, I followed her stoic lead, this time away from her.

⚔

I flip the bookstore's sign to Closed. The angel song fades like a rapid sunset. I'm colder and empty without it. I try a breath, another. I blink, and tears track down my face.

Turning the signet ring around my little finger relieves some of the pressure in my chest. The crossed feather and sword of my family crest is a familiar shape under my thumb. Recently, it's become a worry stone. I slip it off, tracing the angelic runes inscribed on the inside of the band. My namesake angel. Cassiel. Their name—our name—always against my skin. It hums with power, my connection to them just as strong as it was before I left my calling behind. I'd wanted to abandon everything. I even left my fated sword. But I didn't want to leave the ring. The angels never hurt me.

In those first days, I checked the ring obsessively, waiting in fear for Cassiel to withdraw their power from it, but they never did. So it was true that a namesake's power only left the ring upon a nephilim's death. Did it mean I wasn't completely lost or merely that Cassiel deigned to put up with me, a failure who shared their name?

As children, we learn that when we die, our namesake takes our soul. We merge with them, becoming one with our angel and all others who've carried that name. It's a divine culmination of the life we're meant to have lived, a moment to be honored. Yet I've always feared it.

When I was old enough to be given my ring, I was seven, and I asked about death. I asked whether I'd forget who I was and what I'd loved. Gabriel turned impatient with me. Of course I would forget. Angelic memory outweighed the blink of a mortal lifespan. And wasn't true knowledge worth infinite lifetimes on this earth? I nodded but remained unsure.

Alone in my bed at night, my feet too cold for me to comfortably fall asleep, I wondered whether Cassiel would notice me if I died without the ring on my finger. If we weren't connected through the ring, maybe they would forget me. My lifespan was a blink, after all. To an angel, what was one mortal death among the hundreds of thousands in a day?

I asked Zuriel what she thought—of the angelic bond and death. Was she afraid too? My back was to her, her hands in my hair as she braided neat rows.

"I think, when I die, I'll finally be beautiful," she said.

My breath caught in my throat. We didn't talk about beauty. To want to be beautiful meant indulging in vanity. It meant the soul was tarnished and therefore weakened. I asked her what she meant.

"If the only way to find true beauty is through a pure soul," she explained, "then when I die, I'll be united with beauty."

I relaxed. Yes, that made sense. Back then, it seemed an admirable thing to want.

I slip the ring back on. Right hand, little finger. We all wear ours the same way.

At least the day is done. I settle the cash drawer and turn out the lights, waiting in the gloom a few beats longer than usual. I gaze back at the books, the eclectic thrifted and gifted shelves, this space I carved for myself out of nothing. Retracing my steps through the shelves, I realize it's the same path I took on the close of opening day.

Three years ago, I took a risk on renting the space, but now I couldn't imagine my store outside of the historic downtown neighborhood. I'd fallen instantly in love with the wood floors and brick walls, the stamped metal ceiling with its filigree patterns. I'd rented the small studio above and thought I was finally seizing my dream. Demon-hunter-turned-bookseller sounded dramatic and wasn't how I thought of myself. I was simply another person escaping their oppressive family.

Though I was only a hunter for a decade, I'd trained my entire life for those years. All-consuming, it meant that I entered the normal world with nothing. Now, at nearly thirty, I was starting my life over in more ways than one, and I felt too old to be doing so. No one would hire, let alone approve a business loan for, someone my age with no history to speak of—no past employment, nothing on my credit record, no alma mater. I was an unknown. In those first months, I felt as if I didn't exist. The world didn't know how to understand me, and I didn't know how to understand it. Leaving started to feel like a mistake after all.

I'd never used my ethereal gifts for anything unrelated to hunting, but I found that I needed them out here too. It was the only power I had. So I returned to the places that had declined me, and when I smiled very sweetly and projected divine goodness and grace, it woke people up. I was valuable and worthy where I hadn't been before. I gained some things I shouldn't have had according to a world not made for me. I felt guilty and conflicted and angry, but eventually those feelings subsided. I could survive.

You'll come back, Zuriel had said. She was so sure.

Few of us leave. Everyone who does returns willingly when they stop hearing the angels, when they realize they're too much of a target alone, when they *feel* alone. The outside world can't support us the way family can.

I've witnessed the reunion rituals, the cleansings. Gabriel, as the family head, facilitates them. Nephilim make pilgrimages to our home from all over, their lost children in tow. That's when I realized my mother's power. It wasn't her cold efficiency in a fight. It was the way she called us all home.

I lock the back door and enter the night the way Gabriel taught us. *Everywhere is home to a spirit*, she said. *Be silent. Listen. Feel.* An old habit, and hard to break when I'm on edge. The autumn wind rises, biting through the exposed leggings between my coat and boots. I think of warm tea, of huddling in my wingback chair, but restlessness calls me out into the city, into the dark.

The orange light from the streetlamps is sour on my face. Few people are about. The temperature dropped suddenly this week, boding a vicious winter, and only those with necessary business brave the outdoors. They walk fast, eyes down, braced against the wind. I pass an empty bus stop lit for no one. Through a too-bright window, I spy a lonely convenience store clerk staring blankly out over aisles of bright packages. The dark windows of cars parade by. I reach an intersection, and when I pause for the light, a shiver rips up my spine. *Listen. Feel.*

Across the street, a woman stands with her red coat open to the feral wind. She's still, unfazed by the cold as it tears through her. A mass of dark curls obscures her face, but I know she watches me as I watch her. My pulse turns to a roar in my ears, muting the world. Muscle memory grips me, and I reach for my falcata only for my hand to close around air where my sword's hilt once was. But that was years ago, and I'm a hunter no more.

I don't *want* to be a hunter.

I was too weak to be a hunter.

The signal turns for us, but the demon doesn't move, and neither do I. The numbers count down, blinking urgency. The demon tilts her chin up. Traffic starts again. I step away from the intersection, turning back the way I came. I cast a glance over my shoulder, but she doesn't move. I turn down the nearest street and run.

The ground is nothing beneath my feet. The wind is nothing.

I have no weapon, but I am not defenseless. I have my light, but it's a match I will strike only as a last resort.

No one pursues me. I return home breathless but unscathed. And that's what's wrong. That's what puts me on edge.

Demons in a city are far from unusual. As the days turn colder and the nights longer, I've sensed more shadowy auras at the edge of my awareness, but most, knowing what I am, have given me a wide berth. Until now, it seems.

I climb the iron staircase to my apartment, pausing at the landing to reach into the dark, feeling for any sign of the demon. Nothing. Nearby there's a burst of laughter, and three friends come into view, their arms linked around one another. Their backs are to me as they continue down the alley, oblivious to my presence. I watch them until an angle of shadow cast by the building across the lot hides them again. Finally, I stop procrastinating and let myself inside.

I flip on the light by the door, hang my coat and keys, and wait.

For the first year of my new life, my apartment had been nearly bare. I had my bed with only plain white sheets and a small dining table with two chairs. Nothing decorating the walls, no bookshelves, no sofa or soft chairs. No character to suggest the person who lived here. I'd still been holding rigidly to every tenet, thinking I could make a new life by following old rules. I knew the stories of how the angels stopped speaking when nephilim left home, and I wanted to do as little as possible to displease them. Asking for constant reassurance seemed as likely to provoke silence as having too-nice things. So I hadn't asked them for anything, and I hadn't acquired anything. I didn't realize how brittle the emptiness made me until one night, after closing the store, I felt the hollow space deep in my chest and cried. The tears felt like permission.

I tested my interpretation gradually, like a child glancing back at a parent after taking a tentative, wobbling step. I chose only what was practical, opting for sturdy antiques made from old wood. I reupholstered chairs in sienna and sage. I polished and varnished scarred shelves and took in weathered books like strays, cleaning and mending them with the skills I learned tending our family's archive. I could fix something, if not the past.

My apartment remains undisturbed, but there is a new energetic pulse.

Not quite *new*. It's always been here, a background hum like that of the fridge, but now I pick it out of all the ordinariness around me. Where I could ignore it before, it's become magnetized, calling me to it like fate.

The old wood floor creaks under my steps as I make my way to the chest at the foot of my bed. It's a thrifted antique, one of the first things I fell in love with when I allowed myself other furniture. It's the kind that looks as if it's been hauled aboard old sailing ships, as if it's seen the world. It felt like adventure, the kind of energy I wanted to invite into my life.

Below the closed lid, below my knitting and bookbinding projects lies the source of the hum. I put a hand to the lid of the chest, and the old energy sings, inviting me back into its embrace.

I withdraw. So I'm not lost yet, but the guidance is clear. The only way to solve my problem, to protect myself, is through the old ways.

I kneel and crack the lid of the trunk just enough to hear the hinges whine.

Three years. I've held out three years.

I reach for my light, and it springs to my command as it always has, radiant and full despite my lengthy and intentional neglect. Gold and blue flash behind my eyes. Static zips through my body, raising goosebumps along my skin. I taste mint and ice and pear. None of these sensations are real, I know, but they're the product of a mortal body comprehending ethereal power. I've let it rest dormant for so long that the sensations are stronger than they ever were.

I am hot and cold at once. I feel my body rising, weightless, floating above itself even though I know I'm firmly grounded.

I let the lid fall closed.

I tamp down the light, though this time it's difficult to wrangle. As with everything else from my past, I'm out of practice. I visualize packing all that radiance away, folding and compressing it inside myself until it's only a spark. A spark can start a fire, but I've been so careful not to give it any fuel.

I sit back against the chest. I'm breathing hard. My forehead is damp. I know the exertion will pass. The hum from within the chest settles to its former resting state. I slip the ring from my finger. I want to throw it into the lake and never see it again. I want its sigils carved into my bones so we'll be bonded forever. I return it to my pinky. It glimmers in my reflection as I brush my teeth. I crawl into bed, and I hold it against my heart.

TWO

I KNOW THE DIFFERENCE between nightmares and hauntings, and this is a haunting. I dream of golden eyes, pupils like the dangerous edge of a knife. They watch me. I startle awake to a weight atop the blanket. Before my mind is fully freed from the dizzying influence of the dream, it's gone, as if it were only a trick of sleep. I know better. I throw out a hand, find lingering heat, click on the bedside lamp, and discover the distinct impression of a body beside where I lie.

In an instant, I'm out of bed. Sheets tangle around my ankles. I stumble, but fear has made me a primal creature. I don't fall. Dulled senses flare to life, an aura of ethereal light ghosting across my skin as a weak shield. My heart speeds. I hug myself, digging my fingers into the soft flesh at my sides as I back away from the bed. There's no smoke or fire, but the air stings my eyes and dries my throat. My breath sounds harsh in the empty room, but I'm certain I'm only recently alone.

◆

Times like this make me wish I were fully human, that I could brush off the encounter as the result of horror novels and simple nightmares, but too much happened last night for me to believe anything but the truth. I'd thought, naively, that if I left that world alone, it wouldn't come for me. I thought I could set aside my mother's teachings as human children leave behind their parents' beliefs. But the things my mother taught me extend beyond belief.

Gabriel kept us safe. She showed us how to transcend our bodies in service to our mission, and we grew stronger for it. After losing our father, Gabriel seemed to think that if she became as unforgiving as the demons we hunted, no one else in our family could die on the hunt. We learned how to forgo sleep for ritual, how to transmute hunger into sharp focus. We were safe, and we were strong, and she took care of us. I thought I could cultivate something new on my own, but the only lessons that will help me now are hers.

I dredge the past and find that the old words of protection and their rhythms are only as far away as my light was. So much time spent thinking I was outpacing the past when it was right behind me all along. I merely had to look over my shoulder and choose to see it.

In the early morning gloom, I clasp my shaking hands and walk the perimeter of my small studio apartment, laying down wards as I go. That done, I pull my bed away from the wall just enough to chalk a protective circle onto the old wood floor around its frame. My mind blanks on the last of the appropriate sigils, and I look back to the chest and the insistent hum within. Though I abandoned blessings and fated relics when I left home, I couldn't leave this. This—and the ring. I didn't want to believe it, but I knew I'd need them.

You'll come back, she'd said.

I want to prove her wrong. This is one *isolated* problem. I can solve it on my own and return to normal. Or return to *building* my normal.

I rummage past hand-stitched quilts, complicated cable knits, and fragile bookbinding projects, carelessly tossing aside these small triumphs of my new life as the obstacles they've become to sorting out my past once and for all. If I have to go back there and look Gabriel in the eyes as she burns the tarnish from my soul, it'll be Zuriel's fault—for not believing in our strength *together*, for not believing in me.

My hand brushes the cover of an old leather book, and I go still, all my righteous fury turning cold. A mantle of reverence settles over me. I haven't moved the tome since I buried it here, and like everything in the past few hours, its energy affects me more than usual. I rise with it grasped tightly in my hands. It's heavy and not just because of its comprehensive length. Its weight recalls hours of solitary study in the west wing of my childhood home, candlelit rituals in my parents' cellar, the burden of needing to don a cloak of protection.

My fingers find the appropriate page from memory. The pages are fragile and yellowed but will never crumble. The ink is ancient but will not fade. The diagram I'm looking for encompasses the two-page spread, margin notes detailing the effect of each mark. I try not to think about the meaning, copy the shapes as if they are a formula I don't understand from an advanced mathematics text. Once complete, the circle surges with pale light. I set the chalk and book aside and press my hands to the circle to seal it. It pulses once, then fades back to what appears to be mundane chalk. I hope not to see its light again, dread what its reactivation would mean.

I check the local news sites as I have every morning for the past two weeks but find no updates on the story I've been following, a preconcert disaster that's confounded everyone investigating it: a fire that blazed too hot and too long, never spread but resisted all firefighting efforts, and then went out as suddenly as it had started. The key piece that few would know: only hellfire burns like that, and only greater demons can wield it. No attendees had been injured, but the headlining artist was reported missing. Likely, I thought, they were dead, their soul claimed that night.

I tap over to my messages. There are only two contact threads. One is for Ana, the single person I could come close to calling a friend. The other is Zuriel's. My last message to her—*Are you okay?*—is still on read from two weeks ago.

Fresh anger rises with concern, mingling until I have to put the phone down. I sit on the lid of the chest, head in my hands, and breathe. Does she think because I left that I don't care? Does she think I don't miss her? Does she not miss me?

Best to go about the day as usual. Better than watching my wards and anxiously checking my phone. Better than remembering those eyes. I hope the normalcy of my work routine will soothe me, tire me so that I can fall easily into a restful sleep later tonight.

Autumn sunrise is just beginning to brighten the room. I have plenty of time before opening hours and so take a long bath. I try to read a paperback as I soak but instead feel only the heavy ritual tome fatiguing my hands. The words on the page shift and swim and rearrange their lines into warding sigils. Dazed, I watch them. A splash startles me back to reality. The sigils scatter, and I'm suddenly watching my book sink under a froth of bubbles. I bite back a curse and retrieve it, knowing it's ruined. I've never damaged a book, not like this, and it's enough to sour the rest of my plans for a relaxing morning. I splash out of the bath, drain the water, and dry in an uncharacteristic hurry.

My studio, though small, is usually a haven. A wall of shelves holds my personal book collection, though some of it has started to clutter the nearby floor in stacks. My kitchen is stocked with a variety of teas that I like to indulge in after a day in the store. I have more soft cushions and chairs than is necessary for a studio with one occupant. But despite the new morning light and the reliable heat of the radiator, the space has lost its usual cozy charm. I try not to look at the chalk circle as I go to the kitchen for a cup of tea.

While it's brewing, I finger comb my braids out into kinky waves, briefly considering makeup as I do every morning and deciding against it. When I moved to the city, I'd wanted to experience all the life I'd been missing. Makeup had been a forbidden luxury. What business did a nephilim have indulging in vanity? Especially when, besides my family, the others to see me were most often demons. Most hunts happened at night, and so my skin had been a lighter shade of brown back then. I'd unintentionally collected different shades of foundation over time, loathe to throw any of them away. Wastefulness was another source of corruption nephilim were to be on guard against. Though perhaps rejecting indulgence would balance the scales in my favor.

I don an oversized taupe blazer with a soft blue sweater underneath. Sensible wool trousers complete my usual look. It's practically a uniform, a habit I've kept even after leaving home. It's easy to conceal an arsenal of weapons beneath the lines of a blazer and look respectable while doing it. Not that humans ever have anything to fear from our silver throwing knives and daggers, but it's appearances that matter.

I take myself and my tea down the rear stairway to open the bookstore.

I've made a home here, and I wanted to believe I was happy. My old life hasn't intruded much until now.

A flash of movement through the bookstore window catches my attention. Across the street, the coffee shop is bustling. My tea's gone cold in my hands. I set it down on the counter a bit too hard, lock up the store, and leave for a coffee.

The first time I saw Witch's Brew—before the small business loans, before I had an apartment I could call my own—I thought it was only a trendy themed cafe. I knew I was wrong as soon as I stepped over the threshold and the barista met my gaze. She'd seen through me to the radiance humming beneath my skin. Then her surprise melted into a soft smile that said, *I'll let you have your secret, but you can tell me when you're ready.* I've never been ready.

Today, Ana's behind the counter with two of her employees filling the rush of morning orders. The witch of Witch's Brew—as well as its owner and head barista—she shoots me an acknowledging smile as soon as I enter. Bitter coffee and warm milk mingle with spices, florals, and honey in an olfactory latte I've come to think of as the aura of Witch's Brew. The space is lovably cramped in the way local coffee shops often are. Fairy lights strung along the fog-gray walls and ceiling suggest having entered a mystical wood, each table bestowed with an impressive chunk of glittering crystals I don't know the names of. For the fall season, Ana's crowded every spare surface with pumpkins. Each sports a nametag bearing a very human name. I'd asked whether she named them after her favorite customers, and she shook her head and explained that if that were the case, she'd have to devote several pumpkins to my name alone. Not because I was several people, she clarified, but because she liked me so much. I never learned the origins of the names.

In the shop's back corner, a couple peruses the small shelf Ana set up three years ago. Stocked with books that I thought might interest Ana's crowd—queer, artsy, witchy—it's crowned by a hand-lettered sign that reads Support Black-Owned Bookstores in Ana's eclectic print-cursive. We'd coordinated it shortly after I opened, and I made a reciprocal display for her in my store—a tiered table filled with artisan full-leaf tea sachets blended and packaged by Ana's own hands. My similarly enthusiastic sign—Support Latina-Owned Coffee Shops—graces the upper tier. We spent a late night brainstorming their literary-themed labels together, Ana cutting out the paper while I set to work with my fountain pen.

Shortly after leaving home and getting turned down for every job prior to meeting Ana, I'd ultimately decided that I didn't want to work for anyone else anyway. Living a life dictated to me by Gabriel had spoiled my vision of working for or with others, but that night, as Ana and I sat cross-legged at her coffee table, I realized I loved the camaraderie of doing work with another person. Those quiet hours spent talking over herbal tea are still one of my favorite memories.

I hang back by the door until the line has dwindled, observing the new abstract mixed-media paintings on the wall. I bought one of Ana's display pieces on a whim for the bookstore once. Back then, I wasn't running out of shelf space, but I still can't bring myself to take the painting down. It has the suggestion and energy, if not the shape, of wings, and I've become attached to it. When I bought it, Ana had smiled knowingly again but said nothing.

"How are you?" she asks as I step up to the register, the question weighted with significance. This isn't the place for a deeper conversation, but still her care shines through. "Aren't you open a bit early?"

By *a bit*, I suppose she means several hours early.

"I couldn't sleep. I thought I'd get some work done," I say.

"If you're having trouble sleeping, I could put together some herbs for you," she offers, brow still furrowed.

It was a mistake venturing into Ana's shop. She's always a comforting presence—and the menu is excellent—but she's too insightful when all I want to do is hide. I never understood her generous care until I met her family. She's always driving home to the suburbs to see her parents and abuela, a curandera who makes sure Ana doesn't leave without a batch of conchas and herbal blends for her to keep on hand *just in case*. Without fail, Ana shares them with me—when I have a sniffle, when I seem especially down, when I'm out of my favorite tea. Her abuela's openheartedness in her energy work, Ana says, is part of why she felt called to brujería. I met her family once when they'd stopped by Ana's shop, and in only ten minutes, I felt as if they wanted to adopt me even though I'd done nothing to make myself seem interesting and am nearly thirty. Ana's obvious affection for me was enough for them. It was the first time I felt that warmth. The first time I felt I could be enough.

"I'll be okay," I insist. "Occasional insomnia isn't out of the ordinary for me."

She lets it drop. I'm sure I'll get a text later. "Your usual?" she asks.

"Yes, please."

With the whir of the coffee grinder, I fall back into my thoughts. The demon who decided to *lounge in my bed* clearly isn't a free-floating spirit seeking a body to possess—and in any case, possessing an inhabited nephilim body is too much of a challenge for most. That doesn't mean they're not a danger to me though. They're corporeal and therefore a physical as well as spiritual threat.

I turn away from the counter, staring at my store across the street as I think. Among the traffic and general bustle of pedestrians, I don't immediately interpret the movement just beyond my window as being *inside* the store. Perhaps it's someone's shadow.

But the light is all wrong for it to be cast by a person, and even though I'm certain I locked up before I left, the movement is certainly inside. A dark figure pauses squarely in the middle of the window as if they *want* me to see them, but no one else spares so much as a glance. I freeze as my heart launches into a frantic rhythm, my breath catching in my throat. Though I don't *know*, instinct tells me it's the demon from last night. I try to catalog what I can of her appearance: a graceful form; full, lush hair. It's all I can gain from a silhouette alone.

Graceful. Lush—my thoughts ping back to the ease with which the description popped into my head. It lasts a second. A *significant* second.

Automatically I'm weighing how fast I could get across the street without an obvious supernatural display, whether it's even wise to go after a demon near a crowded street in broad daylight, whether this is a trap—

The figure moves, waving—waving at *me* in a manner I could only describe as *cheeky*, and yet the sight sends fresh adrenaline coursing through my veins. Ana, distantly, calls my name. Says it again, higher and questioning, as I fully turn from the coffee she's offered me to push back out into the cold. My body moves on instinct, weaving, swift and precise, through the traffic. A chorus of honking rises in my wake, but I don't care. I've been trained to dodge worse. My heartbeat is in my ears. A hint of smoke hits my nose like an insidious fire, and I think, *No, you won't take this from me. Not my books, not my store, not my life.* I taste metal as I pull the door.

Locked. A useless precaution to worry about humans, and now I've only delayed myself in addressing a real threat. I release a breath and with shaking hands find my keys. Inside, though, everything is as I left it. The scent of smoke is fading fast. The demon is gone. I make several rounds, searching for the telltale acid-rot of an infernal curse and find nothing so obvious.

This demon has never been subtle. She wants me to know she's here and seems to enjoy getting a reaction out of me only to retreat at the last moment. The strategy's off. Most demons don't reveal themselves so soon. And most, once their presence is known, turn vicious. I've trained to recognize the slow spiritual creep that often heralds the beginnings of possession, whether of house or body. It begins with brain fog, fatigue, a general grayness of space, body, and mind. But the air is just as clear as it's always been.

In the time it takes to make another frustrated sweep of the store, even the scent of smoke is gone. I'm tapping my nails on the front counter, their rhythm increasingly agitated, when I spy the only change.

The cover of my notebook is stained red. Not with blood, but with a flirtatious smear of what could only be lipstick.

Here, imprinted on my favorite shade of green, is the shape of a demon's lips. My heart speeds with a new feeling, awe and fear inextricably tangled in a way

I've only felt when locked in the direst of fights, when witnessing a demon's red wings slicing the midnight sky, or when falling under the hypnotic spell of an infernal song. This quiet moment carries that same charge, the reminder that they were angels, that they were beautiful. *Are*, sometimes, beautiful.

I press a finger to the stain and inspect my skin. The red doesn't transfer.

I lift the upper corner of the notebook to my lips, a mere inch from where hers recently were. She'd stood here, where I stand now. She'd looked across the street and seen me, but I'm not sure what person she saw—the ex–demon hunter, or the bookstore owner, or someone entirely different. Someone more than the sum of those surface descriptions. I hesitate a second more before kissing where her lips touched, a charged reenactment of an ambiguous crime scene. Embarrassed heat rises to my face as I return the notebook to the counter.

If she's not correctly inhabiting her role, then neither am I.

I lose track of time. Ana brings my coffee over eventually, snapping me out of my spiral.

"Everything okay?" she asks, clearly worried.

"I forgot something. I'm an inconvenience. I'm so sorry. You didn't have to," I say, taking the offered coffee.

Ana gives me a look. "I feel like I should be bringing you more than coffee."

I try to laugh it off. "I'm just a little scattered after a bad night's sleep is all. Your coffee is a gift."

"But you paid for it."

"You know what I mean."

I spend the rest of the day in a daze, returning again and again to my sparse text thread with my sister and deleting everything I try to say.

I think there's a demon . . . I start.

Do you know if anything's happened lately? Backspace.

Something weird is happening in my store. Delete. I want to confess: *Something weird is happening in me.*

Would you mind coming to keep me company for a while? Again, I clear the text box.

I miss you.

I don't delete it, but I don't tap Send.

⸎

That night, my wards jolt me from sleep. The circle around the bed burns bright white, blindingly so. I don't have to wonder what's activated it. A dark shape looms above me, golden eyes sharp within her silhouette, her curls an undulating cloak of shadow. Her form warps the light from the circle. She's negative space, a black hole. She doesn't touch me, only watches, but I feel the pressure of her aura. A hungry, feral thing, it has a will separate from hers, one that she wrestles with. *Succubus. She's a succubus.* I don't know why she's holding herself back, caging the instinct that's her greatest weapon. Humans, even nephilim like me, would blearily walk into the trap that is her aura, a trap of pleasure. The unsuspecting could drown in it like poisoned honey and think they're enjoying every moment, even as she devours their soul.

The flash of her teeth reminds me of the truth, kicking the fear back to the front of my mind. Whatever reason she has to suppress her aura, she's still a predator. She's still the enemy. I need to move—to attack her? To run away? I'm not sure—but I find she's used one of the weapons at her disposal. Sleep paralysis holds me in its claws.

She notices my intent and seems amused. I struggle against the force of her, succeeding only in riling my pulse. She leaves my side to walk a slow circle around the bed, watching me intently as if deliberating her next step.

I reach for my light—I can't be thoughtful now about what choosing it means—and find it distant, removed. The spark floats somewhere high above and beyond my body as if I'm perceiving it from the bottom of a murky sea. I strain for it, confusion turning to panic. I've never lost the spark. I could shove it aside, ignore it, choose to forget it, but it was never *gone.*

Around the spark, a mirror world materializes above, showing me reality. Me in my bed, asleep within the lit circle. A figure sitting beside me, her hand to my temple.

I'm in a dream.

I don't know what the rules here are. We don't have stories about this, about demons removing our minds from space and time.

She's stopped at the bedside once more to observe me. Silent, calculating. I scream and thrash. To me, it manifests as a muffled cry. But my body in the mirror world remains still as death.

"What do you want?" I scream through a mouth clenched shut, with a tongue that won't obey.

Yet she seems to understand.

She leans over me, the first time she's come so close. Though I know I can't move, instinct tries to scurry me away, to raise my arms to shield myself from her. She hushes me as one would a distressed child, putting a finger to my lips. Her touch is feverishly hot, not the cold I'd expect from such deep shadow. She smells like the beginnings of a fire, like danger.

Her touch slips down my throat, burning a trail to my heart, and I forget this isn't reality. I'm convinced she'll tear my heart from me. I'm convinced this is how I'll die.

Tears track down my face, soaking into my hair. I try for my light again, and it's so far. I'm so far. I need to wake up.

She wipes the tears away, hushes me gently, and begins to hum. It reaches me through my panic. I know this song. At first, I think it's an old lullaby before recognizing its cadence. Without the words, I'd nearly mistaken it. This is angel song. It's been transposed into something deeper and slower, the crisp notes smoothed over, but the same song.

She smiles at my recognition, sharp white teeth within the void of her face. Gathering my right hand in hers, she places it against the heat of her chest. I don't understand—how she knows this song or what she's trying to communicate—and then I feel it. There's a heart within the shadow of her, and it beats, slower than any human's but a heart all the same. She replaces her hand over my heart, and we remain like this, experiencing the simplest measure of our lives.

Humming again, she cautiously lowers herself to a seat beside me. She watches my face for any sign of panic, and when I remain still, she lifts my hand to her mouth. I tense—or I would if I could move—and she notices. She waits and closes her eyes and hums.

"What do you want?" I ask, but my lips can't move. The sound is useless.

She bends her head to kiss each knuckle, avoiding the one bearing my ring. She smooths my hair and brushes a hand down my cheek, leaving a ghost of warmth behind. I feel—*cherished* would be the word in another context. No one's ever touched me so gently and with such attention.

She stands.

"Where are you going? Why did you come here?" I try.

She releases a resigned sigh as if I've placed a burden on her, but when she smiles again, this time, the eeriness of it seems almost tender. She walks unaffected through the glow of the wards, and I fall back into a gentle dream.

⬥

I wake with a gasp, my clothes soaked through with sweat. Without her at the helm, the dream she left me with turned nightmarish. I stumble out of bed. Don't register the cool wood underfoot or the early morning birdsong at my window. I strip out of my clothes, flee to the bathroom, and slam the door behind me. Anything to be away from the evidence of demonic haunting. I shower until my skin is red and shut off the tap only after the water turns cold. I curl into the solidity of the tub.

My father was killed by a demon before I was old enough to remember him. I've seen my siblings maimed on the hunt. I know how possession can break a mind. I watched my sister's months-long recovery into a personality that was never the same as the old. I was prepared for all those eventualities to come for me, but not this.

This is the first time a demon has ever haunted me, something that never happened even when I was a hunter.

Knowing she'd been near was one thing. Witnessing her presence at a distance, another. Meeting those sharp eyes, feeling the weight of her soul above me . . . A double panic rises. There's the *correct* fear—for my safety, of her immunity to my wards—and the fear of myself, my curiosity.

The fact that everything appears the same makes the world feel wrong when I emerge. I pick my clothes from the floor and toss them in the wash. Rip off the bedclothes and throw them in after. Habit steers me to the kitchen and the promise of a warm cup of tea. I find one already waiting for me, steaming in a delicate china cup and saucer I've never owned, let alone seen in my life. I don't expect the scream that rips from me, don't expect to sweep the innocently offending thing into the sink where it splashes and shatters. So solid. And real. The corner of the counter bites hard into my hip as I back away.

Before I can process what I'm doing, I'm snatching clothes out of the closet and tripping down the back stairs. The air is crisp, and I've neglected a coat in my haste. People hurrying to their jobs downtown eye me but say nothing. Only when something sharp stabs into my foot do I realize I neglected shoes as well. Perhaps someone who recognizes me calls out, but I don't hear them. I'm walking. I'm moving. I'm getting away.

Eventually, I start to feel the cold because my body numbs, and the tips of my fingers purple. I look at them wonderingly, try to squeeze the color from the flesh. These are my hands, but they feel separate from me and my concerns—their manicure frivolous, the nails too brittle against what threatens me.

My body returns me home, where I soothe myself with the mundane cleansing of chores. I transfer my laundry without feeling it. I move my stacks of books instead of vacuuming around them as I've always done, conscientiousness born of numb procrastination. When I can't ignore it any longer, I inspect the chalk circle and find it complete and unsmudged. I check the sink and find it empty. But where the teacup once was, I find two dainty truffles. One dark chocolate, one milk. In a show of defiance, I take one in hand, peel away the paper, take a bite. It's as solid and real as the teacup and creamy as it dissolves on my tongue. I wait for something to happen. Nothing does. I eat the rest of the first, leave the second. My body tingles with the return of heat but nothing more.

With the dryer humming in the background, I take a quilt from the chest and curl up to sleep.

—◇—

My nightmares are ordinary this time. Each moment I startle awake, I'm comfortingly alone in the room. I fall into fitful sleep again and dream of her eyes.

The sun is high when I fully wake. I stare at the ceiling and watch the light change. A cup of steaming tea on my bedside table never cools, perfuming the room with the scent of crushed red petals and bloody ripe berries. I study the teacup's painted flowers, return my gaze to the ceiling.

"Is this"—I realize—"an apology?"

I take the tea in shaking hands, clattering the cup and saucer together. All I've had to eat is the truffle. A single infernal truffle. Raising the tea to my lips, I pause to savor the fragrant plume of steam.

Once a demon breaks past wards, it's imperative to act quickly and decisively. I've done neither. I don't know how to be a demon's target in this way. She's never threatened any violence toward me, and all the responses I've learned are violence.

I think of her golden eyes, an omen of danger and . . . something else. I want to see the rest of her, as if knowing what she looks like beyond the veil of shadow will provide any true clarity. The memory recalls the heat of her presence and, with it, the hungry weight of her aura. The want. Hers or mine, I don't know. Like heading off the spread of a curse, I shut down the thought.

The tea is mildly sweetened. Herbal, as if the demon is concerned about ruining my sleep with caffeine. I burn my tongue on it, drink it in a sloppy haste, and fall back into a restless sleep.

Daylight seems the same when I regain consciousness. I'm not sure how long I've existed like this, on elusive dreams and demon treats, but I feel clear, rested. The opposite of haunted. The tea at my bedside has been refilled. Three truffles wait in a delicate saucer. I peel away their papers and eat them together in a single bite—raspberry and almond and rose mingling on my tongue—and down the red floral tea in two gulps. Outside my window, the sky is pale and bright. I wander over to it, squinting against the light.

A shrill noise cuts through my short-lived peace.

I find my phone buzzing a frenzy on the kitchen counter and stare at its screen, struggling to process letters into meaning. Zuriel. My sister. My sister is calling me—for the first time in a year. I accept the call and raise the phone carefully to my ear.

"Cass," she says. Distant and familiar. She waits.

I remember the first time Zuriel called me *Cass*. We were in the sparring room, both tumbled over and laughing. Most likely, I'd tripped into her, and she'd caught me only for me to take her down too. And the name slipped out. Gabriel stomped over to us. We both went rigid, still clutching each other, our grasps turned sharp. We thought she was going to demand more discipline from us. Instead, she wanted to know what Zuriel had said. She repeated the nickname. Gabriel asked where she'd heard it, and Zuriel explained that she'd read a book where the older sister gave her younger sister a nickname.

Gabriel reprimanded her. Our names were too sacred to shorten, she said. Zuriel had robbed me of my connection to my namesake angel by chopping the sound. We nodded gravely and said nothing else during that practice, trading slow, soft blows, more dancing than fighting.

Gabriel burned the book. Zuriel never found out what happened to the sisters.

That night, she tiptoed to my room to apologize to me for harming my name. I told her I was fine, that I liked the sound. It was the first time my identity shifted, became more mine—all because of her. I loved the angels, but everything I had and did was because of them. This name was possibility. I asked her to say it again.

"Hello?" I say politely and barely stop myself from rattling off, *You've reached New Haven Books.*

"Your neighbor at the coffee shop says you haven't opened recently. Said she saw you wandering around downtown looking confused and underdressed."

I force a smile into my voice. "I'm fine. A little sick is all."

"What day is it?"

"Wednesday," I try. "But I've been busy inventorying and lost—"

"I've been trying your phone since yesterday morning."

I'm opening my mouth to speak when Zuriel cuts me off.

"I'm outside your door now. Let me in."

The call disconnects, and I'm left staring at a wall of notifications I'd somehow not heard.

A pounding knock startles me back into motion. Halfway to the door, I notice my rumpled clothes, my flattened curls. I think briefly of changing, but the next knock sounds as if Zuriel will break the door down. I open it.

"You look—" Zuriel's eyes blink wide at the sight of me. Without waiting for an invitation, she pushes her way inside, her gaze sweeping me up and down as she passes. "You look terrible."

She's dressed, as always, in an impeccably tailored suit, and I feel even shabbier beside her. She has our father's height, something I envied when I was younger. I'm the shortest in the family along with our mother, but unlike Gabriel, I feel every inch that Zuriel has on me. She's six feet of perfect posture and poise, never curling her shoulders, never ducking her head as became my habit. Unlike me, she looks the part of a warrior—the determined set of her full lips, the hawklike clarity in her round eyes. On the occasions we did interact with people, they squared their shoulders and sat up straighter when she came around. Like Gabriel, she could command. She could lead. The dense curls of her hair are cropped short, the only hairstyle she's ever had. Easy to maintain. Little for something to grab onto. Doesn't get in the way on the hunt.

Zuriel's attention immediately lands on the circle in the center of the room, and she stops short.

"Why didn't you tell us?" she demands, and if anyone in my family can make a demand also sound gentle and concerned, it's Zuriel. "Why didn't you come home?"

You never answered. How could I go back if I didn't know you'd welcome me?

When I struggle to answer, Zuriel closes the door and cups my chin, forcing me to meet her gaze.

"What kind are they?" she asks. "What did they do to you?"

"She has golden eyes," I say, noting that this information is irrelevant as I say it. Eyes that would be beautiful if they weren't terrifying, my mind unhelpfully supplies. "A succubus."

Zuriel inspects the circle and seems puzzled when she finds it correct and intact. "Succubi shouldn't be able to break this."

I put my head in my hands. Outside the sheltered moments of angel song, I never allow myself to cry. The past few days have ruined my usual restraint, but now would be an inconvenient time. Zuriel would misinterpret me. I'm not sad. I'm not even scared, I realize. I'm overwhelmed.

Zuriel's voice is beside me again. I didn't hear her cross the room. The floor usually creaks.

"How many times have you seen her?" she asks.

"Twice." Do I count the other times I saw her from a distance? It would make things seem more dire. I worry Zuriel would judge me more harshly.

Zuriel takes my hands away from my face, holds them gently in her own. She meets my gaze again, and ethereal light shines through her eyes. It shouldn't startle me, but I haven't seen her do this in years.

"It doesn't seem like she's attempted to drain you," Zuriel decides eventually, and if she was baffled before, it's obvious now. The cold light fades, and her eyes are their normal deep brown again. "Are you sure it's not something else?"

"I know the difference between a demonic presence and a nightmare," I say, unable to summon the energy to be offended by the suggestion that I imagined the past few days.

"Something's happening," Zuriel says, low and quiet as if she can keep a secret from whatever infernal forces might be listening in. "Ever since that fire, we've caught and killed minor demons lurking just beyond the family estate's wards. They stopped sniffing around a few days before Ana called about you. It all has to be connected." She hesitates before adding, "Won't you come back home?"

At that, I pull away. I may be a Gotwenn, but that estate isn't my home. "I can figure it out."

Zuriel looks back at the useless circle, and it's enough for me to understand her point. I ignore it.

"I'm not going back to Gabriel. What she did to you—"

"I recovered."

"But you didn't."

"At least I'm not away in the city pretending that I don't know the truth of what's out there. Even when it comes for me. At least I'm fighting."

I draw a shaky breath, back away. *I watched you die twice. I watched the spirit break you.*

She's changed since I left, become more like Gabriel in my absence. Guilt settles cold in my chest. How could I leave her there after what happened?

Zuriel sighs and changes her approach. "Have you eaten?"

"Tea and truffles," I answer.

Her confusion returns.

"She apologized."

"Who? Cass, who?"

I can't look at my sister when I say it. "The succubus."

"No. Cassiel, you're coming back with me," says Zuriel, starting forward as if to grab me.

"I won't!" I scream.

I watched you die twice. Twice, in that place.

Silence falls heavy between us. We're on the stairs again, destined for different paths. I'm running away from my sister because I witnessed death and knew I couldn't face it when it came again. She's staying because she endured death and had acquired other fears.

Zuriel reaches into her coat and withdraws a gleaming silver dagger. "It's blessed," she says, even though we both know what it is. Zuriel waits for me to object. I've renounced all of their weapons and armor—every hunter's tool with the exception of the tome. When I neither accept nor reject the dagger, she sets it on the counter. Its ornate hilt gleams in the sunlight.

"Why don't you get yourself cleaned up while I cook," she offers.

I nod and close myself into the bathroom. A gentle clatter sounds from the kitchen as Zuriel goes about opening cabinets and retrieving pots. Distantly, the practical part of my mind remembers that I have little to cook and thinks that Zuriel will need to go out for ingredients. I'm relieved by these mundane thoughts when I glimpse on the windowsill a teacup and saucer that had not been there before.

——◆——

I spoon Zuriel's soup into my mouth but couldn't say what its ingredients are or what it tastes like. Yet while normal food is bland, the taste of the demon's tea, of red petals and darker berries, is still strong on my tongue.

It's strange to sit with someone else at my dining table. I only have space for the two chairs, but the second has always been empty. Zuriel watches me as if I'm fragile. Is this how I looked at her after the demon took her soul and crushed it, when she walked hollow-eyed through the great halls of our parents' home?

She mercifully doesn't interrogate the lack of my usual enthusiasm for food. We both know what it feels like to experience and remember too much to stay grounded in our bodies.

My spoon scrapes the bottom of the bowl. "What do the local hunters think?" I make myself ask. Maybe there's more information I can arm myself with. Unless I want to tiptoe closer to the realm of Gabriel's influence, this is the only time I'm going to learn what's actually happening. There's only so much I can piece together from news coverage.

Zuriel looks suddenly tired. "Human hunters don't want any part in this. With greater demons involved, you know most won't take that kind of risk. Especially after Dad."

I focus on stirring my soup so I don't have to meet her gaze. Dad. Of course. Zuriel was barely old enough to begin our training when he was killed. Only Gabriel and Aunt Raphael, the two nephilim in the party, survived that hunt. News of his death was a shock to the regional hunter community. Some packed their weapons away forever. Dad was one of those rare humans like Ana, the ones who could feel a shimmer of the beyond. If he, despite his insight and precognition, could die like that, those without his abilities didn't stand a chance. The story of that ill-fated hunt still lingered like a cautionary tale.

And so our allies dwindled until only our immediate family was left to shoulder the brunt of the responsibility for the whole Midwestern US. We were stretched thin. And then I left.

Guilt twists my stomach. I set my spoon down.

Finally, I ask the real question. "What happened, Zuriel? Hellfire on the North Side? We've always been more discreet than this. We've never made the news."

"*We*," she starts, emphasizing my absence, "did the best we could. I don't need you *and* Gabriel coming down on me."

"I'm not blaming you," I hurry to say. "I'm only confused."

Zuriel scrubs a hand over her face, her frustration cooling. "Sorry." She sighs. "Big singer. Faustian contract. It must've been a very desirable soul because some greater demons came to collect. We didn't expect *two*. I shot one of them, but not before the place went up in flames."

"I'm glad you're safe," I say. I'm glad I finally get to say it to her face.

"I'm sorry for leaving you on read. I was feeling a lot."

"It's okay. I understand."

She nods.

I remember too well how shaken I was after some hunts. Zuriel always stayed with me. Now, I wonder whether it helped her to have someone else's fear to focus on soothing.

"Did you tell Gabriel you were coming?" I ask.

"I had to."

"She's going to summon me, isn't she?" I ask, miserable about staying here, miserable about the prospect of returning.

A summons is different than a polite request of the type Zuriel had offered. It was binding. To refuse meant to give up my light, the ethereal energy that made me a nephilim. I might have given up hunting. I didn't want to relinquish my connection to the angels, no matter how heavy a birthright it had become.

Zuriel opens her palms toward me as if I thought she might be hiding something. "I didn't bring a summoning token," she says.

"You wouldn't have to," I say.

She returns her hands to her lap. "We could've used you there, Cass."

"What about the Gordons?" I say too quickly.

"They've got their hands full down South." She hesitates. "Chamuel was killed recently."

"Oh. I—"

I almost say, *No one told me*. But of course no one would have. Aunt Raphael's son. Our cousin. Gone.

The news sits heavy between us, a reminder of the fact that even we nephilim are vulnerable. Chamuel was near our age and still in his early years as a hunter. We're more likely to die during our first and final decades—the first because of inexperience and the fear that comes with it, the final because even though we age slower and live longer than humans, even our reflexes deteriorate. I've been away from our work for three critical years during my first decade and never had the same natural fortitude or athleticism as Zuriel. Taking up my sword again would likely show that my skills have shamefully dulled.

Zuriel stands. She looks ready to make another case for me to come with her, but instead, she touches the dagger. "You remember how?" she says simply.

I nod, unable to meet her gaze.

"And—I understand why you left even if the others don't," she adds. "I'm sorry."

Something in my chest eases. "Thank you."

"I'll answer this time if you call to check in." Zuriel tries to offer a smile, but her gaze flicks to the dagger between us. I brace for the look that sometimes crosses her, the evidence of what the demon attack left behind, but it doesn't come. Not in this light.

The moment stretches. Finally, Zuriel turns to leave.

"You've come all this way," I blurt, cutting myself off before I can make my own counteroffer. I can't go with her. But maybe she could stay here. Just for a little while. Zuriel catches the unspoken invitation anyway.

She pauses at the door, huffing a tired laugh. "We can't rehash this. I made my choice. You made yours."

"But this is different. Isn't it?" I try.

She crosses her arms and raises an eyebrow, instantly transforming into the indulgent older sister, disapproving but willing to hear me out.

"If Gabriel's concerned, you should stay and gather more information, right? It'll be like any other scouting mission."

Zuriel hums skeptically, but it's encouragement to continue.

"Maybe just a day or two, like we used to do. Then you can be confident when you report back that everything's fine."

"And split the strength we'd have in numbers?" she says. *If you'd just come with me*, I can nearly hear her say.

"We've done it before."

She's quiet for a moment. "I know what you're doing. Nothing you show me is going to convince me to stay out here. Especially not now."

"But you will? Stay for a little while, I mean."

She rolls her eyes. "I have been curious about your store," she admits grudgingly.

"Thank you," I say, clasping my hands in gratitude to restrain myself from throwing my arms around her.

THREE

I'M SO HAPPY TO have my sister back.

We live as if we've reentered our single carefree summer—when our Aunt Raphael spirited us South and away from Gabriel's influence, when we were allowed food with spices and sauces and adorned ourselves with glittery plastic jewelry. We were seven and nine and kids for the first time.

Within thirty minutes, Zuriel's planned an exuberant dinner menu for tonight. She composes a grocery list of items I've never had the culinary prowess to stock in my kitchen, largely because I've been so busy and tired, relying on either takeout or Ana's proclivity to cook as if she's feeding a family of five.

On the way out to retrieve her ingredients, Zuriel pauses to run her fingers through my hair.

"Jumbo box braids?" she suggests. "In a cute little bob. It'd suit your face."

I can almost smell the coconut and shea on her hands from all those years ago. "I'd love that," I say.

"What color?"

"Natural this time."

She laughs. "You used to demand lavender. Or pastel pink."

I haven't heard her laugh in years, and I'm relieved to find that as Gabriel's Zuriel falls away, my sister is still underneath. I miss sharing our memories.

Her joy is contagious, and I smile. "Maybe next time," I say.

But it was the wrong thing to say. Her laugh dies. Her smile falters. She recovers it, but it's dimmer than before. "Natural. Got it. I'll find a beauty supply store on the way."

Neither of us acknowledges the moment. Then the door clicks shut. I'm alone again.

Rumination sets in. I start to worry my ring. I never thought I'd get this moment with Zuriel, and I don't want to ruin it.

Distracting myself with light cleaning, I retrieve the sheets from the dryer and make the bed. I find what kitchen tools I think Zuriel will need for her recipe and set them out so she doesn't have to search for them—though she'll need to buy a zester. I think to gather my styling products too.

It's been so long since I've looked forward to anything, and I lose myself in a daydream of sitting on the steps of Aunt Raphael's porch. I'm trying to eat a popsicle before it melts in the heat. Zuriel's hands are in my hair. Her braids were clumsy, but I loved them. With our cousin Cambiel's direction, Zuriel quickly improved, excelling as she did at everything.

That summer was the most I'd ever seen her smile. She was always better than me at molding herself into the vision of what Gabriel and the moment demanded. But with Aunt Raphael, the only request seemed to be that we be ourselves and that we enjoy it. At first, it wasn't a request we knew how to fulfill. We'd been told we were going South to train with our extended family. There were skills even Gabriel didn't possess, and the Gordons' protective glamours were unmatched.

But Aunt Raphael wasn't who I expected. And I didn't know what to make of Gabriel's reaction to her.

She arrived at our doorstep in a white linen jumpsuit, her hair styled in long thin braids that swayed around her hips as she moved. Like Gabriel, she had the same petite build that belied her strength, her presence bigger than her body's proportions. And her skin! A rich brown that was radiant with the sun's attention. My eyes stung with the daylight that spilled into our house with her. We were spirits of the night like the demons we hunted.

"Your hair is long," were Gabriel's first words to her sister, a clipped observation. Wary disapproval.

That tone never preceded good things, but Raphael breezed past it as if Gabriel were merely grumpy, not passing an implicit judgment on her dedication to our path.

Instead of defending herself, Raphael smiled pleasantly and said, "The house is just as I remember it." But I couldn't imagine it being so lightless with her around.

As we crossed the state line out of Illinois, Aunt Raphael broke the silence in the car as if we were finally out of Gabriel's earshot. Glancing at Zuriel and me in the rearview mirror, at our rigid posture and tightly clasped hands, she sighed. She asked whether Gabriel was still grieving. We didn't know how to answer her. Gabriel was always cold and distant, an anger we couldn't comprehend always simmering just beneath the facade. I looked to Zuriel for answers, and she shook her head.

Raphael rummaged in a shopping bag on the passenger seat and pressed cool cans into our hands. Their surfaces beaded with condensation. I held mine in a death grip and said nothing. The bright, swirling colors on the packaging were foreign to me, and I didn't understand the expectation behind why she'd given them to us. Zuriel, bravely, eventually asked what it was.

"We'll be on the road for a while," our aunt explained. "I thought I'd get you girls some drinks."

"But what is it?" Zuriel asked again.

I didn't understand the look that crossed Raphael's face back then. I thought she was upset with Zuriel for not understanding or for speaking without permission. Zuriel nudged me, then pried one of my hands off the can, squeezing it back into her own.

"You're going to crush it," she whispered in my ear.

But we didn't know Aunt Raphael very well. We didn't know what she was capable of. If she was an adult and she was Gabriel's sister, maybe she had the same outbursts. I wished Zuriel would be quiet. The more we interacted, the more upset Raphael's expression became.

"It's bubbly water. My girls like it. I thought you would too," she said.

Zuriel turned the can in her hands. "How do you open it?" she asked.

Raphael gave us instructions, but by then, my thoughts were too loud and jumbled for me to follow her directions. The pop and hiss of Zuriel's can startled me.

"It's fine, Cass," Zuriel tried to soothe me, the nickname slipping out. Then she went still, her gaze darting to Raphael to see whether she'd noticed.

Instead, she only said gently, "Try yours, Cassiel."

I shook my head. I held the can too tight again.

Raphael pulled over, and I was certain that I'd made her angry. We were in the middle of nowhere: empty blue sky, flat green fields, and an endless stretch of highway. But despite the openness, I felt trapped.

"I want to go home," I said, my first words of the entire trip and the first thing I ever said to Raphael. I didn't want to go home. What I wanted was familiarity, and at least with Gabriel, I knew how to read her moods.

"We're not far. I could drive y'all back if you want," she said, leaning over the center console to face me. Her voice was soft, but she was frowning. I didn't know what to make of the contrast.

The choices Gabriel offered were often a trap or a test. And if I disappointed Raphael, I'd be disappointing Gabriel. What would she think if she'd sent us off for specialized training, the first time she'd trusted us out of her sight, and I returned home a coward?

"But," Raphael added. "I think the long drive would be worth it. You've never met your cousins. They're excited to see you. And I've been looking forward to getting to know my nieces."

She didn't mention the training.

"Here." She held her hand out to me. I gave her back the can. "Watch. It's easy." After popping it open, she handed it back to me. The car turned quiet.

The water fizzed in my hands. Finally, Raphael spoke again, her tone firm but gentle. "Gabriel's not here," she said.

Mantras, as much as Ana espoused their power, weren't a regular part of my life. What Raphael said in the car all those years ago, however, came rushing forward again when I left home. When a clerk at a cosmetic store shadowed my eyes for the first time—*Gabriel's not here*. When I stood in the aisles of grocery stores for the first time, overwhelmed by their bountiful choices—*Gabriel's not here*. Eventually, it became a triumphant realization.

I want Zuriel to feel it as well.

But *Gabriel's not here* could never become *Gabriel has no power here*. I waited so long to leave because of how Gabriel made an example of her sister at the end of that summer, because I knew Gabriel played waiting games, baiting us all like simple demons. I felt as if Zuriel and I were bad luck, that we'd brought her anger down on the Gordons too.

Lost as I am in memory and old guilt, I don't register the unnatural warmth of the doorknob until it's too late, until I've swung the bathroom door wide and find myself staring down a wall of impenetrable shadow.

I scramble back, dropping automatically into a defensive stance. But my sword arm is empty, the dagger too far away.

I'm staring down the demon from my dream.

The darkness doesn't advance, only swirls patiently on the other side of the threshold. She's watching me and making some decision as she did in the dream, but I don't know what it could possibly be, why she doesn't attack when she's found me unarmed.

The shadows pull back, collapsing into a vanishing point. The air is clear. Nothing in the bathroom is changed but for an ornate decanter of faceted glass on the countertop. I approach it warily, but like everything else she's sent me, it doesn't hold any malice. Inside, golden oil shines behind the facets. On my palm, it carries the same red floral scent as the tea. I smooth it through my hair, and after days of neglect, the kinks are instantly softer, the curls defined.

"Why are you doing this to me?" I ask my reflection, helpless in the face of yet another demonic visitation that didn't go as it should.

When Zuriel returns an hour later, I'm still wondering at the crystal decanter in my hands. I hide it away in a cabinet and go help her with the bags.

———◆———

Raphael and her family joined us for a hunt nearly two decades later. She didn't bring the sun with her, arriving instead under the cover of night. Her hair was cut to the scalp, shorter even than Zuriel's and mine. She didn't have to do that. It was a rebellious statement of the kind Gabriel couldn't technically take issue with, though I didn't understand what Raphael was trying to say. When she smiled, the forced pleasantness of before was gone. She was baring her teeth. On the hunt, whenever Gabriel turned away, Raphael's gaze bored into her as if a look alone could smite.

Hate was a wound, we were taught, and therefore it was important not to hate our enemies. Else every night we would walk onto the battlefield already bloodied. Our tenets said nothing about hating each other. Until I witnessed Raphael, I didn't realize we could.

"All done," Zuriel says, handing me a mirror.

My face is transformed by her work, and for a moment, I forget my ruminations. I feel as if I've stepped into a new identity, this Cassiel more confident and in step with the world. Zuriel's incorporated a thread of gold into one of the braids at my temple, a tiny regal flair. I shake my head and watch the braids sway, mesmerized by how flatteringly they skim my shoulders and taper toward my chin.

"Now dinner," Zuriel says, practically leaping for the kitchen.

I look from my reflection to Zuriel and back. "You've already done so much today."

Her back is to me as she lines ingredients up on the counter. "It's not often I get to do things for you anymore," she says, her voice soft.

I think she does this for herself as much as she does it for me, but I keep the observation to myself. At home, my only outlet for creativity was restoring the manuscripts in the archive, and Gabriel always thought I spent too long on my work. Zuriel had little. Maybe today she's doing too much, pushing too hard because she's trying to fit so much life into so little time. And with things she could love and savor and have every day of her life if she let herself. It makes me sad.

"I'm glad you're here," I say over the soft clatter of her prep work.

She doesn't respond. Her hands go eerily still over the cutting board. I think of the demon and cursed objects, worrying there's something she tampered with while enthralling me with gifts.

But once I'm at Zuriel's side, I see the tears on her cheeks. Cupped in her hands, fresh sprigs of rosemary perfume the air around us. I know this feeling well.

She looks down at me as if seeing me for the first time. "It's Zuriel," she breathes, "singing."

As we eat our food, as we wash up after dinner, as we settle in to sleep, I want to ask her about the song. My heart screams that it's a sign, but Zuriel will barely look at me now, her warmth and enthusiasm turned somber. In the dark with her once more, I fight for the courage to speak the truth I see. I turn on my pillow to face her, but she speaks first.

Staring up at the ceiling, her misery palpable even in the dark, she says, "How do I atone for a small, rare happiness?"

The question lodges deep. I want to tell her she doesn't, but every day I stare down that same doubt. I spend so long fighting for an answer to a question I've been asking for years that Zuriel seems to give up on me, rolling over without another word.

In those very first weeks before I met Ana, while I drifted through the city searching for a sign and purpose, I couldn't banish Gabriel's terse whisper from my ears. She followed me into stores, down sidewalks, into cheap rented rooms and dreams. Always, I had her counsel.

I was worried I'd never escape her. Her voice was a spirit, and I was a haunted child.

My first day away from home, I wanted so badly to look like everyone around me. Not necessarily their style but their easy confidence. So reassured that their bodies were safe and their own that it wasn't a thought in the first place.

The nights had already turned cold, and I ducked into a thrift store for a better coat. Others had had a similar idea because few choices remained. As I was flipping through oversized sweaters to layer with, a sundress on the sales rack caught my eye. I couldn't buy it. The money I had was strictly for necessities, and I was very cold, having abandoned most of my old clothes and the memories embedded in them like old stains. But I could try the dress on.

Shaking, I closed myself into a dressing room, hanging the dress on a hook and contemplating it for so long that I considered putting it back where I'd found it. But finally, I slipped its impractical, airy fabric over my head. In the mirror, my skin turned radiant and beautiful against its cheery orange hue. I ran my hands down the skirt, awed. But the brush of cool air on my shoulders felt foreign and drew too much anxious attention to the straps, to my exposed skin.

There was Gabriel's voice again, lecturing me on the dangers of vanity and indulgence. My body existed for a cause, not for the enjoyment of myself or others.

Over the years, her voice did fade. I wasn't sure whether it was due simply to the passage of time or avoidance of the things that reliably conjured her.

Outside of Ana, I didn't have other reliable voices to replace Gabriel's. Despite my honest hopes when embarking on my new life, Gabriel's echo still shamed and scared me into a lesser adherence. I carried the memory of that friendless September just under my skin.

Without Zuriel, I knew what it was to be truly alone for the first time. We'd been isolated before, yes, but now, living among the most people I ever had, I understood the temperature of loneliness. Zuriel's presence had been the way I made sense of our lives, and without her, I'd often felt like an arrow without a bow.

Now, suddenly, she's back. With her, a fleeting glimmer of warmth.

I dress out of sight of the bathroom mirror as I always have. It's easier this way. Our family home had no mirrors, and it took months to get used to seeing my reflection so often and clearly. I hid my body from myself, shy, as if I were a stranger.

I pause to take sips of tea as I get ready, thinking of the night before and Zuriel's willingness to leave some of Gabriel aside. She'd closed up again after hearing the angel song, as if she had to compensate and reassert Gabriel's rigid boundaries—as if she thought the song was a warning. It'd seemed too sensitive to ask how often she heard from her namesake and gravely taboo to offer an unsolicited interpretation of the song's meaning.

I take another sip of tea and startle when I register what it's in. It's one of her cups.

Finding it on the counter beside the sink had seemed so natural. Of course I drink mysteriously delivered tea from dainty little cups. Of course.

Zuriel quirks an eyebrow from the kitchen as I open the bathroom door. "Do you always brew your tea in the shower?" she asks, setting two plates of fried eggs and toast on the table.

"No," I snap defensively, having been oblivious to my mood until confronted.

She's suddenly hunter-observant as I take the chair across from hers. I set my cup down and keep my eyes on my plate, scrambling for something to fix the mood.

"I'm sorry. The past week has been so stressful," I say.

"At least there was no demonic activity last night," she notes casually, and that makes me look up. "Did you notice anything?"

I shake my head. "No," I say, cradling my tea close.

"That smells lovely," says Zuriel. "A gift from Ana?"

I'm happy for the excuse. "She sometimes brings me tea from her visits home."

Zuriel looks toward the kitchen. "Which cabinet is it in?"

"I brewed the last of it just now," I say.

But I've never been able to successfully lie to Zuriel, or anyone for that matter.

Her stare doesn't leave me. "Remind me. When was the last time you saw this demon?"

My hands are shaking, and of course, Zuriel notices. Anyone would notice. I press my palms to my lap, fighting to level myself before I speak. Maybe I'm lying, but I still hate what she's doing.

"Stop acting like Gabriel," I say.

She stabs at an egg, and the yolk runs free. "I don't know what you mean."

"Asking a million unrelated questions like you're trying to catch me in a lie. You know how easy it is to put me on edge, how she'd use it against me."

"I'm just trying to figure out what happened here. You asked me to stay, to investigate. You're out of practice. I'm doing this to make sure you're safe."

A stinging rush of tears blurs my vision. I'm not sad. I'm angry. How many times did Gabriel walk me into a verbal trap and then insist it was for my own good? I gulp the rest of my tea to drown any protests that might form in my mouth. I want to return to last night when Zuriel was Zuriel, her care genuine and warm.

I stand. "I have to—"

But Zuriel holds an arm out, blocking my path.

"I can't purge anything," I snap, "because I couldn't eat anything because you wanted to interrogate me!"

I slam the bathroom door and sit shaking on the edge of the bathtub, suddenly hating that my apartment is one room, that I have to retreat to the bathroom if I want privacy. I could've gone downstairs and taken refuge in the store's back room, but the capacity for rational, balanced thought in the heat of the moment has never been a strength of mine, the reason I was never a good hunter. I hate that I cry when I'm angry. I hate all my weaknesses. Most of all, I hate that they're so transparent.

I once told my family I was fasting. Truly, I was hiding from our mother, trying to hide my body from her. The night before, she'd commented that I had taken too large a portion at dinner. She commented on my curves. I was enduring puberty and didn't know how. I hated my body changing shape. I hated that she noticed. I stopped eating for a week. She praised my diligence until I fainted during training. Zuriel had to shepherd me back to my room while my mother and brothers continued.

"Your vision turns black when you stand." Zuriel repeated my words back to me. "You see dancing lights when you turn your head."

"The fasting is working. The angels must see me," I said. "They're delivering a vision, but I can't fully see it yet."

Zuriel handed me a glass of water and sat with me on the edge of the bed. She looked as if she was about to deliver bad news. "That's not the angels, Cass. You're starving yourself. What you're seeing—it's your body shutting down."

"No," I said. My hands shook. They wouldn't stop shaking. I'd been shivery for a week. I set the glass aside. "I'm fasting."

"You need to eat. If this happened on a hunt—we could lose you."

I started crying then. I wanted to be close to the angels. I thought, maybe, I'd found the answer. I would hear their messages, and Gabriel would give me that small, approving smile again. She'd stop frowning at me as if I were broken. The next day, when Zuriel convinced me to break my fast, I turned sick in the sparring room. I'd eaten too much, too fast, to get it over with. I felt shameful, but afterward, I was empty. I felt better. I thought I'd stumbled on a solution. For three years, I hid that solution from my sister.

My past and present body become one. I climb into the now with the same dizziness, the same secrets, the same shame.

I breathe the way Ana taught me until the shaking subsides. I blow my nose, rinse my face, and return to the table. Zuriel's back is to me as she washes dishes.

I know she's heard me crying, but she says nothing. I finish the breakfast she made. She wouldn't let me *not* finish it. We don't abide wastefulness, and I don't want to fight with her again. When she hears my fork hit the plate a final time, she retrieves my dishes to wash. I keep my eyes down. I've returned to a state where food is no longer enjoyable, where it's simply a necessity for staying alive for a mission.

When Zuriel finally shuts off the tap, the silence becomes unbearable.

"I'm sorry," she says. She doesn't say for what. If she's learned so much about speaking from Gabriel since I left, then she'll never fault herself. *I'm sorry you're a failure* all Gabriel's apologies seemed to say.

"It'll be time for me to open soon," I say, standing. "I should get downstairs."

I consider telling Zuriel to leave, that I'm fine on my own, that I don't need her help. But the person I really want to say those things to isn't here. My sister is, and maybe I have one more chance to convince her to my side.

"You were curious about the store?" I offer.

"I was."

"Come with me," I say, the only context in which I can say those words.

Zuriel sets the dish towel aside. "Your dagger," she reminds me gently. "If you believe there's something after you, you should always be prepared."

I look back to where the dagger glints on the bedside table, stifling my arguments as I retrieve it. This is a small thing to go along with and means we'll make it downstairs in peace.

The sky is gray with a storm that may land here or may pass on, but the store's golden light beats out the gloom. Zuriel trails me on the way to the counter, lingering briefly to observe my handmade signage. Papercrafts had come naturally to me, and I spent a day repurposing pages from damaged books into collages.

"Everything I touch in the archives these days seems to be falling apart. I'm sure the manuscripts miss your attention," Zuriel comments behind me.

I try for an acknowledging laugh, but it comes out nervous. Zuriel peers over my shoulder at my business email. Two orders came in last night, and a vendor is having a sale. I click into the new orders.

"I can show you around while I grab these," I say.

Zuriel frowns at some of the spines as we walk. "Do you read all these?" she asks.

I laugh and don't answer at first, thinking it's the same tired joke all booksellers and librarians hear. Then I realize Zuriel's being genuine.

"I've read something from every genre I sell, and I have to at least keep up to date with what's popular and what people are asking for. One of my favorite things is hand selling."

As we go, Zuriel lets me stack books in her arms, holding them without complaint as I search the shelves.

"Is it difficult to keep a public place warded all the time?" she asks.

"I don't," I say, bracing for critique and glad to have something to do with my hands.

"Why wouldn't you?"

"I don't want to work that kind of energy anymore. Upstairs was an emergency," I answer, bustling off to the horror shelves.

"Really, Cass? What's the difference between your apartment and here?"

I sigh at a face-out anthology. "Don't tell me how to run my business."

"I'm not telling you how to run your business. I'm being practical about your safety. Normal people become targets all the time. Leaving us obviously doesn't mean anything."

"And that's the last one," I say, placing the final book atop the stack in Zuriel's arms. I scan the list in my hands one last time and turn back toward the counter.

When I don't engage, Zuriel relents. "Show me how this works," she says, gesturing at the point-of-sale screen.

Gabriel couldn't stave off adopting technology for long. We always had the cars. It was a practicality, and practicality always won with Gabriel. When we started our ghost hunting business as a front to get more potential information about occult activity in the region, the internet and smartphones became a necessity. Still, Gabriel remained bad at navigating them, leaving most of that work to Zuriel.

Between customers, she quickly catches on with the software, and we work together in peaceful silence as we used to, the sharp beep of the scanner punctuating the moment. I sticker the new inventory as she hands the books to me, and we pick up a rhythm. Her stack shrinks while, on the other side of the counter, mine builds, new titles neatly stacked and ready to shelve. It's a task I could do in my sleep but reinvigorated through partnership.

We've always worked so well together. And Zuriel likes the store. *I've been curious.* I can picture us here, like this, not just today, but every other. Zuriel's always been good with documentation and keeping order. Poring over small details was the kind of work that soothed her, that she excelled at. And my books are chaos, the part of business owning that's unfortunately crucial and that I like least.

The window of opportunity is closing. When will I be in her presence like this again? To speak to her so honestly and share my life with her? She'll go back to Gabriel, and we'll return to our chilly texts. I want to keep this peaceful moment, but if I also want a chance at the vision of the future playing out in my mind, I have to make my bid now.

"I was thinking," I begin, hoping I sound casual though my mouth is already dry.

She hands me another book, and the nervous tremble in my hands betrays me. Zuriel zeroes in on it with a hunter's sharp perception but just as smoothly takes up another book to scan into the system, her back to me, waiting for my move and careful not to telegraph her own.

Fine. So it's like this, then.

I've never bested Zuriel in any fight, whether with my words or my sword. She's always had Gabriel's gift for sharp calculation and, when necessary, her cold decisiveness.

"I've been wanting some help around the store, and since I've already gotten things established, it would be easy for you to step in if you wanted. If you like it here."

"I'm not going to be your *employee*," she says, and I can practically hear the accompanying eye roll.

"No, of course not!" I hurry to correct. "We'd be co-owners."

She keeps scanning, her fingers efficient across the keyboard. The books pile up on my side, awaiting their stickers. My part of the job is admittedly easiest, but I struggle to keep up with her, to place the stickers just so. Eventually, I give up, pressing my palms into the counter.

"I have a job," she says quietly, her tone effectively drained of any emotion.

"You don't have to give up hunting if you don't want to," I say. "But you could stay out here. With me. If you— If it's . . ."

I shut up. I've always had an embarrassment of emotion. Out of everyone in our family, I never mastered how to speak while locking myself away.

She stops scanning, her fingers perfectly relaxed against the home keys while I bite my lip and fidget my ring around and around on my finger.

Finally, she turns to face me fully. "I have a job, and I have a duty to see it through," she says, her face impassive.

"I still hear the angels," I say. I'm showing my hand, I'm cracking, but the window is closing. "Even out here, I hear them. They haven't abandoned me."

Zuriel stands, the movement turned so efficient it's almost robotic. "I'm happy for you," she says without a wrinkle of mirth on her face. "It's getting late. Since I've found nothing on this *scouting mission*, I should report back to Gabriel."

I trail her from behind the desk, rifling through my thoughts for anything to make her stop. To make her *feel*. I don't want my last memory of her to be this colder version our mother cultivated. Not again.

"What about French Cassiel?" I blurt.

When I say the name, it evokes Gabriel's face flickering between the flames in the courtyard and smooth vellum under my fingertips. I'm back at my family estate, skulking around in dark corridors with forbidden manuscripts clutched to my chest.

Zuriel's halfway to the door. She stops abruptly. I nearly run into her, then tiptoe to her side as if afraid to disturb the air around her. But for a twitch of muscle in her jaw, she's retained her mask.

"You promised me you were done with that. You swore a binding oath to Gabriel."

A binding oath I bore the scar from. Merely saying the name irritates my throat.

French Cassiel—so named by my teenage self for the only two things I knew about them: that they wrote in French and that they shared my name. Their manuscript mentioned little about their life. Like an astronomer, their concern was with the heavens.

I discovered them in our estate archives, the loose pages of their manuscript tossed haphazardly at the bottom of a splintering box. French Cassiel had questions I'd never heard asked aloud, and they'd formulated them in another time, likely a continent away. I felt distant and near to them, not just through the connection of our namesake but because they, too, had wanted answers. Because of them, I learned that many of us in the past, upon learning the knowledge passed down about the angels, became not hunters but philosophers.

Their manuscript referenced a raging debate around why nephilim continued to be born at all, what our function in the world was. I could piece together just enough in my intermediate French to be hooked but not enough to understand the depth of their argument. I'd spend hours with a paragraph, their cramped cursive challenging me at every turn, and come away frustrated and confused. I wished I could ask questions, wished that sharing a namesake meant I had a direct line of communication to them.

I wished our self wasn't subsumed upon death.

It was a passing thought, but it scared me back then. It seemed blasphemous at worst and disrespectful to my namesake at best. Of course I wanted to be united with them. But I also wanted to know.

I set the manuscript aside for a week after that, scared of what I was prying open. I understood that our knowledge was part of what made us different from other people. This Cassiel's thoughts, then, would make me different even from my family. I didn't know whether I wanted to change. But I wanted knowledge, so change was inevitable.

Many words didn't have translations at all but seemed to be terminology understood within this community of philosopher nephilim. So much foundational knowledge of other theories was assumed that I'd spend a week with one page to come away with very little enlightenment.

When I realized what I'd found, I abandoned my book restoration projects, though continued using them as an excuse for extended time alone in the archive. I knew instinctively that my finding had to remain a secret. Through their examples, I gleaned that French Cassiel had lived a life I wasn't allowed. In questioning the purpose of existence, they looked to humans, engaging in their pleasures as often as they turned to extreme asceticism. When were they happiest? What made them feel fulfilled? When did the angels sing? It was an experiment to them, tests that needed to be run. Should we live as monks or kings?

I never learned their conclusions if they came to any. When Gabriel began to question my slow progress on restoring the books, I returned to my designated task and snuck the manuscript out of the archive to read in my room after bedtime. Until my lack of sleep began to show . . .

"This Cassiel is no more. Their thoughts don't matter," Gabriel had said to me, shaking the pages angrily in my face.

I never spoke up against Gabriel. She wanted to keep us safe. She knew the truth and what was right, but as she threatened the manuscript, I felt as if she was stealing a part of my identity away that I'd only just discovered, a glimmer of what I could be. Unlike Zuriel, I showed little promise as a hunter. She would be stepping into her role in only a year and I in three, yet I couldn't picture it for myself the way I could for her. I was clumsy and skittish and slow—Gabriel's own words for my shortcomings—the clear disappointment among my siblings.

But French Cassiel was a philosopher and, it seemed, good at it. I was good at restoring the books, at organizing them, at thinking my own thoughts when given the time. I could be like the old nephilim. There was a place in the world for someone like me.

"Why do we keep all these old texts if they don't matter?" I'd demanded, ready, for the first time in my life, to fight.

My brothers stood at the door to my room, looking on with restrained amusement. They knew how this would play out. They thought they knew what came next. Zuriel stood behind them, her eyes wide at my challenge.

I knew Gabriel would slap me. I knew. Her strike was always passionless and cold and preceded by a long, impassive stare. But I had never challenged her so directly, and this time she slapped me so hard I fell. Dazed, I pressed a hand to my burning cheek and was surprised when it came away smeared with blood. Gabriel's signet ring glinted in the candlelight, and all I could do was stare at it, at the crest, and wonder what French Cassiel would think.

How did we, my family, live? Why did we exist, and why did we exist like this?

"It is blasphemous," Gabriel explained, as if she hadn't slapped me, as if I weren't reeling on the floor, "to be as concerned as you are with the line of your namesake. The body and its individual thoughts don't matter once we're united. We are collective, but your obsession has led you to think only of yourself and your desires. Lost in those whims, you've neglected your duties to your family. You've not only lied once but persisted in calculated deception. Do you disagree?"

I shook my head, unable to meet her gaze. Whenever she found fault with me, she'd pose this question to bring me back into alignment with her. It was a mercy to be on Gabriel's side again.

"Do you disagree?" she repeated.

I'd been too shocked to verbalize, too struck by my own wrongness. I'd never lied, never thought I had the capacity to *persist in calculated deception*. But that was what I'd done, wasn't it? I'd thought desire was only a bodily thing and had unwittingly stumbled into it because Cassiel felt safe. They were me, in a way, weren't they? And I wouldn't lie to myself. I wouldn't make myself wrong.

But that was the error in my thinking, as Gabriel laid out. I couldn't trust myself, could I? It was blasphemous.

"I don't," I said, my throat so tight with guilt I thought I'd choke. I wished for an instant that I could stop existing just so I could escape the concentrated gaze of my family members. I'd never been so humiliated, but Gabriel hated tears, so I didn't cry.

She turned to leave, the manuscript pages still clutched in her hand. My siblings hurried apart to let her through the doorway, eyes lowered as if meeting her gaze would turn her wrath on them.

"Where are you taking them?" I called after her, because despite the pain of the moment, fear was stronger.

Gabriel didn't answer. The sound of her heels rang sharp as she descended the stairway. I ran from the room, and Zuriel caught me.

"Don't," she hissed, her grip tight on my wrist.

I fought her, calling down the stairs with rising panic, "What will you do with them?"

When I clearly had no intention of giving up my struggle, Zuriel pulled me against her, pinning my arms to my sides. If I'd been thinking rationally, it'd have been an easy lock to get out of, but I wasn't rational.

I was a liar fueled by desire.

I scratched and bit and stomped my heel into her foot. I howled and turned feral. My brothers stepped back from me as if I'd been suddenly possessed. Zuriel dropped me. I'd become too much trouble. I bolted for the stairs, following the click of Gabriel's heels and the sound of the courtyard door creaking open.

I stumbled into the twilit yard just in time to see Gabriel summon a ring of radiant fire with a flick of her hand and feed the manuscript pages to the flames. I screamed. I threw myself at the fire. Zuriel was there again to catch me. I strained against her, punched at her back as she tried to carry me away from the searing heat, kicked at her shins. She held fast until I tired, enduring my onslaught by whispering into my ear how it would all be okay. But it wasn't okay. I would never know now.

Gabriel watched me from the other side of the divine fire, her face distorted by the heat. At dawn, she'd carve a cleansing sigil into my skin. My behavior befitted one of the possessed. Something in my soul was clearly inferior, something that pain would cleanse.

The memory plays across Zuriel's face in a flash, breaking her emotionless mask.

"What if the other Cassiel was right?" I ask in a rush. "What if the angels live through us vicariously? What if we *know* somehow, intuitively, how our namesakes want us to live because we are each other? Maybe that's why the day I opened the store, I heard the song. Maybe—"

"You're falling," says Zuriel, her voice breaking on the words.

"I'm—" I can't repeat the word.

Nephilim can't fall in the angelic sense. We're already human, and that makes us fallen enough. But that hasn't stopped families from disowning those they deem so, those who've rolled around in the mess of the world and gained a tarnish beyond cleansing.

"Only a fallen nephilim would think they were so important that *angels* live through them to benefit from *human* experience. It's hubris. This thinking is what caused the war. This is what made demons. It's why we're still fighting today."

I try to backtrack and stumble over myself. "You have to have questions too. You were curious about my life here, why Cassiel still talks to me."

"I think you're confused," Zuriel says as if breaking difficult news.

"*You think I'm confused,*" I repeat, each word louder than the previous. I'm on the floor of my childhood bedroom again. Gabriel's ring is bloodstained. The manuscript pages are clutched in her fist. "Did she say I'd try to lie to keep you here?"

Nephilim don't lie about hearing the angels. If Zuriel believes I am—and worse, that it's a lie with the intention to manipulate her—then she truly believes I'm lost.

Her expression is soft, pitying. "You always had trouble when we were growing up, and it's gotten worse since you've been out here. You're imagining succubi. You think your namesake lives through you."

Her words take the air out of the room. I don't hear her; I hear Gabriel. The scar on my back aches, and I need to escape the pain. I need to be good so I never have to feel pain again.

"Come back with me before it's too late," she's saying. "We can help you. We can cleanse you."

I step back from her.

"You have to come home eventually, Cassiel," she says. Not *Cass. Cassiel.* "You're having nightmares about a demon of lust. Don't you see why I'm worried?"

But she's real, I nearly say. Nearly. The ambiguity of her intentions restrains me.

"We can help you banish these thoughts," she continues, genuine concern in her voice.

Zuriel is so certain. And even if I know I didn't imagine the succubus, I don't want to be alone anymore. I've never felt completely at peace out in the world. Maybe I was right. Maybe this is the sign to return home. I'd be with my sister again. I'd return to my calling and all my doubts would evaporate.

"I'll need time to arrange things here if I'm leaving," I say, hedging. But I can't imagine closing the store. I can't imagine Ana's face when I tell her.

Zuriel hugs me, rubbing my back as she does. Her hand passes over the scar. It aches at her touch.

"I'll come get you anytime," she promises. "I've missed you."

"I've missed you too." I'm happy to say it, finally.

She sighs with relief. "I knew you'd find the way back someday."

But why do I feel dread as I cling to her? I know, even as I play with the possibility, that I can't go back. She's right about me. I am a liar.

"I'll tell Gabriel to expect you," she says.

I break away from her. "This isn't about Gabriel. I—"

I hate her, I was about to say, the first time this feeling has crystalized into words. I hate her for the way she took care of us. I hate her for trying to make me strong. But I hate her for destroying the manuscript most of all. It'd been too terrible a feeling to name before now, and I'd hoped running away would diminish it. Hate can wound a soul, and I am wounded. Avoiding tending to it hasn't healed me.

"If I came back, it would be for you," I say, trying to hold close all the ways I'm hurt.

"I want to make sure you're well," she says, still gentle. "What matters most is your soul. I only mentioned Gabriel because if she's going to prepare the cleansing ritual, she needs at least five days of meditation—"

"I'm not leaving in five days!"

The door chimes, and Zuriel and I are immediately pleasant. "Let me know if I can help you find anything," I say automatically.

The woman nods, wandering off toward nonfiction.

Once she's out of sight, Zuriel says, "I'm leaving now, but I'll come back for you. Okay?"

"Stay here. Please," I try again.

She weaves around my display of seasonal candles and tea on the way to the door. "You know I can't."

"Then"—the window has closed—"at least tell me how you stayed there with her and forgot about me."

It's mean and unfair, I know. As soon as the words leave my mouth, I regret them, but they're my genuine feelings, not only a final insulting jab. I didn't hear from her for six months after I left. My letters and calls tapered off. Her avoidance was pointed. We'd been united by our common mission, not our sisterhood.

Zuriel, always the reasonable one, merely says, "I'll welcome you home."

And then she's gone. I don't hear the door ring her exit. I watch her until she's disappeared down the sidewalk. I turn my ring around my finger, and I don't cry. Gabriel hates tears.

I ring out the customer, bidding her a good day through the dread growing inside me. From behind the counter, I watch the Open sign, consider turning it to Closed, but I'm rooted to where I stand.

I remember witnessing my cousin's cleansing. This was before I found Cassiel's manuscript, before I'd endured a minor cleansing of my own. I remember watching the blood run from the blessed sigil cut into their chest. I remember Gabriel's rare smile as she threaded binding energy through the wound, healing it into a scar. Some of us believed that those who returned were made stronger through the ritual, that it fortified our commitment to our namesake and our path. The scar, like many of our scars, was worn with honor. But the blood had terrified me in a way it hadn't before. Perhaps because I was realizing Gabriel terrified me.

A rising note of angel song intrudes on my memories. This time, it's different.

I know Cassiel's voice as I know my own. They're not leading this chorus, but still it winds around my heart. I follow its command, a spirit seeking the divine. As I listen, an ache opens in my chest like a bottomless well. I feel lost even as I near the source of the sound. I want to climb inside the voice and never be without it. I want to sacrifice everything to its beauty.

Dimly, through the swell of my longing, I realize the song is a *sound*. Angel song is grounding, but it is never grounded. It exists fully in the realm of the mind-spirit. But this song is entering my heart through my ears. I'm at the threshold of the store's back room when the realization settles too late. The darkened doorway yawns like the entrance to a cave, the ordinary darkness replaced by something eternal and sentient. The song fades at my realization. It's done its work in luring me here. I reach for the light, click the switch, and nothing happens. The darkness endures.

I could run, but that seems dangerous. I'm within reach of the shadows. Zuriel is long gone. My phone is at the desk. There's no one in the store I could call to—not that I'd want to involve anyone else. This is my fight. I lay a hand against the dagger hidden in my blazer. Our standoff stretches on. I have no doubt about who I'm facing, though I've never been so close to her, not while awake.

"Don't let her take you back there," she says, the power of her voice ringing through me. It carries the wisdom of one who's seen great civilizations fall and stood unaffected in the rubble, the authority of one who's commanded a thousand kings to kneel before her. All her attention is turned toward me, and I'm swept up in the sound's resonance. It's been so long since I've heard a demon speak in their true voice, and I'm reminded once more that they were angels. But for all its power, her voice is also soft and husky, as if she's casually exhaled a breath of smoke before turning to give a friend hard advice.

I stand squarely in the light cast through the doorway, not daring to venture near the shadows. The dark shifts. She moves toward me, the world bending to her step.

Finally, I find my voice. "You shouldn't be here."

I didn't know darkness could smile, but it does. I feel it.

"Whether I should or shouldn't depends entirely on what you want. It's clear you don't want to go back. I can show you something different."

A hand reaches into my square of light. Shockingly ordinary brown-gold skin, elegantly long fingers that end in black claws. I look up to see the dense silhouette of her, gold eyes shining out at me just as in the dream. I reach tentatively for her, my hand hovering over hers, when . . .

"You're trying to seduce me," I say. Because if she's not trying to kill me, that must be what this is. It's the obvious conclusion with a succubus, but I wouldn't have expected such a careful, drawn-out approach. Demons are impatient.

She laughs at that, so sharp and sudden it makes me jump. "Of course I'm seducing you, little angel," she says, drawing the words out indulgently. "It seems to be working. I remain unstabbed."

I look back to her hand, an offer. Open, waiting. I can imagine the heat of her touch, can imagine lacing our fingers, how we'd fit together.

I retreat, backing away from the unnatural darkness she's conjured, from her waiting grasp. I'm sick with the thought that I nearly placed my hand in hers. I almost wish she'd attacked me. It would be easier than this. It would be black-and-white, the way Gabriel taught us.

I close my hand around the hilt of the dagger. The demon showed me that even the deepest darkness has a heart, and now I know exactly where to aim.

She lingers at the threshold of light, her hand outstretched a moment longer.

"Why did you hold me down? In the dream," I ask, suddenly overwhelmed by the memory, by the loss of my light.

She lowers her hand. "You would've killed me if I didn't," she says, and she sounds *hurt*. "Just like you think you want to kill me now."

"I have to if you come back. So—don't."

She treads the line of light, coming as near as she can without revealing herself. "*Why* do you have to?" she says, her voice turning agitated. "So you can fulfill expectations you rejected?"

The sentence hits me like a slap, unleashing every pent-up emotion I've harbored for the past week. "You don't know anything about me! I left my life behind to build this! And then *you* show up, and you ruin—"

The store bell rings. I hear the front door fall shut, the small sound so distant and irrelevant. I glance to the back room and find its shadows empty.

Whoever entered the store either doesn't find what they're looking for or doesn't find me and leaves.

FOUR

T IDYING MY APARTMENT AFTER work reveals that I have the beginnings of a nice, if mismatched, tea set. I stack the cups and saucers carefully on the kitchen counter, studying the fine blue feathers painted on one cup, the blush pink flowers on the other.

I can still hear her laugh. *Little angel* she'd called me.

My limited cabinet space is already packed full, but I find myself consolidating and throwing things out until there's a little corner for the china to nest in. I'm excited to have something so fragile and impractical, so different from my sturdy earthenware mug. I stand back to observe the pieces in their new place as if appraising a rare piece of art before the sobering truth of them returns.

I can still hear her hurt too. Of course I would've killed her. There was one script.

I grab the china down again in a sudden fit of frustration and march the pieces to the trash, summoning every remaining shred of hunter detachment to throw them in. Instead, I find myself standing over the bin and feeling alarmingly conflicted. I hug the china to my chest like a precious gift someone's unfairly demanding I give up. I want to cry, angry with myself for wanting anything at all.

I dress just enough for the cold and stomp down the stairs to the dumpster, the china clinking together the entire way down. Such a soft, dainty sound to be so loud. I tamp down the rising thoughts of protest and hurl one of the saucers into the dumpster. Its shatter against the metal is dramatic and furious. I throw a cup in after it and hate the sound, how it turns into a visceral sensation like crunching broken glass between my teeth.

My throat tightens. The autumn wind stings my face and aids the tears, and soon they're tracking down my cheeks. I toss the final pieces in at once, and when the crash fades, something ugly and desperate rises. I scream, kicking the side of the dumpster so hard that I leave a dent, the metal reverberating its injury. I gulp cold air until it hurts, until I feel dizzy and racked with regret.

I tell myself over and over that this was the right decision. Innocent as they seemed, they were fabricated by a demon and therefore infernal artifacts. I could've easily cursed myself. I was lucky.

The excuse rings hollow. Zuriel didn't even notice them. They were fine.

They were gifts.

But demons aren't altruistic. They aren't kind and they can't be.

I need to see her again. I need to be prepared.

◆

Perhaps the problem was never with my wards but with *me*.

Nothing in our knowledge indicates this as a possibility, but there are few other recorded cases like mine, nephilim who have retained their light but broken away from family to live among normal people. It isn't done. It isn't responsible. I was born knowing my calling, and I've selfishly given it up.

One more thing remains to try.

Night draws close. My plan has brought on old memories, old energy. I know that my family, miles away, is speaking the same angelic words and performing the same sacred motions. Though I haven't moved or spoken this way in years, I fall back into the rhythm of the ritual as if the last time I performed it was only yesterday. Grounding and centering before a hunt is imperative for safety and success. We at once need to remember and forget our human bodies, to exist in the serene in-between. Maybe, when I put down the wards initially, I wasn't focused enough. Few believe living a modern life is compatible with our work, another reason to close ourselves off from the world.

I plant my feet and draw a breath, summoning a ring of light into being. Forming itself into a ring of angelic sigils, it turns a slow circle around me. I know the next line in the angels' song, could never forget it, but standing in the space between my bedroom and kitchen feels anything but sacred. I see now why we had rooms dedicated to this work. Nothing on the walls, no unnecessary furnishings. Just darkness and incense. I don't have the right incense or any at all. Maybe there are some tealights in a drawer—

The ring of light destabilizes, flickering down. I refocus, find the flow of light within myself, feel the cadence of song on my breath. The ring steadies, reflecting its cold light up into my face. I reach into it, find the slender tails of the sigils, and pinch them between my fingers like delicate threads. Drawing one up and one down, they form two additional rings, creating an insulating field of light. I sing for protection and guidance, invoking my angelic namesake to close the ritual. Radiating outward into the air, the rings project a lingering shimmer of ethereal energy into my small apartment.

While the energy is high, I retrace and reseal the warding circles, bending all my concentration to the meaning behind the sigils. *My soul's light is a shield against the infernal enemy*, I think fervently, gripping the piece of chalk so hard it snaps. Taking up the other half, I continue. *None bearing ill will shall exist within.* I stand and dust my hands, jittery from the energy and exertion. But as soon as I step back, the dam against my thoughts breaks and I'm awash in a tide of all the questions I have about her that if this works—hopefully this works—will never be answered now.

One question rises to the surface. Where would she have led me if I'd taken her hand?

When my line of thinking progresses from idle wonder to indecent, shiver-inducing curiosity about her fangs, I realize maybe Zuriel's right. Maybe I'm not well.

These thoughts are too human.

———◈———

I sleep with the dagger under my pillow, one hand on its hilt, the other on its sheath, ready to pull it free. She shouldn't appear—she *shouldn't*—but still I wait, trying to feign sleep. My entire body is tense with anticipation. Or at least, anticipation is what I've chosen to name it. To acknowledge anything else feels like sabotage.

Faint at first, the scent of smoke returns. I think all my anxious wanting has made me imagine it until heat and oppressive shadow follow. The circle blazes to life, but beneath the glow, the wards lie dormant. She's here.

Am I so fallen that my light does nothing to repel the damned?

I tug the blade free, thrusting upward to bring its edge to bear against the form solidifying above me. Shadow melts from the figure like clearing fog until a woman materializes from its depths, her skin a flawless and radiant brown and her hair a long spill of silky black ringlets. And those golden eyes. I know, when I meet them, that I've hesitated a beat too long.

"I've never been held at knifepoint while trying to seduce someone." She leans into the edge of the blade as if it's a silly flirtation. The silver gleams bright against her neck. "I didn't mean to upset you," she says, suddenly all sincerity. "I should've properly introduced myself sooner."

"Why are you doing this to me?" I demand.

"I was sent to find you, watch you. When it was clear you weren't a big scary angel with a thousand eyes, I thought maybe I could reveal I was here, let you decide how you wanted this to go."

She leans closer, and I let her, keeping the blade steady at her throat but not pushing back. My training screams against this restraint. I remember what happened to Zuriel. I know the price of offering softness to a demon.

"You're different than the ones I've heard stories about," she says. "I could like you. As much as a demon could like a nephilim."

I make myself press the blade into her neck, a warning. Against a human, it'd draw a trickle of blood. With a flick of my wrist, I could kill her body and send her soul back to Hell. A blessed blade alone can't inflict a mortal wound, but it's enough to banish a demon from the physical plane.

She's unbothered by my threat, and I hate that we both know it's not serious. Despite the heat that radiates from her, I shiver. She smells like the darkness after a candle's been snuffed, like the close of a ritual, like dying light. I've never met a demon civil enough to talk to for any length of time, let alone one who wanted to flirt with me. I wonder whether this is always the form she takes or whether she's chosen a body aligned with what I find attractive.

"I see what you want. Desire is my specialty, remember?" She says it without threat. "Can I touch you?" she asks.

That she asks for permission startles me. It's not binding magic, not a trick, just a simple question. A demon's never asked me such a gentle question before.

I manage to hold the unnatural intensity of her gaze. She lets me think, patient. I wonder whether succubi are like vampires, whether they need an innocent invitation, a welcome, before they can enact their violence. But her eyes hold the same open curiosity I feel, a hope that this meeting doesn't have to play out the way we both know it should, that we can discard our roles—at least for now.

Against every instinct, I nod.

She reaches confidently for my free hand, heedless of the dagger, and sweeps her thumb over the skin of my inner wrist, pressing it into the bed. Her touch is feverishly warm, as if she's recently emerged from hellfire.

"You deserve to feel good," she says. "I can at least give you that. Make up for before."

The dagger trembles in my grasp. Like the first night she spoke to me, she's reined her aura in, its hunger defanged for now. I'm not under its influence, but I'm surprised to discover the truth in what she says, how much I want her.

Everything falls apart if I say *yes*, and I feel seconds away from ruin.

Her brow creases with concern. "I wouldn't hurt you, but I understand. Of course it's different for us," she says, all lust and heat evaporating as if she'd merely been inhabiting a role. "But do me a favor." She grasps my knife-wielding hand, and I let her also press it down into the bed. I'm pinned. She looms, and I'm hyperaware of my exposed chest and neck. "Take your pleasure if you want it," she says, flashing a fanged yet unthreatening smile.

Then I blink, and the room is dark again, and the demon is gone.

Hot tea steams at my bedside in the morning. Beside it, three more truffles are artfully arranged on a saucer amid camellia blossoms. The hilt of the dagger is still a grounding weight in my hand.

I don't understand.

No one as careless as I've been should survive a demonic encounter. No demon merely teases and vanishes without exacting a toll. But my mind and body are whole. I'm not even hungry.

I sheathe the dagger and spend the morning scrubbing away the chalk circle. I'm not a hunter anymore, and I clearly can't solve my problems like one. I don't want to think of my failed circle as yet more evidence of my shortcomings. Best to be rid of it. Best to move on. It feels good to move my body after so much sleep. I push my bed back to its original place.

The tea and truffles still wait for me on the bedside table. Besides the flowers, there's something different this time. I draw a slip of paper from beneath the saucer. *I promise to be good*, reads the sharp cursive.

But when I reach for the chocolates, my fingertips tingle. One practically gleams with demonic energy. It's obvious that she hasn't tried to disguise it, knows that I will easily sense it, wants me to sense it. An invitation.

Gingerly, I take it between my thumb and forefinger, and there's a spark at the first contact, our opposing energies bent on resisting each other.

Take your pleasure if you want it.

An apology. An invitation. A seduction.

I place it back among the camellias, get ready for work, and take the herbal tea down with me.

———◆———

The bookstore is the same as always. No sister efficiently tapping away at the keyboard. No demon shadow in the back room. I walk among the shelves, running my hands across familiar spines and opening the same computer windows in the same order as I do every morning. When I finally flip the sign on the front door to Open, Ana appears in an instant.

"Thank god you're okay," she says as soon as she's through the door. "You didn't answer my texts, and I was trying not to be a clingy friend."

I stare at her. Here is a human person. In the daylight. Speaking to me. The normal part of me registers that Ana is looking even witchier as Halloween nears. Her long dark hair has the new shape of thick bangs, and she's donned a cloak-like velvet coat. On a normal day, I might have complimented her on her lovely lace blouse or impeccable eye makeup. Her skin is flawless as always, as if she blends a shot of beauty potion into her morning coffee. By the time I've thought all these things, I've forgotten what Ana said and have been staring at her in silence for a few embarrassing seconds.

"You called my emergency contact?" is not what I mean to say first, but I do.

"I know you don't like your family and told me only to use it as a last resort thing, but— I was worried for you. You weren't answering your phone. When I called to you on the street the other day, you didn't seem . . ." She trails off.

"No, it's okay." I look down at the tea in my hands, its fragrant steam still rising pleasantly. Ana looks at it, too, and I suddenly want to hide it away, as if it tells too much of what's happened to me.

"Are you feeling any better?" Ana tries again.

I nod. "Just stressed. Holiday season approaching, you know."

Ana looks incredulous, then changes the subject. "My coven is hosting a circle soon. If you want to come."

"I'm not a witch," I say, struggling to piece together the conversational leap.

"There are nights where we join with people outside our coven, a kind of open-magic night, if you will." She seems very proud of her pun, but I know this forced casual tone. It's the one she uses when she tries to convince me to go to support groups. "You don't have to be a witch. All sorts of energy workers join us."

I fold my hands on the counter, covering my ring with my left hand. I've gotten too close to her, and by doing so, she's gotten too close to my secret. Ana's suspected everything else, but she's never proposed a supernatural explanation.

"You've never invited me to these before," I say carefully.

"I wasn't sure before."

"Sure about . . . what?"

"There are more people than you think who've left toxic covens. But you don't have to stop practicing just because you left."

"I'm not— I don't have magic, Ana."

But my weak protests are useless.

"I know something's going on with you," she says. "You don't have to hide it to spare me worry. If you need shelter from bad energy, we've dealt with this before. Whoever's after you can't scare us."

"It's not so simple," I say, realizing too late that this is as good as an admission.

"Then *tell me*, Cass."

It's my family, the angels, the demons. Most of all, it's *her*.

"I . . . can't," I say.

"If they've bound your speech—"

"It's nothing like that."

I'm rescued from our conversation by one of my regular customers stopping by to pick up a special order and am grateful for the opportunity to escape to the back room. I ring out the customer and sigh as soon as I think I'm alone again, but Ana reappears from the fiction shelves.

I brace myself for more questions. Instead, she only says, "I'm just across the street if you ever need anything. If you want to talk."

I force a smile. "Thank you."

I watch Ana until she disappears into the coffee shop again, then go about opening the mail, thinking about the truffle all the while.

<hr>

During a lull in customers, I dash upstairs for the tome. I've uncovered it more times in one week than I have in all three years. Flipping through for the entry on succubi, I can barely maintain the careful, respectful manner that's instinctive with handling a text this old and precious. Even if I didn't know what it was, I'd still know that it's the kind of book that demands respect.

Only half a page of information exists on succubi. Everything written here I already know. Most *everyone* already knows what's written here. People are perceptive, and myths exist for a reason, whether by the names we currently call them or something else.

I've only touched demons with the edge of my sword, but with her, the thing I want most is to feel her curls between my fingers. I imagine cupping her face in my hands and letting her draw me into a kiss. Every time, I stop short of imagining the heat of her mouth on mine.

I don't know how to understand the precarious link between us. Nothing since French Cassiel's manuscripts has made me feel this way—the glimmer of deeper possibility, the potential of waking to my full self. As with French Cassiel, understanding her could rewrite my world. And just as before, perhaps that's the real fear. Not that she's a demon, not that we should be enemies, but that letting her in means accepting new knowledge, and accepting new knowledge means change. Last time, it ended in fire.

I can't refocus on work after my short break. I drop things. Trip around the corners of shelves I could normally navigate with my eyes closed. I ring up a customer's books but forget to tell them the price until they awkwardly prompt. I become so lost in my thoughts that I nearly lock up with a customer inside who I didn't realize was still browsing. It's been a slow, typical day, and still, I'm frazzled.

When I finally return to my apartment in the evening, the room is red with sunset. I don't turn the lights on, take my time putting away my shoes and cardigan, needlessly straighten the things in the closet.

Before ascending the stairs, I'd decided.

Energy sparks when I take the chocolate in my hands. I roll it between my fingers. So small. So ordinary. I press it to my lips, and it warms my skin. For the first time all day, I feel hungry.

"I don't even know your name," I whisper to the empty room. "Would you trust someone like me with your name, the way I've trusted you with my body?"

The pressure of a shadow forms at my back. I move to turn my head, but she taps a black claw against my cheek, halting me. She remains just out of view.

"Avitue," she says against my ear.

I repeat the name in wonder. By the power in it, I know it's true. I've never simply asked and had a demon give their name.

"Now you have all you need to bind or banish me. If you're skilled enough, which I've no doubt you are, you could destroy me."

"Then why tell me?"

Her shadow is hot against my back, a strange comfort in the chill of autumn. "You're sweet *and* dangerous. A rare combination of traits in a mortal. And I'm in the mood for a high-stakes seduction."

She vanishes, leaving a cool void in her absence. I push the truffle into my mouth.

This one is dark. Bitter chocolate and black cherry chased by the metallic sting of blood. My body prickles with warmth, and I gasp at the jolt of arousal, how it strikes hot and fast. "Avitue," I breathe on a shaky exhale. Can I summon her back? Would she guide me through this maze of novel sensations? I suddenly need to be free of my clothes, need to feel my skin under my hands. When I've stripped away every scrap of fabric, I lie back on the bed, blissfully unselfconscious of my body for the first time in my life. I cup my breasts and test the sensation of my nipples, squeezing just to the edge of pain. Whatever moans or gasps come to me, I let myself have them, let myself breathe, let myself feel. This isn't artful. The influence that's taken me doesn't know delay or pace. It's hungry and it wants.

My thighs are already slick with arousal, my flesh swollen and hot. I find the point of pleasure with my fingers, massage into it. I gasp. My hips buck. *Avitue.* Amid the wash of pleasure, I'm only dimly aware of the spreading dampness beneath me. This, in any other state of mind, would have elicited shame, then panic. I'd have sought immediate atonement. But here, under the demon's spell, I'm freed. My body is my own, a new geography to explore. I test the sensation of my fingers inside me, moan, spread my thighs. Never in my life have I had this relationship to my body, not when a mere thought was always enough to send me spiraling into guilt. I feel sharp and fragile. My flesh is urgent, every point of me electrified. I want something, need something inside me.

I sweep a desperate hand across the bedside table, searching, and knock the saucer to the floor. Its shatter seems distant, muffled; I don't care. *Avitue.* My hand lands on the sheathed dagger, and I grasp it, curl my fingers over the crossguard, thrust its silver hilt into me. The flare of the pommel is delicious, the ridges of the rounded hilt exquisite. The metal is icy in comparison to my fevered body, and I gasp at the shock. Thrust and pressure together bring me off. My body tenses, relaxes, tenses. I cry out, my limbs loose, my core unspooled. The tang of blood on my tongue fades, settling me back into myself. I'm suddenly aware of the sheen of sweat on my body as it cools, the earthy scent of arousal in the air, the evidence of my orgasm on my hands.

For a moment, I'm frozen, shivery cold. Something leaden and heavy settles in my stomach. I register the dagger, slippery wet in my hand.

My vision blurs. I stand, hot desire replaced by something cold and automatic. I crunch across the porcelain shards, and if they stab into my feet, I think I deserve it. From under the bathroom counter, I withdraw an ancient wooden box. It's not something I've had to touch in months, and the rattle of the implements inside brings me back home. These are tools for returning one's sense of discipline and self-control. My thumb is on the latch.

A hand grips my wrist.

"Cassiel." The voice at my ear is alarmed this time.

I choke on a sob and try to wrestle my arm free, but I'm weak. I've always been weak. Avitue presses her body into my back and wraps an arm securely around me.

"Oh, angel," the endearment slips out on a breath against my neck. "What they've done to you is worse than much of what we could." She continues to hold my wrist gently but firmly where she caught it. Holds me *lovingly*, some distant part of my brain supplies. I swat the thought away before it can fully bloom and overtake my chest like a weed.

Avitue kisses the nape of my neck, comes around to take the box from me, and vanishes it all as if it never existed. I can't look at her. She strokes my cheek, her dark claws a delicate trace along my skin.

"Why?" she asks.

"A weak body weakens the soul," I recite. "A weak soul is unfit for a warrior."

"Desire isn't weakness. It's human," whispers Avitue. "You're—"

"A nephilim," I finish bitterly.

I register the barest shake of Avitue's head in the dark. She's here now, standing full and corporeal beside me. No haze of shadow. I could turn toward her, truly see her. Find her golden eyes. I don't.

"If I'd known—" Avitue starts.

"It's nothing," I say. "I wanted it, wanted to feel good, I mean, but— It's conditioning. The atonement is."

Avitue waits, then says, "Every time?" The words are soft as if the suggestion of what they imply will break me.

I swipe at my tears. "It's necessary. To resist temptation. If we're to survive the hunt."

"Did you even want to be a hunter?"

"Please," I sigh.

"I'm only angry for you."

The room feels suddenly too small for our silence.

I try to push past Avitue for the door but hiss at the sharp reminder of the shards in my feet.

"Let me," she offers, approaching as if I'm an injured animal. She scoops me easily into her arms and carries me back to the bed. I keep my eyes down, shamed as if the dagger, wrinkled sheets, and broken china are evidence of a crime. Avitue settles me on the edge of the bed and kneels to smooth her hands over my feet. Her healing touch first stings like an insect, but in the time it takes to gasp surprise, the pain is gone and the flesh healed.

We stay like that for a moment, with Avitue bowed at my feet. She wears a luxurious drape of black fabric and, but for the glow of her eyes, would blend into the deepening shadows. Each second that passes, I grow painfully more conscious of my body. I've never undressed with another person before. I long to wrap myself in a towel, a blanket, anything for modesty, but this moment is too fragile to disturb.

"I'm sorry," she says. "I need to be more careful with you."

"Why are you doing this?" I ask again.

She grins up at me. "Dangerous to entrust that information to a nephilim."

"But I already know your name."

"Destroying me—" Avitue shrugs. "I can be replaced. I'm only a small piece of all this."

"Of what?" I ask, my heart fast as I say the words.

Her coy laugh startles me. "Our eternal war, little angel. Heaven and Hell will not stop for us." She turns the full gleam of her gaze on me as she stands. The room is dark, and still, I feel I'm in her shadow. I look up at her and think of a different kind of power. "I don't want to leave you like this," she says.

I run my thumb over my ring, tracing the familiar contours of my family crest. "And I don't want you to leave," I admit to my lap.

Avitue doesn't move, and I can't look at her. Our meetings are emotional standoffs, each of us weighing the costs of trading one vulnerability for another. Gaining ground only brings us dangerously closer.

"Okay," she says, and I jump at the small word. Her finger is under my chin, raising my gaze to hers. The point of her claw bites into the soft flesh at my throat. I swallow, and it hurts, and I witness the slightest dilation of her pupils. She takes a slow step toward me, looming, and I stop breathing.

Her hands find my shoulders and squeeze, and it's painfully luxurious. "You're so tense," she whispers. "I could practically see all these knots from across the street."

I huff a laugh. "Is that what you were thinking when you broke into my store?"

"I broke nothing," she teases, beginning to knead the tension from my muscles.

I sigh, the heat of her hands unwinding me. I let my eyes drift closed, let myself trust.

"Would you like a massage? Would that be . . . comforting?" she ventures.

I nod, surprising even myself as I agree.

"I can get your back if you lie down."

I hesitate. We resume the standoff, but this time, it's brief.

"I can't keep turning my back to the enemy," I try to joke.

"Are we enemies?" she asks seriously.

"I don't know."

Avitue hums thoughtfully, sweeping behind me to the other side of the bed. I turn to watch her, and my heart stutters when she picks up the dagger.

I've never seen a demon handle a blessed weapon or *any* blessed object, but that discovery is far from my mind. I wish for a blanket again, this time to hide from mortification.

"*Fuck*," she hisses, dropping it to the floor with a metallic clamor.

The hem of her sleeve is singed. So she'd tried to handle it through the fabric to no avail.

"Why did you— What did you think would happen?" I ask, scientific curiosity winning out over embarrassment.

"I had a theory that you'd ruined the blessing. But maybe it's more interesting that you can't unbless something by having a good time."

I repeat her words under my breath, considering.

"Does anything nullify blessings on objects?" she asks.

"Some can lose their strength over time and need refreshing, but a blessing never completely fades."

"Well, then," she says. "You maintain the ability to not-quite-fatally stab me if the massage isn't to your liking. So?"

I'm still mulling over blessings as I settle onto my stomach. Avitue sits carefully beside me as if this is still warded space, and I realize she's the first person to ever share my bed like this. I've never had a partner or sought anyone I could be so vulnerable with. It's an accident that we've arrived here. Not a fatal one, I hope.

She begins with my scalp, applying just enough of her nails to be invigorating before working down to my shoulders again. At my upper back, she pauses, brushing her hand over the skin enough to leave a trace of warmth but nothing more.

Her voice is quiet. "Can I ask about these?"

And I remember. "Oh." I sit up as if she can unsee the line of scars across my back.

"Who did that to you?" she asks, concern and anger warring in her features.

"It's fine," I say, palming the intricate scar on my left shoulder. "They're"—I search for a word—"traditional."

"Did you want them?"

"I wanted this one," I say, stroking the sigil under my palm. "It was my first. My sister did it."

Avitue's frown doesn't leave. "The sister who tried to take you back?"

"It was different with us before," I say. I don't want Avitue to think badly of her no matter how complicated our relationship is now. "It's the angelic sigil for—"

"*Unknown one*," she says.

I drop my hand. "How do you know?"

"Falling didn't give me amnesia. Maybe I can't speak it anymore, but I can read."

"Oh." I wince. "Sorry."

Of course she knows the angelic tongue. I've heard her hum their songs, the words stripped from them, from her.

"No, I'm sorry," she says as if the word is unfamiliar to her. "*Surprise!* This demon is touchy about the fall." Her eye roll is self-deprecating. "You were explaining."

Unknown one—a loose translation of a complex angelic feeling—was the closest we could find to *sister*. It carries the connotation of wishing to learn about a person until they are known, a longing to connect. We entered the world unknown to each other and endeavored to understand. Less so recently.

"The back is the best canvas a body has. We collect our blessings here and the stories of our lives," I explain. "My sister and I were close before. We wanted to have something like a pact, just the two of us."

Some scars hurt and some do not. The story across my shoulders is short, befitting nearly three decades. There is the angelic rune my sister did, a web of loops and circles. In the middle, my first cleansing scar, set by Gabriel. On the right, a blessing for my first hunt. Curving jagged over my side is another scar, not a sigil but a reminder of a wound that could've been fatal had Zuriel not pulled me out of the path of a demon frenzied by the new moon.

Down my left thigh is a column of neatly spaced horizontal lines, the scars done by my own hand, one for each time I was compelled to mark an impure thought. Even out here, there were times I resorted to the cleansing and recentering power of our old tools. I don't ask Avitue what she's done with them. Even though their absence disturbs my comfort, I'd rather not know where I can reburden myself with those habits. I've had the box for as long as I can remember. It was, like most things passed down to us, given to me on my birthday. The wood of the handles was worn smooth from centuries of nephilim hands, but without any special care, the blades remained rustless and forever sharp. No one ever had to instruct me on what to do with these ancient tools, their blades too small and wrongly curved for use against any enemy other than one's own deficient flesh. Self-discipline was a mantra. Self-loathing was easy.

Avitue takes in every mark, lingering over the simple lines the longest—a perverse and personal record of my shortcomings. I'm worried she'll ask more questions, but her attention returns to the sigils on my back. "The second one? *Loyal mind, pure soul.*"

Gabriel's. Two integrated sigils carved over my spine. I cross my arms over my chest as if I can hide from the memory. "I swore I'd never talk about it again," I say.

Avitue nods as if she understands. She probably heard most of my conversation with Zuriel and has pieced at least part of the story together. Or she knows that, sometimes, when others command us not to speak, it's for the best. Some experiences we'd rather not relive in words.

"That night when you held my hand to your heart, I think I understand now," I say.

She tilts her head. "Yeah?"

"Yeah."

Avitue studies me, her eyes glinting like a cat's in the dark. This moment, like my life out in the world, seems impossible, and I want to grasp it while I can.

"What do I want?" I ask her because it's easier than naming desire.

She closes the space between us, drawing me into a kiss that's both fierce and tender. Even though it's exactly what I've asked for, I gasp against her, unprepared for the way her touch wakes my body again. For so long, I tried to numb myself that now I don't know how to endure feeling. She threads her fingers in the braids at the nape of my neck and holds firm, grounding me with the gentlest edge of pain. I breathe her in, her scent a memory of fire. I want to live here, but too soon, she pulls away.

"What's wrong?" I ask, worried I've ruined something.

"Nothing's wrong," she says, though she won't look at me anymore. Her hands are fisted in the sheets in a way that's certainly not safe for the fabric. "I don't want to push too far. After, you know."

"Did I make you uncomfortable?"

She laughs. "No, little angel. Quite the opposite."

"You're . . . very comfortable?"

"I'm very hungry," she says. "And I don't think we should confront that right now." Before I can react to what that implies, she says, "*I* was in the middle of comforting *you*."

We return to where we were before. The scents of rose and lavender and other flowers I can't quite identify perfume the air as Avitue massages scented oil into my back. I don't know where she got the massage oil, but if she can conjure tea and truffles . . . The press of her hands feels practiced, and I relax into their warmth. She's careful to avoid touching me in a way that might feel sexual, and I turn my face into the pillow and cry silently. I've never had such gentleness enacted upon my body by another. This kindness, I think, will be my true downfall. A soft temptation with a featherlight fall.

FIVE

I'M VAGUELY AWARE OF Avitue's presence through the night. She keeps a respectful distance from the bed as if she's realized something and made a decision she hasn't shared with me. I toss and turn, thinking foggily of questions I want to ask once I'm conscious enough to form them coherently. I don't know whether I dream her eyes or simply catch her looking at me during brief snatches of waking.

Exhaustion still weighs on me when I finally rouse sometime in the late morning, but I know Avitue, for once, had nothing to do with my poor sleep. When my eyes finally focus, I spy her across the room with my heavy edition of Shakespeare's collected works cradled in her lap. Her eyes are intent on the page, and she's settled into an easy sprawl, one leg kicked over the side of the chair, an arm resting on its back. Her mouth twitches in a smile.

Daylight brings my first clear look at her, and once I've seen her, I can't look away. I'm happy to be charmed, to let myself be swept away by admiration. She makes such an innocent picture. A *normal* picture, if not for the anachronistic black robes. Her features are feline sharp, softened by heart-shaped lips and a round nose. Without the creep of shadow at her edges, her curls seem even longer, spilling goddess-like down her chest and across the arm of the chair. My chest fills with longing. Not the frantic lust of the night before but something warm and comforting.

When I sit up in bed, Avitue's gaze is immediately on me. She hefts the book shut and rockets to her feet as if she's been caught in the act of something more nefarious than perusing classic literature.

"Which one is your favorite?" I ask, and it feels so easy. When have I had a casual, friendly conversation outside of Ana? I moved away to start a human life, yes, but I've hardly made an effort to reach out to anyone.

"Back in the day, I liked attending the comedies," Avitue answers. She shifts the book in her arms as if she doesn't know what to do with it. "It's rare that I get a chance to reread them."

A realization clicks in my mind for the first time. I push my blankets back, lean forward. This is the clearest my mind has been in Avitue's presence, and it's as if I'm truly hearing her for the first time. When she spoke to me from the shadows, I'd been so distracted by the power in her voice that I hadn't noticed the accent.

"Are you English?" I blurt.

"Because I like Shakespeare?"

Now it's my turn to be confused. "No. You have a London accent."

"Demons don't have nationalities?" There's the upturn of a question in her statement. "This is just what I settled on. For when I'm speaking English, anyway."

I run my hands through my sleep-mussed hair. These are not the questions I wanted to ask. There's something about the sunlight and the way Avitue was sitting there, an easy picture of domestic warmth that I've dreamed of but never had. A life I've always wanted.

"You wear desire beautifully," Avitue says. Her eyebrows lift, and she peers through me, observing something immaterial. "I can see," she says, "everything you want." It's an unthreatening fact. She tilts her head as if trying to get a better view, steps forward.

I lean away, and Avitue blinks, stops.

"I'm sorry." She looks down at Shakespeare's collected works. "I'm invasive. It's my job. I've never had reason not to be."

I clasp my hands tight beneath the blankets. "Why are you here? Why did you stay?"

Avitue doesn't seem to have considered this herself. When she answers, it's as if she's thinking out loud. "I wanted to make sure you were okay. After yesterday. I feel responsible. I *am* responsible," she corrects.

"What do you do now? This can't be what you've been sent to do. Aren't you supposed to"—I swallow—"feed on me? Weaken me? Eventually claim my soul?"

Avitue hisses frustration and turns to replace the book where she found it. She's all sharp contours from what I can tell despite the loose robes, but when she hefts the book above her head, the sleeves fall back, and there's a pull of muscle that suggests the physical strength she used to carry me the night before.

She's still facing the books when she says, "You're so beautiful I want to ruin you. I do. There's this thing about being a succubus. A hunger. An emptiness that convinces you the next soul will fill you. It's a lie. I know that. I don't have to act on it."

"What happens if you don't?" I ask carefully.

These are the answers the tome doesn't have on demonology. Succubi are usually subtle nocturnal hunters who are picky about their targets. No one in my family has ever hunted one, not when there are more destructive, gratuitous demons. Avitue's honesty would give me even more leverage over her and others like her.

"Unless I feed my soul with the energy of another's, I will wither until I don't exist. No destruction needed on your part. We're the unluckiest of the damned." I'm about to respond when Avitue finally faces me. "Why did you eventually eat the food if you knew it was from me?"

This is easier than responding to Avitue's admission. I'll take it. "I was scared the first time because I didn't expect it. I still wasn't sure of your intentions. With the first chocolates, I was just so exhausted. And on some unconscious level, I knew there was nothing malicious about them. But they still weren't normal," I say, realizing it only now. "No one can live for days on tea and a handful of truffles and not feel like they're starving at the end of it."

This makes Avitue smile, which I'm shyly happy to see again.

My phone rings. I startle and feel sick at the spike of adrenaline. Suddenly, the noise is no longer coming from across the room but instead from Avitue's hand. She approaches me slowly and hands the phone off. Zuriel.

"I have to take—" I start, but Avitue is gone.

I answer.

"I let Gabriel know you'd be back with us."

I'm lightheaded. The whiplash—from a casual chat with a demon that I *definitely shouldn't be having* to an unnerving call from my sister wherein I have to pretend to bend to our mother's will.

"Thank you," I say because saying anything else, anything more, will betray me.

"And the succubus?"

So we're not acknowledging the fight.

"Gone," I say. It's true for now.

"Killed her body?"

"Yes," I lie. A small word, but it's bitter on my tongue.

"Worried she'll come back?" says Zuriel, sensing the unease in my voice. "I can bring something more permanent. Your sword is where you left it."

"Don't," I say too fast.

"Cassiel, what happened?"

The silence stretches. There's nothing I can tell my sister. I decide to say as much. "I don't want to talk about this over the phone. I'll call you when I'm ready."

She softens, some of the old Zuriel coming through in her voice. "I just need to know you're safe."

"I am," I say and hope it's not a lie.

❦

I don't open the store. I can't make a habit of this, but at least I've managed to put an appropriate notice on the door this time and update the social media accounts. When Avitue returns to me, I'm propped up on pillows and curled around the tome, staring down at the entry on succubi. Like any good student, I have the urge to make notes, to add what Avitue's revealed to me—an academic distraction from a personal and existential problem. I tense when she bends to peer at it, and she backs off. While the tome is written in Old English—ensuring that any average person stumbling upon it wouldn't glean much—I'm sure Avitue would have no problem reading it.

"Right. Boundaries. I should knock or something?" She fidgets, and I don't know what to make of that. Outside the context of seduction, Avitue seems utterly lost, unsure of what to do with her body.

I hate this dance we're doing. This not-quite-trust. We're no longer enemies—enemies don't apologize and comfort and heal each other—but we can't be friends. We're wary companions, united only in that we're reluctant to happily follow the path set out for us by our respective sides. Reluctant to hurt one another. It's a low bar—to ask not to be hurt and to agree not to hurt another—but it's not something even my family provided me. I don't know what to do with the sudden flare of anger that overtakes me at the fact that my own mother hurt me and yet a demon tried, in some small way, to undo that harm. It's beyond my current processing. It doesn't fit into the carefully crafted worldview of my family.

I close the tome and sit up. "What made you change your mind about what you were sent here to do? Is that something I can ask?"

Avitue settles onto a nearby cushion. Beneath all the charm—without conscious attention toward grace and seduction—she's awkwardly lanky in the most endearing way.

"I hadn't seen an angel since the fall," she says.

"I'm not an angel," I say. "You know that."

"You're, what, one percent angel?" says Avitue, and briefly, she's back in her element of flirtation and quirked eyebrows. Turning serious again, she says, "When a lord of Hell warns you of an angelic threat, you take them seriously. When they send you after that threat, you wonder what duke you personally offended. From all I'd heard about you nephilim, it sounded like a death sentence they were trying to sell as a grand opportunity."

A joyless laugh escapes me. "And when you tested me with a couple scares and realized I wasn't a threat at all, you took pity on me?"

Avitue frowns. "No, Cassiel. I never wanted to scare you, and I'd never insult you with pity. Would you have believed me if I'd left a little note? *Hi, I'm a demon, but I promise I just want to have a nice chat. How about next afternoon?* I knew it would scare you, but I had to show you somehow that I was here and wasn't going to harm you. I had to know how you would react."

"In the dream. That was when you made your final decision," I say, recalling her burdened sigh.

When she smiles, the expression is tired and resigned as if she's looking through me to a fate on the horizon, one that she's summoned but also doesn't want. "I was told you were out of practice. I was told you were alone. I could tell at a glance you were lonely. I was never sent to kill you outright. There are plenty of other demons who could do that job better than I can. This was always going to be a seduction," Avitue says emphatically, watching for what her words do to me. "But you weren't what I expected. Your pain had a familiar shape that I couldn't ignore, something I never thought I'd see in a nephilim. It seemed a shame to go through with the original plan. So a seduction on my own terms."

"On your own terms," I echo. "Meaning?"

The confident smirk returns. "I want your heart for myself, little angel."

For a moment—a moment—the confession stymies me. I pull us back to my original question. "And Hell's terms?" I ask. "Won't there be consequences when they find out you've deviated?"

Avitue shrugs and makes a noise in the back of her throat. "Let me worry about that."

"Thank you," I try, "for telling me what you have."

There's so much about her, about this situation, that I don't understand, but I realize I want to deserve her trust. I left home to be among normal people only to find that the walls I'd built to protect myself were the only thing keeping me standing. I couldn't so much as stumble, not out here, not alone. There was no one I trusted to catch me—not because I thought they wouldn't want to but because I thought they couldn't understand how. But Avitue, impossibly, was the person to both break through the walls restraining me *and* catch me when I inevitably fell. Someone who would do that was worth knowing. And, I hoped, worth trusting.

I smooth my hand over the old leather cover of the tome. "This is everything my family knows about demonology," I offer. I don't know where I'm going, just keep talking. I have Avitue's attention now, but she watches me warily. "All of my siblings have one. When we're training, we memorize it from cover to cover. Every tactic, every sigil, every ritual and weakness." I turn to the diagram of the circle I used, placing it right side up in front of Avitue. "This one is standard. It didn't affect you."

Avitue recoils as if the mere sight of it might hurt her, then she leans in. Her hand hovers over the page. She glances to me, her frown deepening. "Why would you show me this?"

I turn over several hundred pages, back to the beginning of the book, back to the index of angels. I feel reckless. I feel wild hope. I've spent so long hiding myself, so long drowning in secrets that I couldn't imagine another way. For the first time in a long time, I feel alive as I flip through the pages of the tome. Like a dam breaking, there's no stopping this. I don't want to stop. I want to express every secret until I can take a breath again.

"All of us are named after them," I say, nodding to a page dominated by an illustration of a multiwinged, many-eyed seraph who wields a sword alight with holy radiance.

Avitue looks from the illustration to me and back again. "Too bad you don't get all the wings," she says, but the joke is flat.

I close my eyes for a moment, worrying the ring on my little finger. "Some of us do. If we're disciplined enough to draw deeply on our ethereal nature. The demons who've witnessed the transformation don't survive. So your side wouldn't know."

Avitue doesn't blink, doesn't breathe. "Have you?"

"Once. When I was pure, I accessed that power for a moment, but I still couldn't manifest wings."

I remember only fractured images from that hunt. It was one of my first—before the fear of death, of demons, of our own mother, wore me down so completely that running away seemed the only option.

Zuriel had already been on the hunt for a year. At seventeen, I was just venturing out into a world that had seemed simultaneously inevitable and impossible for most of my life, even as I trained late into the night to prepare for that fate. My sister would find me in the hours before we were set to leave and braid my hair, distracting me with a story as she did. As soon as she was done, I'd be nervous again. I still had to go out there and face some new menace that wanted me and my family and others dead. Or worse. But Zuriel would squeeze the tension out of my shoulders and tell me that whenever I felt lost or scared, I should look to her and follow her lead.

And so later that night, when I looked up from where I'd been knocked to the floor of some dilapidated warehouse, I didn't scan for threats first. I found Zuriel. For a few slow seconds, I watched her summon an ethereal arrow to her bow, and I thought that if I had the strength to fight for something real, it would be for her.

The world turned bright and buoyant as I stood, still dazed, still processing how I'd ended up on the floor. But Zuriel's smile seemed brighter than it all. She'd darted over to cover me and shouted something. Only then did I notice I was holding the source of the light—a bright shield made of my own soul's radiance.

But that happened only once. I pack the memory away.

Gingerly, Avitue finally lays a hand on the book and traces a column of names. "If you ever trusted me, would you show me your wings?" she asks, voice hushed as if we inhabit sacred space.

A war of emotions surges through me. There's the reckless hope that wants to finally stop hiding the nonhuman part of me, to share it with the only other person outside my family who might understand. But there's also the fear, the insistent voice that says I'm not good enough to deserve anything—not kindness, or admiration, and certainly not my angelic inheritance. Before I can check it, the insecure part of me speaks.

"You know I can't," I snap. "After what's happened, I'm not worthy of wings."

Angry tears suddenly blur my vision, and Avitue is a black smudge moving toward me. I'm not angry with her. I'm angry with myself. Scared. Disappointed. Maybe Zuriel was right. How much farther can I fall?

"Cassiel, purity isn't—"

"You're not a nephilim. You don't know our teachings. You don't know how it works!"

The pressure of Avitue's hands on my shoulders might have been comforting before, but now the touch seems to burn me through my clothes. I swipe them away.

"Leave!" I say.

I don't want her to see me cry again. I don't want to keep falling apart in front of her.

"But I meant—"

"Leave me alone!"

The heat of her withdraws. The floor creaks. When I can see clearly again, the room is empty, and I'm desperate for the familiar, ugly relief of the wooden box.

❖

87

I want to call my sister.

Cocooned under layers of blankets, I feel raw from crying. Chest aching. Face swollen. My skin sensitive from wiping at so many tears.

I wish I hadn't sent Avitue away.

I want to call my sister, but I don't know how, not about this, not after how we parted. The days when we used to confide in each other are gone and have been for years. Yet she's the first person I think of.

You're falling, she'd said.

Nephilim don't seek pleasure, and sexual pleasure for the sake of it is our greatest taboo. According to Gabriel, we were not like the nephilim I'd read about in the old manuscripts. They didn't hunt demons. They had abandoned their duties to the angels, shirked their responsibilities in our war against Hell. Being already lost, their survival didn't depend on their purity. Not as it did for us. Now, what recourse did I have to ward the demon off? I was lucky Avitue had listened to me when I told her to leave. But what was the point? Zuriel was right. I was falling.

For once, I call Ana. Maybe our regular brunches do add up to something. Maybe we can talk about more than how work is going, at least for my part. Ana's always been happy to talk about her family, and I've been happy to listen, asking questions to avoid ever having to say much about my own.

But even as she picks up, I'm already ironing out the tone of my voice, automatically smoothing the edges.

"What's wrong?" Ana asks, immediately seeing through my attempt. The small clattering noises on the other end make me imagine her in the kitchen, setting a pot on the stove to boil. She's talked at length about kitchen witchcraft, about recipes passed down to her from all the women in her family. I suddenly worry I'm interrupting something important.

"Are you busy? I can call back—"

"Don't you run away from me, Cass," she scolds gently. "You *never* call me. This must be important."

I don't even know where to begin. I sigh.

"I feel like—" I begin, then cut myself off. What *do* I feel? Everything. I try to untangle it. "I don't know what I'm doing anymore."

"I sense this isn't about work," Ana observes, perceptive as always, the distinct sound of a knife against a cutting board punctuating her words.

"It's not," I say, still considering what to say, what to hold back.

Ana's quiet, waiting for me. She's good at that, at giving space.

"I thought I could be okay, moving here. But I haven't been. I've just been hiding. And suddenly, all the reasons I left home— I have to deal with them."

It's quiet on Ana's end. Either she's finished chopping or set the knife aside. I worry she'll bring up her challenge to me in the store, the accusation that she knows what I'm hiding from her. I relax when she doesn't.

"I shouldn't have called your sister," she says, voice heavy.

"No, it's not that. You did the right thing. It's the kind of emergency I should've called her about myself."

"Then . . ." Ana pauses. "I want to help you, Cass. I just don't know how. You're so hard to read, and I'm always worried about pushing." Another pause. "So this isn't about your sister?"

Ana's always been so perceptive that I've never had to ask for help outright, but I know it's not fair to her or to me. I do need help. I've always needed help. I want to scream the word, but Gabriel taught us to ground our emotions by disciplining our bodies into numbness. Then the soul could be free. Then we could access our true strength and wouldn't need to rely on others.

Why did I let Avitue take the box? In the moment, it felt right. I felt freed from its burden, its mere presence suggesting that I was broken and would inevitably fail again. But I am broken, and I have failed.

I trail my fingertips down the scars on my thigh—a short, neat ladder to perfection, to worthiness. Opening the box—inhaling the scent of the old wood, choosing the appropriate tool—was an instant wash of relief. I knew, with bloodletting, I'd be pure again. I consider the other tools at my disposal: razors, bright-handled paring knives, the box cutters downstairs.

"Cass?" Ana says when my silence stretches.

"I—" I consider making an excuse, running away from her again.

"Are you safe, Cass?" she asks next.

The tears rush back. I shake my head. I choke down a sob.

I've let a demon into my life, into my heart, and now I'll never find my wings.

"I'm coming over," Ana says, shuffling in the background. "Stay on the phone with me. I'll walk you back to my place."

I let Ana in minutes later, dragging my body from the nest of blankets. I can tell she's trying not to stare at the scars exposed by my camisole when I turn away from her to pull a sweater over my head. I can't explain them again, can't tell her that one I still cherish and another still hurts. Among nephilim, our scars are unremarkable. We all have them. But out in the world, scars tell a different kind of story. I wanted to keep mine close. If my head were clearer, I would've thought to dress before, but my head isn't clear, and that's how I've landed in this moment.

I gasp at the swell of wind outside my door and hug my coat tighter. The air invades my chest, chilling all the tears I'm holding in. Ana scrunches her shoulders up near her ears. I've never seen her dressed so casually. Her only makeup is a smudge of eyeliner. She's tied her hair up in a messily elegant bun and wears a black hoodie and leggings combo that makes me believe she's about to pop over to a very chic yoga studio—not rescue her secretive friend from an anxiety she's only vaguely aware of.

"Thank you for answering," I say, shivering away one layer of fear. If I were truly a burden, she wouldn't be here. She wouldn't have picked up the phone. "I had a fight with my sister," I add because it's the part I can explain, the part that makes sense.

Ana's feet pound the steps. "Zuriel didn't help you?" she asks, her words infused with indignation.

"She tried. I wouldn't let her."

"What did helping look like?"

"She wanted me to come back home. Close the store. Return to our family business." The euphemism we always used to refer to demon hunting—*family business*.

Ana releases a frustrated huff. "Telling you to give up what makes you happy and go back to living with your weird mom isn't helping."

It's another cloudy, viciously windy day. Out of the shelter of buildings, the wind cuts into us again. Ana looks both ways before stepping into the crosswalk, and I remember my reckless dash across the street in pursuit of Avitue. When I told her to go away, did she think I meant forever?

Like me, Ana's also taken the small apartment above her business. Every time I visit, it smells like freshly burned palo santo, as if she's just closed a ritual moments before my appearance. Snaking ivy and pothos spill down bookshelves and across windowsills. A snake plant and lucky bamboo crowd together on an end table while colorful succulents adorn a terrarium on the coffee table. Beside them, a stack of coasters reads "Plant Mom," the words written in flowering vines. On the kitchen counter, measuring cups of steaming tinctures sit beside mounds of dried herbs and flowers.

"What are you working on?" I say, nodding at the ingredients as I slip off my shoes in the doorway.

Ana smiles shyly. "A little something for Día de los Muertos. It's an old recipe some of the great-great-grands liked, but it's best if you infuse a little of your own taste into the recipe. It facilitates communication, helps them get to know you better. The right ingredients can tell a story." She shivers and rubs her hands together. "Let me make you a lavender something?" she suggests.

"I'd love that," I say, settling in my usual spot on the wicker daybed under the window.

"I'm sorry for what I said before," she says, the words bursting from her like a difficult confession. She takes up a cluster of little spoons and a French press only to immediately set them back down. "I just— I've seen a lot of bad shit happen among witches. Magic that requires sacrifices no one should have to make. Covens that turn into cults. I've lost friends to them. One I never found again, and I hate that I didn't try harder for her." She clasps her hands. "I don't want to see it happen to you."

"I'm not going back there," I promise, holding eye contact with her.

She bites her lip. "My family's helped a lot of witches out of these situations. I know the signs, is all. Once you've seen it happen before, you get worried."

"It's not just my family that's the problem," I say, studying my ring. *You wanted honesty. You want to be real,* I remind myself. "There's someone I met. My family wouldn't like her, and I haven't known her long at all. But she's changed everything. I don't know if I can keep going the way I have been."

"That sounds huge. And scary, if I'm sensing correctly."

"I'm terrified."

"If your family wouldn't like her, isn't that good? From what you've told me, it doesn't sound like they've treated you well."

I squeeze my eyes shut. I feel like someone's thrown sand in them.

"The thing is, I really shouldn't be talking to her at all. But suddenly, she's in my life, and I don't want her to leave, and there's all this other stuff that's come up because of it."

I really, truly can't explain this in human terms.

"I see why you're conflicted," sighs Ana. She thinks. "Would you be open to a reading? Maybe the cards could give you some clarity."

I huff a mirthless laugh. "You'd draw something like Death or The Devil."

Now Ana laughs. "That's just movies. And those cards don't mean what you think they mean."

"I'm pretty sure your cards would combust if you tried to read for either of us." I say it with the tone of a joke, but Ana takes it seriously.

"Who are you, Cass?" she asks gently.

From Ana, the question is a feeling, as if she's cut an incision in some metaphysical law of the universe in order to stare me down.

I shiver. "I'm still trying to figure that out."

SIX

I LOOK UP HOPEFULLY whenever someone passes the shop window, which is often—as if Avitue will just saunter through the door and up to the counter to request my most complete edition of Shakespeare's collected works. I wonder who else she enjoys, whether she also finds Chaucer amusing. Very likely. Perhaps I'm stereotyping based on a sample size of one, but outdated bawdy humor seems exactly the taste you'd expect from a demon of lust. I wish there were a way to contact her, to smooth over the way we parted. For a wild moment, I consider summoning her. I do have her name. But the etiquette here, I'm unsure of. Is it rude to pull someone from wherever they are for a friendly chat? It would only take—

The chime on the door announces Ana, a paper coffee cup in one hand and a takeout container in the other. "I brought you something for lunch." She smiles shyly. "I wanted to make sure you're eating."

Over lunch at the store's cramped backroom table, Ana presses me to start seriously looking into hiring someone else to help me with the store. I've given her the chair while I perch on the edge of the desk, boxes and stacks of to-be-sorted inventory crowding the floor around us.

"I know it's nerve racking," she says as I take the last bite of a croissant sandwich. "No one else will care about the place as much as you do, but especially now, I'm sure you can see how it'd be useful. You can't expect yourself to work every day forever without a break."

I nod because what else can I say? She isn't wrong.

"I'd be up for helping you out, too, if you wanted. I've had to go through figuring this out, and I could offer any advice I can. Hiring can be its own stress, but it's worth it."

"I'll see about it when I can pull myself together a bit more," I say, snapping the empty container shut. "Thank you for everything. Really."

It's because of seeing Ana's success that I wanted to give my impossible dream of running a bookstore a try, and she'd been the only person to encourage me. After leaving the control of my mother, I didn't fancy working for anyone else—and maybe, after hunting with my family my entire life, I have a bit of hesitation around working *with* anyone else too.

But Ana's right. My entire life is this store. Which means I don't have much space for living. Perhaps that's the intention, that I fell into the familiar comfort of workaholism because I didn't know how to live.

I'm well acquainted with strategizing, and that mindset transfers to work well. I can't apply that to friendships or hobbies. Not unless I want to seem even weirder than I already do. So I avoided them in favor of giving myself over fully to my work. But even before Avitue's appearance, I was tired. Now, I need a break and—employee situation aside—don't know how to take one.

I'm waving goodbye to Ana from behind the front counter when I glimpse a dark figure on the opposite sidewalk turning down an alley and out of sight.

⊷◆⊶

Two days have passed since I sent Avitue away. I'm beginning to worry she won't come back, and what a worry to have—that I might not be able to see where an ill-defined and inadvisable relationship with a literal demon might've led.

I do what I'm good at and distract myself with work. I reevaluate what I've been doing with my displays of sideline items. As the weather turns cold, people seem more interested in candles. I could rotate those closer to the counter. I make a list of titles to pull from the shelves for discount or donation, titles that have been sitting unsold for a year or more. Between serving customers, I stand overwhelmed in the back room, looking at a towering shelf of advance reader copies I need to do something with, the stacks and boxes of shipping materials that have gotten a little out of hand.

Finally, I attempt a first draft of a flyer to put on the front door announcing that I'm looking to hire. One employee? Two? I've only been able to start paying myself a salary in the last few months. I'll have to look at the numbers again, see what I can fairly pay, think about how many hours I'd ask from someone. And what kind of person would they be?

Maybe someone where I was years ago, someone who might not have all the things on paper but needed someplace to begin, someone to see them and give them a chance. So one person. More hours, if they wanted them, would make it more meaningful.

Assembling a plan always makes me feel in control, and I close for the day feeling better. That feeling dulls, however, when I lock the doors and start up the stairway to my studio. Maybe I have a plan for one aspect of my life, but now, in my off hours, I have plenty of time to ruminate over my family, to try not to check the news.

And to worry about what's happened with Avitue.

The sun has just set when a soft knock sounds.

"It's me," Avitue's voice carries muffled from just outside the door. A smile twitches my lips. Unnecessary for her to knock, but I suppose she's making a human attempt at boundaries.

I'm glad I don't have to raise my voice for her to hear. I don't know whether I could. My throat feels tight.

"I know," I say. No one else knocks on my door besides Ana, and she only comes over to pick me up for our weekly brunches.

"Have you . . . eaten anything today?"

"I don't want your chocolate. I'm sick of chocolate."

I feel petulant. I feel exposed. I feel scraped hollow.

"I could cook something?" Again, the uptick.

"Demons can't cook," I say.

I suppose they could, technically, as much as they could do any other human thing, but the lack of necessity would mean a learning curve.

Avitue doesn't defend her culinary skills. "I could go out for something. Whatever your favorite is."

"You can see everything I want," I remind her. *Let her put her prodding to good use.*

There's nothing else from the other side of the door. When Avitue knocks twenty minutes later, it's with a bag of Chinese takeout in hand. She's changed her outfit to a shockingly modern leather jacket and jeans. A pair of cat-eye sunglasses shield her serpentine eyes. The claws, though shorter, still look just as sharp. Perhaps at a distance, someone might mistake them for high-maintenance acrylics.

"You left them, Cassiel," Avitue begins carefully. "You left for a reason. You were unhappy there. With their rules. Why hold yourself to those standards?"

I feel small. I've never asked myself that question for a reason.

"You have your store. You have neighbors. This whole community of people," Avitue continues. "Here's a new way of being for you."

"I feel foolish for leaving."

"Leaving took strength."

"And I've used all I have." I don't want to cry in front of her again. "Thank you for the food," I say, tucking into the bag and withdrawing containers and chopsticks. I can't look at her. "Share with me? If you can eat."

We sit at my small table, a spread of food between us. This is the second time this week I've gotten to share my table with someone, already more times than I have all year. Avitue takes a single broccoli floret and leaves the rest for me. I can't help but hum contentedly through the first bites. Gratitude fills my chest. Not one but two people have thought to check in on me today and make sure I'm okay. I hold to that and try not to think of how my mother would shame me for enjoying food, how she'd make me feel guilty over the soft curves of my stomach and hips.

"Thank you," I say again, managing a grateful smile for Avitue.

We finish the meal in silence, Avitue watching me eat as if it's the most fascinating thing she's ever seen. At any other time, with any other person, I'd feel uncomfortable under the focused attention, but it's freeing not to have to hide, not to feel as if I'm committing some shameful act by nourishing myself.

She clears the containers with a wave of her hand, saying, "I should go."

The abruptness of it startles me out of the warm feelings I'd nestled into. "Why?"

"When you sent me away, I realized it's probably for the best if I don't stick around. I just wanted to see you one last time, make sure you were okay."

"Oh."

What could I argue against that? Our problem is resolved. What would a demon and a nephilim do together?

"So—" Avitue stands, nods. She's unbalanced again, fidgety. I wish I could see her eyes.

"Stay."

Avitue raises an eyebrow.

"Please stay," I say more confidently. I go to her, reaching for the glasses. "May I?"

Avitue doesn't answer but doesn't back away. I remove them and find—

"Your eyes are different."

I state the obvious because I'm surprised. The vivid gold of her irises has expanded to fill the whole of her eyes, and there's a tension around them that wasn't present before. She isn't breathing again, seems to be waiting on me. When the realization settles, I force myself not to step back, to hold her intensified gaze.

"How often do you usually feed?"

A muscle in her jaw tenses. She tries for casual and fails. "Usually? Nightly. I've pushed it to three nights before."

"It's been a week," I say unnecessarily.

"Yes."

"You've been here a week."

Avitue reaches for her glasses, and I return them to her, but she doesn't put them on.

"Since you've been with me, have you not fed from anyone?"

"No."

"Could you . . . do it without hurting me?"

I ask it just like that, surprising her and myself. Avitue's mouth pops open at my question, and I can't help but focus on her fangs. My last shred of self-preservation screams that she's a monster.

She tilts her chin up as if she's scented fresh blood, the line of her neck taut with restraint. "I don't doubt your strength, but I want you to be sure this is what you want," she says.

"You healed me. Now I want to help you," I say.

"You wouldn't have needed healing if it weren't for me."

"I've never felt good in my body or about my body. That's started to change because of you."

"I was being a careless flirt. I meant it as a gift, but—"

"And it *was* a gift. More than you know."

"But your wings," Avitue says, her voice so gentle.

"If I've given up being a hunter, there's no point holding on to the past." It's scary to finally admit, but there it is in the space between us. It feels like the loss of something I've never had, but I don't want to mourn. I want to keep moving forward the way I started to years ago. "I want to help you," I repeat, certain.

Avitue's eyes widen as if she has, in fact, had an encounter with an angel.

"So," I say just as the anxiety of what I've agreed to starts to set in. "How does this work?"

She considers me for a long moment, and when I manage to hold her gaze, she relents. "There are several ways. You're a nephilim, so you have reserves of energy that humans don't. Energy that I can't access because it would destroy me. It might be . . . difficult in the moment, but if you drew on your ethereal energy, you'd be unaffected."

"And you'd be satisfied?"

"As content as if I'd fully drained someone."

There's a tragic reality behind those simple words. I imagine a soulless husk of a body and corpses drained of blood. We've never encountered a succubus, but I know the stories from other hunters who've witnessed the aftermath of a demon's feeding. In cases where the succubus doesn't kill, the victims are left with strange nightmares. Those dreamers, upon waking, are plagued by malaise and haunted visions that consume their hours. Without an intervention, some will turn into skeletal shells of their former selves, obsessed with the demon who ruined them, wasting their lives on a vain search for a cursed but beautiful lover.

I twist my ring around my finger, finally allowing myself to step out of Avitue's space. Her hunger makes the air heavy.

I'm certain she knows what I'm thinking but doesn't try to deny or soften what she does to survive. She lets me have my fears, saying only, "You're angel-touched. I was warned that your bodies don't succumb the way humans' do, not with a soul like that."

"If I can do this for you and it doesn't affect me, then it would spare others. Wouldn't it?"

"Look at you," she says, grinning. "Fearlessly selfless. A true angel." She closes the space between us again, testing me, and I hold my ground. Her touch is feverish when she cups my face in her hands, searching me with a predator's stare. Though my breath turns shallow, I meet it. "It sounds like you're proposing a long-term arrangement," she says.

A chorus of desire sings through me, the thought so bare that I know she can see. "Maybe," I say, surprised that my voice is still strong.

Her teasing relents. "Can you tell if I'm lying to you? Is that something nephilim can do?"

"Are you?" I ask. Then it clicks. "The circle didn't work because I'd used the sigil for *intention*. It activated because it detected demonic presence, but you could exist within it because you had no *intention* to harm. You weren't an enemy."

"You're much too excited by the prospect of trusting a demon."

"I want to trust *you*."

Avitue makes a surprised noise in her throat, and I take her hands and lead her to the bed. We sit facing each other, and the long, dark angles of Avitue's limbs are a sharp contrast to the earth tones of my blankets. Despite her rigid posture, I sense her stretching free from a long time spent stiff and cramped, all languid and indulgent, a long, breathy sigh. The feeling reaches and curls around me, sensuous and heavy. I'm back to worrying my ring, distracted by the growing warmth and wet between my thighs. Avitue hasn't even made a move toward me, and I have to push back against the shame attempting to creep in.

"Are you doing something to me right now?" I ask, and it comes out too breathily, too needy. I'm struck by the strong urge to press my body against Avitue's. I want to feel her breath against my neck.

"Not consciously," she answers. "My energy affects nearby humans when I'm intending to feed." She licks her lips. "Prepares them for me."

"Oh." I might drown in this.

"Do you feel you're still able to say *no* if you need to? If I accidentally push you too far?"

"Yes," I say, biting down hard against the sound that threatens to follow.

"If you want me to stop for any reason, say my name and say it truly."

Even through the haze of lust, I'm startled by the request. I've watched Gabriel command a demon with their true name, witnessed her unmake them. I still remember the viscera, the blood that spattered my face, the not-sound of a soul rending. Even for a demon, it was a cruel fate and one that Gabriel had reveled in. For months, it plagued my nightmares. I knew it was one tool in our arsenal that I couldn't resort to. A name seemed too personal.

"What if I hurt you?" I say. "I only know invocations for—"

"Just my name. Nothing else and you can't go wrong," she reassures me.

"I don't think I could," I say, fear and lust a tangled mess.

"I'm asking for your safety. I haven't been this hungry in a long time."

Despite the flush consuming my body, I shiver. "Okay," I agree.

Avitue turns unnaturally still again—watching me, making some judgment. "You're strong against it. Are you resisting? If you are, it'll hurt when I try to draw from you."

"Oh."

"That bit of trivia not in your tome either?"

I force myself to focus on the question. The air around us is too thick. I press my thighs together. "No, actually, no it's not."

Avitue's slouch is tense, her hunger the only thing holding her up. "I want you to undress me," she says suddenly.

I don't remember closing the space between us, but my hands are on Avitue's lapels, and I'm tugging the jacket free of her arms. I fumble her shirt over her head. I feel dizzy. Time skips forward in frames. My body is feverish, shaky, my movements urgent, all focus bent on Avitue's request.

"Angel." Hot hands cup my face, steady me. Golden eyes. Such beautiful golden eyes. My head swims with the image of them. Avitue's voice reaches me as if through water. "You can't resist me, but you also have to focus."

"I want you," I moan, and the sound feels obscene in my mouth, as if something else is speaking for me.

"That's enough," says Avitue, and the fog draws back. The air clears. The room opens. The strained look returns.

I'm breathing harder than I should be. "Did you . . . ?"

"That's only the effect of my aura."

I sigh. "There's not an in-between for me. Either I resist it, or I don't."

I hate having such a technical conversation while I'm mildly aroused and Avitue is half undressed. This entire time she's been wearing some complicatedly strappy lingerie under her shirt like a deadly secret, and I didn't realize how devastating it could be to witness strips of black satin plunging into her cleavage. The initial tide of demonic energy left me weak for her, but this small detail is what will ruin me.

I feel as if I've been sent out into the field and forgotten all my training. It feels silly to be here like this, in my own space, frustrated because I can't properly offer myself to a demon.

"We don't have to do this now. Or ever," says Avitue.

"But you're tired."

"That doesn't matter."

"I want to try. Let me get used to your aura so I can figure it out."

"You're saying you want to practice this?" Avitue clarifies.

I nod.

"Then I'll ask you something like before, and you can . . . figure it out?"

I nod again.

This time is not a gradual unwinding. One moment, the room is normal, and the next, I can see only Avitue's body, can feel only my own lust.

"Kiss me," says Avitue, and time skips again.

In the next moment I manage to grab hold of, my lips are already against hers. In the next, my back is pressed into the mattress, and Avitue is above me. I moan into her mouth and deepen the kiss, heedless of her fangs—

It's over again. The room is bright and clear. I'm still on my back and breathing hard. Avitue is topless but composed on the edge of the bed, watching me. My mouth tastes metallic, and when I swipe a hand over my lips, it comes away smeared red.

"I lose time when I'm in there," I pant. "If I can stop losing time, I can focus." I sit up. "I want to try again."

"Once more," Avitue concedes. "Then rest."

Before Avitue's aura washes over me again, I close my eyes and fall into myself, locating that glimmer of white-blue light. When I surface, the world is watery and dense. Avitue is within reach, and I *desire her*, but the rest of the room still exists, though blurry around the edges.

"Kiss me," Avitue says again, and there's no rush to comply. I move because I want to, and this time, I can enjoy her. Can brush a hand over her chest and down her ribs. Can choose to raise a hand and tangle my fingers in her hair as our lips meet.

"Your eyes are glowing," Avitue says against my lips. "Are you yourself?"

"Yes," I say and rejoin us in a kiss.

Avitue undresses me, and in the heady space of the aura, I don't have the presence of mind to be self-conscious. The choice to let her pull me deeper into this experience seems like an obvious one. She's careful with me, dusting my throat with kisses before moving back to meet my eyes. To check that my focus remains. She thrills at pinning me to the bed and straddling me, grinding the heat of her body into mine. She is smoke and shadow, her corporeal form phasing in and out. Her side or shoulder is a stretch of shadow for the span of a blink, and then she's flesh again.

Avitue draws a silk ribbon from her hair that wasn't there before. It's black as her claws, and she holds it in her teeth as she dips a hand between my thighs, tracing light fingertips over my skin. She's careful with her claws, but the barest press of their edges against my sensitive flesh sends a delicious shiver through me. I can't help the moan that escapes my throat, and Avitue grins around the ribbon, white fangs sharp against the fabric. She curls her fingers, pressing into the wetness between my thighs, eliciting a whimper from my mouth. With a hum of approval, she takes the ribbon from her mouth.

It's only now that I realize it's not just me; I can feel how wet Avitue is. She's so apparently unbothered otherwise, so cool, so composed, and my stomach twists at the knowledge that my body could entice a succubus. I grind my hips up into Avitue, and her eyes flutter shut for a moment. Only a moment. Then her hands brace on either side of my head, and she searches my eyes again.

"I think you're ready," she says against my neck. "I'd like to bind you for this, if you don't mind."

I reach up while I still can, trace the line of Avitue's lips with my thumb, and marvel at her softness. Her mouth parts at the touch, and I run the pad of my finger over the point of a fang. Her tongue darts out, tastes me, then draws my finger into her mouth. It's a long, forked tongue, a true devil's tongue. I'm prey in the mouth of a predator, and I've invited it. Avitue shoots me another grin before there's a stab of pain at my fingertip. She hums, shuts her eyes, sucks harder.

"You have lovely blood. Just as I expected," she pronounces.

The compliment brings new warmth to my face. I never would've imagined myself blushing over *what lovely blood I have*, but the old Cassiel wouldn't have invited a demon to bed either.

The ribbon is cool and soft against my skin when Avitue loops it around my wrists and through the space in the headboard. The sheets and pillows are shredded where she's rested her weight. Wings darken and solidify above us, shadow made solid. Her cheekbones seem inhumanly sharper, and when she speaks, it's with lengthened fangs.

"You've been so good for me. I need you to stay focused." The point of a claw traces from my cheek to the soft hollow of my throat, and she pauses, looking me over again, wide eyed, as if I'm a miracle. "Remember what I told you. If you're scared, if I hurt you, you have my name."

My heart flutters. I nod.

And then Avitue's moving down my body, pushing my legs open, and settling between my thighs. The heat of her mouth and press of her tongue pull a cry from my throat. She grips my thighs, claws digging into my flesh. The jolt of pleasure immediately drains me. I moan. Time slips forward.

"Focus, Cassiel," she growls a warning. "Or I will stop."

I fight to ground myself in the sharp pressure of her claws against my thighs, anything that isn't pleasure. I retreat into myself as years of training have taught me, find the wave of blue-white light, and grasp hold of it. But Avitue's work is soul deep, my pleasured body a doorway for her to access my deepest self. When I gasp, it's with my entire being, tand time melts again. I understand only pain, pleasure, power. I stare down her soul, that shadow heat of our early meetings. I am falling into darkness, into her. I am a ribbon unraveling. I am my blood, my sweat. I am an immolating burst of pleasure, a sun into a black hole. The drain is instant and greedy and vicious.

"Cassiel." My name calls me back to my body. Avitue is above me but out of focus, blurry through tears. "*Cassiel*," she repeats, insistent.

I find the light again, hold on to it with all my strength—and am renewed.

The room is brighter than normal. I sit up—Avitue must have untied me—and find myself staring at an awestruck demon on the other end of the bed. As I discover the edges of my body again, I take in the shredded sheets and exposed downy stuffing spilling from the pillows. My hair is sweat damp against my forehead. I examine the smeared blood on my body, strangely unmoved.

"Cassiel," says Avitue again, and I register the blue glow reflected in her eyes.

A shimmer of white-blue light haloes my shoulders, and finally, I look up and around me. Radiant, ethereal wings span the room—and they're mine. They're attached to *me*. I flutter them, marveling at the way they catch and push the air. They feel as natural as my arms, as if I've always had them and known how to move with them. When I look back at Avitue, her curls stir on the gentle breeze created by my wings, and her own have become a solid presence at her back. Iridescent black feathers shine in the light I cast, a dark rainbow that shifts with her movement. They were angels. She was an angel. I long to see her wings stretched to their full span, under moonlight, in daylight. I want to catalog every feather and write an ode to their shimmer.

Avitue speaks her admiration first. "They're beautiful," she says. "You're beautiful." She closes the space between us and cups my face in her hands. "Thank you." She kisses my cheeks and forehead. "Thank you."

I bury my face in the crook of Avitue's neck, and she puts her arms around me, careful not to touch my wings. Her aura is just as present as before, only now it settles around me like a mantle, no longer jagged and desperate. It's turned comforting, a raging beast pacified into a warm, purring cat. I am happy to have done this for her, warm in the afterglow of transformation through sacrifice.

I sigh, breathing in the smoky scent of Avitue's skin. Nothing about this moment seems real. "I don't understand. Why now? When I've practiced for years and was never worthy enough. I shouldn't be able to manifest wings. I'm not good enough. I'm not—"

"Don't," Avitue soothes, knowing where my ramble is going. She squeezes me close. "You're perfect. We'll figure out how your wings work. Together, if you want."

"But if someone like me is worthy of wings, what else have our teachings gotten wrong?"

Avitue smooths a hand over my hair, but I don't miss the way she tenses. "If you're going to ask your questions, be careful." There's something beneath the surface of the statement that I'm too tired to prod right now.

"It must be so late," I murmur. I've processed too much of the supernatural, too much soul stuff, and the only surviving piece of my brain is the dully practical one. "I should go to bed. I should open the store tomorrow. Get new pillows."

Avitue giggles—demons can giggle!—and I like the way it rumbles through her chest. It's such an honest noise.

"Well, maybe I was slightly wrong," she says. "It seems this can make you a *little* tired."

I pull back. "Won't you stay?"

Avitue blinks at me.

"If it's not boring for you, I'd like the company."

Avitue takes my hand with a level of tenderness and trepidation that would suggest we've never so much as kissed. "Of course, angel."

I leave Avitue with the full intention of preparing for bed but quickly forget brushing my teeth or showering or any human thing when I glimpse my wings in the bathroom mirror. I'm tired, but I've never felt so strong. I brush my hands down the length of the feathers. They feel like glass and water and sunlight. I fold them close against my back, then fan them out again, over and over, just to see how the light shifts. I feel like a celestial body, like a star. The light reflects off all the bright, polished surfaces of the bathroom and overwhelms my vision until the shape of wings is bright even when I close my eyes. I smile until my cheeks hurt. I laugh, full of joy and relief and faith. Maybe I didn't make a mistake. Maybe I can trust myself after all.

A soft knock comes from the door, and Avitue's voice drifts through. "Are you all right? You sound like you've gone mad."

"I'm fine!" I call back, half-laughing and half-crying. "It's all fine."

"Okay," says Avitue, her tone incredulous.

"I'm an ethereal being of light cramped into a studio bathroom!" I exclaim, falling into another fit of giggles. "Did the angels foretell this? Can they see me?"

"Do you mean, like, in a prophecy way, or . . . ?" says Avitue.

I throw open the door and pull her into a hug. "I want to be beautiful with you forever," I say, not thinking, only feeling.

"Well, that's—"

"You are *so* nice!"

Avitue softens into my embrace. "No one's ever told me that," she says quietly.

The high of discovery eventually wears down. I brush my teeth and shower while Avitue waits at the edge of the bed and flips through all the books on the bedside table. I don't want to let go of my wings, but once I'm back in my rational mind, I worry that they could hurt Avitue. I'm not sure what direct contact with ethereal energy would do to her. And so I let that thread slacken and retreat, returning to a form I try not to think of as lesser.

I emerge clean from the bathroom only to more clearly face down the fact that we *have* made a mess. This time, the bed undeniably looks like a crime scene. Bloodstained sheets dragging the floor, long tears and punctures that would suggest an attack. But in contrast to the brutality of it, the kindly assailant sits reading serenely among the wreck, still dressed in her very distracting lingerie. A couple feathers have caught endearingly in her hair.

I pick one free and earn her smile. "I hate to disturb you in the middle of a good read, but if we're going to sleep, I have to fix this."

She sets her book aside. Emily Dickinson this time. I'm about to ask her something about poetry when she bites down on the grin spreading across her face.

"What?" I say.

"I did wonder what you'd taste like," she says, no longer trying to hide her smirk.

I shield my face with my hands. "So you are, in fact, still trying to murder me," I groan.

She takes my hands away from my face, and I'm exposed again. Her hold on my wrists communicates intention, and I allow her to position my body where she wants, following her silent direction as if it's second nature. She sets my palms flat against the mattress so that I'm bent over the bed, and I stop breathing. Taking my chin between her thumb and finger, she appraises me and says, "I like you like this. Maybe next time?"

She is trying to murder me.

I shift without thinking, and in an instant, she's kicked her leg over my back, pressing her heel down into my spine.

"I didn't say you could move," she says, deadly serious, her eyes searching my face. Finally, she breaks out into a smile again. "Breathe, little angel."

I do, and she's so close, and all I can smell is her. The lines of her lingerie draw my gaze down—past her breasts which are very much in my face, down the curve of her stomach and hips. She pinches my chin, and I snap my attention back to her face.

"Do you know what you taste like?" she asks.

My face is hot. My thoughts are melted. "I don't know," I say, small beneath her, lost in her shadow, her beauty, her power.

But then she laughs, and her foot slips from my back, and I don't know whether I'm allowed to move or not. She laughs so long and so hard she loses her words, and I'm content to witness her mirth and wait.

"I can't say it with a straight face," she says eventually.

"Then say it laughing," I say, because I love her laugh, its luscious villainy.

"I was gonna say—" She's lost in another round of giggles before speech returns. "You taste like Heaven!"

I giggle-snort surprise, but I don't break my pose. "I thought you were being serious!"

"I *was* serious, but then I realized it sounded like a joke, and I couldn't find another way to say it."

I stop laughing. "So I . . . do?"

"You look terrified!" she says through her laughter.

"It's not the news I was expecting."

She pats my shoulders. "Come sit. Poor angel."

I sit. She pillows her head in my lap, and I can't tell whether she's still flirting or serious. "You have to explain," I say.

"I remember the way Heaven used to smell. It clings to you."

"Then what does Heaven smell like?"

She thinks, closing her eyes. Sleepily and unhelpfully, she says, "You."

The rise and fall of her chest is slow like her heartbeat, slower than any human's could be. I observe the gentle motion of her, running my fingers through her hair. She hums contentedly.

"Are you falling asleep?" I ask when she doesn't rouse.

"It is a misconception that evil never sleeps," she says. "My preferred method of indulging in sloth, as a being who doesn't need rest, is to sleep."

"Do you dream?" I ask.

"I'm a lucid dreamer."

"What was your last dream?"

She hushes me and smiles. "Inappropriate for delicate angel sensibilities. Hey, get down here. I'll play big spoon."

It's too late to change the sheets, and I'm too tired. I nestle into the bend of Avitue's body, grateful not to be alone. The smoke-heat of her scent envelops me, and as sleep descends, I realize how much comfort I find in something that should signal danger.

I wake to the cold light of early dawn and a pit of dread in my stomach. Avitue is still nestled at my back, and for all appearances seems to be genuinely asleep. Her black ringlets are an inky wave across the sheets, her full lips parted on a quiet breath. Even in sleep, she draws me in, a perfect temptation at all times.

Last night comes drifting back to me. After a lifetime of fruitless attempts, I found my wings because of Avitue. I'd also been ready to give up hope of ever finding them for her.

I've risked so much for a small moment of kindness. I feel pathetic for it but hungrier still. I'm surprised to realize I regret nothing. I only want answers and reassurance. Against all reason, her tenderness alone makes me trust her. Maybe it's foolish to think a millennia-old demon *wouldn't* be a skilled actor and an adept liar. She's a creature of seduction. She can discern any need and offer to fill it. But I want to think that the care she's shown me can't be faked.

I ease myself out of bed so as not to wake her and pad across the cold floor. Everything feels urgent, and I can't process as long as she's pressed against me, not when the memory of last night is such a distraction. I've never had sex with anyone, never planned to, but if I had, that certainly wasn't how I'd expected it would happen.

When I turn back to glance at Avitue, I find her sitting up, golden eyes intense on me. I startle and immediately start rambling. "Sorry to wake you. The floors are creaky, and I'm so used to being alone and not having anyone to disturb."

Avitue drops her gaze. "Cassiel," she says, and there's a weight behind the way she says my name. Her grip on the edge of the mattress tightens before she seems to remember her claws. She flexes her hands, folds them in her lap, then runs them through her hair. "I can't give you what you want."

"What do I want?" I ask.

She watches me as if seeing through to my pounding heart. "I can't stay with you," she says.

"Oh. Of course. No, I wouldn't expect—" I flounder over a response until Avitue stops me.

"I didn't say I didn't want to," she says with the tone of one trying to gently deliver terrible news. "I said I can't."

"That means," I start carefully, "that you . . . do want to stay?"

She grits her teeth through a weary hiss. "When you've lived for an eternity, you learn not to look too hard at the paths you wish you could've taken."

"So. What can we have?"

She slips from the bed, still fully nude and unconcerned by it. I might've spent the night with her breasts pressed against my back, but it seems terribly impolite to so much as glance at them when I feel painfully sober. For once, it's a challenge to hold her hypnotic gaze, to not admire the curves of her, the casual sway of her hips as she walks. I take an automatic step back as she nears, too overcome to exist within reach of her.

A sly grin reveals her fangs. "You can look if you want, little angel. I'm not shy."

"I don't think I can," I say, staring resolutely at her face.

She tosses her curls back with a dramatic sigh but is obviously reveling in my mental squirming. "I thought we'd fucked your shyness away last night," she coos innocently.

My face is embarrassingly hot. "You're very pretty, and I don't know how to deal with that."

"Only pretty?" Avitue pouts, cocking her head like a predator trying to better discern its prey.

"I said *very*."

She smiles. "Horny bards have written hundreds of songs across the centuries proclaiming my unmatched beauty, and yet I meet a precious angel who I *adore*, and she offers me only an unadorned disyllabic *pretty*. I'm quite offended."

She envelops me in the smoky scent of her embrace and sighs into my hair. The heat of her body banishes the morning chill, and I melt against her again. I've never had the space or the luxury to consider the attractiveness of other people's bodies at much length. It's novel, taboo, like so much in the past few days. I feel as if I need to learn how to see as other people do. To look and desire without trepidation is not a freedom that's ever felt within my reach.

"I've never tried to seduce someone as hungry for kindness as you. If I can grant you any happiness, no matter how small, it would be the greatest thing I've ever done. Tell me, since our time is limited, what would you want to experience together?"

My heartbeat is wild in my chest. "How much time?" I ask.

Her hands slip down my torso to press heat into my back. "Tell me," she whispers, grazing my neck with her fangs.

"I'd want to share my favorite books with you, go to a play. Maybe even . . ."

"Yes?"

"A date? As if we're normal people going to a restaurant."

"Hmm," she hums, amused. "Very bold of you to invite your sworn enemy on a date."

And that *is* what I've done, isn't it?

"It's a slippery slope from hunting someone to dating them," I try to joke, but Avitue's pressing a kiss against my throat, and the words come out strangled. While I'm in the habit of being bold, I press forward, saying, "Maybe we could just have . . . normal sex?"

"You keep using the word *normal*. I feel called out." She draws back, and there's a teasing smile playing across her lips.

I can't quite join in on her mood. "Why is our time limited?"

"I can't put this off forever, Cassiel," she sighs. "We might be demons, but when a lord of Hell tells you to do something, they expect *punctuality*. They expect results. And I won't have any to deliver."

"You never fully told me what you were sent here to do," I say carefully. "If this is connected to the fire."

"It's connected, yes."

"Then you're here with me because . . ."

My head spins with possibilities. I wasn't present at that hunt, but now our family home is being stalked by demons. They might've been able to claim the soul they were owed, but . . .

"My sister killed a greater demon. They want revenge."

I can't escape association with my family, it seems. I haven't killed a demon in years, but I doubt that matters to them.

"You're here," I continue, "for revenge."

Avitue frowns. "I said I wouldn't hurt you."

"Which is why I'm worried about what happens to *you* when you don't turn up with my soul."

Avitue runs a fang over her lower lip. "They'll find out I'm a traitor," she says, as if it's simple. I can't imagine betraying a lord of Hell is easy—but *I'm* the reason she thinks it's worthwhile.

"You don't sound concerned," I say, and it's a fight to keep my voice level.

"Eh." She rolls her eyes. "Working myself into a panic over something I can't help isn't exactly sexy, is it? It's fine. I've lived long enough."

"You've lived long enough," I echo, letting the true meaning behind the words settle. "You've lived forever, and now you're just . . ."

I struggle with Avitue's nonchalance and the revelation that we have so little time, that soon, the demons will know of her betrayal. I don't know what to say first. Could I offer to protect her? *Could* I even protect her from a hoard of demons? How many would be hurt because of Hell's plan?

"I-I have to get ready for work," I say with all the panic that I feel.

Avitue blinks at me. "Yeah, er, if that's—yeah."

I don't mean to, but I slam the bathroom door behind me.

❖

"I have the sense that Halloween's going to be really big this year," Ana's saying, but I barely hear her. It's when she asks, "Do you have any plans?" that I stop poking at the shelves below the register and stand up.

"What did you say, dear?"

"Do you have any plans? For Halloween?"

"When is that now?"

Ana taps into the calendar on her phone. "It lands on a Saturday this year. Lucky that we get a weekend Halloween this time around. I'm going to throw a party again if you'd like to drop by."

She looks hopeful, and I return to fussing with the computer to avoid her gaze. This will be the third time I have to awkwardly decline her invitation. I make a vaguely interested but noncommittal sound, and I don't miss the way her expression falls. She's known me long enough to understand all the ways I say *no* without ever using the word. I feel bad for pushing her away again.

Once more, I try for something approaching honesty.

"When I said before that the holidays are stressful for me, I didn't mean Thanksgiving or Christmas," I say, finally meeting her gaze.

"Oh," says Ana, the look on her face shifting from disappointment to confusion.

"Halloween was a big deal to my mom. It still is, I guess. A lot of family traditions I didn't enjoy." I shrug. "So I just like to stay in."

Traditions, meaning the longest hunting night of the year. Like any natural cycle, there are times during the year when the energetic connection between realms shifts. Every Halloween, there is a spike in crossings to and from Hell, and as Halloween night nears, spirits have more influence in the world, meaning plenty of work to keep hunters busy.

"Should I . . . not ask?" says Ana.

"It's complicated," I say.

Ana's brow furrows. "I'm sorry. It's always been my favorite time of year with both Day of the Dead and Halloween. My family has a lot of traditions too, just . . . ones I've always enjoyed. I shouldn't have assumed—"

"No, please," I say. "I should've said something earlier. Thank you for always thinking of me."

She tries a smile. "Like I said before—" She gestures across the street. "I'm just there."

When Ana leaves, I sense Avitue's presence as a gathering pressure and find her just behind me. She's dressed again in her black leather jacket, but today she's decided on a severe V-neck that flaunts the swell of her breasts. She watches Ana's retreating form through the window.

"A party sounds nice," she says. "Why did you tell her you don't want to go if you do?"

So she's read me again.

"I'd feel *guilty*," I say. "I could never enjoy myself while knowing there's people I'm not helping."

"But you don't go out anyway."

"No," I say slowly.

"So. Live your life. This cycle goes on with or without us. If I were a mortal, there's no party I'd miss."

"But if I went to a party, I'd have to talk to people."

Avitue grins. "You don't have to talk to people to dance. Or drink. Or get high. Or, if the chemistry is just right, to f—"

"I don't think Ana's throwing that kind of party," I hastily interrupt.

Avitue laughs, a joyous mouth-wide-open kind of laugh. I'm entranced by the music of it, her mouth, her teeth.

"You become so prettily flustered. I'd love to go to a party with you," she sighs. "We could start off easy. A mild level of depravity and work our way up. What's a mortal soul without a little tarnish? It gives *character*."

"Are you tempting me?" I ask, settling into the flirtation as if this is something I've done before.

"Is it working?" Avitue asks, tickling her claws up my sides. "Your heart's all aflutter."

"I'm sure I'd disappoint you. Or worse, bore you."

"Absolutely not," she says, pinning me again with her amber gaze. "There's something fun about picking the wallflowers."

I'm about to fall completely into the daydream I've found in her eyes when a flicker of movement beyond the window snaps me back to reality. Avitue gives me an amused look and disappears as if she were never here.

"Hello!" I say a little too brightly as a new customer enters and receive an awkward smile in return. My brain takes a full minute to reset before I can decipher the to-do list stuck to my monitor.

Halfway through the day, I'm wondering where Avitue's gone and round a wall of shelves to find her emerging from the children's section perusing a board book on butterfly life cycles. The little book seems wrong in her sharp hands.

"You know, I invented the slutty version of every Halloween costume," Avitue says without a glance up from the book.

"What?" It's not what I'd expected her to say.

"If you search your heart, you'll find what I say to be true." She winks, turning to disappear into the shelves again.

Everyone who comes into the store asks about her.

"Is she famous or something?" my tenth customer whispers, setting down her books on the counter. I sigh, glance back at Avitue, and do a double take. She's slouched sideways in my favorite armchair and tapping away on a smartphone.

"No," I huff.

"She looks famous," insists the customer.

I ring up her purchases and give the price, but she's too busy staring at Avitue to notice. I repeat myself but don't know how to ask a third time in a way that doesn't make me feel horribly impolite. Once I manage to get the woman out of the shop, I go to Avitue. She quirks an eyebrow to acknowledge my presence but doesn't look up from what appears to be her Instagram feed.

"Jealous, angel?" she says.

"No. Just mildly inconvenienced."

Avitue allows a mischievous smile to spread across her face. "Trust me, this is, in fact, mild. I don't even have to lift a finger around you humans and you're falling over yourselves."

"I suppose you're very proud of that."

"Oh, the things I've done to you would earn me bragging rights in Hell." She licks her lips suggestively, and I can't help my blush. The comment doesn't settle right though. I want to say something. I turn my pinky ring once, twice. Avitue tries to fall back into whatever she was wasting time with on her phone, but her brow wrinkles into a frown when she realizes why I'm hovering. She pockets the phone. "I'm sorry, angel. I'm such a disaster." She sits up properly and reaches for my hand as if she's about to propose. "I really do value what you did for me. Your trust." Impossibly, this makes me blush more. "Your pleasure tastes delicious," she murmurs against my knuckles.

It's too much, and I pull my hand back. "Don't make me want you while I'm working," I scold.

She gives me a positively evil smile. "When's your lunch break?" she asks.

Face hot, I shoo her away, leaving her cackling in her chair.

Between a lull in customers, I find her in the occult section, a poorly lit corner of the shop, snickering and taking selfies in front of the shelves. I should've known she would find it eventually. I wait silently for her verdict.

"The lighting here could be better," she says, flicking her curls over her shoulder. "But angel, this is a *gold mine*. Why didn't you tell me you had a sense of humor?" she asks, grin wide and sharp.

"I don't know what you're talking about," I say, allowing a conspiratorial smile.

She pulls a heavy red book from the shelf. "*Demonology 101*," she reads, raising an eyebrow at me. "I don't know why you've not replaced your big book upstairs with this one, honestly. *How to Summon Spirits. Satanism Today. The Book of Demons.*" She runs her fingertip down the spines, reading out an entire shelf. "Absolute bollocks, all of it," she pronounces, delighted. "Do you know how many of these go on about salt circles?"

"It's been a staple in the human imagination," I say.

"But *this one*," she says, selecting a thin white book no bigger than a contemporary poetry collection. "Everything in this one is suspiciously true." Entitled *Everyday Spiritual Safety*, it's authorless and self-published. "Sneakily disseminating truth among the mortals, are we?"

"So I've been caught," I say.

She snaps another selfie with *Demonology 101*. "If you became a bestseller, maybe they'd get possessed less."

I take my little book from her, smooth a hand over the cover, and return it to the bottom shelf. There's no title on the spine, and with the flashier books at eye level, people rarely notice it. In two years of business, I've only given away three copies.

"Why are you taking so many selfies with my books?" I ask.

"*Angel*." Avitue heaves a long-suffering sigh. "It's *publicity*. People will buy things if they're encouraged by a pretty face."

"And you're the pretty face."

"Obviously." She poses for another shot with the book held just below her cleavage. "Are you going to get that?" she asks.

"Get what?" I ask, bewildered.

"Your door. Your new customer. Seriously, Cassiel, I can try my best at what I do, but it's up to you to maintain customer service standards," she teases.

Somehow, she'd become so charming I missed the door chime.

"Oh!" I say, turning.

But Avitue grasps my shoulder, pulling me back to her and kissing me. Hard. I'm dazed when she lets me go.

"Good luck out there!" she says, smiling deviously before returning her attention to the shelf.

⸺◆⸺

I know we're ignoring it. Well—I am, anyway. I've become comfortable in avoidance. It's why I haven't returned to my family estate since I left. It's why, until very recently, I left my hunter's tome buried at the bottom of a chest. It's how I can turn away from the odd shadows I sense in my daily life, go about my day as a normal human, and hope nothing too terribly bad happens.

It's obvious that Avitue is waiting on my lead to resume our conversation from this morning.

I want to—I do—but all my nervousness expresses itself in bustling around the shop as if it's any other day and there's nothing so pressing as an infernal plot looming in the near future. As if I'm not soon going to lose the one person in the world I've connected with on a literally spiritual level.

I'm saying goodbye to another customer just after lunch when Avitue's arms snake around my middle. The scent of leather and smoke rolls over me. She waits for the bell to quiet before she speaks.

"One normal day," she says.

I turn in her arms, bringing us face to face, and neither of us would have to move much to kiss.

"Let's just give ourselves today, and we'll talk about everything tomorrow. One day to live like everything's fine. Could you relax then? If I give you permission to not worry about responding to me?"

But you're going to die. You're going to die because of me.

"No, not that face again," tuts Avitue. "This isn't your fault."

Suddenly all my fears of my own death at the hands of some cruel demon are projected onto Avitue. Those nightmares turned me sleepless for months, and it was only after a year of leaving home that they finally stopped. Now, I feel the full force of them again. Except there's no dream to wake up from.

"I have to save you," I say, realizing that I'm willing to fight for the *possibility* of what we might have.

"You can't fight a lord of Hell on my behalf," she says as if I'm being tedious. "You just met me."

"*You* just met *me*," I say, "and you're going to *betray* a lord of Hell."

"That's different."

"No, it's not!"

Avitue squeezes her eyes shut for a moment. "Let's do that thing you wanted. 'Normal people going to a restaurant,' you said. Let's do it tonight."

"But we should—"

"*I* want to have fun with my final days, if you don't mind." She tries for a grin and, when I don't return it, adds, "Please, Cassiel. For me?"

"I can't imagine a date with me is the best way to say goodbye to an immortal life."

"It is. And it's what I want." She raises an eyebrow. "Indulge me?"

I let out a breath. Under ordinary circumstances—not that I'd have met Avitue under ordinary circumstances—I would be incredibly flattered if someone like her wanted to go on a date with me. For her sake, I try to locate that emotion, imagining what I might feel like until a bit of that reality can shine through. "Okay. I think I'd like that."

SEVEN

W HEN CLOSING TIME NEARS, an old black car sits conspicuously at the curb in front of the bookshop. *Old* might not be quite the right word. Although I know nothing about cars, I know it's so old and well taken care of as to be decidedly *classic*.

It really shouldn't surprise me when, after I finish locking up, Avitue saunters confidently to the car's passenger side and opens the door for me. Apparently, demons can not only own smartphones, they can also drive cars.

She's also changed her outfit for the evening, though I don't know when. A black bodycon dress accentuates her curves, her long legs. She's paired it with sleek heels, their soles flashing red with every step.

Avitue watches me process all this with a growing smirk but only comments on the car. "1970 Chevelle," she provides proudly.

"Why do you have a car when you're a spirit unbound by the laws of physics? Where do you keep it?"

She only answers the first question. "Sometimes you're in the mood for a good old-fashioned human-style seduction. Take them out for dinner first, and all. And while teleportation is convenient, nothing beats a good joyride."

A couple people on the sidewalk stare with undisguised envy as they walk by, unabashedly looking back over their shoulders as they pass. Avitue practically drinks in the waves of lust rolling off them.

I don't ask where we're going, folding my hands in my lap as Avitue slides into the driver's seat. The interior of the car is as deep red as the soles of her shoes, its leather bench seat as pristine as the day it was manufactured.

My composure doesn't last once we're on the road.

When I suggest for the fourth time that maybe it would really be best if we slowed down, Avitue asks, "You trusted me with your soul, but you don't trust me to drive us to dinner?"

We weave recklessly through crowded traffic, but no one dares honk their horn at her, opting instead to merge obediently out of her path. Space always appears when she needs it, everyday things bending to her will. We miraculously escape several close calls, and even though I recognize the magic at work, I can't bear to watch.

In lieu of an answer, a high-pitched, strained noise escapes my throat, and I cover my eyes for the rest of the drive, fishing for a conversation topic to distract myself.

"Do you always look like this, or do you choose your appearance based on what the person you're with finds attractive?" I ask, peeking through my fingers enough to see that my question has amused her. Her mouth quirks in an uneven grin, revealing one lovely fang.

"I've had thousands of bodies and infinite genders, but this is one of my favorite looks. I'm flattered I didn't have to change anything for you."

That piques my interest enough to forget my nerves. I lower my hands a fraction. Avitue's smile widens.

"Succubi and incubi are the same. People were the ones who tried to assign and name distinctions," she explains. "Most of us enjoy a bit of genderfuckery. I don't think I identify with the having-a-gender thing. I just like this body, and that means she/her pronouns seem easiest for you humans."

"Things are different now. There are more people who wouldn't assume. Do you want me to use something else?" I ask.

She considers, then says, "Not really. You're very sweet for asking. I think you might be the first person to ever ask a demon about their pronouns."

We arrive in front of an Italian restaurant on the other side of town in record time. I don't realize I'm shaking until Avitue comes to open my door and takes my hand. "Sorry, angel," she says, but I'm not sure she completely means it this time. When I step out of the car, however, the cool breeze grounds me. How unreal it is to be in public hand-in-hand with Avitue. I'd thought the normalcy of it would resist us somehow.

It's early evening and pedestrians are beginning to crowd the sidewalks, people on their way to restaurants or shows. Many of them stare at us. We're an odd couple, I know, but they'll never know just *how* odd. I don't have much time to dwell on worrying what others think about us though. I'm captured again by Avitue's smirk, the teasing sway of her hips.

Our table is in a private corner of the restaurant, and I'm relieved for it. I'd like a quiet evening, and Avitue can't help but draw attention wherever she goes—including mine. The low amber light of the restaurant and its hues of cream and gold make her eyes shine. As if her beauty needed any assistance.

She smiles. "I love how you admire me, and I'm loath to ask you to divert your attention, but the waiter may be disappointed if we never order anything."

"Oh!"

I find the menu unopened in front of me, and when I take it in my hands, the paper is a delightful satiny weight. Avitue has ignored her dinner menu in favor of perusing the wine selection. Eventually, I decide on a pasta, and when I return my menu to the table, Avitue looks up and through me. Then she blinks, resettling in her own thoughts.

"If you're having alfredo, we could do a bottle of chardonnay?" she suggests.

I believed her when she said reading desires was a simple reflex, a habit she carries from the way she's had to exist. It's still no less strange having my thoughts read for something as commonplace as a dinner order, something she could easily ask for and receive. It's an odd intimacy.

"I'm sorry," she says as soon as she realizes what she's done. She looks genuinely apologetic, maybe even anxious, as if she's been caught doing some objectively worse evil demon thing.

"No, I'm not upset. Just surprised. I'm not used to it."

"I'm really trying not to be a nosy bitch," she sighs.

"It's how you process the world," I say, understanding. "Just use your power for good."

"It's very cute that you want to reform me."

"You're the one who said you wanted to be good," I say, remembering the note she left with the tea.

Confusion flickers across her face before she bursts into an indecently loud howl of a laugh. "That was a smutty double entendre, angel."

I press my hands over my heating face, hiding from her.

"No, no, come back," Avitue pleads, still laughing. "You're very sweet. The truest angel I've ever met."

I'm laughing behind my hands now. "I can't face you after this."

"But you can. I love your face." When she wrangles her laughter, she adds, "And I might've been flirting, but I did and still do mean that I only intend good things for you."

I peek at her and finally lower my hands. Her expression is serious again. "Wine?" she asks.

"Oh," I say again, fumbling my words. "I've never drunk before."

"I . . . should've known that. If you don't want—"

"I'd like to try it," I say, and her smile returns.

Avitue doesn't order any food for herself, instead requesting two bottles of wine, one white and one red, when the waiter appears.

"I don't think I can manage an entire bottle of wine on my own," I tell her once we're alone again.

She grins as if I've said something very amusing. "Definitely not. You're likely a terrible lightweight. I'll pour you a glass, but the rest is for me. I adore a good red."

"Aren't two bottles of wine a lot? If you're going to drive?"

"Cassiel, my little ray of sunshine," she sighs, propping an elbow on the table. "It takes more than two bottles of wine to get me anywhere near drunk. You have to remember I've lived an eternal life of debauchery. I know this body's limits."

When the food arrives, I've only recently recovered from the adrenaline of the drive. The mushroom alfredo, however, fully distracts me from any lingering anxieties regarding having to get back in the car for the drive home. I slowly acclimate to my glass of wine, sipping and contemplating between bites of pasta, and decide near the end that I like it. Avitue was right; I am a lightweight. My body is fizzy with warmth. My muscles looser. Laughing is easier. Meanwhile, Avitue drinks her wine like water and, true to her word, behaves no differently for it. Her cabernet is as dark and red as her lipstick—makeup I've never seen her without—and I'm caught staring. Again. Her gaze flicks from my fork, laden with pasta and halfway to my mouth, and back to my face. A slow smile quirks her lips.

"You're wonderful company," she says. "And I promise I'm not saying that just because I like the attention."

"But I'm not doing anything," I say, fearing again all the ways I'm inadequate, boring. The anxiety wells up until it's tumbling from my mouth. "There's nothing interesting about me. I open my shop. I buy groceries. I read books in bed until I fall asleep."

"Maybe that's what you see. I see someone figuring out who she is and who she wants to be. That's a hard thing to do and far from boring." Avitue looks down into her drink, her smile turning almost *shy*. "It's why I like humans."

"You like us?"

"I like some of you. I like *you* especially. There aren't an abundance of people someone like me could have a quiet, comfortable dinner with."

I wish I could see into her desires the way she can with mine. "You've lived forever, and this is what you want?"

"I've spilled a lot of blood on the command of others," she says, pouring the remaining wine into her glass and filling it to the brim. I'm thankful this is the most chaotic thing she's done since we sat down. "Sometimes it's fun. But maybe I want a different pace."

She tips the wine back, not pausing until she's finished off her glass. Continuing to watch her seems suddenly indecent, so I return to my food. For the next few minutes, she seems lost in thought, drumming her nails restlessly on the table, staring out at the other diners as if they suddenly perplex her. I'm taking my last bite of pasta when I feel her gaze return to me.

"Dear?"

"I love that you call me that," Avitue murmurs. The intensity remains.

I sit back in my chair.

"I know you call everyone that, but no one's ever thought to use an endearment with me. Not that I court endearment."

"But you're lovely," I blurt.

"Pretty sure that's not the first impression I made on you. And I don't often have the opportunity for second and third impressions."

She summons her phone to her hand, taps the screen a couple times, and pushes it across the table to me. The grid resolves into a series of pictures, all of the same beautiful demon with gorgeous hair. I take the phone in my hands.

"You're"—I squint at the screen—"xXxHellfireHottiexXx?"

"It's retro humor," she laughs. "No judgment formed against me shall prosper."

I scroll through. A photo of Avitue deepthroating a strangely shaped dildo at a party. Another of Avitue's naked body bathed in money, her fanged mouth half-open and dripping blood. One of her smiling with gleeful innocence in the background as she holds a fresh human heart to the camera.

Before the terror of it can fully register, Avitue peers over at the phone and comments, "Oh, he was a wanker. Don't feel bad for him."

"Does this violate the terms of service?" I ask numbly.

"There's terms of service?"

"You have to say *yes* when you sign up."

Avitue shrugs. "They must not apply to me. As an expert in contracts, I think I'd know when I'm bound by something."

"They're not going to issue *that kind* of contract," I clarify.

She smiles sweetly. "*That kind* of contract is the only sort that matters."

I scroll farther. Each post has hundreds of thousands of Likes. The ones she posted from the bookstore have already garnered several thousand. "You have so many Followers. You must not be making too many bad impressions."

"People like sexy bad girls, but they don't *like* sexy bad girls, you know? I can show my fangs online, but it's another thing in person." She's suddenly on her feet and pulling her chair around the table to sit next to me. "Here, let's you and me take one."

"What?" I say, an edge of panic in my voice.

"Nothing *intense*, just, like, a fun picture. Show my Followers that I'm not always covered in blood." Avitue throws an arm over the back of my chair and leans into my space, frowning at the camera until she finds an angle that she likes. "Don't look terrified. Smile."

I do as I'm told, but I look as if I'm sitting for a professional photo as a librarian next to Avitue with her practiced flirty wink.

"Um . . ." I start as Avitue begins tapping at the phone again.

date nite!! ;) look at this cute angel i found. she's so precious and not at all as naughty as me lol, she types under our selfie, and it's posted before I can make any protests about looking like a stuffy librarian.

"Your eyes are visible in all of them," I say instead.

"People think everything is contacts and good makeup and body mods these days. Back in the day, humans were more willing to believe in monsters." She pauses, returning briefly to her phone. "Look, we're already getting Likes. People love you!" she says, holding up her notifications as proof.

Seeing Avitue's assembled posts baffles me, as if I'm looking at another person, someone trying very hard to seem tough and cool and careless. I scroll back to the picture of us together, Avitue's forked tongue out, one golden eye closed in a suggestive wink. I'm a stark contrast next to her.

"Let's take a normal one," I suggest.

Avitue rolls her eyes dramatically. "You're obsessed with normal," she grumbles good-naturedly.

Avitue lets me hold the phone for the second photo, and I tap the shutter button just as she turns away, face nuzzling softly into my hair, all the sharpness of her obscured. She stares at the photo when I return the phone.

"Is this how you see me?" she says, her vision of herself shifting before my eyes. We keep the photo for ourselves, don't post it.

But the image of her holding the heart won't leave my mind. The little square continues to cast a shadow over the moment.

"Can I ask you something?" I say.

Avitue eyes the way I'm turning my ring around my finger, and I stop. She looks wary for the first time all night, and it's like those uneasy first encounters. I miss the heat of her as she straightens, moving ever so slightly away from me.

"Yes," she says, her gaze somewhere over my head.

"Are you—?"

"I am trying," she starts as if in the middle of some task that requires deep concentration, "not to look at what you want to know."

"Oh." A nervous laugh pops from my mouth. "I was remembering last night. When you said you hadn't fed from anyone since we'd met."

"Yes," she prompts.

"And the picture of the—"

"Heart I stole," she finishes for me, relaxing back into her chair with a coy smile that she immediately purses when she sees my face. "You can't expect me to be an upstanding citizen like you."

"It's not that . . . It's just— You seem to enjoy, you know."

"Blood? Violence? Murder?" she rattles off dispassionately. "I'm a *demon*, Cassiel. I thought you already understood this."

The words have the tone of *I thought you wouldn't judge me*, and I realize what's happened. Avitue was reaching for vulnerability through flirtation. She knew that, unlike her Followers, I'd see those pictures for what they are. It was an implicit question. Am I okay with who she truly is?

"I do," I rush to say, to soothe, and it's technically true. It's why I was scared of her in the beginning. I thought she'd turn that violent excess against me. I try to backtrack to my original question. "I was only wondering how you, um."

Her attention turns sharp, gaze flicking from my lips to my throat, and I realize my heart's quickened with nerves. For a moment, she's utterly hypnotized.

Then I break the spell. "I was wondering how you choose your victims."

At that, her gaze snaps back to my eyes. "My *victims*," she repeats quietly, her tone disappointed. She sinks in her chair, her attention drifting away from me for the first time since our conversation started.

Released from the pressure of her attention, I see the restaurant again. The tables nearest to us have new diners. I was so wrapped up in her presence that I neither noticed our old neighbors leave nor the new ones arrive. At some point, our plates were cleared.

"You know the little fish who eat trash?" Avitue says.

I nod skeptically, unsure how this answers my question.

"It took me a long time to realize what I was doing to myself," she says. "I mean *embarrassingly* long. Like, centuries. Back then, I could blame the post-fall depression. Most of us didn't survive being thrown out of Heaven with our self-worth intact. I wanted to die and feel alive at the same time. So I'd find these terrible men." She drifts off in thought again, and by the time she resumes, dread has pooled in the pit of my stomach. "You can tell the ones who think women are literally disposable. I don't even have to read them."

I reach for her as if I can head off the inevitable, ward away a past that's already happened.

"I can't die, little angel," she reassures me. "That's the whole point."

"But they'd try," I say, my voice thinned by the horror of what she's implying.

I picture a night creature, covered in her own blood and rising vengefully from the dead.

"Some would." Her shrug is followed by a predatory flash of teeth. "And I'm a very generous lover, so I'd always reciprocate." She's back in my space. "Is that moral enough for you?"

I only realize my hands are shaking when I raise them to cup her face. She blinks in surprise, an eternity of bitter anger draining at my touch.

"No one will hurt you ever again," I promise, not expecting the vehemence in my voice.

Avitue looks awed. "That's so hot," she whispers, and I think she means *thank you*—for seeing her, for caring.

The waiter appears at our table with the check, and we break apart—Avitue with the focus of setting her sights on new prey and I with nerves. She tugs the waiter down by his tie and, like a sleight of hand trick, tucks a fold of bills that definitely wasn't in her hand moments ago into his chest pocket. He looks dazed as she releases him with a wink.

"I don't think that's how you pay at restaurants," I say, watching the waiter pause every few steps to get his bearings.

"So by the book," she sighs, grinning at me.

"Was that a pun on my occupation?" I ask.

She rises, offering her hand to me. "You decide."

"You have to be nice to people," I say under my breath as we weave around the tables and toward the door.

"I didn't skip out on the check or murder anyone," she says.

"Being nice is more than not being mean," I try to explain. "You said you like humans."

"I said I like *some* of you. You're generally very amusing folk."

I stop in the restaurant foyer, and Avitue turns back to me, perplexed. Summoning my courage, I say, "If we're going to be together, you have to respect people."

She tilts her head as if this is the strangest thing I've said all night. "What are you talking about?"

"People aren't *things*. You can't will them out of your way like they're an inconvenience. Or treat them like they only exist to entertain you."

She makes a face like I've presented her with a complex math problem. "But what if they *are* inconveniencing me?"

"That's not the point."

"Then . . . ?"

"You see *me* as a person deserving of care, someone who has my own concerns, someone to respect. You have to do that for everyone."

"Is *that* why you're so tired? Is this your angelic burden or something?"

"No, that's just— It's part of existing in society."

She wrinkles her nose. "I have bad news for you about human nature then."

"Avitue, please," I say, exasperated.

"Is this our first lover's quarrel?" she says brightly.

"You have to be nice to people. You can't treat others like things," I reiterate.

"Do you want me to copy that down one hundred times? No, okay, I get it," she adds quickly when I frown. "I will endeavor to develop *morality*."

"This is important to me," I say, lowering my voice as another couple sweeps past us on the way into the restaurant. Their attention lands on Avitue, skipping over me entirely.

Avitue seems not to notice them. Her pout turns grave. She appraises me, smoothing her hands down my sleeves as she thinks. "Okay, angel," she sighs, tugging me gently out the door by my lapel.

And like that, she's back to flirting. Those few steps knock my thoughts and breath from my body, the world narrowing down to her once more.

"You're so fun," she says, releasing my blazer to capture my wrist in her grasp.

We're very much *not* holding hands. She's leading. I'm following, a body happy to dance to the whims of her puppet master. The wind whips her curls across her face as she looks down at me, and I zero in on the dark-red lipstick, the fangs revealed by her smirk. I don't know whether I want her to kiss me or bite me, but—irrationally—I want it now. Her grasp on my wrist is a brand, and I want it elsewhere.

Avitue stops, and I realize she's holding the car door open for me. I look from her to the car, unsure of how we arrived here so soon. As if waking from a dream, I fold myself into the seat. The snap of the closing door begins to ground me.

"You okay?" Avitue asks as she settles into the driver's seat.

I'm staring through the windshield, still stymied. "It was such a strange feeling. When you did that."

She laughs as if I've told a joke. "It's called being horny, babe."

"Oh," I say, my face suddenly very warm.

She slouches in her seat and props an elbow on the window ledge. Even with bad posture, she manages to remain alluring. Her dress has ridden up her thighs, and with effort, I drag my attention back up to her face. There was something we were talking about before. Something important.

She notes my distraction with a flash of a grin but doesn't tease me again. "Cassiel," she starts. That tired look crosses her face, not as dire as last night, but there still. "I'm not a happy person or a good person. I've done bad things, most of which I don't regret. For however long this lasts, can you deal with that?"

"You can always change."

"If demons had redemption arcs, we'd be angels again," she says. I don't miss the bitterness in her tone. "And I don't need redeeming from anything."

I change tack. "When we met, you decided things would be different."

"That's because you're you. No other reason." Her slouch turns tense. Her nails drum pinpricks into the upholstery. When she notices, she brushes a hand over the damage, wiping it pristine. "Angels—and from what I understand, nephilim too—believe they're good because they've bound themselves by certain rules. Your kind aren't nice, either. But I sense that you are. And that interests me."

I think of Gabriel and our tenets. I think of Zuriel, choosing rules over sisterhood. I think of Aunt Raphael, the only model I ever had for making room within those rules, and the repercussions of daring to do so.

"Is it enough that I want to be good to you? I won't be around long enough for the other stuff to matter much anyway," she adds under her breath, her hand tight on the steering wheel as if to prevent more absentminded damage.

The reminder hurts deep in my chest. So much of her is fathomless. She is at once more comprehensible than the angels—so human shaped and *here* that I can almost forget she was one of them—yet she inhabits their same gravity. Trying to argue my point seems suddenly futile. She's had eons to think these thoughts and calcify a self around them. I'm sad for her, though I don't know whether it's because she believes her truth is so immutable she's given up or because people and experiences and survival convinced her that trying wasn't worthwhile anymore. She would hate for me to be sad for her, though, would probably find it insulting.

I pack my thoughts away, and I hope, maybe, something gets through to her when I say, "You're enough."

It's what Ana says to me, something I struggle to believe but want to. I want to believe it for Avitue too. Her face doesn't change, and I worry I've misunderstood her, but then she's across the seat and straddling my lap in an instant. I'm dizzy with the heat of her, the weight and press of her body against mine. She cradles my face in her hands, her usually sharp pupils blown wide.

"Can I kiss you?" she asks, her voice heavy with want.

"I think I'm going to die," I whisper. Because every moment with her is more than I could've ever imagined allowing myself.

"Is that a *no*?"

"It's a *yes*."

Her smile ruins me. "Put your hands on me," she commands.

"Where?" I ask, terrified of all the possibility she's offered.

"Anywhere," she hisses impatiently, and I rest my hands tentatively against her hips.

She ducks her head to nuzzle my pulse, sighing against my throat. "Thank you," she says.

"Of course."

She kisses me with all the hunger I witnessed in her eyes. Her hand closes lightly around my throat, her thumb pressing into my quickened pulse. The claim of the gesture thrills me where I should be afraid of her, of this. Instead, it urges me forward. She hums, and I open my mouth to her, her forked tongue flicking curiously against mine.

I think I'm going to die.

She kisses me slow and deep, and we breathe each other in, the moment stretching deliciously until I feel the coil of heat low in my belly.

I break the kiss, feeling as if I'm surfacing from deep underwater. I find the gold of her eyes in the gathering dark, and there's tension around them again. This time, concern.

"You're okay," she soothes.

But outside the shelter of her aura, desire still feels different. Dangerous. I take a breath.

"Home?" she suggests.

I nod, and she untangles herself from me to resettle behind the steering wheel. She threads her fingers through mine, the concern plain on her face until I speak.

"I'm not used to feeling alive in my body like this."

"You're afraid to like it," she says.

"I think so. But I do."

Despite what she claims about herself, she's a more considerate driver on the way back. She even allows someone to merge into the lane ahead of her without so much as eye roll. She is *inconvenienced* several times—by pedestrians and stoplights and one-way streets. None provoke a reaction. Her thoughts seem elsewhere.

I have to untie her from her fate. I want to see what happens when she lets herself change, because I think she too is standing at her own precipice. Because she's *interesting*. Even if she doesn't want to believe it, the hedonistic chaos of her is tempered by something else.

She was an angel, and I have dedicated my life to understanding angels.

When we return to my apartment, we don't turn on the lights. We don't have normal sex or any sex at all. I'm surprised to find the bed clean and intact again.

"Thought I'd play house while you were busy downstairs," explains Avitue.

I thank her, and she pulls me down to the fresh linens before I can make anything of it.

She applies the heat of her hands to my shoulders, massaging the tension from them. "How did they feel?" she asks. "Your wings."

"They felt like they've always been part of me, just waiting to be found. I felt bright."

"You *were* bright. Damn near burned my eyes," Avitue chuckles.

I smile at her over my shoulder. "I would have warned you if I knew it'd happen."

"Do you think you could find them again whenever you like?"

I close my eyes, and I can sense the shape and weight of their light like phantom limbs. I try to grasp at it, but it's as if my hand passes through. "I can *see* them, but I don't think I can make it happen just because I want it to."

"Maybe they manifested because your body perceived a threat?"

"It didn't feel like that," I say. "Something else triggered it."

Avitue scrapes her nails ticklishly slow down my back. "Bet it was the amazing orgasm I gave you."

"It was not!" I nearly shriek, turning to slap playfully at Avitue's hands.

When we calm, Avitue places a kiss against the scar on my shoulder, tender and sincere. It's a stark contrast to the kiss in the bookstore, to her obnoxious flirtation. She moves easily between the two, although I suspect the sincerity is rarer. I'm thinking about what it means, about her care with me, when I say, "Last night, I've never done that before."

"What? Fucked a demon?" Avitue says, laughing.

"No, I mean . . ."

She recognizes what I'm trying to say and pulls me against her. "You were perfect, and I don't know how to thank you."

"I wasn't boring?" I ask, thankful for the dark, that I don't have to face her as I ask.

A slow and unique horror dawns. If there's anyone in the world who could rate sexual encounters on some objective scale of worst to best, it'd be Avitue. I feel suddenly on uneven ground, as if there's no way I could ever satisfy her if this weren't life-or-death.

"You are easily the *least* boring person I've had sex with."

"But is there something I should do? Something you'd like?"

Avitue shifts, pushing me down on the bed and straddling my hips. I blink up at her, suddenly and thoroughly overwhelmed.

"What I like—" she says, tracing the point of a claw down the line of my neck to my heart, "is for you to lie back and make all your pretty noises just for me."

Heat blooms in my chest. My pulse turns hot. I recall last night and that dark moment I let go, the burst of pleasure before her teeth pierced my soul. The memory unfurls inside me like a tea leaf, its essence swirling like blood in water. Avitue strokes my cheek, cupping my face in her hands as she leans down. Her hair curtains the world away, and all I can see is the glint in her eyes.

"Now," she adds, glancing to my throat, my lips. "Is that something you'd like, angel?"

My heartbeat thrums in my ears. "Yes," I whisper.

"Good." She sits back, and I can breathe again. "One of the greatest pleasures of my immortal life has been topping pretty girls like you."

My thoughts ricochet between *immortal life* and *topping pretty girls like you*, and I'm stymied to silence. Avitue waits, a satisfied look on her face as I hope for one of my thoughts to finally reach my mouth.

"There's so much I want to learn about you, but there's no time."

"What do you want to know?" she asks, as if it's that easy.

"Everything."

"I can't cover thousands of years in one night, but I can give you the highlights."

She moves again, gesturing for me to pillow my head in her lap. I do, reveling in the scent and heat of her.

"I have this certainty that being made a succubus was a special punishment. I wasn't like others who fell. I didn't participate in the rebellion, but I was guilty by association."

"A special punishment for what?" I ask.

She combs a hand through my hair. "I guess I asked the wrong kinds of questions, wanted to know why we angels could manifest physical bodies if seeking and indulging in pleasure betrayed our devotion. Now all the sensations of the world are open to me, but I'll die if I don't indulge the destructive pleasure of feeding."

I understand now why Avitue was so gentle with me and so angry on my behalf.

"That seems cruel," I say.

Avitue shrugs. "It's how things went. Other questions?"

I try to think of something neutral, happy even. "Your favorite part about life in this realm?"

"I was a patron to a lot of lady artists."

"Oh! That's nice of you."

"They seemed to think so too." She smirks until her second meaning registers on my face, then breezes on. "Endorsed some mystics. I might've gotten out of hand with Benedetta in the seventeenth century, but it was a good time."

"The nun?" I clarify.

"The nun. And that was all in my free time. Don't ask me about all the shit Beelzebub had me doing. Half of my work is playing femme fatale and ruining some politician. Demeaning work that I barely needed to use my power for. Those men already have a foot in Hell. They fall easy. But when you're a succubus, you're the lowest of the low to other demons. That's why I liked this realm. I wasn't part of a hierarchy anymore. I could use my power the way I wanted, make things better for some people and worse for others. But playing along with Lucifer's plan got me my current rank, got me here."

I find, when Avitue takes me through history, that she marks the passage of time by local fashions. Some big historical events she knows little about personally but can recount the itch of whatever fabric was common where she'd settled. Eventually, she's standing up and turning the whole affair into a fashion show, snapping her fingers through hundreds of years of representative outfits. I let her, laughing at her poses and exaggerated accents.

This is easier than talking about celestial and infernal forces. Easier for Avitue, I suppose, than recounting the bloody details of an unfathomably long life enacting and witnessing cruelty. The clothes were a source of joy, a distraction, a way for her to assume a new identity and pretend for a little while that she was *normal*. Avitue doesn't fail to notice when I turn pensive, and soon she's rustling over to me in layers of skirts and lace.

"You were lonely," I say.

"Yes."

"Heaven threw you away, and then Hell—"

"I want to sleep, Cassiel. It's late."

I don't argue that demons don't need to sleep. I don't protest when Avitue tumbles into bed in a full evening gown. She throws a lace-gloved hand across me and pulls me close.

"You're so old." I speak the realization aloud as it settles. Of course I know she's old. Of course. *Knowing* she's old is one thing, but *comprehending* how much she's lived through is impossible. It's the narrow lens of a mortal mind. There are two realities. One: I'm here with Avitue, a person who cares for me in whatever way she can. Two: an ageless being of unknowable power holds my fragile, finite body in her grasp. The gulf between the two seems unnavigable.

"So old," I repeat, awed.

"Ouch," laughs Avitue, feigning offense.

"No, I mean you're . . . It's impossible to imagine so many years."

Avitue hums thoughtfully. "Aren't you ever scared? Of, you know."

"Dying?" I say. It seems strange for her to tiptoe around this.

"Of knowing you don't have that much time, no matter what you do."

"I always imagined I'd die on the hunt, so I didn't think much about the time I had left. That's how most nephilim go eventually. Some of us settle down when we age, but a lot of us feel too guilty giving up hunting when we know we can still protect people."

"So . . . you're not scared?"

"Everyone knows a hunter who's died. Every time we'd go out, I was terrified. Eventually, it wore me down so much, I quit and decided to live with the guilt. As far as normal mortality, it just is."

She's silent for a while before she says, "I can't imagine it."

I turn over to face her. Her eyes are so beautiful in the dark. This time, when I look into them, I realize I'm just as willing to endanger everything I have for her—for the mere possibility of exploring what we might have together—as she is to give up everything for me. The knowledge settles like a destiny I always knew I had. I'm no less scared, but I'm jumping off the cliff.

Avitue witnesses the realization through the desire embedded at the core of it. She opens her mouth as if to protest, but I speak first.

"Do you remember everything? If we survive this, will you remember me?"

She looks pained and hopeful all at once, the truth of what she's been carrying all day finally bleeding through. We kiss, tentative and cautious, as if it's the first. I linger in the warmth of her, breathing her in.

Against my lips, she whispers, "I could never forget you, Cassiel."

EIGHT

A REEK OF SULFUR startles me awake. *Demon*, my training tells me. I can't move, can't make a sound. I struggle vainly against the force holding me. Just out of sight, I hear the scrape of a heavy boot against the floor. Avitue's heat is no longer beside me.

"You look glowy," a voice grumbles.

"Drained her recently," comes Avitue's easy answer.

I stop struggling. Force myself not to panic. They don't know yet. They haven't come for her.

"Good work," says the second demon, and the boots clunk their way across the floor to the side of the bed, eclipsing the moonlight and throwing their heavy shadow over me.

"Your sisters say they're best just after their connection to the angels has been broken, when the light turns. Rich as blood but unlike anything you've ever tasted before. You have that to look forward to before you deliver the soul."

I'm glad I can't scream because there's suddenly a grubby hand in my hair, and the sulfur smell threatens to overwhelm. The demon tugs until they can see my face.

"This one looks cherubic," they sneer. "She put up a fight at all?"

"A bit. But she was easy enough," Avitue purrs.

"Good. Be careful when you finally break her. You know how our master likes these ones."

"Of course."

"Any sign of the tome?"

"If you haven't noticed, there are a lot of books to go through between here and downstairs."

The demon drops me and stalks back to Avitue. "Get it done. Shouldn't be that hard. It'd have some gaudy angelic glow. You've had how long?"

"Performing a temptation on a nephilim is a delicate—"

There's a *thump* followed by the sound of books tumbling from the shelves and spilling open across the floor.

"If there's something you neglect, Beelzebub can find a thousand others eager to replace you."

"No one else knows this realm like I do."

"And no one else is as vulnerable as you are either. There's a reason none of you succubi are critical to the plan. I don't know why Beelzebub's bothering with the risk."

"I'm sure if you want to question Beelzebub's methods, he can find a thousand others eager to replace you," Avitue echoes the demon's threat.

A step. A mocking laugh. "Wait until you have the rank before you make bold claims."

Avitue spits a vicious hiss. "Get your fucking hands off me, and let me do my job. I know how to run a temptation."

"For your sake, I hope that you do. You're running out of time."

The sulfur smell evaporates all at once, and the hold of Avitue's sleep paralysis relents shortly afterward. I curl protectively into myself. Avitue, in her modern clothes again, kneels at the bedside and smooths my disheveled hair. I flinch at the touch, remembering that demon's hands. Avitue draws back.

"What are they going to do to me?" I ask.

"I won't let that happen, remember?"

"What did they mean? What do they do to people like me? Why do they want the tome?"

"You don't need to know that. Nothing's going to happen to you."

"But the other nephilim. The ones who fall on the hunt."

At that, Avitue won't meet my gaze.

I think of my sister. What would have happened to her if Gabriel hadn't shown up? I think of my father, killed before I could properly remember him. What do they have planned for Avitue when she inevitably fails the task they've given her? I don't often think of violence, but the words are spilling out before I can consider what I'm saying.

"I'll kill them if they come back. I'll kill them, and your sleep paralysis trick won't stop me."

Unlike my brothers, I've never gotten any pleasure from the hunt. I don't enjoy killing. Even at the peak of my abilities, I was soft. This feeling is different. A threat to someone I care about outside of my family is a new thing for me. I'm not fighting vaguely for humanity anymore. There's someone I want to protect, someone I want to keep.

Avitue blinks, the only expression of her surprise. "Don't make yourself seem like a threat to them. Not now. Trust me."

"I *have* been trusting you."

She sighs that burdened sigh again, the one from the dream. "I know."

"When they come for you, I'll kill them."

Avitue sighs. "You can't fend off all of Hell. I'm not doing this so that you can become an avenging angel and get yourself killed." She pauses, then says low as if someone will overhear, "If you want to do something, if you trust me, then let's make a plan, you and me."

"That means you'll have to tell me what Hell wants."

She sits back, looking suddenly very tired. "Revenge, like you said. Your sister killed one of ours, so . . . we take someone important to her. Killing you outright would be unsatisfying to them. Physical pain would be too easy. That's why they didn't send a short-tempered brute like Belial. You know how to deal with them. Beelzebub wanted something more psychological and delicate, something you wouldn't be prepared for. That's my expertise." She gives me a weary look. "Please don't ask me to describe more than that."

Even though I'd asked before, I decide I don't actually want to know the details of spiritual torture.

"How do we get out of this?" I ask instead.

A low hiss builds in her throat like a sigh. "I've never successfully convinced a lord of Hell that he doesn't want what he wants. I might be able to negotiate a more favorable outcome, but it wouldn't completely change the current course. And I'd have to give him something else that's desirable to compensate."

I rest my face in my hands for a moment. It's just after three in the morning, and I *am* tired. "A deal with the devil by proxy," I observe.

A lord of Hell wants my soul claimed. That seems the nonnegotiable piece. But maybe, if I want to protect Avitue, I don't have to die for it.

"In theory," I start, emerging from the shelter of my hands.

Her attention perks up at the words. "In theory," she repeats, watching me closely. It's that predator's stare again, the single-minded focus, the unnatural stillness. I'm meeting the gaze of a large cat without glass or bars separating us.

"Can you make a claim on a soul and not . . . do anything about it?"

"Are you offering me your soul, Cassiel?" she asks. She's quiet, no hint of teeth. But that stare. It carries the same restrained hunger as before she fed from me. She said she was in the mood for a high-risk seduction, and if this were a game, getting away with my soul would be the ultimate prize.

This is dangerous territory. Even more dangerous because it doesn't feel that way. People have been tricked into terrible binding contracts with less straightforward language, but even without her impish smirk, I understand that this is still flirtation. I have nothing to fear from her sharp edges, but *my soul* and *eternity* are such large concepts that I don't trust myself to understand what I'm promising.

"In theory," I whisper.

Now, the teeth. "It's like you know how this goes." She shifts, and the tension breaks. "There's certain etiquette every demon abides by. If you've been granted permission to claim a soul and you do, no one else can challenge or question that claim. So if I happen to favor your soul in your body for another hundred and twenty years, that's my business."

"And then after? When I die?"

"Then we're together forever. In whatever way you want to be."

"What do you mean?"

Avitue frowns. Even for her, there's apparently a limit to how fun flirting about death can be. "Do you really want to talk about the gory details now? When you're not even sure?"

I nod. "Now is when it's important. So I know what I'm getting into. So I know what to choose." Already, my heart is hammering in my chest.

"Could mean a lot of things. Of course, I'll do whatever you want, what's least unpleasant."

I swallow. "Is it always painful?"

"Among all the options, there are only two I would consider. First, I could make you one of us. You'd live forever unless you had an unfortunate run-in with one of your family's relics. But I could see how becoming a demon wouldn't be the most appealing choice, considering."

"And the second option?" I ask.

"I could carry your soul with me for eternity. Keep you right next to my heart. You could see what I see and communicate with me, but you wouldn't have much influence in the outside world." She thinks. "Actually, there are three."

"And the third would be?"

"You die, and there's no afterlife. You just"—she shrugs—"stop existing."

I can tell she's being careful not to give weight to any of the choices she's presented, careful not to make me feel pressured into the option she wants. While I consider, she adds, "You don't need to decide now." With a grimace, she continues, "Being with a demon isn't too appealing in the end. But it means no one will come for us while you're alive."

Even though we're discussing the fate of my eternal soul, I feel oddly detached from it all. I wonder whether the weight will settle the older I get, once I've lived past a century and begin to feel my mortality.

"What would you choose?" I ask.

Avitue looks as if she's about to protest my question, but instead, she asks, "If our roles were reversed?"

I nod.

"If you were one of us, we could keep living together like this. You'd still get to experience the world. But it's the most painful path. Falling hurts a soul. And you come out changed."

"Changed how?"

"You'd be like me and also not—what myths call a vampire, a human soul changed by occult ceremony. I don't know if a nephilim could stand this kind of hunger for the humans they've spent their lives protecting. Inevitably you'd mess up. One day, you might intend to feed, and you might not stop until it's too late for them."

I back away from that vision. I'll confront that moral crisis later. Later, when all the pieces are assembled and I can see every path forward.

"What would you have to give them in return for claiming my soul?"

She thinks. "Maybe your sister's longbow. Or a similar relic. The ones that can kill our souls and not just our bodies. It would put them at ease, having one less mortal threat in this realm."

"Like my falcata?"

She sits up straighter. "You never mentioned that you wielded one of the angelic weapons."

"It's the one I showed you in the tome, remember? Inherited from the angels themselves, radiance and all."

"You'd be giving up a lot for this, Cassiel," Avitue says. "Risking a lot. Forfeiting your inheritance for nothing."

"For you," I remind her.

"Even worse. I don't think demon hunters are supposed to be saving demons."

"Ex–demon hunter," I remind her. "I'll save whoever I want."

"We have time," she says, though I doubt it based on our recent guest's visit. "Think it over. I can go to Beelzebub and propose our idea just to see if there's a chance at all, but . . . promise me you'll think on it."

This first agreement is the easiest one I'll make with her. I promise.

<hr/>

I cradle the tome in my hands the next morning, laying down select wards that won't harm or banish Avitue. To the uninitiated, I'm sure the process looks like a lot of monotonous pacing and muttering, but from where she lounges in bed, Avitue tracks my every movement with the rapt attention of a cat watching a songbird.

Her outfit of the moment is composed wholly of a lacy black thong and gold nipple rings.

I ignore her for now, frowning down at the tome as I recite the final line to set the ward. When I hold up my hand, there's a pulse of white-blue light through the room that blankets every surface before it dissipates. Avitue shivers at the effect but nothing more.

"I hate that," she says. "Feels like a swarm of little crawly things."

I close the tome and return it to its place at the bottom of the chest. "You can't complain about it much when it'll keep your colleague from paying us another visit."

When I finally turn to her, she's holding up what I *think* might be a dildo—a red monstrosity with conjoined phalluses and two heads. I don't give her the satisfaction of a reaction. "Why do they want the tome?" I ask when I rejoin her on the bed.

"As you humans say, knowledge is power. If we can destroy even one of them, we weaken your ability to pass on your knowledge. The less future nephilim know, the easier our work becomes. The more we know about what you know, the stronger we become."

"That's why you were so shocked when I showed you the tome. I'd handed you half your objective, and you didn't even have to do anything."

Avitue taps the dildo thoughtfully against her lips as if it's only an ink pen. "It was the trust that shocked me, but yes. I wasn't even sure exactly what I was looking for. None of us have seen them. We're only aware that you have old written records of your knowledge."

"It didn't even cross your mind to take it."

"When I realized I *didn't* consider it, I did think that I must be bloody losing it."

I sigh, finally give in, and ask the question Avitue obviously wants me to ask. "Why is it shaped like that?"

"It's a devil phallus. Because I'm a devil."

"It seems a bit . . . large, don't you think?"

She turns it as if considering, and the silicone length sways menacingly in her hand. "It's average?" Whatever my face does in response makes her choke on a laugh. "I see. We'll ease you into debauchery yet." She sets the toy aside, and it vanishes without her touch. "Before I leave you, may I grant your other wish?" she asks, cupping my face gently in the heat of her hands. Her gaze is sharp, and for a moment, I forget to breathe.

"Yes," I whisper.

She blinks, and then she's seeing through me, turning over desires and fears to seek what's underneath. I experience it as a tug in my chest, bidding my heart to come undone and spill all its hoarded secrets. My pulse speeds, sending heat between my legs. Her search is gentle and curious, and I open to her, laying bare the bloody pulp of myself.

When she refocuses on me, my breathing is fast and shallow.

"Thank you," she says, her voice soft, tender. "Yesterday, you were scared of yourself, of wanting. May I show you something?"

I nod.

The morning is still early enough that light hasn't found us yet. Avitue rises, and when she opens her right hand, there's a red votive candle in her palm. She sets it on the floor a few feet from the bed and lights it with a flame that's sprung from her index finger. Continuing this way, she encircles us in candles where I'd once chalked warding sigils against her. I never knew demons could create sacred space, but this couldn't be anything else. I feel in my bones when a ritual has opened.

At the foot of the bed, Avitue holds out her hands as if bracing something, and when she turns to me, an ornate gold mirror flashes my reflection. It looks as if it could've been stolen from Versailles, and I'm stunned to be framed by something so beautiful. I can't speak. I don't know the words to this ritual.

Avitue is transformed by the soft glow of the candlelight, and when she returns to the bed, I feel like a goddess has descended upon me. She kisses my lips, my cheeks, my throat. I guide her hands down to the hem of my shirt, and she undresses me like a priceless gift, each scrap of clothing discarded as if it was an affront to my beauty. Avitue places another kiss against my breastbone before returning to my throat, her tongue chasing my pulse. I tilt my head back for her, bracing for the pinch of her fangs, but she only lays a final kiss against my neck.

"This is for you, Cassiel. Not me," she murmurs into my skin.

She gathers me against her, my back to her chest so that we both face the mirror.

"You're so precious," she whispers to my ear, and I shiver. She smooths her hands down my arms, chasing the goosebumps away. "When you're ready, I want you to open your legs for me."

My heart races at the request, sending fresh heat below. Avitue kisses my shoulder and waits. Together, we breathe for a minute, two. I observe the mirror, my body framed in gold. Avitue's hair cascades down my chest from where she's pillowed her head in the crook of my shoulder. The candlelight holds steady, not a single frame flickering. Slowly, I part my legs, sheets whispering across my skin.

"Good. How does that feel?" she asks.

The air is cool against the exposed wet heat. I feel raw. Pink blossoms at my center. I've never seen myself like this before. Suddenly, I can't meet my reflection.

"Do you want to stop?" asks Avitue.

I'm breathing fast. With fear, with want. "No," I say. "What do you want me to do next?"

She doesn't answer immediately. "First, tell me what you want."

"I want you to touch me again," I answer.

Her eyes glint in the mirror, and I'm drawn back to our reflections. "Do you know how hungry you make me?" she asks.

The question is a knife, and I tread its dangerous edge. My heart pounds. "Tell me."

She hums against the pulse in my neck and trails her fingers between my breasts, down my belly, until she finds the ache between my thighs. I gasp at her touch, arching against her. "Your soul is the brightest star in the night," she says. "Your blood tastes like perfection brewed in Eden. I could spend all my lifetimes searching for you and never lose faith." She tells me I am beautiful and precious and good, channeling her belief into touch. I let my head fall back against her, sigh into her hair, breathe her name.

I know when hunger overtakes her, splitting her focus. While her attention between my thighs remains insistent but careful, her right hand keeps a desperate hold on my hip. It will bruise, but like last night, her claim excites me. I gasp when her claws break the skin, and that calls her back to herself. She blinks as if woken from a heady daydream and replaces both hands gently on my shoulders, one slick with arousal, the other with blood.

A broken whimper escapes me when she withdraws. "Please," I beg.

"I have one final request," she says, meeting my gaze in the mirror.

"Anything."

She's sharp again, her hunger shining through. "I want you to pleasure yourself for me," she says, as if she's the one desperate for release. "And I don't want you to look away."

I obey, stoking the fire she started. Our bodies are two hot stars in the darkness, and as she holds me, I wonder whether my pleasure passes through to her. She sighs against me as if it were her body I touched. Her fangs skim my neck, but all that follows is the ghost of her breath, a kiss, a cry muffled into my skin. My pulse turns heavy, the sound of her enough to drive me over the edge.

Without the insatiable pull of her aura, I can concentrate on Avitue this time, feel the way her energy moves, the way it grasps possessively—something one might expect from a demon—but there are flashes of something else. A softer devotion. My light leaps to mingle with it.

Her name fills my mouth, both warning and pleasured cry.

She senses the pressurized shift, releasing me just as two pairs of ethereal wings burst into existence. For a fleeting moment, they feel strong. The mirror strains to reflect them as if the light is too massive. My eyes burn. I can't see myself for my wings.

Without Avitue's aura to stave it off, shame follows close behind, the plummet sharp. I'm barely out of the heat of my climax when it lodges in my chest and turns me brittle. The flow of light ruptures with the force of it. A shiver runs through my wings, gossamer-fine cracks in the radiance, and they shatter like glass, their shards fading away on the air.

I cry, and it's messy, and Avitue holds me through it.

She apologizes, and I hate that she feels as if she's done something wrong. *Cherished* was the right word before. She was so tender, and I felt cherished.

I manage to say through my sobs, "I just wanted to feel good with you."

An ache rises in me to atone, and Avitue holds me tighter, sensing the destructive desire hook its claws in.

"I'm going to stay with you until you're safe," she says.

She runs a luxurious bath for me, puts on a record she finds of Chopin's nocturnes, and sits beside the bathtub, our hands clasped beneath the bubbles until the water begins to cool. My face is puffy from crying when I whisper, "Thank you."

"Anything, angel," Avitue says. "Anything."

⊷◇⊶

We leave for the park on foot. I feel so exposed outdoors, but Avitue insists that the walk will do me good—change of scenery, a necessary reset. "I know it's not what you *want*, but I sense it's what you need," she'd said.

Out of the shadow of the tall buildings, I do begin to feel better. A cold wind gusts off the Chicago River. Not many people are out. A couple joggers finish their runs shortly after we arrive. Even the gulls seem to have stayed home. It's quiet without them. The sunlight has already started to take on the muted quality of winter, the Earth tilting away from warmth. We face the water, and I try to breathe. The tome is heavy in my shoulder bag, a weight I can no longer afford to leave behind. The past is creeping back in like a rising tide, and soon enough, I'll have to walk into it.

"Do you want to talk, or do you need quiet?" asks Avitue.

"I don't know," I respond, so we're quiet.

Avitue and the wind and the sunlight and the water are my entire world for a few precious moments, and I let myself have this peace. The ache in my chest eases. I reach for Avitue's hand, and she lets herself be held. I feel her gaze on me, a question, but I look only at the river. I force myself to take a deep breath.

Avitue tentatively breaks the silence. "I've been thinking," she begins. "What do you feel when you come? Just before the wings appear?"

I shoot her a look, but when I search her face, there's no suggestive teasing there. She's sharp in her earnestness.

"I feel close to you, and I feel what you feel."

Avitue frowns as if I've presented her with a disappointing puzzle. "Is that all?"

I stare at her. Doesn't she know the name of her feelings? I've seen it in new couples who wander into my store, the budding and delicate thing between them as evident as light.

Maybe, for demons, it's different. Falling changed them. But what else could my wings be so drawn to?

"It's everything," I answer her.

———◆———

Now that we're out, I don't want to go back to the apartment. As always, when the weather turns cold, the studio begins to feel cramped. So we walk, wandering the sidewalks with no destination in mind. Eventually, Avitue pulls me into a diner, both to warm me up and convince me to eat something.

We're seated at a booth in the front where broad windows look out on an intersection. I barely glance at the menu, ordering only to appease Avitue, who doesn't ask for anything at all. Even so, the server lingers, staring at her as if she's both a bad omen and a miracle. Where everyone else is sniffling as they escape the chill wind, faces red and skin dry, Avitue glows as if she's just stepped in from a beach vacation.

"Nothing for me," Avitue repeats, enunciating each word carefully.

Finally, the server blinks and turns to go, staring mildly dazed at her notepad. As I watch her retreat into the kitchen, I reconsider having chosen the side of fruit. Out of season, it probably won't taste like much. The thought is faded as if it belongs to someone else. I look across the table at Avitue. She taps her blunted nails on the table, agitated as she watches the pedestrians pass.

"Will she be okay?" I ask, concerned for the server. The detached feeling lingers as I speak.

"She'll think she had a weird day at work and won't know why. She should bounce back when I'm gone." Avitue narrows her eyes at me, clearly weighing something. "Will you tell me what you're thinking?"

I stare down at my lap. "I wish I didn't cry so much."

"You can cry as much as you need to."

"It's embarrassing."

"It's a response to being hurt."

I turn my ring around my finger. "Your aura . . ." I start.

153

But the server is setting down a plate of scrambled eggs and toast in front of me. There's a little bowl of fruit on the side.

The normal world is quickly turning surreal. I wonder if anyone else has ever sat across from the demon they're unwisely falling for in a nondescript diner booth and attempted to eat brunch like any ordinary day.

Avitue is careful to avoid making eye contact with the server again. Chin in hand, she faces the window, her expression blank. It might seem rude if I didn't know she was trying to spare the woman another awkward moment. I try my best at a smile as I thank the server, and she hurries away, glancing at Avitue as if trying to determine whether she saw her properly before.

When Avitue turns back to me, it's with a concerned frown. "What were you saying?"

I take a breath and, in a rush, admit, "Being with you is the safest I've ever felt in my body, the most I've ever been able to trust myself to feel. When I'm held in your aura, it's like everything that's weighed me down is gone."

"Nothing about me has ever been safe for anyone," she says as if resistant to the idea.

I see the shift happen again, the same kind as on our date.

"I like being with you, Avitue," I say because I realize I've never said it before. "I like *you*."

I've asked her to stay with me. I've invited her on a date. I've trusted her with my body and soul, but I've never told her the simplest piece underlying it all.

Her troubled frown doesn't budge. This, out of everything, seems the most difficult piece to assimilate. "I like you too," she says.

Her solemn mood doesn't lift. I force myself to eat, not tasting the food but feeling less shaky by the end of it. My phone pings. Ana.

A reminder to actually RELAX on the one day you've given yourself off. Don't make me come over there and bake you cookies because you know I will. Her message is followed by heart, knife, smiley face, and cookie emojis.

"What's made you smile?" Avitue asks.

"My friend Ana," I say, putting down the phone. "She loves to send knife emojis when she's concerned."

Avitue's eyes practically sparkle. "Exactly my kind of person."

"She wants to threaten me into self-care."

On the walk back to the apartment, I tell Avitue the story of how I became friends with Ana. Answering her curiosity is an easy distraction, but when we climb the stairs to my door, something is off again. Instead of following me, Avitue waits at the landing's edge.

Key in hand, I return to her. "What's wrong?"

"I should really ask someone about what we discussed. Better sooner than later when a soul is involved."

My soul. My soul is involved.

Recalling our plan from last night, I ask, "Where are you going?"

Unimaginatively, I picture Avitue in a dark alley meeting up with some grimy demon disguised as a man. Maybe the same grimy man who put his hands all in my hair. I stop trying to picture it.

"I'd rather not, you know, open a gate to Hell in your bedroom," she says.

"Oh."

She grimaces, revealing fangs. Even her discomfort looks deadly.

"What does a gate involve?" I ask.

I've tracked down and sealed the rifts left behind with my family before, but we've never come across anyone entering or exiting an active portal.

"If you're not in spirit form? Mostly lots of blood."

"Yours or?"

"You have to decorporealize to enter, so." She shrugs. "Spirits only."

I piece my thoughts together aloud. "You use your own blood to open a gate, and you can't enter with a body, meaning you sort of—die?"

"It's grim."

"But you can come back? With your body?"

"This realm prefers souls to have a physical anchor. When you cross over from Hell, the gate"—she waves her hands vaguely—"can interpret a human body for your soul. If you return to Hell through the gate, it holds the body you sacrificed until you're ready to make another trip to Earth. It's a sentient force, both the bridge and the tollkeeper, and the more often you cross, the more it gets to know your soul, your preferences, how you present when you interact with the physical world. Returning to Earth after your body's been killed somewhere in this realm and not just reabsorbed by the portal is a pain. Crossing always leaves you weak, but it's worse when your body is new too."

I consider. "Which is why possessions happen?"

"Some of us are lazy, skip making our own body, and go the possession route. It's risky, existing too long outside our realm without a permanent anchor here. You start to forget things. You get lost, desperate. I'd guess those spirits are the ones most hunters go after."

I file that information away like a good student, as if I'll have to recite it later.

"You can't talk to the demon who was here before? Get him to relay the message?"

"It'll be better if I go straight to Beelzebub. I'll look committed, at least. It's been a couple years since I made the crossing."

"How do I know if you're okay? What if something goes wrong?"

Avitue thinks. "Don't try to summon me. You *could*, and it'd work wherever I was, but it'd make me look bad. We're not supposed to go about telling humans our names. If someone can summon us whenever, that means we're not fully in control, and we can't be counted on. But I can give you this."

She steps back, cupping her hands together as if concealing something inside. A zing of infernal energy cracks the air, leaving behind a taste at the back of my throat that I can describe only as *red*. She extends what looks like a silver coin to me, a crimson sigil on its face. I take it. As with the truffle, there's an initial spark, but this shot of energy stings my hand and forearm numb as if I've bumped my elbow hard. Avitue apologizes when I wince.

"What is it?" I ask, turning it over to find the same symbol on the other side.

"That's my name," she says, tapping a claw against the sigil. "It's a very general locator, of sorts. Right now, we're close together in the same realm, so it's bright.

Farther away, and it fades. If I'm not in this realm at all, it's fully silver. And if it tarnishes, maybe summon me then."

My pulse jumps. "What does it mean if it tarnishes?"

"I'm not in a great spot, that's for sure. Summons will override almost everything else, so you should probably be able to get me out of whatever mess I've gotten into. But that's unlikely. I've made this trip a thousand times. I know how to bargain."

I'm holding the coin too tightly. I relax my fingers and study its face again.

"Your sigil is so pretty," I say.

The line of it is one gentle, unbroken curve like an ampersand or treble clef.

"If by *pretty*, you mean *very intimidating and demonic*, then thank you," she says, her teasing grin returning for a few precious seconds.

We're still outside my door, still staring at each other, waiting for one of us to finally say goodbye.

Avitue speaks first. "Time is different in Hell. Give it a couple days here before you worry about me. Okay?"

"I can't promise not to worry."

"Then just . . . wait for me."

I don't have a choice, but I don't say that. There are no more words. I hug her. She's so warm. So impossibly warm.

When I let her go, she turns as if to walk down the steps, then disappears as if she were never here. I watch her sigil fade through hues of red until it's dusty pink. It settles there as I let myself into the apartment and stand with my back against the door, unable to remove my coat or shoes. Minutes turn into an hour. I keep watching the sigil, rooted where I stand. Doing anything else when I know she's sacrificing herself to a Hellgate would be impossible, and standing vigil feels like *doing something*. I steer my imagination away from gruesome thoughts more than once. Even after a soul has passed through a portal into Hell, the infernal rifts left behind are still dangerous. Days can pass before they naturally fade, and meanwhile, they remain hungry for any soul who draws near. I don't want to think of those grasping tendrils around Avitue.

In the span of a blink, her sigil drains to silver. I release a heavy breath.

⸺◦⸺

I'm changing into my pajamas that night when I notice the fresh purple of a bruise on my hip. It's out of sight, so no one would question it, but I know it's here. A reminder of her. I marvel at it in the ornate gold mirror, pressing my fingertips into the skin to ease back into the sharp clarity of the moment her claws pierced me. I gasp and draw my hand away. When I glance back to my reflection, I'm startled to recognize a glimmer of hunger.

I turn off the lights and settle under the covers, placing the silver disk beside the pillow. Hours later, it's still pale. I eye it as if hope alone will return its color. Too early to worry, I tell myself, rolling over to observe the long shadows the streetlamps cast across the ceiling.

Closing my eyes sharpens my focus on the deep hum of the silver. Not an audible hum, a spiritual one. Unmistakably Avitue, recognizable like a lover's favorite perfume. I settle into the resonance of it and try to remember what felt good about that first time her energy woke my body and set my skin on fire.

Touching myself isn't easy without her, a more cautious exploration than the first time. I think of the way she looks at me as if I'm the most perfect thing in the world, and for a few precious minutes, it's a shield against the storm of anxiety that threatens at the edge of my thoughts. I brush my hand down between my legs, through the curls there, gasp. Stop. My breath is fast in the lonely dark of the room.

I turn over, waiting to feel something awful, waiting for either the shame or detachment to descend on me again. It doesn't. I take one breath, another. The disk remains silver. Whole and safe, I fall asleep.

⸺◦⸺

I wake five minutes before my alarm. Taking stock of the room, I expect to find Avitue lazing in one of my chairs like on that first morning, but I'm alone, and the tracker is still pale.

Too early to worry, I tell myself again.

This is the most normal morning I've had since Avitue appeared and disrupted everything. I try to fall back into the safety of my old routine but find that I've lost the rhythm. I'm thinking too much, feeling too much. Nothing is rote and easy. Everything takes longer. By the time I take my first sip of tea and find I've forgotten to sweeten it, I'm already standing at the store's front computer, and it's too late.

My phone pings with a notification from Ana. *Can I bring you something?*

I reply, and just after I've welcomed my first customer, Ana appears with a sachet of herbs.

"What's this?" I ask, turning the hand-sewn fabric over in my hands.

Ana squares her shoulders and tosses back her hair as if preparing to deliver a very serious speech. "Ever since that fire, something's felt different about the city. I didn't want to scare you, but you're caught up in the energy shift too. I wanted to bring you this. For protection." She nods toward the herbs. "Carry it with you."

I smile, feeling a tug of emotion in my chest. There's a low energetic hum, like a watchful shield waiting to spring forth. It'd perhaps rescue me from bad luck like slipping on a patch of ice. Or ward off a would-be thief. It's strong enough, even, to redirect the kind of curses Ana's mentioned untangling from people before. It's tuned to earthbound magic, not energy from other planes—though I don't doubt Ana's abilities there. Still, its value to me is greater than whatever power it holds or what it can do. It's physical evidence that someone's paying attention to me, that someone cares. I thank her, warmed by the thought.

All day, I think about sacrifice. Mine, Avitue's. My family's. For so much of our history, nephilim have given up the ability to lead normal, human lives in order to protect others from a threat they don't even know exists. Now I've forsaken that vow to forge a far more personal one.

Leaving my sword behind was one thing. Giving it up entirely—and to forces I'd devoted my life to fighting—had been unthinkable. The falcata was fated for me. I know that path. I don't know the new one I'm drafting for myself. Would I give up my past, my future, my fate, for merely the *chance* to discover happiness? And with someone with whom it felt impossible? The question returns every few minutes as if I haven't already decided. As if I haven't always known.

My heart's answer is resoundingly clear, and that's the terrifying piece. I know the right answer even as I'm backing away from it, as my voice of reason screams at me to keep things as they are.

A second, more practical problem: I'd have to return home to retrieve the sword; and so, in trying to step into my new life, I'd return to the old. The understanding that I'll have to face everything I left there, whether Gabriel summons me or not, looms over the entire day. I briefly toy with the idea of asking Zuriel to bring my sword as she offered before. But then, Gabriel is keeping a close watch on us now. I'd rather get the sword myself and not risk involving someone else or having to answer questions.

Every box I move feels heavier. Each polite smile becomes more strained. I fight the urge to close early.

As I always have, I make it through the day. I survive.

NINE

A T THE WITCHING HOUR, Avitue returns to me smelling scorched and faintly of sulfur. I rouse as soon as I sense the warning crackle of energy in the wards before they settle dormant again.

A perturbed hiss comes from the dark, and I roll over to see Avitue stepping into the square of moonlight cast on the floor.

The sight of her snaps me fully awake. I sit up so fast the world briefly spins.

"Are you okay? What did they say?" I ask.

She's tired; I can tell—her confident strut gone, the flirtatious quirk of her lips now downturned and bitter. She throws herself across the foot of the bed, turning motionless and quiet, a mass of tangled curls obscuring her face. But while she seems languid and exhausted, her aura is sharp and feral. She holds it close as she did before, all her energy put toward leashing it.

"Avitue?" I say, heart beating fast.

She mutters something frustrated and infernal. The words don't carry power, but they do sound like a curse. "Fuck," she hisses, returning to English. Her hair stirs with a breath, and she's quiet again.

"They said *no*?" I guess, hands clenching so hard my nails bite into my palms.

"They said *yes*. They were just brutal about it."

I don't know whether to relax or not.

"Did they hurt you?" I ask.

"Only my ego," she says, her eyes shining through her mass of hair. She takes a moment before she speaks again. "Crossing twice in such a short amount of time isn't easy."

"Do you need—"

"No," she interrupts, knowing what I'd been about to offer. "Too dangerous right now."

"Dangerous how?"

"Bloodlust. A spirit-body disconnect that comes with crossing. The soul's fatigue tells the new physical body that it's starving. I know it's not as dire as it feels, but I don't need to do anything to aggravate that." She heaves herself up to sitting. "I wanted to tell you as soon as I could, but I probably won't stay here tonight."

I crawl to meet her at the foot of the bed. Her curls are uncharacteristically tangled and messy, their silky sheen lost. I can't properly see her face.

"I'm happy you're here. May I?" I ask, raising my hands.

She hesitates before nodding. Carefully, I comb out the worst of the tangles with my fingers, starting at the ends.

"You don't have to do that," she says, her golden eyes watching me. "It'll settle as I reacclimate to this realm."

"But I want to see you before you go," I say.

As I begin to push her hair out of her face, I find that her cheekbones have taken on that inhuman sharpness again. Her fangs are lengthened too, but I don't shy away. Her lips seem oddly drained of color until I realize she's only missing the wine-red lipstick I've never seen her without. At this point, I doubt it's makeup. Its staying power through kissing and drinking and sleeping is supernatural.

Warily, she watches me work.

"Cassiel—"

She says my name just as my fingers catch on something rigid and bony at her hairline. She hisses as if the light touch has pained her.

"Are these—?"

"My horns," she says, ducking her head as if shy of them. All the hair I've worked out of her face falls back into it.

"I'm sorry," I say. "Do you not like them?"

"I hate them. Just after crossing is the only time I can't hide them."

In contrast to much of Avitue's usual sleek, polished look, her horns seem as if they were carved haphazardly by someone who took neither care nor time. Two entirely different shapes, they look as if they were taken from separate pairs. One sweeps back in a spiraled arch. The other points skyward, its point cleaved off. Nicks and scratches scar their length. I sense a story here, one that she's sensitive about.

"I'm sorry," I say again.

She meets my eyes through her tangled hair. "You're the only human who's seen them."

I don't know what she wants me to say to that. The answer seems important.

She continues. "I tried to hack them off after the fall. They seemed so ugly. I'm embarrassed by my reaction now. The damage was permanent."

So rare for her to mention the fall. I speak carefully. An ageless and unhealed wound exists here.

"You were trying to cope," I say.

"I didn't know how to feel. But you understand."

Maybe I do, in my own human way. This is so big that all I can do is nod.

"You've seen monsters that don't even exist in most people's nightmares. More than anyone else, you understand the life I've lived," she says. Tentatively, she reaches for my hand as if it's an exercise in self-control. Then I remember the bloodlust. I study our entwined fingers, how her nails could now only be described as claws. "You're sacrificing a lot for this," she says, just as she said before.

"I'm certain," I say.

"Returning home for the sword—will it be hard for you?"

"I know where I left it in my room. It's my inheritance. By our laws, no one can keep me from it."

"But emotionally. There's a lot of pain there. They hurt you. And I won't be able to go with you into warded space."

"I can do it because I need to. For us."

Avitue's shadowed face is grim. "There's something else I should tell you."

The guilt behind the words makes me sit back. Her hand tightens around mine reflexively before she lets me go. Her posture wilts, body curving around a secret or a wound.

"Things were so fragile in the beginning. I didn't want you to doubt me."

"But there were so many things you did say."

"Yes. When I felt reckless or when I felt safe. And then the more I started to like you, the more I worried I'd say something wrong again and you'd send me away for good. The angels mean so much to you."

My mouth is dry. "Please just tell me," I say, unable to wait out the building dread.

"Lucifer restricts the finer details of his plan to those in the lower circles, but as I advanced in Hell's hierarchy, I was privy to the most basic details of his revenge. This small thing that's happened with your family is just a conveniently unexpected piece in a long timeline."

"You want war with the angels again," I say. This is known, obvious.

"But how do you lure angels out of Heaven? We can't reach them. They don't seem to care if we cause havoc on Earth."

This is still within the realm of what I know. "So you go after us. Their avatars," I say, my thoughts leaping ahead of her to where this possibly leads.

"But when Belial talked about breaking nephilim souls—it's not just torture. A soul is ruined that way, gone. It never unites with its angel, and we learned that interrupting the union prevents that nephilim's angel from ever making another connection in this realm. Because you have all become so spread out over time and love to cut each other off over philosophical differences, no one recognizes how badly we've broken the angelic lineages. And with lifetimes so short, who's keeping an appropriate record of whether a Barachiel or Cambriel returns to Earth? Information is so easy to destroy."

The tome, my sword, my soul. All small pieces in destroying the nephilim for good and inciting a war that, even to me, has seemed mythical up until now. I think of our ill-kept family archive, the water-damaged and mold-spotted manuscripts Aunt Raphael found on her travels. I remember Gabriel and fire and wonder how much of a hand nephilim have had in our own destruction, how shifting ideologies have led us to literally burn our past.

I think of Chamuel, the news of his death that much more tragic within the knowledge that there will not be another Chamuel born to some family unknown to us. We are an endangered species, and none of us knew.

Any choice I make to stay with Avitue becomes another knife in a body already bleeding out. I would be complicit in our destruction. The final Cassiel. How much would that hurt my namesake?

Avitue watches me think with a deepening frown. When I stay quiet, she adds, "We've tracked Gabriel's nephilim forever, but there's never been a convergence of archangels like this. Gabriel, Zuriel, Michael, Raphael, you—all in one family. Something is happening in Heaven. It's the sign Lucifer's been waiting for. Your angel might not have led the charge against us, but the ones close to them did. Claiming your soul might be enough to destabilize Zuriel, and in turn, Gabriel, Raphael. If we can unsettle them enough, maybe their angels will take notice."

A convergence on Earth reflecting events in Heaven. And without records, we couldn't have known just how significant our family was.

My entire life, I felt drafted into a war I didn't want to fight, and now I learn not only that it's inescapable but that we reside at its center.

I hold my ring to my chest and feel my wild heartbeat beneath. I could be angry with Avitue for doling out half truths in pieces, but I know they'd kill her for this without a moment's hesitation. I know where fear and rules have led me, but Avitue has lived with them forever.

"Before you knew who I was, did you want this?" I ask.

Her eyes flash, and I watch an old conflict play out on her face. "Here's the truth, then," she says, the weariness of an eternity packed into those short words.

"I wanted angel blood on my hands as much as the next demon, but the greats hold their plans close. If I succeeded in this, I could be among them. I could do something about all these feelings besides taking them out on insignificant humans. I could be someone other than a lowly succubus, a no one in Hell's ranks because I spend all my time in this realm trying to survive. So many of us succubi are fiercely independent out of necessity. We can only depend on our loyalty to ourselves." She softens with a breath. "And then I met you, and you weren't at all what we'd been told nephilim were. You'd been hurt like we were, in the name of goodness."

"I want to believe Cassiel never hurt anyone," I say.

Avitue's attention flicks to my ring and then back to my face. I let her take my hand, and she appraises the ring, a conflicted look on her face. "It was selfish of me to ever ask anything of you, especially when I knew what it would mean," she says.

"Would you have claimed my soul without telling me this?"

"I didn't tell you before because I didn't think there was a chance for us. Making my petition to Beelzebub was the first time I felt hope. That's when I knew for certain that I had to."

"For your conscience or for me?"

"I have no conscience."

"I don't believe that."

She drops her gaze. "We wanted to do this for a chance at a future, but what would the point of it be if you didn't know what it was built on? You deserve everything. More than the angels or I could give."

I find an ember of hope in her words. "You said I could live forever," I say.

"As a demon, Cassiel," Avitue reminds me gravely, as if I could forget.

"But I could exist in this realm. I could go back to my archival work. I could travel like Aunt Raphael did, find other nephilim, and record their histories. If I lived forever, I could help piece us back together."

Avitue looks sad for me. "They might've been your people, but they'd kill you on sight. They wouldn't understand what you were."

"But you convinced me you weren't here to hurt me."

"I was lucky with you. You were different from what I'd been told."

"There have to be others like me. There were in the past."

"Take time to think," says Avitue, and I can tell she's not yet convinced. "We don't have to move. Not yet."

"How will you rest?" I ask.

"I'll go back to the rift where the gate was. The lingering energy soothes the pain of crossing."

"But that's risky," I say, understanding now why we always found spirits gathered around the rifts.

She grins. "Don't worry about me, little angel. I've done this before."

I can't fall asleep after she leaves. I spend the rest of the night watching the minutes tick by, watching the tracker. Her sigil remains bright red, and I reassure myself that she's safe, that she's not far.

<hr>

Avitue lounges naked in bed as I get ready the next day, her sensitivity from last night replaced by her usual confidence. Time, as she said, has smoothed her body back down to its human proportions, packing away all her messy edges. In the daylight, it seems wrong to return to the vulnerability unveiled under the shelter of darkness, so we don't. I'm happy to have her back, jittery with the knowledge that, yes, maybe, we can explore a future together. Maybe I'm not a hunter, but I can help in a way that's real and substantial and suited to me. Even if it does mean facing down my past.

As I bustle through my morning routine, her eyes track my every movement like a deceptively calm cat—except provoking her into pouncing would most likely end in shredded clothes and missing the start of opening hours.

"You look like a Renaissance painting this morning," I comment, laying out my clothes on the chest as I pull them out of the closet. "One of the Venus ones."

She raises an eyebrow. "Oh yeah?" She laces her fingers behind her head. "Wanna paint me?"

I laugh. "Remind me after I go acquire any artistic skill."

My comment spoils her levity. She sits up, tucking her legs beneath her. "I've seen your bookbinding projects, the lettering. You don't arrive at calligraphy like that without any artistic skill."

"It's only a joke," I say. "Being a calligrapher doesn't make me a painter. And anyway, it's practical knowledge. My brothers were never going to be the ones to restore the old manuscripts in the family archives."

"Even so . . ." Avitue begins. "Putting yourself down seems a bit too easy."

I take my time removing my coat from its hanger, my back to Avitue.

"Don't apologize," she says, and I know she's read me. Then, tenderly but firmly, she adds, "Come here."

Her voice shoots a thrill through my chest and straight between my legs. My breath caught in my throat, I turn to face her, and suddenly all concerns of tardiness flee my thoughts.

I don't have to puzzle out the expression in her eyes. She wants to devour me. Where days ago, it startled me, now it draws me to her like gravity. I still don't understand how anyone could want me as soul deep as she does, but as long as I'm holding her gaze, I'm blessedly free of questions. When I reach her, she folds my hands into hers and studies me.

"Kneel," she says, her voice still soft.

I follow her command, and she cups my face. "You're beautiful perfection. I'd tell you every moment of every day if I could."

I swallow. My eyes water as if I'm staring into the sun. "Every day," I repeat, stuck on the possibility in it.

Avitue sighs. "I shouldn't have—"

"Don't apologize," I say, echoing her, my throat tight. I still want to hope.

She releases me, and I miss the warmth of her hands and her gaze.

"What's that there?" she asks, pointing to an emerald A-line dress hanging to the far side of the closet, nearly out of sight. It's one of the few dresses I own, something I bought online when I was more devoted to making a radical break from my old life and my old self. I'd tried it on, liked it so much it terrified me, and never put it on again. My usual uniform was safe, boring, comforting. If I wore something too nice, people would notice me, and I didn't want to be noticed.

Avitue retrieves it from the closet and runs an admiring hand down the fabric. Thoughtful, she holds it up to me.

"It looks gorgeous against your skin," she says.

I pair it with wool stockings and throw on my long coat, and we head down to open the store. She's a warm shadow at my back as I unlock the doors, and for a dangerous moment, I begin to imagine what my life could be like with her always at my side. I've never imagined myself with either a partner in business or in life, but now I want it, and I can't get comfortable in that thought, not when there's still work to do.

I quash the feeling before it can grow, hoping that it wasn't enough of a desire or the right kind of desire for her to perceive.

I have enough time to ward the store before opening hours and find it easiest to do so in the dark. It puts me back in the headspace of ritual, of standing in a circle with my mother and siblings, of looking across the room to see a familiar face turned eerie by candlelight. I set a stick of incense to burn at the register and walk the perimeter of the store and down the rows of shelves, reciting memorized fragments of the angelic tongue. Every few feet, I bend to chalk warding sigils on the undersides of the lower shelves where they can do their work while remaining hidden and unsmudged.

As I'm completing my rounds, I find Avitue in one of the reading nook's chairs, gripping the arms as if holding onto it for dear life.

"Oh, my dear," I say, rushing over to her. "You could've waited outside until I was done. I didn't think."

She gives me a strained smile. "Maybe I'm a slut for pain."

If she can tease, she must be fine. I roll my eyes fondly. "In that case, don't enjoy yourself too much," I say, returning to the front counter to sweep away the incense ashes and start the computer.

The day begins slowly. It's half past eleven when the first customer appears. I glance up from placing an order to greet them, and my *hello* dies on my tongue as soon as our eyes meet. It's not quite like when Ana looks at me, but there's undoubtedly something there. Weak, but still present. I register their appearance last—cropped hair mostly hidden by a beanie, a denim coat with a rainbow of patches. A they/them pin affixed to the chest pocket.

"Hello," I finally say, offering a smile. "Let me know if you need anything."

"Yeah, um." They nod, then smile awkwardly, disappearing into the shelves.

I'm wondering what they're here for when an older man comes in to pick up a special order, and my musings are forgotten. He's followed by a tired mother with two exuberant children.

"I'm so sorry," she says to me as she tries to wrangle them.

"No worries," I say, sending a discreet sparkle of grace her way.

The two children find Avitue in the armchair I've already come to think of as hers. She's perusing a book on local birds when the children start bouncing around her, the little girl apparently enamored with Avitue's nails.

"Are you a goth?" I overhear her question, bright and curious.

The mother rushes over to apologize and herd the children away, leaving Avitue staring after them with a look of puzzled disbelief. When the three return to the counter with a stack of novels, the mother's standing a little straighter and looking a little less weary.

Avitue appears beside me when they leave. "The small humans," she whispers.

"The children?" I laugh.

"They liked me?"

"I've told you you're very likable."

"They shouldn't. Aren't children more perceptive? That's what people say."

"Some are. This only proves my point."

My first customer approaches the counter again, their head down as they study the cover of the small book in their hands. I recognize it immediately and feel a tug in my chest. Avitue sees the customer before they see her and backs away into the shelves again as if she were never here.

"How much is this one? It doesn't have a sticker," they say, holding up the book for me to see.

I try for my best customer service smile. "It's free."

"Oh, wow." They flip through the pages. "Thanks!" they say, smiling up at me as if I've given them a gift. I hope it'll turn out to be as good as that.

Once they're out the door, Avitue reappears.

"So you noticed it too?" I ask, watching them until they're past the window and out of sight.

"You don't live on this earth as long as I have and not get a sense for which humans might be able to see what you really are."

I turn my ring around my little finger. "Of course," I say, quiet.

"Why don't you give them a better cover? Why not put them front and center at the register? You'd move more of them. But it seems like you didn't want them to take it."

I lean heavily on the counter. "I don't make them flashy for a reason. I don't want people to notice them. They should feel called to the knowledge, to know it's what they need. But . . . I can't know if it actually makes them safer or endangers them."

"How would it endanger them?"

"Some people don't just want to help themselves. They want to help others. They seek out a community, more knowledge. They become hunters." I tell her about the fate of many human hunters. I tell her about my father.

"I see," she says quietly.

Work picks up toward closing. I retrieve an online order from the back to ring up, take a delivery of several heavy boxes, and try to locate a book for a customer who can't remember the title or author but informs me that the cover was blue.

When the shop is quiet again, Avitue returns to my side, picking up one of my new boxes as if it has contained only air this whole time.

"Need me to move these? Open anything?" she offers, tapping a claw against the strip of tape.

"Actually, if you could help me get them to the back room, that'd be really helpful."

"No problem, angel," she says, hefting all three boxes into an effortlessly balanced stack. She moves as if unburdened, and as I watch her shoulder open the door to the back, I think my heart melts. The longing from this morning returns in full force, the wish that this could be every day, that the universe would allow us this.

Satisfied with my total for the day, I'm closing everything out and shutting down the computer when a flash of infernal energy surges through the shop.

"Avitue!" I call, panic and years of training waking my light to the surface like that first night. I run for the back, fearing that something's broken through the wards, that they've come for me or Avitue when—

"I've got a surprise for you, angel!" Avitue announces when I arrive in the doorway.

She's safe and beaming, and nothing in the overcrowded room seems out of place. I collapse against the doorframe, the spike of panic leaving me shaky.

"Shit. Did I scare you? You're all glowy. I'm sorry," she says.

I heave a sigh. "I'm okay. Give me a moment."

"Note to self: no demon magic without a warning."

"What did you do?" I ask.

She smiles, gesturing around the corner. I step into the room, and my mouth drops open.

"I extended your space!" she announces proudly.

The far wall is very obviously not where it was before. Where I once had a small closet of a room, I now have something that looks like a narrow hall, the brick wall I share with the neighboring property pushed into their space.

My panic returns. "Avitue!"

"You were out of shelf space—and floor space, actually—and there was nowhere to put the boxes, so I—"

"But that's the art studio's space," I protest, wondering what this must look like on their side, already trying to figure out how I could even explain this to them or our landlord.

"They still have their space. This is a pocket dimension."

"A *pocket dimension*," I repeat, every moment of this becoming more stress inducing.

"What? Pocket dimensions are a sensible storage solution."

"I can't have a pocket dimension in my store!"

"Why not?"

I stumble over my response. I don't *dislike* the extra space. "What if someone sees it and asks questions?"

"Who comes back here besides you?"

"But it smells demonic. What if someone senses it?"

"Regular people can't— Wait, what does demonic energy smell like to you?"

"Well, it's like—"

Again, I realize Avitue is different. Where evidence of demonic presence is usually unsettling, her energy isn't.

"It's not really a smell. More like . . ." I struggle to find a proper description. "It's a feeling that's present enough to seem like a smell."

"Well, when you're done feeling your angel feelings, you should come check it out," she says, stepping into the new space as if to demonstrate its structural soundness.

I creep forward, feeling for the threshold where the physical meets the supernatural. I shiver when I cross it, a full-body realization. Avitue holds her hand out as if inviting to guide me into unknown territory. I've let her before. It seems silly to stop now. I take her hand and let her pull me against her, peering back to see what's become of the old space.

Desaturated but just as I left it, the old room looks like a photograph someone's turned down the lights on.

"Wow," I breathe. "It's like we're in our own little world."

"Do you like it?" she asks.

"It's weird. I'll think about it," I say.

"I should've asked."

I shake my head, trying to comprehend. "How are you this powerful? How are you not some greater demon every hunter knows about?"

She shrugs. "Who's considered a greater demon is as much about influence before the fall as it is about strength, and Hell's hierarchies are based in cronyism and arcane bureaucracy I couldn't bother to give a shit about. I didn't fall because I wanted power, so I'm not in with the popular girls."

"The popular girls?" I echo.

"You know. Luci and Bel," she says, her lips quirked as if she's made some very clever joke.

Seconds tick by before I put it together. "Did you just call every hunter's worst nightmare Luci and Bel?"

"Only if you never tell them I said that."

I can't help it. I do laugh. There's never any levity among hunters. We can't afford laughter and then we forget how to. Even among newbies, the bloodiness of the hunt weighs a spirit down fast. There's something freeing in the way Avitue diminishes the greater demons and the shadows they cast over our lives, and I realize that this is how her spirit survived.

As she watches me laugh, her attention shifts from amusement into sharp-edged thirst. It's moments like this that I see her—truly see her, past the ease of her facade and into the ageless truth of her spirit. There's a well there, eternally deep, that I could fall into forever if I looked too long. She sees me seeing her and lets the facade fall. Or, more accurately, recklessly tosses it aside. There's no use pretending, not here. Being known excites her.

Avitue pushes me up against the wall and draws me into a deep kiss. Her hand closes around my throat like a collar, possessive and tender all at once, and I sigh into the warmth of her. Bright golden eyes pin me when she moves back.

"Are you hungry?" I ask breathlessly.

"Always," she says, the end of the word a hiss.

The sound kicks my heart into a new rhythm. It's not fear; it's want. Another revelation, this one stronger than the first, crashes into me. I don't want her *despite* her monstrousness but *because of* it. Avitue must hear my wild heart, must see something on my face, because she grins with those beautifully sharp teeth.

She releases me to trail the points of her nails down my arms as she kneels before me. It's heady seeing someone as strong as Avitue on her knees, and when she looks up at me, her gaze is still piercing, impossible to diminish. I'm pinned again by that look, my heart hammering with some primal recognition of danger even as my body thrums with need. One hand braces against my hip, her touch a brand through the fabric. She keeps her attention trained on my face, clearly waiting for my permission. I nod, and she relaxes, her aura twining around us like tendrils of smoke. The edges of the world turn pale and blurred, everything narrowing down to her.

She slips a hand beneath the skirt of my dress, her nails drawing sharp lines up my thigh. I gasp, reach for her, and in an instant, her hands are locked around my wrists, pressing my palms back against the brick—a clear command. *Stay.* I flex my fingers, itching to bury them instead in her silky hair. The brick is too rough. Comfortless. I want *her*. She watches me squirm and struggle to stay put, to follow through on such a simple order. My body has become a list of needs.

"You are evil," I breathe.

She grins at that. "Poor thing. You've just now realized?"

I let my head fall back against the wall, finally breaking eye contact with her. It doesn't bring any relief. Her hands are back on my thighs, teasing slow circles. I shiver.

"Avitue," I beg.

She ignores me, and I peer down to find her lapping up a trickle of blood from the trail of scratches on my thigh. Her grip on me tightens. She moans, throwing her hair back, savoring the taste. I watch her lick her bloodstained lips, mesmerized. Then she's turning back to me, newly urgent, as if the blood has awakened something. I'm no longer the only desperate one.

She pushes my skirt up, fisting one hand in the emerald fabric. It seems suddenly too fragile, too delicate. Her dark nails are a stark contrast against the white of my underwear, and in her eagerness to pull them away, she shreds the cotton as if it were only tissue paper. And then her mouth is on me, and my ability to concentrate on anything so trivial is lost. Avitue is relentless, her forked tongue prodding into me, tasting me. I sigh her name, my hands balling to fists against the wall. I ache to touch her. I stay put. But when she finally turns her full attention to my clit, I buck against her, fighting to stay standing. It's not long before my legs begin to tremble, before my head feels light and fuzzy. Her name is broken in my mouth, a blasphemous prayer. She answers it, and my body is a burst of pleasure and light.

When coherent thought returns, I've steadied myself with my wings. Avitue is on her feet again, cupping my face in her hands.

"Good girl," she purrs, and my chest surges with warmth.

In the haze of my postorgasm thoughts, I'm relieved that I could satisfy her again. The aura is different. Sated now, it pulls and clings to me less, settling lightly instead. When it withdraws, the room opens up once more, and I let myself fall into the strength of Avitue's embrace. She strokes my back, murmuring sweet words into my hair.

"Thank you," she says. "You look so delicious in this dress."

"I think we might've made a mess of it," I say, half-sighing, half-laughing.

"That's what I mean," says Avitue, grinning.

I chipped a nail at some point while clenching my hands against the brick. The skirt of the dress is shredded on one side and dappled with blood. My wings toppled a precarious stack of books at some point. I'm righting them when a familiar voice sounds from the front of the shop. Ana.

Panicked, I turn to Avitue. "I can't go out there like this!" I stage-whisper.

Cool as always, Avitue hands me my coat from where it hangs on a hook. I shrug into it, though a few inches of ripped hemline remain visible. I can only hope it's not noticeable enough. Avitue, though, is smirking. She maintains eye contact as she retrieves my ripped panties from the floor and tucks them into her inner jacket pocket.

Face burning, I tug open the door and hurry to meet Ana. She's hovering by the register, craning her neck around the shelves until she spots me bustling toward her.

"I noticed your lights were on late and—"

She stops short when she sees Avitue emerge with me, eyes darting questioningly between us. I know when Ana's put together the information from all my vague anxious rambling because her expression shifts from concern to understanding.

"Ana, this is—" I cut myself off, remembering at the last second that *Avitue* is her true name. Like giving out someone's social security number to a stranger, it seems worse than rude. "This is a friend. Helping me with the store."

Which only serves to remind me that we still haven't named our relationship or what we're doing together.

"If I'm working here, does that make me an employee? I've never been an employee before," Avitue says, eyes bright as if she's suddenly discovered her calling.

I give her a look, but Ana is graceful enough not to comment. Instead, she gives her name and extends her hand to Avitue, saying, "I run the coffee shop across the street. Cass and I have known each other a couple years now."

Avitue doesn't give her name or even bother to make one up, but she shakes Ana's hand enthusiastically, the sharp points of her claws still intact. I don't know what it means that Avitue's not *trying at all* here, not trying to play human in the least. Has she misinterpreted my comfort with Ana? Does she think Ana knows the truth about me? Avitue seems to be having too much fun until something in Ana's face changes at the contact. Suddenly they're both staring each other down as if this meeting has turned into a challenge, their hands clasped too tightly, one waiting for the other to give in.

"How did you and Cass meet again?" Ana asks, withdrawing her hand from Avitue's abruptly.

"I was looking for a book," Avitue answers easily.

It's not a lie, I note.

"You have *really interesting* energy," Ana says, looking pointedly from Avitue to me.

Avitue smiles, fangs and all.

"Both of you do," Ana adds.

"I'm not interesting," I hurry to say.

"I'm a witch," she says sharply. "Not a fool. Why are you so insistent on being a mysterious loner? Is there something I've done to make you not trust me? We have codes of secrecy to protect ourselves too, but I've always been open with you about what I am."

"I wanted to start over and be normal," I say, struggling to come up with the right words. "You wanted to be a witch. I didn't choose to be—this."

Who are you, Cass? she'd asked.

Avitue hugs me to her, once more a warm, supportive presence.

Ana's frustration cools. "I'm sorry," she says, tugging at the sleeve of her coat. "I came over to check on you, not interrogate you. I want to help when you reach out, but that's hard sometimes."

"I don't mean to be distant," I say. "I don't know how to talk about it all."

Ana nods once. "Okay," she says, drawing a breath. "I get it." She tries to smile, eyes darting to Avitue and then away. "Whenever you're able to, though, I hope you know I'd listen."

The door chimes her exit, and I turn to bury my face in Avitue's hair.

⸺◆⸺

I feel heavy. I fall into the nearest chair as soon as we're back in the apartment. It's already dark. The sun is setting too early.

We neglect to turn on the lights again, and Avitue could almost disappear into the shadows of the room. She paces the small apartment like a too-big cat in a tiny cage. I follow her by the sound of her heels on the wood, the way the shadows darken with her passage.

"Ordinarily, that'd have been delicious," she says.

"What?" I say, distracted by my ruminations about Ana.

"She's jealous of me."

I sit up. "I didn't think she ever felt that way about me. If I'd known—"

"Friends get jealous too."

I sink back miserably. Of course. Ana's supported me for years. Then out of nowhere, Avitue shows up, and from a brief interaction, it's clear that I've trusted her more than I've ever trusted Ana.

"You've told me everything," Avitue says. "How is she different? Even if she is a witch, there's less risk in telling her than telling me."

"You understand what I am more than anyone. You're part of this history. You know what it's like to . . ."

"Fall?"

I wish I could see her face clearly. Instead, she's cloaked herself in shadow, just as she was when we met.

"It doesn't compare. Forgive me for being careless," I say.

"You have your wings now. It'll be different for you."

I turn over her words. "Cassiel's been quiet."

"We all prepare to fight differently."

"Do you really think they will? With us? Angels rarely leave Heaven."

"I would leave Heaven for you."

I search for the glint of her eyes and can't find even that. Why would she declare something like that and turn away from me?

"I can't see your face," I say.

The room is quiet. I breathe in the stillness. And then I understand. In the beginning, this is how she entered vulnerability.

"I would fall again if it meant I landed here," she adds.

I don't have the time she's had. There's nothing equal I could give.

"Cassiel. Your soul is priceless," she reminds me.

I've preferred the shortened *Cass* since I've been out in the world, but in Avitue's mouth, *Cassiel* is remade. She says it with the accented emphasis of a language not from Earth, a gentle hiss followed by the swift ripple of the vowels. It sounds simultaneously closer to its divine origins and different. Like Zuriel's shortening of the name years ago, Avitue makes the sound my own.

"Would you say my name again?" I whisper.

She doesn't ask why. "Cassiel," she repeats, turning my name reverent. "Cassiel." I let the sound wash over me like angel song. Avitue steps into the yellow light cast by the streetlamp outside, returning us from the hold of her shadow world.

"People used to try and worship nephilim as minor gods when they found out what we were, so we hid ourselves for our benefit and theirs," I say, recalling why, before Avitue, I kept my secrets. "Obviously, that's not what I'm worried about with Ana, but I don't want her to see me differently."

"She already sees you differently than other people. It seems she has for a long time."

I remember the first time I walked into Witch's Brew. "I know," I admit. "But when you come to a new place determined to start over, the last thing you want is to immediately dredge up the past you're trying to leave behind."

"But you didn't try to avoid her. You kept her in your life even though you knew she would always know. There's a reason for that."

"She was the first person who tried to help me," I say. "I had only a few dollars left after being alone in the city for a month. She gave me a free coffee the moment I walked in her shop and abandoned everything to talk to me. She let me sleep on her couch for weeks while I got my life together. I was just a scared stranger, and she was so kind. If it weren't for her, I would've gone back to Gabriel even more embarrassed and ashamed. Ana saved me. She's been so open and gracious, and all I've done is hide from her."

I find Avitue's gaze, a mirrored gold in the dark.

"If things don't work out for us, I'm glad you have her," she says.

"Please don't say that."

"Okay," Avitue says, her tone apologetic. A brief silence settles.

"Why didn't you disguise yourself around her?" I ask next.

"Some humans are more perceptive than others. It's not worth bothering with those types. They see through it all anyway. And it's fun to watch them try and puzzle it out."

"Did she guess correctly?"

Avitue hums thoughtfully. "Maybe I'm a witch who committed a gruesome blood sacrifice to gain immortality."

"Can people do that?" I ask, shocked.

"I've never seen it work. But it hasn't stopped humans from trying. People are always getting lured in by tricky demonic contracts that were only ever going to end in getting their souls eaten. But every new wannabe thinks they're going to be the one to outsmart a demon."

"Have people tried that with you?"

Avitue advances, bending to rest her hands on the arms of my chair. I sink into the cushions, looking up to meet her gaze. An unfathomably long lifetime's worth of memories clouds her face. She kisses my forehead.

"Don't give yourself nightmares, angel."

I only now realize just what I asked for. A series of bloody accounts. A list of every person who lost their soul to her. Too much to demand so lightly.

I wonder what it will feel like to willingly give my soul over to her.

She extends a hand to me as she withdraws. "Let's find your dinner."

"I don't have an appetite," I say.

"But you should eat."

"Would you hold me?" I ask.

But tonight, not even curling up in Avitue's arms can stop the weight of doom descending on me. My phone pings on the bedside table. Rare to get a text at all. I shift to peek at it, expecting Ana. Zuriel. *Gabriel's going to make a move soon. I don't know what the plan is yet. Be ready.* I turn my phone off. I want to shut out the world. I want time to stop.

Avitue nuzzles the pulse at my throat.

"Do you want to feed again?" I ask.

"Don't spoil me," she jokingly chides. But when she moves back to look me full in the face, her brow creases. "I'm not feeding from you if you're this conflicted. It's too dangerous. And not what you really want."

"I'm not conflicted," I say. "And what I want is you."

"You want complete certainty that if I can stay, everything will be all right. You want security. That's different."

I turn into the heat of her. "I'm scared," I say.

"I know," she says, petting my hair. "You don't have to do this."

"I do. I want to."

TEN

SOMETIME IN THE EARLY morning, I must've finally drifted to sleep. I wake up, tangled possessively in Avitue's limbs. My eyes are still sleep heavy, but I make myself check the time. My phone's lock screen reads—

"Oh my god, work!" I exclaim, dislodging myself from Avitue and throwing off the covers.

Avitue rouses lazily, blinking at me like a disgruntled cat who's lost the warmth of a good lap.

"I'm sorry! I should've opened half an hour ago!" I explain as I hurry to the bathroom.

We'd talked long into the night, and I'd forgotten to set my alarm. Trying to date a demon hasn't done any favors for my reliability. I settle for a lukewarm shower—the hot water takes notoriously long—before dashing out in a towel to grab clothes from the closet.

Avitue stops scrolling on her phone when I emerge, vanishing it from her hand. "I'm so sad that you're bothering with a towel." She pouts dramatically. "I do enjoy looking at you."

"It's cold," I say, so frantic to get out the door that I begin dressing in the wrong order.

Clothes successfully on, I forgo tea and forget my coat—the cardigan will do; I only have to get down the steps—when simultaneously my phone pings and an ethereal bolt of energy electrifies the air.

Ears ringing, I freeze. This is the doom I felt last night.

"Cassiel," Avitue says behind me. "What the hell was that?"

"My mother wants to see me," I say, caught between numbness and panic.

Now beside me, Avitue says, "So she sends a lightning bolt like she's God?"

"This is serious. Binding. It's not an invitation."

Another question is forming on Avitue's lips when I jerk open the door. As I expected, it's there on the step, an emblem of wings glinting gold in the morning light.

I swipe it up and pocket it as if Avitue hasn't already seen it. A quick glance reveals all else is the same. No visitors, only the small lot behind the bookstore and the back of another shop across from that.

"I'd like to braid your hair," I say, and I can tell by the look on Avitue's face that it's not at all what she expected. "It's so beautiful, and I'd just like to touch it before—before . . ."

"Tell me what's going on," Avitue says gently.

"I need to sit," I say, bracing against the railing to lower myself to the steps. Avitue settles on the step below mine. "Can I?" I ask.

She offers her best attempt at a flirtatious hair flip, but she's too tense for it to look genuine. For a few quiet moments, I comb my fingers through Avitue's luxurious curls and memorize how they shine in the sun. Eventually, I separate a section on her left and begin to braid with shaking hands.

Avitue is about to turn to look at me before she stops herself at the last second so as not to disrupt my work. "No one's ever braided my hair before," she says.

"*Avitue*," an unfamiliar voice, raspy as if from too much smoke, speaks from somewhere within her jacket. She winces and gingerly withdraws her phone. Suddenly, it's a haunted object of the kind my family would uncover in houses seized by demonic influence. Electronics were always the strangest, the infernal energy and electrical signals mixing and disturbing each other in unsettling ways. Garbled voices over static. Flickering lights. Images and sound at the uncanny edges of mortal understanding. Avitue's phone is the clearest example I've ever witnessed.

She gives me a meaningful look and puts a finger to her lips. "Yeah," she answers without putting it to her ear, suddenly all confidence.

"Belial's spooked them," the voice continues. "We think they're going to call her back soon. Her soul is already yours if you can pull this off. Make sure she can't regroup with them, whatever it takes. We need to move now, and I don't want to be surprised by another nephilim."

"But—do we know where they keep the tome?"

"We have a vague location. It looks like they have a network of underground chambers. What I need to know is if your part is covered."

When Avitue hesitates a beat too long, the voice returns with an edge. "Don't tell me you haven't managed to break her yet. You said you had control of her. That's what we were counting on."

Avitue's eyes dart to me and away. She stands, gripping the stair rail until I can see the strain in her hand. "Look, I'd have had her by the time I promised, it's just—"

"We expected some amount of difficulty given her nature, but a succubus of your prowess should have been able to claim her by now. She's out of practice."

"I know."

"And alone. Where is she now?"

Avitue grits her teeth. "I have it handled."

"*Where* is she, Avitue?"

She turns her back to me. I could weather this easier if I could at least see her face. It's only now, as I'm feeling desperate for air, that I realize I've been holding my breath, that I'm gripping the grimy iron stair with all my strength.

"She received their summons before I could get to her. She slipped me."

The pause that follows feels dangerous. "So she's on her way back to the estate."

"Yes," Avitue says as if it hurts her.

"When."

"Just—just now."

"I hope, for your sake, that you have sights on her."

Avitue looks up into the innocently blue sky and shoves one hand into her pocket. "I do, yeah."

"Your deal with Beelzebub," the voice begins, and I feel my pulse in my skull. "If you still want her soul for yourself, you're going to have to make up for this."

A beat of silence passes. "Tell me what to do," Avitue says, voice flat.

"Get control of her before she reunites with her family." The voice pauses. "It'd only be fitting if Belial helped you, since he's responsible for this."

"I don't need Belial," Avitue snaps.

The other demon seems to take a moment to process this. "Get control of her when she goes back to them. If you want her soul, make her bring us the rest of the relics in addition to the sword."

"But that's—"

"*You* wanted the extra work. If it's no longer worth it to you, the original assignment still stands."

"I'll get the relics," Avitue says, a frustrated growl bleeding into her voice.

"Don't fail us."

A static screech follows, and the phone is quiet. I rise, shaking, to my feet. Avitue is within reach. I could touch her. I don't. I wait for her.

But that's impossible, I'm sure she'd been about to say—and I agree. There's no way I could possibly get my hands on my family's relics, let alone live with myself for handing them over. Giving up my sword is one thing. Stealing the inheritances of my family members would be an unthinkable betrayal. Just as things had begun to feel possible, the reality of our situation closes back in.

This was never going to work.

There's no asking her to run away with me, not when both Heaven and Hell have expectations of us. We'd always be found.

"I'll come up with something," Avitue says, trying to convince me as much as herself. "But for now, we have to make this look real while I buy time to think."

"Make *what* look real?" I ask.

"You have to go back to your family," Avitue says carefully. "I have to stop you. As long as you don't do anything fatal . . ."

"I can't."

Her face is carefully blank. "If you want to go, I'll let you go. I'll tell Beelzebub I couldn't."

"I'm not asking you to *sacrifice yourself* for me," I amend when I realize how deeply she's misunderstood. "I mean that I don't know how I could possibly make attacking you look real."

"You still have the dagger, don't you?"

Any other time, I would've blushed at the memory associated with it. "I put it away with the tome."

"When I attack you, use the dagger. They'll see that you're stronger than me, and I'll be reprimanded, but my soul will survive. Hopefully, by the time I can make the crossing again, I'll have figured out alternatives."

"Won't it hurt you?" I ask, knowing that, based on the look of the demons who've met with a blessed blade, it hurts terribly. It's as bloody and visceral as killing a body—because that's what it is.

"It'll sting," says Avitue, wielding dismissiveness as her own weapon. She must know too; she has to know how much this hurts a soul.

"And what if I can't?" I ask.

Discussing this on such a beautiful day feels surreal. Only moments ago, we were in bed together, each other's bodies the only thing in the world. Yesterday, we were laughing together in the store. Days before, we went on a date. It already feels like forever ago when Avitue miraculously healed me and made me feel worthy of care. The golden wings feel heavy and cold in my pocket.

"If you can't kill me, then we need to have someone come to your aid. Make it look like I could be reasonably overwhelmed if I don't back down." She thinks. "Let's do both. I'll meet you in the surrounding woods. You see me, you run. I'll let you get close enough to the house that someone can hear you and come running. Meanwhile, you need to at least make a show of attempting to kill me when I catch up to you. We do our thing until there are others within sight, then I'll back off."

"I haven't fought in years," I say. "And I've sparred against my family, but I've never attempted to kill anyone I care about. I don't even think I could pretend."

"You're not killing me. Don't think of it that way. We're just making it look like I gave a shit about my job."

I shiver. I can feel in my hands the memory of flesh and bone giving way under the force of my sword.

"I know I can't do it."

"The alternative is worse for you, Cassiel."

I force myself not to look away. "The alternative?"

"If you can't make your part look convincing, I can." She says it so gently, like an offering, as if she's sparing me something. It still chills me.

I swallow. "I don't want to see you that way, even if I know it's not real."

Avitue breathes a heavy sigh, takes a backward step down the stairs, and looks out over the lot. "Fuck. Okay, new plan," she says, but doesn't follow with anything.

My phone chimes again, and my heart stutters into a frantic rhythm. Avitue seems too consumed by her thoughts to notice. When I tap into my phone, I see the name of the sender and go still. *Gabriel.* My hands shake so badly that it takes an entire minute to type a response. *Yes. Received summons.*

"No time for another plan," I say, moving to pocket my phone. It slips from my hand and through a gap in the stairs. I watch, unmoved, as it plummets to the concrete below. Halfway down, it vanishes, and then Avitue's extending it to me. I take it in both hands and squeeze its hard edges into my palms. "I need to find a way there now."

"I'd offer to drive you, but, well."

"Of course. I'll try asking Ana," I say. "And if you can come back to me after all this, meet me at the gazebo on the abandoned property next door."

Avitue nods, the muscle in her jaw tight. Then she's suddenly stepping back up to clutch me into a desperate kiss. "After we meet at the estate, don't remember me that way. Remember me like this. Please," she says against my lips.

All my words are gone. I want to cling to Avitue and breathe in the smoky warmth of her and not move forward into this future that's been thrust upon us.

"Don't forget the tome," she says. "Keep it close." Then she's away down the stairs, her saunter turned stiff.

I dial Ana as I grab my shoulder bag and begin distractedly shoving in whatever clothes my hands land on. Briefly, I consider packing Avitue's coin and decide against it. My family would notice it straightaway, and I don't want to unwittingly give them something that would endanger her. The bag stuffed full, I press the tome atop it all and wrestle the clasps shut.

Ana picks up in three rings.

"Lucky you caught me on my day off," she says, and the unworried ease of her tone confuses me for a moment. "We need to get you some help so you can take a full weekend every once in a while."

"Ana," I say, words a rush. "I need a huge favor. And I'll be as honest as I can this time."

"What's wrong?" she asks, serious in an instant.

"Family emergency. And I don't have a car—"

"I'll be right over. You're home, right?"

Ana is at my doorstep in minutes, her blue compact waiting in the tiny lot below. I thank her profusely, and when we're settled in the car, Ana asks where we're going.

I worry the shoulder strap of my bag. "My family home, actually."

Ana frowns, and I realize the small amount of information I've given her about my past will work against me now.

"I'll take you where you need, but will you be safe there?" she asks. "You said you wouldn't go back."

"I'm not going to rejoin them," I reassure her. "I'm going so that I can break away for good, and I won't be alone," I say. "Someone outside my family is meeting me there."

Ana steers us onto the road and considers her next question. "Is it the woman you've been hanging out with the past few days? The one I met at the bookstore?"

"Yes," I say, preparing myself to tell more truths after so long spent hiding as a reflex.

"It's not just the family stuff that's had you on edge recently. It's something to do with her too, isn't it?"

I nod.

"She said she came in looking for a book, but I know it's more than that. How did you two actually meet?"

"She's— You said you sensed something interesting about her. What was it?"

"She seems . . ." Ana searches for a word. "Not *evil*, but she's weighed down by a lot of negative things. Maybe even dangerous things. But when I saw you two on the sidewalk the other day, you looked so happy. And she seemed different. Less burdened. Because of you."

"And what about me? Since you've known me, what have you sensed?"

"Well, you never wanted me to do a reading for you or anything like that. I think I can understand why now." She glances briefly from the road to me. "Energetically, you're the opposite of her. Your aura is unlike any other person's I've seen. But you're weighed down too."

"Avitue and I"—I accidentally say her name without thinking—"neither of us is quite human. Well, I'm more human than she is if we're thinking about this on a spectrum."

"Oh," says Ana, focusing very intensely on the road. "What a thing to learn while driving."

"I'm sorry."

"Don't be. I've been asking questions," she says. "It makes sense that you wouldn't associate much with people if you're, you know, something else."

I've been worrying my ring so fiercely that I've made the skin beneath sensitive. I force myself to stop.

"Nephilim," I say quietly. "I'm a nephilim."

"Well, you're obviously not a giant—unless you are? Can giants make themselves not giant?"

Ana's confusion confuses me for a moment, and when I realize where we've missed each other, my tension melts into anxious laughter. Because it's as simple as who I am, I'd never considered that finally telling my giant secret would need to come with a brief mythology lesson.

"Some interpretations call us warrior giants. The warrior part is right. Some say fallen angels. The angel part is right. The first of us were half-angel and half-human. Of course, it's been ages since angels walked this plane. We're distantly related to them now, but the connection to the ethereal remains. We have our own angelic power, and our namesake angels are patrons of sorts. They look out for us and sometimes intercede. But their will and their opinions can be unknowable."

"So you're *divine*," Ana says, her face lighting up as if she's uncovered the universe's greatest mystery.

My original fear, the reason I never wanted to tell her, surfaces. "Not divine," I correct. "Just someone with old connections. Please don't treat me any differently. I don't want some special status. I just want to keep being your friend."

That brings her down. "Oh, Cass, I'm sorry. I only reacted that way because everything about you makes sense now."

"It does?"

"Your aura confused me. I thought maybe someone powerful loved you *a lot*, but the more we got to know each other, I was sure the good energy I felt was also *yours*. I always wondered why someone who felt so good and likable would shrink themselves."

I register the pinch in my upper back, how I'm curling my shoulders inward even as she speaks. With effort, I sit up taller. "To Gabriel, my namesake was all that mattered, never me. When I left, I wanted to be liked for who I was, not because of Cassiel." Stating that simple truth aloud threatens to block my throat. I blink back tears and turn to watch the traffic move around us. "Even though I love my namesake, it hurts to be so worthless without them."

"I'm certain your angel doesn't think you're worthless," Ana says, her voice firm but kind.

The pang in my chest is immediate and overwhelming. Gold sears my vision, and tears follow. No chorus this time. Cassiel alone sings for me. Their song comprises one enduring spectral note. They're a sun within an arm's reach, their presence bending space and time.

Am I still your chosen? All my fears spill from that simple wish. *Show me the path. Don't leave me with this. Help me protect her.*

I am in smiting range and worry I deserve it. Imploring an angel to help a demon is so high an offense that it's unwritten. But the sun blazes on mere inches from my face. I might think they were indifferent but for their gentle warmth. The space between us tenses as if Heaven pulls them back. When I dare to reach for the sun, the vision folds, a dizzying collapse that finds me staring back at infinite selves.

I'm unsure how or when I return to my body, but when I do, Ana is parked crookedly in a cramped convenience store lot. She's slumped over her steering wheel and drawing deep, shaking breaths. "Is it always so easy to draw their attention?" she asks.

My tongue feels like a foreign object in my mouth. "I usually don't try."

She heaves a long sigh.

"Did you see them?" I ask.

"No, but I definitely *felt* something." She takes another steadying breath. "Are you okay?"

I remember the warmth. "I think so."

Ana sits back in her seat. "Was my assessment right?"

My ring is warmer. Not too hot. Just as warm as the sun.

"I hope so," I say.

❖

At a stoplight, Ana returns to piecing together her discoveries. "If you're angel-touched, that makes Avitue . . . ?" She hangs on the end of the sentence as if not wanting to assume.

"A demon." I force myself to say it as if it's just another word.

This draws her eyes from the road again. I can see the questions forming by the furrow of her brows, but traffic resumes, and I have to direct her to the right interchange ramp.

Once out of the city traffic and on the highway, Ana speaks again, "You seem like an unlikely pair."

"You don't know just *how* unlikely. The family business I said I didn't want a part of— It's demon hunting."

Ana opens her mouth. Closes it. Tries again. "So you're meeting your demon girlfriend at your demon-hunting family's house?"

I choose not to comment on the *girlfriend* bit. Ana can read energy between people, but she wouldn't need psychic abilities to see what was going on between Avitue and me.

"It's complicated."

"Sounds like," Ana sighs. When several cars pass us, Ana glances down at the speedometer to see she's far below the limit. She speeds up. "Now I'm worried for both of you."

"We have a plan," I say. "Then we can live how we want."

We're quiet for a long stretch of highway, just the wind noise, the steady hum of the engine, and the wall of goldening trees on either side. I notice the smoky incense scent of the car's interior for the first time since getting in, and it makes me ache for Avitue.

"You don't have to tell me more, but . . . text me? To let me know you're both okay."

"I will."

"And your store? Need me to check on anything?"

I'd forgotten all about the store. I drop my spare key in Ana's cupholder. "If you could bring in the mail. That's really all that should need tending to. I'll only be gone for, well, a couple days." I point. "It'll be this exit here."

There's nothing around it, no signs for gas stations or restaurants. We leave behind the openness of farmland, and the trees close in again.

"Your family really is out in the middle of nowhere," Ana comments.

"Secrets will make you do that. We have warded safe houses within the city where we can stay before or after a local hunt. It's all well thought out. Strategic. Even more so now that Gabriel is the family head." I go back to twisting my ring even though it hurts now.

"Is it okay for you to be telling me all this?"

"The rules I was trying to follow don't matter anymore."

We take a sharp and poorly marked curve, and Ana taps a little too hard on the brakes. "Sorry," she says, grimacing.

"There'll be a narrow, unmarked road just up here on the right. It winds through the trees for a couple more miles, and then we should be at the gate." I fight to keep my voice neutral, trying and failing at staving off a wave of fear as I anticipate seeing the gates again and facing what's beyond them.

Ana slows to a crawl and finds the path, overgrown and intentionally easy to miss. It's unpaved, and I feel the need to apologize for how rough the ride suddenly becomes.

"If you want to just drop me here," I start.

"No way. I offered to drive you, and I'll take you as far as I can." She tries to give me a smile, but the lines of her face are tight. "I feel like I'm turning you over to an executioner or something. Not helping you."

I'm quick to reassure her. "You are helping."

For the rest of the drive up to the gate, we each sink into our own thoughts. I return to worrying the strap of my bag, pressing wrinkles down the length of the fabric. Soon, I will see Avitue, and she will be different. *Remember me like this. Please.* I remember our first meetings, how my fear was based only on the knowledge that she was a demon with unknown intentions. This encounter would be different than that.

The way ahead widens, and around the curve, a small fleet of sleek black SUVs lines the space in front of a tall iron gate. Angel statues cloaked in moss stand vigil to either side.

Ana lets out a breath at the sight and eases the car to a stop. "You really will be okay?" she asks, and it's then that my awareness prickles faintly.

I glance at the car's mirrors, a quick flick of my eyes that makes Ana frown again. Two demons are trying very hard to suppress their auras—and one is practically tapping me on the shoulder. Avitue.

"Yes," I answer distractedly.

Ana's hand lands on mine. "Cassiel—"

"Thank you for doing this on such short notice. You've been such a dear friend, and I should have reached out to you more."

"You sound like you're saying—"

"That we should do something together. When I get back. Yes."

Ana doesn't look reassured, but I need her to go. "Please have a safe drive back. Like I said, I'll text you," I say, gathering my bag and hurrying from the car.

"Okay. Yeah."

I try my best to smile as I bend to make eye contact with Ana through the open door. "Be safe," I say, warding both the car and Ana with a discreet flick of my wrist. Ana notices, nods. I shut the door, turn to the gates, and don't look back until the hum of Ana's engine has faded. Then, with an unusually steady hand, I grip the cold metal of the gate and let myself through.

The sharp clang of the lock once I'm on the other side cleaves everything into a sharp before and after. The sun is beginning its fall toward the horizon, and the rustle of dead leaves at my feet is the only noise as I walk through the trees. The house isn't within sight yet. I'll walk for another quarter mile.

Avitue gives me a metaphysical tap every few steps. *I'm here.* The only comfort she can provide, but it's also foreboding. We both know what comes at the end of it.

When I'm sure I'll see the house through the trees any moment, Avitue vanishes, a blip on my radar that ceases to be. My step falters. I want to postpone this. I want to turn back. I step forward.

Into the path ahead of me, Avitue emerges from the trees, silent as a shadow. I stop and almost let her name slip, but there's the barest shake of her head. This isn't a reunion. This is not my Avitue. But the unfinished braid is still there, frizzy and tousled as if she's been anxiously running her hands through her hair and catching her fingers on it, forgetting again and again that it's there but deciding each time that it's worth keeping.

Run, she mouths, and I do, gripping the strap of my bag in one hand and drawing the dagger with the other.

I scream for help, but the words are too strained and don't carry. In my bag, the book thumps against my hip as I run. Amber eyes flash in the trees, there and gone. A streak of black hair like an ominous storm threatening to overtake me. I scream again, scream for my sister Zuriel as she'd once cried out to me for help all those years ago. My boots slide on the fallen leaves, and just as I lose my footing, something catches me from behind.

I'm slammed back into a tree, knocking the air from my lungs and cutting short my call for help. Suddenly, I look up into the glow of Avitue's eyes, utterly cold and empty of recognition.

I breathe hard. When Avitue told me it had to look real, I didn't think I'd feel as if I'd lost her. I didn't think I'd feel this panic.

Too late, I remember the dagger in my hand and flick it upward only for Avitue to knock my hand away, sending the blade flying into a pile of leaves. I scream for help again, genuinely this time, and Avitue covers my mouth with a sharp hand, her claws biting into my cheek. I scream against it and am surprised to feel tears track down my face. Avitue rips her hand away as if the touch of them burns. I scramble away from her only to catch my toe on an exposed root. I scrape a shin and elbow in my fall, but the pain doesn't register.

All I can focus on is Avitue looming, advancing, and our plan is gone from my mind. I'm scared. This feels real.

"Avitue."

I know I shouldn't say it, but her name slips from my mouth. A plea. That stops her, and for a second, there's *my* Avitue, mirroring my own fear. She unfurls her wings, summoning an inky sphere of darkness around us. I don't know whether I'm dreaming or awake, but for now, we share a small ephemeral universe.

"Can I—?" she asks.

"Yes," I say. I don't know to what, but I desperately want her close.

Avitue is kneeling beside me in an instant. "I'm so sorry," she says, running her hands over my scraped skin. Her touch burns like the seconds before drawing a hand away from open flame, but when it's over, I'm healed.

"I saw Cassiel. Just before I arrived, I saw them," I say.

Avitue's eyes are wide. "What did they say?"

"It's not that simple."

"Never is with angels." She turns her head as if listening for something. "Your rescue party is on the way. I need to go."

I clutch her to me. "Please come back. Promise me."

"I will always find you, Cassiel," she says, drawing back to catch me in the fire of her eyes. "For now, though, you need to sleep."

I nod, my heart thrumming a frantic rhythm.

I want Avitue to hold my gaze, but she's staring beyond me, watching for something I can't see. She taps a finger against my temple, and true darkness descends.

———◆———

My dreams are empty. I feel empty. How long I float in and out of sleep, I don't know. When I stir for the final time, something solid and heavy lands near my head.

"Why did I give you this if you can't hold onto it?" A voice. Zuriel's.

I blink open my eyes from one darkness into another. The air is thick with incense. All smoke makes me think of Avitue. I try to sit up. My muscles burn with weakness.

Zuriel's weight settles on the edge of the bed. "I'm sorry I doubted you before. That succubus came back for you."

My pulse pounds in my head. I fight to stay upright. In the low light, the dagger glints next to my pillow. I can't think of anything to say for a moment.

"She finally had you in her grasp, and all she did was put you into a deep sleep. Whatever her motivations are, she's the most baffling demon I've ever encountered. Did you get a good look at her when she attacked you?"

"What happened to her?" I manage.

"Michael and Gabriel were going to go after her, but we needed to get you safe. She must've been desperate to pursue you so close to the house."

"How many days has it been?" I ask. The heaviness in my body tells me I've been asleep for too long.

"Nearly two. You kept talking in your sleep when anyone came near you. It sounded like a name."

A cold weight settles in my stomach. They can't have that name. My family can't have that name.

"A good friend. She's the one who drove me."

"She's lucky the succubus was only after you. What were you thinking bringing an outsider so close to the estate?"

I didn't want to be alone with this secret anymore.

"She wanted to help." I give up on trying to stay seated and recline back onto the pillows.

Zuriel watches me. "You're horribly out of practice, but I feel safer having you back. Not having to worry for you."

I'm too tired to broach this, but thankfully Zuriel doesn't push. I feel for the sides of the bed and find that it's narrower than I expected.

"Are we not upstairs?" I ask.

This room, now that I'm looking at the perimeter of it, is only big enough for the bed, a simple wooden chair, and a dusty shelf. A single candle provides light. There are no windows.

"Because you've been a target, Gabriel thought it safest if you weren't," says Zuriel.

"So I'm down in the crypt for safekeeping. Like a relic."

"Speaking of which," says Zuriel, drawing something long and heavy into her lap. Though I can't see it well, I immediately know what it is. "Gabriel wants you to start practice again as soon as you're able to stand. If they're going to attack us on our own property, you need to be able to defend yourself."

"I'm never going to be like I was before. Especially not in a matter of days. I don't know how you went back to it after that, Zuriel. I can't fail you again, and I know I will."

Zuriel stands and sets the sword in her place. In its curved grip, the gem in the eagle's eye gleams. "You never failed me," she whispers. "Gabriel shouldn't have—"

The door swings open, and Gabriel's familiar silhouette fills the frame. Even in the low light, she's just as I remember her—impeccable suit and curls wrangled back in a severe bun, despite being in her own home. A beat passes before she says anything, and I hate my sudden urge to crawl under the bed and out of her sight.

This silence is on purpose. This silence is a test.

She steps into the room with a familiar wooden box in her hands. My throat tightens. Zuriel bows and excuses herself. I want to call after her to stay, please stay.

"Good to see you awake," Gabriel says first, an imitation of a gentle parent. No acknowledgment that I've been gone for years. Then, "A succubus attacked you, correct?"

As if she didn't know. As if she weren't there.

I nod, unable to find words in my mother's presence.

She sets the box at the foot of the bed. "Make certain you're strong for the fight ahead," she says simply and leaves.

As soon as her steps recede, I grab the thing and shove it in a dark corner under the bed. Even that much movement is too sudden and strenuous because, when I stand, my head goes light and my vision fuzzy. I grip the post of the bed and wait for it to pass. When I look down at my body, I notice that someone's changed my clothes. I'm wearing something long and drapey and white, and in a fit of sudden rage, I rip it off over my head and kick it under the bed with the box. My bag is in the chair in the corner of the room, and I change into my favorite soft blue sweater and a pair of wrinkled chinos. The rest of the bag's contents I dump out on the bed to see what I thought to pack in my frenzy.

The last thing to fall from the bag, a badly rumpled feather, freezes my breath in my lungs. It's iridescent black and long as my forearm. I have no doubt who placed it there. I just don't know when she must've done it. Its barbs are all askew, and its spine is broken from the weight of everything stuffed on top of it, but as I take it in my hands, I find it's still strikingly beautiful. I settle back on the bed to begin the task of meticulously setting the barbs straight. When I'm done, I twirl it in my fingers, raise it to my nose, and find that it still smells faintly of smoke.

Returning to the moment where my faith—in Gabriel, in my family's doctrine, in myself—failed me, I find myself back in rural farm country under a punishing summer sun.

Advertising as exorcists and ghost hunters is an easy way for my family to invite average people to call for our services or pass on word of supernatural activity.

Most hunts are for hauntings.

A teenager performs a summoning on a dare. Someone playing with divination tools gets the attention of a demonic spirit rather than their deceased loved one. New owners of an old home find a suspiciously preserved diary among boxes in the basement.

The job becomes rote, especially for possessions. Evacuate the unaffected. Restrain the possessed. Mark their forehead with the appropriate sigil. Ward the building. Exorcise the spirit. Things can diverge from there. The weaker ones can be banished to Hell with words of power. The stronger ones can fight, and that's when we finally draw weapons. Gabriel's approach to the job when interacting with humans takes on the energy of a particularly charismatic businessperson, and it's a wonder people don't think we're charlatans. But when a demon manifests into the material plane, the false smile drops away, and Gabriel is all cold glee.

Even the head of the Gotwenn family can fall complacent.

In the place where I lost my faith, the corn rose high. I don't know how I ended up in the field. There was an exorcism. The exorcism went wrong. We were unprepared for a child's body to be able to contain a demonic spirit of that magnitude. We were unprepared for the possibility that a demon could possess a nephilim. Everything in the tome points to the impossibility of demonic possessing divine. But, once out of the child, the spirit immediately went for Zuriel. The world broke with the force of it.

The house was shaken to its foundation, but Zuriel rose unaffected from the debris. The shadow of her new form, dark winged and oozing bile, briefly eclipsed the sun.

Was I running away from her or running to her?

Cornstalks obscured the sky. The only person I believed had ever truly loved me faced me between the rows. She didn't move with her usual grace. She jerked and snarled. She was fighting an internal battle, and she was losing. I was unprepared for the way this tactic struck me so precisely, the way it immediately and efficiently dismantled all my trained responses. It was perfect in its psychological cruelty. It emptied me of rationality, of hope. For once, my mind was clear.

My sister will kill me. Or I will kill my sister.

Then, garbled, Zuriel said my name. Said it again, clearer, anguished. Then she vanished, and there was only the demon in her ruined body, charging.

Down in the vast stretch of corridors and rooms beneath the Gotwenn estate, stone dampens the living world above to an eerie silence. Yet even secreted away in this old crypt, I feel the end of something looming near.

The sparring room is empty. I'm happy to be alone with my thoughts and the once-familiar shape of the falcata in my hands. I extend the sword, testing the deadly forward weight of the blade. My arm trembles. My muscles strain to relearn posture and pose. The angelic weapon isn't heavy as swords go, but years of comfort have diminished my endurance. Then there's the lingering effect of the deep sleep I've only recently climbed out of.

It was part of the plan, I tell myself over and over—in the cold spray of the shower, in the dim candlelit room, while pacing the length of cobwebbed corridors. Despite the press of people on the sidewalks and the customers in my shop, I was largely alone in the city, but now I'm truly isolated. Zuriel brings me food. Gabriel makes her alarming check-ins, and the door to the house proper remains warded and bolted against me. I think, based on the arrival of meals, that three days have passed.

I'm not trapped. I might not be able to enter the house, but there are unguarded subterranean passages that lead off estate grounds, that could lead me to Avitue. Only, I'm not sure whether I want to take them yet. Not sure whether I'm strong enough or settled enough. The memory of Avitue's predatory efficiency and the merciless focus of her gaze won't leave me. In those moments, I hold the feather and try to remember warmth. I'm thankful to my past self for thinking to map all my potential exits, inking my estimates of their locations and paths into the blank final pages of my tome.

Even now, finding myself back at the place I thought I'd escaped, I don't want to acknowledge the reason I'd felt compelled to memorize exits all those years ago.

Sheathing the falcata, I settle down for a short rest, one knee to the floor. I'm breathing too hard from cycling through a couple basic forms and resolve to make another attempt just after I catch my breath.

"Why is this demon interested so specifically in you?" comes a voice from behind me.

I whirl to face Gabriel, and the edges of my vision turn dark. My head swims. I fight against the fear that I will collapse right here and draw myself up. "The one who attacked me?"

Gabriel allows nothing to show on her face, but as with everything, this too is a subtle test. "Zuriel says the succubus found and haunted you in the city. Presumably, since Zuriel left the dagger with you, we can assume you've killed her at least once. She must be important for the demons to be so devoted to keeping her in this realm. She must be skilled if they insist on sending her after one of ours." Gabriel cocks her head expectantly. There's a correct answer to her questionless question, but I know neither what she's asking nor its answer and worry that anything I say will endanger Avitue.

"There's no way I could know her rank or what their plan for her is," I say.

"But you've seen her multiple times," says Gabriel, advancing a step.

If it were appropriate, if we were sparring, I'd take a defensive stance. I resist the instinct. "I have."

A frown cracks Gabriel's impassive expression. Something must be very wrong for her mask to slip like this. What's happening upstairs that they're not telling me? "So you must know something about her."

"She resisted my early wards. She's looking for something. I don't know what."

"I want you to lure her out. We know she'll take risks to have you. We'll catch her and make her talk. Then you'll kill her," says Gabriel, nodding to my sword.

Why me? I barely stop myself from saying. *Why do you want* me *to kill her?*

"Michael is more practiced," I say. *Tread carefully.* "I still feel unsteady on my feet."

"You don't need practice for this. You're still able to lift your sword?"

She's mocking me. What else can I do but nod?

"We will restrain her. You put the sword through her heart." With that, Gabriel turns to go, leaving the room even colder than before.

❦

This is the night I plan to find Avitue.

Zuriel arrives with what I think might be dinner. It's impossible to judge the time by what's served. Every plate is the same uninspiring fare, and I eat only because I'm tired of being weak. There's never been much comfort, let alone indulgence, to be found at the Gotwenn estate.

The past two generations let much of the house and grounds fall into disuse as the size of the family dwindled and attitudes turned toward austerity. Since Gabriel became the family head, that's been magnified.

I've known no other way.

Before Zuriel leaves, I reach out to her. "Can you make sure I'm not disturbed for the rest of the night?"

Zuriel pauses with her hand on the door. "Gabriel suspects you of something, you know."

"I know. Tell her I need to meditate. Refocus."

"We've seen that demon again. Twice now. I've never seen one of them so desperate. She seems careless but also hasn't fallen for any of our traps."

I try for casual. "Haniel must be itching to go after her."

"Michael is doing everything to hold him back. Even with demons, I'm not that bloodthirsty." Zuriel moves away from the door and lowers her voice. "You're not planning on going after her by yourself, are you?"

204

I keep my eyes down on the sword in my lap. After three years apart, Zuriel still knows me so well. "Yes. But not to kill her."

"Then why? I'm sure *she* would try to kill *you*."

"I just need to talk to her."

Zuriel's voice turns harsh, and the only reason I don't flinch away is because of the thread of concern running through it. "Not only is that the most foolish thing I've ever heard, but it's also directly against Gabriel."

"Please, Zuriel. She won't hurt me."

"What do you think she was trying to do when she attacked you? Where's your sense gone?"

"I need to trust someone here. I need to trust you." I stand to meet her. "When there was no one else, we had each other."

Zuriel shakes her head. "I want to protect you. And to do that, I can't let you go."

"Please," I try again.

"I need to tell Gabriel. You're a danger to yourself."

Zuriel takes a hurried step toward the door when I grab her.

"I think I love her," I say.

There. The impossible confession fills the space between us.

"You're not well. You're confused," Zuriel says, grasping desperately for an explanation. She tugs out of my grasp. "This is my fault. I *knew* something was wrong, and I never should've left you. I should've told Gabriel then."

"You can't say anything to Gabriel. Please. I'd lose her."

All my pleading has the wrong effect on Zuriel. She looks at me as if I'm not her sister, as if I'm deeply disturbed, as if whatever's possessed me will poison her too.

"Their powers of suggestion and seduction are strong. If you stay here, her influence over you will weaken. You'll be back to normal," she says as if trying to reassure herself.

"It's not demonic influence. I know what that feels like."

"And so the alternative explanation is that you're in love?" Zuriel scoffs.

Though I know what I must sound like to Zuriel, being dismissed still hurts. I push forward and try to ignore the sting. "Do you really sense that I'm under demonic influence? You of all people would know best if there was any evidence of that."

It's Zuriel's sensory gift that allowed the demons we hunted to trick her those years ago. The reason the accident happened. A minor demon. That's what she'd said she sensed, and we'd all believed her. What else but a minor demon could fit its power into such a small vessel? We couldn't know what we were drawing out.

Zuriel sighs and puts a hand against my chest. Closes her eyes. When she opens them, they glow white, and she looks through me into the truth. I hold her radiance and don't look away. The air reverberates with shock, and Zuriel draws her hand back with a gasp. When the light fades from her eyes, she's staring at me as if I'm a stranger.

"You consented to sex with her. You manifested wings in front of her. You showed her the tome. You *planned* for her to do this to you." The truths tumble out in a rush as Zuriel struggles to understand them. She shakes her head. "You'd give up your sword to protect her. I don't know who you are anymore."

That small sentence buries a brutal and severing cut deep in my chest. Zuriel was the first person—and, for so long, the only person—to truly understand me. I've misjudged badly, confusing the trust I wish I could place in her with the reality of all that's changed between us. And now, it could cost me not only my sister but Avitue as well. I can't lose them both.

I start to speak, as if anything I say could pave over the truth, but Zuriel holds up a hand and hushes me. She turns away. Light ripples across her skin and fades. Ripples again. When she speaks, it's in a shaking voice. "You're not under her influence. You're not lying. And from what I can sense from your truth, she's not either."

I dare to let myself feel a glimmer of hope, but I'm afraid speaking will break whatever realization Zuriel's approaching.

"If you haven't betrayed us, then the question becomes why would she betray them?"

"Let me go to her. Please. I can find out more."

Zuriel rests a shoulder against the wall, letting it take some of her weight as the fatigue of truth-seeing settles. "Why didn't you tell me sooner? Why let me believe you were in danger? That you were—" she hesitates, then heaves a frustrated sigh. "I don't know why Cassiel would allow this. It's not right. You can't be well."

I flinch at her words, but I remember what brought me here. I want to decide how I should live. Despite the pain, I meet her eyes as I say, "You saw that I am."

Zuriel drops her gaze as if unable or unwilling to face this version of me. "She's a demon, Cass," she says, more to herself than to me, still processing this new knowledge.

"Please let me go," I say.

Zuriel gestures tiredly at the door as if to say, *I'm not stopping you*, but I wait. I want her on my side, not just to look the other way.

"Gabriel will know what I've done," she says finally. "What do you want me to tell her?"

"Tell her you were checking my condition. Making sure there was no lingering influence hindering my recovery."

"She'll still be suspicious. You're weak, but you're not concerning enough to justify me weakening myself by using my sight."

"She won't have to feel suspicious for long."

"I'll let you go, but you have to tell me what you learn."

I promise.

"You realize you've turned everything upside down for me?"

"Yes." Then, after a moment of consideration, I add, "I'm sorry."

ELEVEN

I PACK MY BAG just in case and belt the falcata to my hip. It's a silly look with my wrinkled contemporary clothes, and as I wander through a dusty cobwebbed corridor, I think of how many nephilim must've wielded the sword through the ages in order to pass it to me. What would they think of me now?

Perhaps, like Zuriel, they wouldn't recognize me.

I draw the sword from its scabbard and wake its radiance just enough to provide light to see by. The walk is longer than I remember, and water pools in the lowest parts of the path. Eventually, the tunnel slopes upward on a gentle incline, and the heavy drone of Gabriel's wards builds. She's been here recently to refresh the sigils. I encounter her work as an invisible wall rippling with vigilant energy. These aren't simple wards. The archangel themself watches.

I shift my sword to my offhand, take a steadying breath, and reach not for my light but for Cassiel. I'm drenched immediately in gold and warmth, the same as in the vision. I am weightless and winged. The sun fills my sight, its rays coalescing into a radiant glove upon my right hand. Cassiel guides me forward, and when my fingertips breach the wall, I witness an eclipse, a heavenly body setting themself between me and Gabriel. In a flash, I pass through the wards safe and unseen. Gold drips from my fingertips like water, angelic power returning to its source. I'm left trembling as if in the wake of an adrenaline surge and wipe tears from my cheeks.

"Thank you," I whisper to the dark, too overcome to move.

Ana and Avitue were right. Cassiel wouldn't abandon me.

Packed earth replaces stone. A crack of light above marks the end. I sheathe the sword, unbolt the old wooden doors, push up, and emerge into a world of frost and moonlight.

I shiver at the touch of the outdoors, but I welcome the fresh breeze after days of nothing but dust and damp. My skin prickles alive. White beams and a peaked roof are just visible through the trees. I hurry for it, my boots crunching over frosted leaves, breath clouding on the air. The gazebo is the same as I remember it, although perhaps more of its white paint has flaked away over the years.

A familiar shape, blissfully unaffected by the chill, paces the gazebo. I steal a couple backward glances as I approach, stretching out my awareness of the surrounding energy. Trees, animals, nothing else. Avitue watches me silently as I approach.

Neither of us moves. Avitue stands in deep shadow under the cover of the roof, but her eyes glow with an inner fire. Even from this distance, the high set of her shoulders and tense stride betray the strain in her. The hunger. The restraint. It's obvious that she hasn't fed since we were together in the shop.

For a moment, I'm scared that this won't be the comforting reunion I'd hoped for. The cold Avitue that hunted me down flashes in my memory.

"You came." Avitue breathes relief. The terrifying vision is broken. "I've waited here for you every night."

I take another tentative step toward her. "I'm sorry."

"I was so scared I'd accidentally hurt you. I was scared I'd misjudged something. And that maybe your family had figured us out and were going to punish you. I don't know what nephilim do, but with demons, punishment is always terrible, and I kept imagining all these things." Her fears come spilling out in a breathless rush. "I thought maybe you'd decided you didn't trust me after all and wouldn't come. Or that if you did, you'd come with—"

The ornate scabbard at my hip catches the moonlight as I walk, and Avitue's gaze darts to it. She takes a step back.

"What's wrong?" I ask.

Even in the dark, I can tell this is more than unease. It's fear she's trying to hide, and Avitue's never been scared of *me*. Then I realize.

"You've never seen one of the relics before," I say.

She heaves a sigh. "I didn't think its presence alone would create this"—she puts a hand over her chest—"pressure. I thought maybe, because I hadn't seen you in a while, I was more sensitive to your energy."

With all our other concerns, I hadn't considered how the sword's presence would affect Avitue. Wielding our sacred weapons on the hunt was one thing; those demons were our enemies. This isn't a fight, but an ancient angelic weapon is clearly still an ancient angelic weapon, no matter how much one trusts the person in possession of it. The demons we fought weren't only afraid of a permanent death. The energy itself set them on edge the same way demon-touched objects did to us, and something directly handed down by the angels clearly magnified that effect.

I unbelt the sword and let it fall into the grass. Unarmed, I step up to join Avitue under the cover of the gazebo, but now she's staring at me with wide-eyed surprise.

"I want to be close to you without making you more uncomfortable." I drop my bag as well and roll the ache out of my shoulder. "I don't sense anyone else here."

Avitue nods, everything about her face and posture turned still and solemn. I miss her confident swagger, her flirtatious ease. If we do this right, I can see that version of her again.

When I look properly into her face, I notice something wrong. Something other than the hunger. I close the space between us and raise a hand to Avitue's face but don't quite touch. One side is marred by a bruise. Her lip is split and newly scabbed over. "What happened?" I ask.

"Belial said my pretty face didn't do its job, so I might as well be ugly like the rest of them."

"He *hit* you?"

"He's a demon," she says matter-of-factly. "He's done worse."

"Can you not heal it?"

"Best not when he's involved. It'll just make him insufferable."

I don't feel true anger often, and when I do, it's often a long and gradual build. But seeing Avitue like this, trying to shrug off something so blatantly awful, makes me want to—in her words—*become an avenging angel*. This isn't unlike what Gabriel's done to me for my failures, but it's different when it's not me. It's different when it's someone I care about.

I think I love her.

"It's sweet that you're concerned, but I don't want to think about Belial when I haven't seen you in days."

"My family spotted you," I blurt. "They said you've seemed careless. Gabriel wants me to . . ."

Avitue's hands come to rest on my shoulders, warm reassurance in the cold autumn night.

I sigh at the touch. "Gabriel wants to use me as bait to catch you. She wants to know the demons' plan, and she wants you dead for your obvious interest in me."

"Well." Avitue squeezes my shoulders, and a little of that reckless smile flickers across her face. "Guess she won't have much luck there."

"But I need to tell them something. Gabriel suspects that I know more than I've let on. And I promised my sister I'd tell her the truth. About our meeting."

Avitue winces at the betrayal. "Why would you promise her that? Why would you even tell her about us?"

Us. There's an us. We hang by this thread together.

"She wasn't going to let me go, so I told her I loved you." I force myself to hold the intensity of Avitue's gaze. "And she didn't believe me, so I let her see everything. She knows about us, and she trusts you too. She let me come here and promised not to tell Gabriel."

Avitue is already shaking her head. "But she's a nephilim."

"*I'm* a nephilim!"

"That's different. You're different."

"My sister is too. She's the only family I trust."

Avitue paces the gazebo, and I let her go, knowing that, eventually, she'll come back to me. Belatedly, it hits her. "Wait. You *love* me?" She makes a noise of disbelief. "I'm a demon, and you're practically an angel, and I'm fallen, which means I can't possibly reciprocate your feelings. You do know that? I'm not good. I can't feel—"

"Avitue," I say gently, and it's enough to stop her rambling. "If you want to love, you can."

She points to herself. "Damned. Fallen. Unforgivable," she lists as if I need reminding. "We got the ability to love ripped out of us along with our grace."

"But you're the reason I can manifest wings."

"That credit solely belongs to you, Cassiel. It's nice that you think of me, but don't let others claim your power."

"I mean that I figured out why I can access my wings. My radiance is attracted to love, and it—" I struggle to explain the metaphysical in concrete terms. "It reaches for you. It's especially overwhelming when—" I cut myself off, unable to speak frankly even as I freeze in the dark, trying to subvert an infernal plot and sidestepping an equally undesirable divine one.

I know Avitue understands when an endearing-yet-evil grin takes over her face. "I was *right* before. It *was* the amazing orgasm."

I'm hiding my face in my hands again when Avitue captures my wrists and sets my hands back at my sides. "Don't hide. I want to see my sexy angel warrior."

My face is burning. "You want to embarrass me to death."

"I know I said I didn't want credit, but also this is the greatest achievement of my life."

I love the pure happiness in her smile, a glimmer of what I hope we'll have on the other side of this. She's so close and beautiful and *perfect* despite what she says about the fall. I want to lose myself again in her eyes, her hunger, her aura.

"I think it happens because it's a moment of pure feeling where I'm not overanalyzing everything. If I practiced, I think I could manifest wings from a source of love."

"Wouldn't I know if I could love? How could you sense something I can't feel?"

"It would be hard to name a feeling if you don't think it can exist."

She turns somber again. "If demons can choose to love, that changes all our ideas about what happened in the fall. But I don't think Belial wants my philosophical musings. He'll be grumpy, to put it lightly, if I'm away much longer."

When I twist my ring around my little finger, I realize the tips of my fingers are turning numb. I rub my hands together and pocket them, but my cardigan is little insulation against the cold. Noticing my vain attempt, Avitue gathers me into a smoky embrace.

"We don't know exactly where the relics are," she says into my hair. "And there's no way we can get closer to the grounds because of the wards. But we're planning to move tomorrow."

"If you don't have the location and you can't get in, then how?"

"I told them you'd come back to look for me. Hear me out. I have another idea."

It's when Avitue suggests possession that I disconnect. I can hear her still talking to me, but the words lose their meaning.

I'm under the summer sun in a cornfield. I cannot move, not because of any supernatural force, but because I'm certain I've witnessed my sister's spiritual murder. Zuriel's empty body charges me. In my memory, it's always those first two steps just before I know Gabriel breaks through the row beside us. I never see Gabriel. It's always my sister's body, empty. Moving fast and slow. Bent on violence.

"Cassiel?" Avitue shakes me gently. "Cassiel."

Summer is gone. The world is dark and cold. I wonder at the sudden space between Avitue and me, the way she's gripping my shoulders as if to shake me awake.

"What was that?" she asks, face pinched in concern.

"I thought I lost my sister." I put my hands to my mouth as if I can hold in the tide of awful things set loose by verbalizing the confession. "I thought I lost her, and then even when she recovered, the memory of it . . . I thought I lost her, and then I left her."

Avitue seems to struggle over the motions for comfort. She starts sentences and then bites them off. Finally, she settles on a simple question. "What happened?"

For the first time, I tell someone.

⸺◆⸺

We've mastered the outward appearances of being human. We can perform our roles if needed. I thought, for many years, that something about our connection to the ethereal made nephilim colder than humans. Less able to feel the full range and depth of human emotions. If any of us were to externalize an emotion, it was because we were conscious of what we wanted to project and what we wanted to elicit as a result of that projection. It's why Gabriel seemed cartoonish in the way she dealt with the humans who called us for help. Too friendly, too optimistic, too kind. Playing a character I didn't recognize as my mother.

In the aftermath of the possession, Gabriel turned kind and comforting. For months, Zuriel didn't recover. Gabriel eventually stopped attempting emotion. She prayed over Zuriel and marked her with blessed oil. She etched sigils into the doorway to her room and over her bed. Zuriel's soul remained beyond. Unreachable. Traumatized out of its body. At all hours, one of us was set to watch for her spirit's return or, more often, to make sure spirits with ill-intent didn't find an uninhabited body and make themselves a new home.

Six months later, Zuriel spoke. I was the one watching over her body when she did. We'd been reunited mere minutes when Gabriel appeared with a list of demands. Necessary ritual cleansings. A plan to build back up to her previous schedule of training. A weak body and a weaker soul endangered us all, she said.

Zuriel didn't relate what happened to her when she was beyond. No one mentioned the possession except to hint that perhaps Zuriel didn't take her training seriously enough. That her soul wasn't pure enough to repel a demonic spirit. It must have chosen her for a reason.

I don't remember the exorcism in the cornfield. Zuriel's possessed form charged me. Then, the rustle of the stalks. Gabriel's back. I don't remember more.

Zuriel's hands shook when she restrung her bow. She trembled when she nocked an arrow. Her shots struck wide. The practice dummy went unharmed. Gabriel watched her, all silent judgment. Would leave her to practice late into the night.

I crept into Zuriel's room one night, slipped into bed beside her, and put an arm around her middle. Our breathing synchronized. It must have been early in the morning, just before sunlight, when Zuriel spoke.

"When I was in the beyond, I knew how to come back," she whispered. "I just didn't want to." She turned over to face me in the dark. "You understand, don't you?"

I nodded.

"I wish I'd had the strength to stay away. I wish I was allowed to be weak. Just this once."

◆

It's late when I'm done, and my body feels as exhausted as if I just returned from a hunt. Three years. Three years away from my family. Three years to be a normal person, to attempt to build the comfort and security I was denied my entire life. In a matter of days, all those reserves are used up.

I curl my numb toes in my boots. I'm not sure how long Zuriel can cover for me. I'd best get back if I don't want to ruin our chance at enacting our plan.

"I never knew what made you leave," says Avitue. She's still careful, quiet, as if she's once again making room for my fragile and sharp-edged memories next to her own.

Even after all this, my hope that Zuriel will leave with me still survives. I push forward, as I always have.

"I think your idea would work," I say.

"It's not something I'd ask, knowing what I do now."

"Tell me everything again," I ask, focused now.

Avitue does. I nod along, make suggestions. "You can magic objects in and out of existence, right? I've seen you do it."

"Yes, but they'd sense if it was something I'd made. It'd have a sort of demonic *something* about it."

"What if I bless it? Would that be enough to make them think it was the real thing? Would it cancel out the fact that you'd made it?"

Avitue thinks. "It'd help to see the real thing. So I at least have an idea of what I'm forging."

I retrieve the falcata and lay it at Avitue's feet. "Try this one."

We settle on either side of the sword. Avitue traces the air above it with her hand as if it will help her memorize the dimensions and artistic flourishes. She's careful not to touch the relic itself. Neither of us knows what would happen if she did. I know that injuries inflicted by the relics will result in the true death of a demon, but there's never been an opportunity to see what would happen were a demon merely to hold one of the relics. Would it hurt but not kill? Would nothing happen at all if there were no mortal wound? My time with Avitue continually reveals more gaps in our knowledge.

"Got it, I think," she says, and in her hand, she's suddenly holding a sword that looks eerily like mine. However, even in the dark, I can see the glaring omission.

"It's missing the inscription," I say. The grooves of ancient text—the representation of the angelic tongue itself—are absent from the spine of the blade.

"Yeah," Avitue says, drawing out the word. "I think it's written into the laws of the universe that demons can't speak or write in the angelic language. I guess trying to reproduce it counts as writing. Good thing we don't have any of the tomes to check the authenticity against. Here, your turn," says Avitue, handing over the fake sword.

I take it and am surprised to find it perfectly balanced, if a little lighter than my own. "This feels good in the hand," I say, almost launching into praise of Avitue's artistry. I refocus, holding the sword in both hands, palms upward. I try to ignore the prickle of discomfort from being out in the cold so long inadequately dressed.

I close my eyes, reach for my light, and whisper a few carefully chosen angelic phrases over the blade. It's not an easy language; it feels closer to singing than speaking and requires me to call on my light to approach anything close to correct pronunciation. I pause to consider my choices so far and add one more for effect.

"What's that last one?" asks Avitue, sensing it.

"Just a little sparkle to make it feel good," I say.

"Feels like a giant Stay Back sign."

"Will it seem more authentic?"

Avitue's mouth twists into a grimace, and she takes the blade back with apprehension. There's a visible spark when her hand meets the hilt, and she startles, clenching it tighter as if daring it to try that again. "Very."

"Take this to them. If they believe you can influence me, maybe they'll let their guard down when they come for the relics. There are three more. My sister's bow, my brother's ax, and my mother's rapier. Do you think you can make something based on illustrations alone?"

"If they're detailed enough."

"They are." I swallow. "To avoid detection by the wards, it's probably best if you're not in a demon's body. So you'll have to possess me before we return to estate grounds."

"Only if it's something you think you're ready for."

"I am," I say, feeling for the spiritual shadow of my wings.

"We don't know for sure how it'll affect you," Avitue reminds me.

"Zuriel's soul was forced from her body. But for a moment, both souls existed together. If we don't oppose each other, it should work. My light seems to like your energy."

When we stand to leave, swords in hand, I pause. There's an ache in Avitue, a desire, but she won't move to fulfill it. She's waiting for me. I step back into the aura of her warmth, and the look on her face strikes me. I want to hold this look. It seems special to see Avitue's want so plainly, when she's the one who can so effortlessly sense mine.

I kiss her, and when I do, I reach for that feeling Avitue will not or cannot name. Light surges into form behind me, and when we break our kiss, we're bathed in the ethereal light of my wings.

"You were right," says Avitue, and I can see once again, just like in the restaurant, that her understanding of herself is shifting before her.

"It feels so easy now," I say.

Years of torturous discipline and denial to discover that it's warmth and connection that unlock my higher self. I will a single feather to fall free. It transforms as it flutters to the ground, shifting to a solid but radiant white. I tuck it into the inner pocket of Avitue's jacket, a promise.

When the falcata chose me as its new wielder, I was seven years old. It was heavy—and not because I was a child and not because I was only used to my training sword. Even though I was young, I sensed the weight of the generations who'd held it before me, knew the burden of wielding an angelic and eternal object with a finite, human body.

A gentle hum first alerted me to the sword's presence. I heard it first, faintly, from the sparring room as I moved through my stances. It sounded like a distant choir, I told Zuriel. I did not say that the choir's voices weren't human. There were certain things I already knew not to say around my family unless I wanted to cause alarm. These voices weren't human, but they were not *bad*. I knew what evil felt like. That's the first lesson any nephilim child learns. Families keep cursed or possessed objects to show their youngest, to tune their senses with things that—if warded and handled correctly—are mostly harmless.

So I knew there were voices that only I could hear and knew they were not evil. I didn't know the words they spoke.

When I found the source, I didn't know where I was or how I got there. It was as if I'd entered a deep trance and awoken on the other side. I stood before a pedestal, a gleaming sword upon it. I knew, intuitively, that all the voices I'd heard belonged to the sword. I wanted to touch it; it pulled at me, called to me. My hand hovered inches away from the hilt when I heard the distinct click of Gabriel's boots behind me. I whirled to face my mother.

"I'm sorry." The words tumbled from my mouth even though I didn't know where I was or what I was about to do or what it would mean for me to touch the singing sword. That seemed like the kind of thing I could be punished for.

Gabriel said nothing. Only nodded toward the door she'd silently entered through. I'd only heard her steps when she'd wanted me to hear them.

I slipped past her, face burning with shame. I was certain now that I'd be punished. I just didn't know how severely or by what means. So when Gabriel led me back to the sparring room and placed the practice sword in my hand, I was surprised. I thought she must be leading up to something, but my mother merely said, "You've practiced only one hour." Then, as she had so many other times, she left me alone.

Over the next weeks, I continued to find myself inexplicably drawn to the sword, turning up before it with no memory of how I got there. Each time, Gabriel found me just before I touched it. I was never punished.

I didn't know what it all meant—this sword was obviously important, and my mother didn't want me near it yet never punished me for abandoning my studies to find it.

The day I finally laid hands on the sword, the chorus was chanting, its rhythm insistent. My fears of punishment and my mother were wiped from my mind. There was just me and the voices and the sword. When I grasped it, there was no fanfare. No burst of light. The voices faded as if with a contented sigh, and I suddenly had a sword and still no answers.

However, when I wandered upstairs, sword in hand, the estate had changed in one subtle but meaningful way. I could understand the inscriptions in doorways, on all the ancient objects in glass cases, below the paintings of angels. Some of them, I realized, were names. I was stumbling over the pronunciation of one, feeling like a child just learning to read all over again, when the click of Gabriel's boots sounded on the old wood floor.

"I-I just—" I started, stumbling to find an explanation for why I'd abandoned my studies and taken a holy relic—that was suddenly obvious to me now—out of safekeeping in the crypt.

"I see that it was, in fact, destined for you," said Gabriel.

During a visit with our extended family, Aunt Raphael told me that I was one of the few nephilim to ever hear their destined relic sing to them so young. I was entrusted with one of the last remaining tomes.

Not even this accomplishment changed Gabriel's attitude toward me. I continued to feel unworthy. I didn't even know to think the word *unloved*.

———◆———

The sword glows in my hand as I descend back into the earth. I've kept my wings. It's cold, and I fluff them around myself to trap what little body heat I still have. With the radiance of my wings and the sword, I'm the lone source of light for a long time.

Zuriel is pacing in front of my door when I round the corner into candlelight. She stops short and stares at me as if surprised that I've returned.

"It's one thing seeing them through the truth-memory and another seeing them in person," Zuriel says eventually. "Not even Gabriel has four."

I sheathe the sword and needlessly adjust my belt as if action will help me sidestep thinking too hard about Gabriel. I draw my wings in close, suddenly shy of them.

"Tell me what happened," Zuriel says, pulling me into the room and shutting the door behind us.

"We're going to give them fake relics," I say. "It'll spare Avitue and make the demons think they have an advantage they don't."

I explain this part of the plan in detail, but Zuriel, shrewd as she is, prompts, "And the part of this that worries you?"

I ease myself onto the bed with a sigh and dismiss my wings. I haven't slept yet, and it's nearly morning. "They think Avitue has influence over me and expect she can infiltrate the estate."

"That's not possible. You know that. They know that. Gabriel herself ensured the borders are unbreakable."

"Not if I shield her."

Zuriel understands immediately. She sits in the chair across from my bed, and it creaks under her. Resting her forearms on her knees, she seems just as tired as I am. "As far as we know, there's never been a benevolent, symbiotic possession."

"I know," I say.

"If you're worried, you shouldn't do it," Zuriel says. It's soft, but it's a warning. *If you don't trust*, she implies.

"I don't want to scare you is all." *You're the only family I have.*

"As long as you're safe," she says.

I don't expect the reply, and it eases some of the knot in my chest.

Zuriel sits up, studies her hands. "I was lost when you left," she says, quiet. "I couldn't focus on the hunt anymore. I got sloppy. No offense, but—" Her mouth quirks in a rueful smile. "I realized I was so vigilant before because I was looking out for you too."

If not for Zuriel, I'd have more nasty scars. On more than one occasion, she's literally been my shield, throwing her body between me and demons without a thought. It happened so often on my first, smaller hunts that Gabriel reprimanded both of us, saying that I'd never learn if Zuriel spared me from every lowly spirit. They sensed weakness, and that's why they targeted me. As long as I froze in battle, I endangered everyone because I couldn't hold my own.

"Gabriel knew why I was off," Zuriel continues. "When I stopped responding to you, it was because Gabriel said that feeling was weakness. And a weak soul—"

"Is unfit for a warrior," I finish, understanding now. Why did I ever think Zuriel didn't want to hear from me anymore? Of course this was Gabriel's doing. I'm about to apologize for claiming that she abandoned me for Gabriel when she continues.

"I had to recommit myself to the path. Gabriel said you were falling and that I would, too, if I followed you. I had Zuriel's name to live up to. I was scared."

"I know," I rush to reassure her. "I'm sorry I doubted that you cared."

But Zuriel doesn't seem to hear my apology. Her hand is tight on the arm of the chair. Another side to this is brewing.

"And now, because I abandoned you, because of my mistake on that hunt, this demon shows up in your life offering a cure for your loneliness and a twisted immortality."

I want to leap to Avitue's defense, to tell Zuriel that what happened because of that hunt isn't her fault, but she will always throw herself between me and my problems.

"If this demon does anything to hurt you, I will personally hunt her down," Zuriel promises.

"I trust Avitue. She wouldn't hurt me," I say, matching her quiet intensity with my own.

Zuriel studies me, then lets the issue go with a sigh. "Gabriel will want me to bring you breakfast soon," she says, looking to the door but not moving.

"Why does she really want to keep me here?" I ask.

To literally keep me in the dark.

"She knows you're not telling her something. She knows Avitue wants you—though I don't think she knows the precise reason. And she knows that capturing Avitue will get her that answer. Get both of you to talk. If you're together, all the better for her really."

I want you to lure her out, Gabriel had said.

I unconsciously mirror Zuriel's tired posture. "I'm doing exactly what she wants me to. Again."

Zuriel's smile is grim, a familiar expression we often shared.

"There's not another option for Avitue."

I think. My phone was missing from my things when I woke, and in any case, reception has never been good this far out and entirely impossible in the basement levels. No one ever bothered wiring this far—hence the lack of electric lights or warm showers.

"Do you think she can hear us?" I ask.

Zuriel shakes her head, but the fact that she doesn't speak doesn't give me much reassurance.

"She chose you to visit me down here for a reason," I say, the sinking feeling in my stomach growing.

"We've always been close." Zuriel reaches the same conclusion. "I shouldn't have let you leave tonight. That's what she wanted *me* to do—make us think we were safe to form our own plans. But this was always her way to learn what she wanted to."

We sit in miserable silence until Zuriel forces herself to her feet. "I want to follow you this time. When you leave," she whispers.

The words I've wanted to hear for years, but the shadow of whatever Gabriel has planned snuffs out the glimmer of hope I felt before.

"She's trying to show us that we can't leave. Not really. That we can't exist happily out there with normal people."

"You did it," Zuriel says.

"What does it matter if we can always be summoned back?"

I haven't often thought of the penalty for ignoring a summons because it's not something I'd even considered before now. We're told of the repercussions once, and children speak of it only in whispers afterward. If we want to abandon our calling, then we must also give up our connection to the ethereal and become human. It's excruciating to have the connection severed, we're told, and it doesn't happen quickly. A nephilim can only be shut off from their light in a several-day ritual. On the other side of it, their life is shortened to a normal human's years, and they're left with the eternal sense that something is missing.

Zuriel doesn't answer, and I know we've had the same thought.

"Whatever she expects, she won't expect me to invite possession," I say.

"She won't," Zuriel agrees, and suddenly the thing we've always feared becomes our hope.

TWELVE

As closely as Nephilim are anchored to Heaven, we don't follow any human religions, having our own records of history and spiritual knowledge. We possess the power and protection of our ancestors, the angels who walked on earth and led half-human lives.

Nephilim rarely speak of gods. In the direst situations, you could call on an angel to intercede on your behalf. A direct messenger.

Always unworthy in Gabriel's eyes, I never made a practice of calling on my namesake, worrying that they would also find me wanting. Still, they did call me to my destined relic early. Maybe I should've known that meant something. Did they want to spend more time with me over my comparatively short life? What must they have thought of me leaving my sword—and by extension, my calling—behind?

I close my eyes. Remember how to take a deep breath. I've been starved for them, unable to let my mind or body rest.

Zuriel doesn't appear with my meal. I know it's morning. Soon, I estimate that noon has slipped by. No Zuriel. No meal.

I still haven't slept, and at this point, I'm unable to.

The door creaks open. Finally, it must be Zuriel—

I open my eyes to meet Gabriel's gaze.

She steps into the room and pulls her coat tighter around herself. "A bit chilly down here," she says.

No matter how many clothes I wear, no matter how many blankets I bundle around myself, I've never felt quite warm. I don't say this. When has anything ever come of voicing a need?

Gabriel always has a point, and I wait for her to reach it.

"If it weren't in your best interest, you know I wouldn't do this," she says, settling on the bed beside me and smoothing a hand over my disheveled hair.

I force myself not to withdraw from the motherliness of the gesture.

"The demon who attacked you—we haven't seen her recently. I want you to come upstairs. See if anything about her behavior changes once she knows for sure that you're here."

I nod, and Gabriel, apparently satisfied, leaves. When I've stuffed my few belongings back into my bag and step into the corridor, I find the door to the upper floors swung wide, sunlight spilling down the steps. I feel as if I'm in a dream when I ascend, relishing the solidity of each step up into warm, fresh air.

The view of the hall from the top of the steps is exactly how I remember it, and I pause here on the threshold. The house is utterly silent. None of my family is to be seen. This solemn hush has always pervaded the estate, the only sound the occasional creaking of the old wood floors. I remember even as a child being afraid to disturb the quiet, memorizing the places I could step so that no one would hear my footsteps.

Muscle memory takes over now as I enter my childhood home for the first time in years. I find the silent places in the wooden boards, stepping fast and light, realizing that I don't want to be seen. The doors to the rooms I pass are shut and locked. I still don't know what's behind most of them.

The grand entryway is bathed in a rainbow of soft light. Up on the first landing, the glow of evening sun through the stained-glass window dazzles me. It has always been my favorite thing about the house, this depiction of an angel rising up from the earth. I climb the stairs and pause in front of it, taking the moment to center myself. Gabriel will be waiting for me.

My room is on the third and final floor. Gabriel stands in the bedroom doorway and steps aside to let me pass. This room feels giant compared to the closet I've been shut away in for the past week. Giant even in comparison to my studio apartment.

My apartment. My daily ritual of brewing tea upstairs and walking down to open the bookstore. I'm surprised to feel something like homesickness spread through me at the thought and force it down. If I don't stay firmly rooted in the present, I'm worried I won't have the strength to make it back there.

Nothing about my childhood room has changed. There's the ancient four-poster bed with no curtains. The heavy desk made of some dark wood. An imposing wardrobe in a similar style. The soft blue linens I picked out as a young teenager are the newest thing in the room and at odds with the heaviness of the furniture.

The curtains are thrown open, allowing sunlight to stream through. Have they been that way since I left, or has Gabriel just opened them? I set my bag down at the foot of the bed and go to the window. With my back to Gabriel, at least I don't have to fight my expression into something neutral.

"Have dinner with the family tonight," Gabriel says from the doorway.

I turn the ring on my little finger once, twice. I look down at the stretch of land I can see from my window. Is Avitue out there? Does she see me?

"I don't have much of an appetite," I lie.

If this is the only thing I'm safe to openly refuse, I will refuse it. I'm very hungry, especially for something other than hard bread, flavorless potatoes, and colorless vegetables—foods that, Gabriel says, force one to turn inward and strengthen the spirit. However, all I can see it as is a punishment for leaving, for being a less than obedient daughter. Gabriel has me back, and she will make me regret leaving, make me believe that comfort has made me soft.

If I am soft, I'm not worthy—of my sword, of my name, of my identity.

I only know Gabriel is gone because of the click of her heels retreating down the hall. Briefly, I wonder whether this is what Gabriel wanted. To put me in a place where I would deny myself something I need. To manipulate me into making myself weak.

Eventually, the house is quiet again. I press a hand to the window, look for a slip of black amid the autumn leaves.

<hr>

It's been dark for hours when I decide it's time to leave.

I've seen none of my family the rest of the day. Not even Zuriel. If a family dinner did happen, it was managed in utter silence.

It's as if the house has been emptied.

I slip into the dark hallway and trace my fingers along the wall, counting each doorway I pass until I come to Zuriel's. It's closed but not latched. I push it open.

A single candle lights the room. Zuriel sits in front of her mirrorless vanity, bow in hand. She lifts her head when I enter.

"She wants us ready for tonight. Won't say for what," Zuriel whispers.

"Of course."

Zuriel stands. "Keep her close."

I squeeze her hand. "I want you to come with us. When we leave."

Zuriel nods. I force myself to let my sister go. Hopefully, not for the last time.

<hr>

Avitue waits for me at the gazebo, and this time, I sense other demons lurking at the edge of my awareness. I've left my sword behind in service of maintaining our lie and barely stop my hand from instinctively going for the absent weapon at my hip.

I need to warn Avitue about Gabriel. We need to be careful. I didn't expect our audience.

As I approach, Avitue gives the barest shake of her head, a warning not to say anything that would give us away. I can't say that I already know.

When Avitue detaches herself from the deep shadows, the concern on her face alone might give us away. Hunger seems to have etched itself deeper into the lines of her, become an immutable quality of her. She walks with hunger, sees with hunger. The pressure of it beckons me closer. I know this isn't conscious on Avitue's part, know that this is distinct from her aura. Sometimes, the body acts apart from the self to survive.

We meet on the frosted leaves. Part of me can't help but note how inadequately Avitue is dressed for the weather, how impractical her heels and soft leather jacket seem for what we need to do. Not that clothes or cold could faze her—and she won't be in her body long anyway. My breath leaves visible puffs on the air. Avitue isn't breathing at all. She takes both my hands in hers, and the tenderness in the gesture spikes worry. The other demons will know, won't they?

Avitue draws me down to the frozen ground, and soon, I understand why.

One moment, I am myself—one consciousness in the only body I've ever known. The next moment, the world's tilted on its side and I'm staring into Avitue's empty eyes. I try to move and realize I've fallen into the grass. I push myself back to sitting and take in the full reality of Avitue's lifeless sprawl. The sight confuses me.

Then, there's something like an incorporeal tap on my shoulder, much like how Avitue had signaled her presence in the woods. *Over here*, comes Avitue's voice, and it feels as normal as one of my own thoughts. *Well, not over so much as in. Ha.* Avitue sighs, seems to stretch out within my body, and some of the tension I sensed in her before eases. *Easier not to be alone in my body when I'm feeling like this*, Avitue says.

My body stands up without me, and it's not a *bad* feeling, just odd. I let Avitue move, not wanting to interrupt her and risk something unpleasant. *Belial will think I'm vain, but...* Avitue easily lifts her own body—suddenly and conspicuously cool to the touch—and carries it over to the gazebo. I wonder at my sudden strength. I've seen possessed people exhibit inhuman strength, but I know my own abilities, and I'm not sure whether it will stop being strange to witness my own body leisurely doing things I'd struggle to otherwise. As Avitue props her body upright against one of the gazebo's wooden posts, I realize why her body feels so unusually cold. The heat has followed Avitue's spirit and is with me now, warding off the autumn chill. For once, I don't feel the cold at all.

Lead the way, Avitue says, and it's as if she's handed over the metaphorical steering wheel to me and moved back. I need to reacquaint myself with my own limbs for a moment, and then, stiffly, I turn us back toward the estate. The demonic presence I sensed fades, as if they were only waiting to see whether Avitue could do what she claimed she could.

I imagine a bubble of protective light into being around the part of me that is Avitue, and we pass through the wards without so much as a glimmer of warning, Cassiel orbiting to shield us.

A prickle of emotion ripples through me, too quick to identify. I belatedly understand that it's Avitue's and not my own.

Remember when I said Gabriel wants to use me to catch you? I say, pulling the old doors shut above us. I expect to be plunged into complete darkness, but having Avitue with me alters my vision. It's not necessarily brighter, but I simply know the boundaries of the space around us.

Yes, says Avitue, her wariness winding through me.

She has plans tonight as well. I don't think she knows any specifics, but she's hoping that letting me think I'm safe will reveal something.

I feel rather than hear Avitue's grumble. *And what's your plan when we encounter her?*

I hesitate. *Gabriel doesn't know that I can access my wings. Is there anything . . . unharmful that you could do to buy us time?*

I could try sleep paralysis? But that'd be a single-use trick. If they're on guard, it won't work, so we'll have to be sure about when.

How long would it last?

If I'm not around to maintain the effect? They'll fight it off, and we'll have a minute at best.

Not good odds. Both of us think it, and neither of us says it.

And the demons? I ask.

They love the sword—by which I mean it creeps them out but they're glad to have it. Definitely redeemed myself with that one. Got them a way in where there wasn't one before.

And the eating-my-soul thing?

Once I get the relics, I'll have leverage. It's not uncommon for a demon to be permitted to claim a soul for themselves as a reward. If I want to wait until your natural death, that's my business.

My natural death. Avitue's easy explanation nearly triggers an existential crisis on the spot. It bothers me that she has to consider it this way, that my death is some inevitable loophole within whatever infernal code demons order their actions by. It taints whatever future discussion we need to have about immortality and what each of us wants from this relationship we've fallen into—if we both survive tonight.

Your bubble doesn't shield me from your doomsday thoughts, you know, says Avitue, attempting and failing at her usual levity. When I say nothing, she continues, *I have no intention of getting us exorcised or worse. We're both getting out of this, and I promise we'll talk about this then, yeah? When we're safe. For now, compartmentalize. It's what's kept me alive since whenever BCE. Trust me. It works.*

We're at the basement door that leads into the house proper. I find my breath again, squash all my doomsday thoughts into a dark corner, and move us forward.

The small archive is on the first floor. The keypad lock is shiny and new in contrast to the original wooden door. It beeps with each keypress, a small sound that's unbearably loud in the still darkness. I listen for the mechanical whir of the lock sliding free and open the door just enough to slip inside before closing it behind us.

Flipping on the lights reveals floor-to-ceiling shelves lining each wall. A long table and a case of scrolls dominate the center of the room. I retrieve the third of the four scrolls and spread it flat on the table, revealing detailed, to-scale illustrations of a rapier, a bow, and an ax.

At my touch, blue script shimmers to life around each illustration, every block of text tied to lines that indicate a single angelic rune inscribed into one of the relics.

That much Old English to translate one rune? I forgot how verbose angels are, Avitue says, tracing my hand over the illustrations. Judging. Estimating. Imagining.

A bow appears atop its illustrated version. Avitue adjusts some of the flourishes with a flick of her hand before moving on to the ax and, finally, the rapier. These replicas are just as impressive as the sword. *Just enough angelic aesthetic to fool whoever wants to inspect them closer and knows what they ought to look for*, says Avitue. *Your turn.*

I lay down the same series of blessings as I bestowed on the sword, and when I'm done, Avitue glances around at the shelves. *Anything here that could pass as a tome?*

If there could be a haven at the estate, this small family archive is the nearest thing for me. Out of all my siblings, I was the only one who spent any voluntary time here, often lingering after my studies to read things that hadn't been assigned to me. I'd spent a particularly boring summer in my teens entertaining myself by cataloging and reshelving everything we had. I'm thankful for that work now.

I know the perfect thing, I say, approaching the wall of shelves opposite the door.

Penned by a forgotten woman mystic in the Middle Ages, the book I select is actually one of my favorites. Its details on occult and ethereal subjects are correct a small fraction of the time, impressive for anything written by a human but not anything that demons wouldn't expect nephilim to know. Collected by a previous family head more for the sake of preserving the history of demonology than for any enlightenment it might provide, it's not dangerous in the wrong hands. Still, I'm hesitant to part with the nameless woman's book. Already so lost to history, this work could be the last remaining proof of her life and work.

Can you make a copy of this? I ask.

Avitue makes a thoughtful noise. *Books are complicated. I could replicate the material of it, but the text would need to be copied down page by page.*

No time, then, I think, attempting to make peace with handing such a treasure over to people who won't appreciate it. I smooth a hand over a vellum page and feel wrong even handling the book without gloves.

Before I can get too attached, I place the book in my bag, set the room back as I found it, and return to the hall with the trio of weapons—the bow slung over my shoulder and the rapier and ax in either hand.

I half expect one of the locked doors to suddenly open as I pass. They do not. The house remains eerily silent, even for the Gotwenn estate. The ground itself is holding its breath, and my own comes shallow. I grip each weapon in my hands as if I might use them if startled. Avitue is quiet as well. Even she is past the point of witty quips.

In the basement, I expect Gabriel around every corner. Each time, we meet only more candlelit gloom. We are back to my chosen exit corridor when Avitue speaks.

It's no good that your people've waited this long. Belial will be just into the trees. I don't want an all-out fight.

That's not what Gabriel wants either. She doesn't care about the demons at all, not anymore. She cares about me and what my choices mean for her.

She's the same as every other insecure power-grabbing duke in Hell, sounds like, says Avitue. *Do you really not want me to go one step above 'unharmful'?*

I've already done enough to get me disowned. I don't elaborate on what that would mean for me. Don't want to think about what will happen when news of what I've done spreads beyond my immediate family. *Compartmentalize,* Avitue said.

Look, I can ditch my body, says Avitue. *If it comes down to it, can you fly us out?*

But then everyone will know, Avitue! Everyone will know about us.

Nausea threatens to sweep through me. The ax and rapier are sweaty in my grip.

Avitue pushes me out of the way, and just like that, the physicality of my panic vanishes.

Find your wings and concentrate on that, says Avitue. She breathes for me, deep cleansing breaths. Wills my heart back into a resting rhythm. *We'll make it out of this. I promise you.*

Avitue reaches up for the door, and I feel the rough, weather-worn wood against my palm.

We emerge into crisp moonlight.

A demon looms at the tree line. Even in the dark, I can see their soot-streaked coat, the scorched hem of it. Hair sticks up from their head like a cursed doll. Avitue strides my body toward them with a confident swagger I don't feel. We pass through the final line of wards, and I let the protective bubble around Avitue fall.

"Got the goods," Avitue calls out, twirling the ax and rapier in my hands with a flourish. It's truly Avitue's voice that comes out of my body, though it feels disconnected from my lungs and throat and tongue. More a projection than regular corporeal speech.

The demon steps forward and with them comes the pungent odor of sulfur. This must be the demon who appeared in my apartment days ago and threatened Avitue. Grotesque boils dot their skin. I'm thankful that Avitue is in control. I've never stood so casually near a demon like this, and my impulse is to skewer them with the rapier.

Instead, Avitue hands the book and all three weapons over into the demon's waiting hands. They hold the book under one arm and immediately wrap the false relics in a length of grubby cloth.

"Disturbing stuff," they mutter as they bundle the weapons out of sight. Their voice is hoarse as if from decades of smoke. "I hate to say it, especially to you, but they'll be pleased with your work."

Avitue dips into a mocking bow. "I'm going back for my body. Don't wait up."

A hole opens amid the shadows. "Not to worry. Didn't plan on it," the demon says before vanishing into the void.

The air immediately feels clearer, less oppressive. I think for a moment that I might sigh in relief—and turn to find Zuriel's bow trained on me. Michael and Haniel, my brothers, step up from behind Zuriel, and suddenly there's a point of cold steel pressed warningly into my back. The true rapier. Gabriel. I freeze.

Zuriel steps forward, bow still drawn. She's only a few paces away, and Zuriel has never needed to be this close to hit her mark. My brothers move with her, eager for a hunt that will surely not last long.

Are you sure *about Zuriel being on your side?* Avitue asks.

Yes.

"In need of an exorcism, it looks like," Gabriel says from behind us, and I wish, for once, that I could see my mother's face. "What is your name, demon?"

"Belial," Avitue supplies.

The tip of the sword presses. "Is that true?" Gabriel asks. "If you lie—and my daughter will know if you do—I'll make sure you lose your vessel."

Fury blazes through me first—Avitue's emotion. My own muted response chases it like ice water. Too slowly, I realize, *I'm* the vessel. My mother would threaten to maim me—kill me?—just to antagonize a demon.

Gabriel has threatened many things during my life, but her approach has always been subtle and never anything so violent as what she suggests now. Even from Gabriel, this feels like a betrayal, and I struggle to process it even as my mother holds me at sword point. Avitue's retort builds like acid in my throat.

Thankfully, Zuriel's answer is quick, her eyes bright with truth-sight. "The demon speaks truth," she lies.

"Then that means you must have a reason to care for this body. You haven't destroyed the soul inside, so you must care for it as well." A pause. Gabriel is waiting for something. A confirmation of some kind. I stay quiet, couldn't speak if I wanted, but Zuriel's carefully blank expression falls. A truth-seer caught by her own lie.

A lie that reveals a greater truth.

Gabriel continues. "Tell me how a demon makes traitors of two daughters."

At that, radiance spears through the air near my ear, and there's a choked sound behind me. I whirl to see Gabriel clutching the shoulder of her sword arm, an arrow of light pierced through the flesh. She stumbles back but doesn't completely lose her footing. Pain and rage twist her features. She clenches the hilt of her rapier but can't push through the shock of Zuriel's ethereal arrow enough to wield it.

"I am the family head," she manages through clenched teeth. "The consequences of rebellion are—"

Zuriel summons another bright arrow to her bow as Haniel and Michael turn on her, and that's when Avitue claps my hands together. Infused with her will, the sound reverberates, louder than such a simple gesture should be. Apart from Zuriel and me, everyone falls limp to the grass. Zuriel, bow still drawn, trains her arrow on one neutralized target, then another, disbelieving.

I find my voice. "Follow us!" I call, running for where Avitue left her body.

We find it unmoved and unharmed. If time weren't against us, I might be more disturbed by the fact that Avitue hadn't closed her body's eyes before we left. I kneel beside the empty vessel and wrap one arm around the railing of the gazebo, bracing myself for Avitue's departure. I know I'm alone because the cold closes in, because the world is darker. Avitue is on her feet too quickly, has suddenly manifested wings, while I'm still dizzy and doubled over from the loss of her. She bends to offer a hand to me. I grasp it, and for a moment, there is only this warm point of contact and the intensity of Avitue's gaze, golden and feline and lovely.

I barely have to think and my wings are unfurling into Avitue's aura of warmth, a blossom of light.

We turn to find Zuriel hanging back, staring at us. I drop Avitue's hand and go to her. "Fly with us," I say.

"You know I can't make wings," Zuriel says, casting a glance back over her shoulder.

"But you're my sister, and I love you," I say, drawing her into a hug. "That's all you need to make wings."

Zuriel cautiously settles her arms around me, returning the embrace. It's awkward but sincere. We've never had much space to give or receive physical affection, have known it only in the form Gabriel bestowed and so had grown wary of it. This is different—an open way forward instead of a looming trap.

An undefined bloom of light gathers at Zuriel's back, forming a silhouette of wings before finding its individual feathers. Zuriel shakes them out as if they've been gathering dust while they waited for her in ethereal space.

"It feels . . ." Zuriel starts.

"Like you've always had them?" I suggest.

Avitue appears at my shoulder. "They've woken up."

The moment breaks.

Under the open night, we lift into the sky. The estate turns small below us. Zuriel doesn't look back. I do, and I think it might be out of a desire to see it minimized, for the trees to cover it all and render it harmless, featureless.

Of the three of us, Avitue is most at ease in the air. When it becomes apparent we won't be pursued, at least not this night, she banks toward the city, spreading her wings to coast on the currents with the confidence of one who has never feared falling. She loops back to me, a graceful black arc among the stars, before surging forward again, charting our path. She does this a couple times, falling back to circle Zuriel and me before moving confidently ahead. If I knew her less, if we'd made this flight under less urgent conditions, I might think she was showing off, but each time she moves back to us, it feels as if she's drawing a circle of protection.

Her distance also grants Zuriel and me privacy to talk, should we want it.

"I've left everything," Zuriel says, just enough to be heard over the wind. "We're really not going back."

The city comes into view in the distance, a starry spread of tiny lights.

"We're not," I say. It's a promise.

Zuriel shivers and wraps her arms around herself. "In all my daydreams about flying, I never imagined it'd be so cold."

We lapse into silence for a while before I say, "I'm glad you're here."

My sister smiles at me, and it's a genuine and precious thing.

The high of our escape and first flight gives way to fatigue by the time we're over the city. Not even Avitue is immune. I don't miss the uncharacteristic gracelessness in her landing, the way she stumbles in her heels. I can no longer feel my face by the time we alight on the rooftop of some luxury apartment building in New Eastside. We're so close to Lake Michigan that I can see the choppy water in the dark, think dazedly that I might fall into it with the way the wind pushes at my back.

"Why are we here?" Zuriel asks.

A sensible question. I try to catch up. I'm thoroughly fatigued—physically, mentally, spiritually. As long as we're far from Gabriel and I can rest soon, I think I can be happy with wherever we've ended up.

"My place has more room than Cassiel's, and Gabriel won't know where to find you, at least for now," Avitue says. "You're welcome to the guest suite, Zuriel."

I find myself stuck on the basic fact that Avitue, apparently, has an apartment in the city. Some luxury penthouse thing she's never thought to mention. And that she's inviting us to stay the night.

There's a pool on the rooftop. Of course there's a pool—very fancy, no doubt—though it appears closed for the season. Avitue walks by it without a glance and holds a door open for us.

"Rest and talk tomorrow?" she offers.

Zuriel stretches her arms above her head and dismisses her wings, moving to the door with a grateful sigh. "Sounds lovely." She yawns, seemingly too tired to question the reality of demons owning perfectly normal, if terribly expensive, apartments.

Avitue meets my gaze, and for a moment, it's just the two of us. Just the tension in Avitue's stance, the hunger in her eyes. I kiss her as if she's a fragile thing—and she might be. How weak has this ordeal made her?

"We should—" I start.

"Later," says Avitue, though by the gleam in her eyes, the kiss has only made her hungrier. There's a flash of lengthened fangs when she speaks, as if her body is slowly giving up its illusion of humanity to conserve what little energy she has left. "I want you to rest first."

Thirteen

T HE ANGEL IS SHAPELESS, an undefined haze, like light through clouds, when they first appear to me in the clear expanse. This place isn't white, but it is clear. Yes. That's what my mind settles on. There's no air. Or at least there's no wind, and I don't need to breathe.

An eye blinks open, followed by several others. All are different sizes and colors and shapes. Some aren't human. I think I spy a horizontal pupil. Another is vertical and sharp, and I think of Avitue, think of reaching for her in sleep, but there's only me and the angel and the clear expanse.

The sharp-pupiled eye moves forward and looks down on me as if understanding that I favor it. This is the one I make eye contact with when the angel speaks.

I would see you move forward without fear, they say.

I have the fleeting realization that this is the angelic tongue. I can understand it in full as a language, see how all its pieces fit together. Only memorized fragments and names have been passed down to us, things I could recite without knowing where one word began and another ended. This sudden knowledge of the whole is a gift not to all nephilim but to me and me alone. A blessing.

Three pairs of radiant wings unfold from the ether, spanning the width of the infinite expanse. Their light sears my eyes, and I hold an arm up to shield my face. There's the fleeting urge to fall to my knees in deference, but the physics of the space don't allow for static concepts like gravity, like up or down.

Keep only the bonds that free you.

The ethereal light of the angel's wings washes over me like a cleansing tide, and I think its radiance might cling to me forever. I'm renewed in a way I'd never gain from food or rest, another smaller blessing.

When the light subsides, the vision settles me gently into my body, bearing my soul back to earth on a warm breeze. The first thing I feel is the weight and heat of Avitue's arm across my middle and silky sheets against my bare skin.

Avitue's bedroom is far from dark. The wall of glass opposite the bed welcomes in the glitter of city lights, and I think I can see the indigo line where water meets sky.

Dawn will arrive soon. I want to meet it.

Avitue sleeps heavily for an immortal being who doesn't need sleep, and I slip carefully from her grasp without her stirring. The room itself feels vast and empty, and I shiver when my feet touch the polished concrete floor. The only furniture is the bed and its side tables. Above that, an ornate gilded frame dominates the length of the wall, holding what looks like some original Renaissance-era painting I've never seen before. Something featuring two winged beings in an ambiguous tangle of limbs. It's a bold look amid the stark minimalism of the rest of the room, but Avitue is nothing if not bold.

I reach for one of the silky black robes hanging on the back of the bedroom door and startle when I see my right hand. My palm glows with the energy of an angelic sigil. My namesake's. Propped in the corner by the door, my falcata gleams faintly, safe in its scabbard. My tome is with it. I stare between the mark and the sword, close my fingers over the sigil, and whisper my thanks.

Before meeting Avitue, I was never visited by an angel or granted a vision. Even for nephilim, such encounters are rare. For this to happen to me now is the confirmation I needed.

My family's will—Gabriel's will—is not necessarily the angels' will. Even for us, some things remain unknowable.

I slip on the robe to find the garment is very short and composed mostly of lace panels, providing only the most essential coverage to be decent in front of company. Not that I'd want to wear this in front of anyone but Avitue. It's closer to lingerie than anything practical.

Out on the balcony, I'm immediately reminded of the season. Especially at dawn, the air is much too cold for a robe so thin, but for a vision of the sunrise, I brave it. My own clothes are in desperate need of a wash, and I don't think I could bear to don them again anyway. They seem so tied to memories I want to distance myself from as soon as possible.

I brace my forearms against the railing and wait, eyes trained on the water. Eventually, traffic picks up below, people hurrying to morning shifts all over the city. The horizon is violet, pink, orange. The first rays of sun don't warm me, but that's okay. I can't feel my fingertips or my toes, but that's okay. I smile and find that my lips tremble. Tears track down my cheeks, and it's not from the wind or the cold. My chest is a tangle of emotions, and I don't have the energy to hold them up to the light, straighten them out, and identify them. Not now. So I let myself feel, let them wash over me like the vision of light. And if I choke on a sob, that's fine. And if I wail, that's fine.

The balcony door slides open behind me, but I don't turn. Avitue presses herself to my back, and when we touch, her skin is the comforting heat of fire against my chilled body. She nuzzles sleepily into the crook of my neck, circles her arms around me, and breathes against my skin. I sniff and relax into the scent of smoke.

She wordlessly coaxes me back to bed—a warm hand finding my cold ones, bodies twining together for support, a tangle of limbs stumbling to the door. It's certainly daylight. We could stay up. We don't. Avitue curls against me and sets her breathing to a human pace. I think of everything I could say. I realize, again and again, that I'm in love and haven't gotten to properly say so to the object of that love.

I roll over to face Avitue, and despite her sharp teeth, her smile is soft. She props herself up on one arm, attentive to what she senses I'm about to say.

A voice carries from the adjacent room. It's not my sister's. It's not human at all.

Only a possessed human could speak this language.

The mere sound of it here, in this place that should be a refuge, feels unreal. My instincts scream at me to react. I reach for Avitue, judging how quickly I could take up my sword.

"We're fine," Avitue whispers, hands calm and steady on my shoulders. "We're fine. They're not here. It's just a message and nothing bad."

I struggle to understand this even as Avitue casually goes to the door and shrugs on the second robe.

"You're safe," she says. "They just want to talk. I'll tell you after." And she's gone.

I pad to the door and listen through it for the conversation in the living room. The demon speaks again, the sound hollow as if through stone. The speaker's smoky rasp lacks intimidation, their cadence a strikingly familiar music. Avitue must pause to think for a moment before responding in kind. I've only ever heard her speak Hell's language in frustrated whispers under her breath, and in hearing her full, clear sentences, I'm drawn to the rhythm and depth of it. A dialect of angel song, I realize, the two languages separated by war. I can almost feel the sounds in my mouth, can nearly grasp the meaning before a syllable takes an unexpected detour. I want to hear more, would happily listen to Avitue say anything. Could she teach me? Their exchange is short, and at the end, Avitue returns to me with something in her hand. She draws me back into bed and holds it up.

"Got your book back," she says and extends it to me.

I take it and stare at the cover. "The mystic's treatise?" I let it fall open, disbelieving. Disturbing the pages reveals that it's picked up a peculiar scent. Iron and burnt hair and a ghost of sulfur. I wrinkle my nose and hope the smell won't stick.

"They said good job but that if this was all you had not to bother with delivering any others," says Avitue.

"Oh." I'm back to smoothing my hand over the cover.

"And . . ." Avitue says with a tone that makes me look up.

I hug the book to my chest, and Avitue closes the space between us. "I've officially been granted claim of one nephilim soul," she says, placing a chaste kiss on my lips. "Though there's a little blood pact we'll need to make it official."

So it's real. Though it's what we planned, it seemed like one of those crossroads that would forever loom in the distance.

"A blood pact?" I echo.

"It's no more blood than I've taken from you before. This time we get a fancy ritual circle. And I promise I'll make it sexy, as all the best rituals are."

I'm about to ask more questions when I hear the distinct sound of water running.

"That'd be your sister in the kitchen," Avitue says, sauntering off to greet her wearing nothing but the lacy robe.

I look fretfully back to the bedroom, retie my own robe, and hurry after her. Zuriel is standing in Avitue's sinfully sleek kitchen—all marble and steel and hard edges—when she turns to us, glass of water in hand. She blinks, chokes down her water, and clears her throat.

Avitue seems to enjoy the reaction and slides easily onto one of the barstools on the other side of the counter. "Sleep well?" she asks.

I keep my eyes down, pulling at the sleeves and hem of the robe. I hover awkwardly beside Avitue, unconvinced that I could sit in any way that would be decent.

Zuriel adjusts her bow sling, and that's the first time I realize she's wearing it. Her right hand doesn't leave it, as if she's worried the apartment air might swallow the bow whole. "Heaviest sleep I've had in a while," she answers, having smoothed over her expression. She turns the glass in her hands as if she can knead it into a different shape. "I need to talk to Cassiel alone."

"Ooh, secret angel stuff, is it?" says Avitue.

Zuriel sets the glass down hard, chipping it against the marble countertop. I startle at the noise, and Avitue rests a steadying hand against the small of my back. Zuriel's attention flicks to the gesture and away just as fast.

She releases the glass as if startled by her own strength. "I'm sorry," she says, her smile strained.

We all stare at the web of cracks in the base, the splintered crystal shards. Avitue waves a hand, dismissing the trouble, and the glass heals itself. Zuriel steps back as if more nefarious energy is at work.

Avitue's expression falls, all trace of her lighthearted teasing evaporating when she sees how deeply Zuriel's discomfort runs.

Hours ago, we escaped Gabriel's grasp together. We left behind our family, our home. To me, that alone had meant so much. But now, after time to think, it's obviously not settling for Zuriel the same way. Did her namesake also appear to her, or did something else put her on edge?

"I'll leave you two to catch up," Avitue says, "but you should probably go back to the guest suite in case Azazel wants to talk again." She nods to the horned statue in the middle of her fashionably sparse living room.

Zuriel immediately looks on guard. "It's a portal?" she asks warily.

"More like a phone."

Zuriel's unease persists. She stares at the statue warily. "A conduit for evil spirits," she mutters, thinking aloud. She's so focused on how she could've missed a hellish aura that she doesn't notice how Avitue's mouth twists, her patience suddenly thin. Zuriel continues, "Last night, I didn't even notice it was there, and I can't sense anything now."

Time with Avitue has calmed my response to her energy, but the statue feels different. I don't think it was made by her or any demon. I watch it over my shoulder as if it will tell me its history.

Avitue drums her claws into the marble countertop, chipping obliviously away at the stone. "Maybe you know less about us than you think," she says.

She's hurt by the assumption under Zuriel's statement, the same one I had when we met, the reason I couldn't figure out why the circle didn't work. Avitue might call herself evil, holding up the ancient judgment as a shield, but it's different when someone else prods the wound. She's a spirit of contradictions, and she's had a long time to develop them.

Zuriel watches Avitue's harmless destruction of the countertop as if it's a sign. "Cass, go put clothes on. We're going out," she declares, leaving no room for protest.

In the shiny elevator, I feel shabby in my wrinkled clothes. Everyone eyes us with either questions or judgment as they board in their expensive suits and designer dresses. Even the most casual outfit probably costs more than I make in a month. Avitue offered new clothes to us, but Zuriel firmly declined and pulled me into the elevator as if we were escaping imminent disaster. No one stares for long though. Zuriel stands with her feet planted and her arms crossed, exuding the energy of a bodyguard who's not to be messed with.

"What's wrong?" I hiss when the door opens into the lobby.

The tired security guard stationed near the reception desk—a block of imposing polished stone—startles to life when he sees Zuriel's bow.

"Ma'am," he barks.

Zuriel turns for a fight before relaxing when she meets the gaze of a wide-eyed receptionist. The security guard is on us in a few swift steps.

"You can't have a weapon—" he starts, but Zuriel's hand is pressed to his chest before he can knock her away. Their eyes lock in a metaphysical exchange, and seconds later, he backs down with a nod. The receptionist's gaze darts from the charmed guard to me and Zuriel, who wears her most practiced dealing-with-humans smile. I'm chilled as she reaches out to the receptionist for a handshake, and the woman, despite her trepidation, is compelled to clasp her hand. The same silent exchange passes between them. I've seen Gabriel do this a dozen times, telling people what they have and haven't seen, what they are and aren't allowed.

"I didn't know you could do that," I say to her, glancing over my shoulder at the receptionist and guard, both back to looking bored by their jobs.

"Gabriel taught me while you were gone," says Zuriel. "Don't judge me. Your girlfriend does the same. I want to keep my bow on me. There's no way I'm leaving it behind in that creepy apartment." She looks me up and down, her annoyance building. "I see you continue to abandon your *ancient, angel-fated relic*."

I ignore the jab. She's anxious. Scared. The world is new to her, and I know what that feels like.

A fountain thunders in the center of the room, providing the cover of white noise. Zuriel glares at it disapprovingly but falls wearily onto a nearby couch, low and square in design like the furniture in Avitue's living room. I remain standing, staring up at the silver tiles that comprise the chandelier as I count down my frustration.

Of course the real Zuriel doesn't live up to my daydreams of us out in the world together. Gabriel's rules are all she's known, and if it took me years to begin dismantling them, I can't expect her to be where I am literally overnight. She's stressed. So much change at once, and the only way we've been taught to handle stress is to train harder, to atone for our failures, and to smite our enemies before they can hurt us. None of that helped me out here. Atonement only pushed me back toward Gabriel, toward shame and fear.

"I can't believe this is happening," Zuriel says, her true emotions finally bleeding through. She sounds thoroughly overwhelmed, as if she wants to curl into a ball. I've never witnessed her like this. "The memories were one thing but seeing her up close in the daylight— She's so real."

"Avitue?" I say, trying to understand Zuriel's distress.

"You just let her touch you like she's normal."

"She is—well, she's . . . It's normal if you like someone," I say.

Zuriel squeezes her eyes shut and pinches the bridge of her nose. "Oh no," she groans.

"I'm going to be okay," I try to reassure her. "Avitue's kind. You'll see."

"I don't want to leave you alone with her."

"You have to trust me. And trust her. She helped us escape Gabriel last night. If she wanted to betray us, there were a thousand times she could've done it by now. Why would she drag this out?"

Zuriel opens her eyes again, freezing me with a disbelieving stare. "She's waiting to forge a pact for your soul. That's what I'm scared of."

I drop my gaze. I'm not *not* scared, but it's for a different reason than Zuriel is. I squeeze my marked hand into a fist and press it over my heart. I could tell Zuriel about the dream, but I don't. I shouldn't have to. It's sacred and mine. I want to keep it to myself for a little longer.

"You're not actually going to go through with it," Zuriel says when I stay quiet. "You were just saying that before. You wouldn't give up— Cass, look at me. Please."

I do, but Zuriel doesn't like what she finds in my eyes.

"No," says Zuriel, the word thick with emotion. "No, I'm not losing you like this. I'm here now, Cass. You're not alone. You don't have to do this."

"I'm not going to stop being your sister," I try to reassure her.

She stands, gripping my shoulders as if she can push her will into me the way she did with the guard and receptionist. "You're not the kind of person who gives their soul to a demon."

Again, her words hurt me. "Well, maybe I am. And maybe I want to."

Zuriel won't give up. "I understand wanting to live in the daylight. I understand wanting your store. I even understand giving up this forever war. But I don't know why you want her or even trust her."

"You trusted her to get us here," I say.

"Because for once I wanted to be on your side!" she says, exasperated. "You always look at me like I wanted to hurt you by staying with Gabriel. I was scared, Cass. I don't want to fall."

"Do you still think I'm falling?" I ask, meeting her gaze, holding my breath.

The fountain crashes behind me. Zuriel lets me go. "When you left me to go meet Avitue last night, all I could think about was how scared I was for us."

"I was scared, too, when I left," I say. "I gave up being a hunter because that choice felt right, but you don't have to. If it's your calling, you can follow it without Gabriel. And once you get used to it, it is better out here. And you wouldn't be alone."

"I'm sorry I ever abandoned you," Zuriel says, pulling me into a genuine hug. I hope we'll have more.

Finally, I relax.

My sister casts her eyes down. "I'm sorry I chose Gabriel."

I squeeze her tight. I can't swallow the lump in my throat. "We can build what we want now," I say.

Zuriel's eyes shine with tears when we break apart. She blinks them back, and I want to tell her it's okay to cry now, that it's good, but she speaks before I can. "I was thinking I might see your friend Ana. The one who can see the future? Maybe a reading from her would help me figure out what to do, where to start."

"I've been friends with Ana long enough to know that she'd be hesitant to say she can *see* the future, but she does give good advice. She's kind and supportive." I think. "I need to thank her too."

"I can let her know you're okay in the meantime, until you see her—or maybe get another phone."

"I don't have a phone anymore, do I?"

Zuriel grimaces. "I searched before I left, but I don't know where Gabriel put it."

"I'll need to head over to the store today. I'm sure I have a tower of boxes waiting for me. Meet me there later? Ana's is the coffee shop called Witch's Brew just across from my store."

I hug Zuriel again before she departs, and already we're becoming more comfortable with affection. The embrace is less awkward than when I helped her find her wings, grounded in the knowledge that we no longer have to hide, no longer need to hold back.

I turn for the elevator only after Zuriel passes through the glass doors and disappears down the sidewalk. I hope her reading goes well. I was never brave enough for one. Now that I'm no longer hiding, maybe I could face whatever the cards illuminate.

Avitue is staring up at the statue of the horned woman when I return. An imagined breeze catches the statue's long straight hair, but other than that, many of the features are eerily familiar to me now. The knowing smirk. The sharp cheekbones. She wears a gauzy robe that demonstrates the sculptor's expert craft with suggesting airiness through stone. I follow the line of the wind through the fabric, drawing my gaze back up the column of her body, lingering on her curves, the way the fabric drapes over her nipples. Her horns are unbroken, unscarred. She looks like a neoclassical Egyptian goddess, as if she too could hold the sun between her horns.

When I step up beside Avitue, she says, "You're making me jealous." She teases, but the lines on her face are tired, sad. I walked in on her remembering a past life. "How do I get you to look at me so unabashedly?"

The sun rises behind the statue, bright through the glass wall. Maybe the placement is just right that the horns do catch the sun for a few minutes in the afternoon.

"I'm learning," I say, keeping the real Avitue in my peripheral vision as I step back to admire the statue at a distance. "It's scary to see someone that way."

Avitue looks back to the statue, its mostly human representation of her but for the horns. "I never told the sculptor what I was, but I didn't completely hide myself either. I think she knew to some degree. Not about the horns, but it's like she could see what I desired, how I wished I'd never ruined them. I was her patron for years. She'd carve these grotesque, twisted figures from myth. I loved what she revealed in the marble, characters ruined by their stories but still beautiful because she saw them that way. And then, one night, she started work on a project she wouldn't let me see. This one. A gift."

"You told Zuriel it was a phone," I say, struggling to connect all the pieces.

A smile twitches Avitue's lips. "Sometimes, when Beelzebub or some other asshole sent me on a quest halfway across the world, I'd still find ways to talk to her. Sometimes it was through dreams. When she was working in the studio, I channeled myself into my likeness. It started out as a fun trick, but I think it changed something about the nature of the statue. Other demons discovered the stone. I had to remove it for her safety. Kept it ever since, and having it here means the others are less likely to put in the effort of a full manifestation when they can speak through an already-open portal."

"What was her name?" I ask.

"Phoebe."

The name closes the door on the past. Avitue turns her back to the statue, and I file the story away. I wonder what other mementos she's kept from her previous lives. The apartment is so empty, a hollowed gallery.

I wait for Avitue to ask about Zuriel, but she doesn't, allowing us our private moment. I trace the edge of the kitchen counter with my finger, unsure of what comes next. The world has opened up to us. We've saved each other. I feel free. Even more so than when I left home to start my bookstore. This time, I know it's for real.

With Zuriel gone, Avitue relaxes her careful control over her aura, turning sharper by degrees.

"You should feed," I say softly.

It feels like a euphemism. Maybe it is. I'm still not used to squarely facing what Avitue's need means for me, for us. With time, I hope that it'll feel like less of an event in my mind. I trust Avitue. After everything we've just endured, how could I not? Still, I have nerves.

Avitue looks as if she wants to devour me on the spot, but instead, she says, "And you should eat something first."

Her sleek refrigerator is empty. Of course it is. Almost everything about the apartment is pretense, an attempt at playing human. I suppose I've played human in my own ways.

I'm turning to inform Avitue that I'll need to go out for something only to find her proffering a flawless apple, her claws black points against its red skin. I might've laughed, but in the next moment, I find myself tenderly snared in Avitue's aura. My focus on the apple sharpens. Suddenly, it's the most enticing food I've ever encountered. Impossibly red. I imagine breaking the skin of it with my teeth, the sweetness within, its juice dripping down my chin.

"Don't just desire. Indulge," Avitue prompts.

I step into her space, and she encircles my waist with an arm, drawing us together. She holds the apple to my lips, her eyes bright with anticipation. I open my mouth obediently, and the fruit is even sweeter than I imagined. A delighted moan escapes me. Unselfconscious, I take another messy bite.

"There," Avitue says, encouraging. "Let go."

When only a sliver of core remains, my lips are sticky with sugar, and I lick the last traces of juice from Avitue's fingers. The aura is heady and intoxicating now. I'm already breathing faster with want. Avitue sweeps me up into her arms as if I weigh nothing more than a doll. I nuzzle into the heat of her, sighing my pleasure.

She deposits me back in the luxurious mess of sheets, and I make a little noise of protest at the loss of contact. Avitue makes me wait, relishing the way my body squirms, all my attention trained on her as she circles the bed, observing and plotting.

"Such a gorgeous thing," breathes Avitue, finally settling beside me and stroking my hair. I lean into the touch, hoping for more, wanting to feel her hands on my skin. Her fingers tighten in my hair, restraining me. "You're getting impatient," she teases, considering. Her aura withdraws, and her face turns serious. "May I take your blood?"

I feel lightheaded, but I'm able to understand. Overcome, all I can manage is a nod. Avitue's aura washes over me again in a wave of warmth, cradling me.

"It will hurt, but only for a moment," she tells me.

Avitue straddles my hips, using one hand to pin my wrists over my head. With the other, she reaches between us to tease my clit. I gasp at the touch, bucking my hips up, seeking more sensation as Avitue presses her lips against my neck, kissing the line of my throat before finding the pulse of a vein with her tongue. The insistent rhythm of her fingers is a successful distraction from the pinch of her fangs, and my startled cry fades to a low moan as Avitue drinks. This drain is different than before, more gradual than when focused around the point of orgasm but no less intense. Her mouth is a delicious wet heat against my neck, and I relish the feel of her pleasured hum through my skin. Soon, the mingled pain and pleasure will push me over the edge.

When I next see Avitue's face, her lips are smeared red with my blood, and all I can think is how beautiful she is, how I would make an offering of my body every day to see the look of pure satisfaction on her face. She kisses me. The taste of my blood and the featherlight touch of her claws against my sensitive, heated flesh send me adrift in a storm of pleasure. I moan into her mouth, and she nips at my lower lip, the point of her fang finding fresh blood.

She releases my wrists as if to withdraw from me, as if she won't ask for more. I reach for her, careful to avoid resting my blessed palm against her.

"You always give me so much. Let me please you," I say before my courage fails me.

Amusement quirks her mouth. "You seem to be forgetting the fact that you're literally my meal. Feeding from someone I like is pleasure enough."

"But—"

I have trouble saying what I mean. Before Avitue, I never had to navigate conversations like this. The awkwardness of it persists.

"Oh. I see," she says, easily reading my desire. Her smile becomes a wicked grin. "Tell me exactly what it is you want."

"But you already know," I say, turning shy without the hungry insistence of her aura.

"It'll be much more fun for me to hear it from your lips," she says, looking down at me expectantly.

"I can't," I say, heat rising to my face.

I feel silly. My skin is damp with my own blood and sweat and arousal, and somehow I can't manage *this*. Avitue's eyes widen a fraction, and it's that look from before, the gaze that looks through me and into what my heart desires. She searches what she's found there like a predator who's caught the scent of blood.

"Look at you, all blushing innocence," Avitue coos, stroking my cheek with her sharp hand. "Won't you do it for me?"

My mouth is suddenly dry. "I want to make you come," I say, a whisper.

"Your imagination is specific. I want every gory detail," she says.

The words are on my tongue when holding her gaze becomes too much, but the moment I break eye contact, she catches my chin and brings me back to her.

"I want all your attention when you speak," she says.

I take a breath and push forward. "I want to taste you and make you come with my mouth. I want you—" I break off.

Avitue takes mercy on me, states bluntly, "You want me to sit on your face."

"Yes," I say, breathless.

"Thank you for indulging me. I want you to get comfortable asking for what you want—in bed or otherwise." She kisses me again. "It'd be cruel to make you beg now, although I do want to hear it. You sound so pretty when you're like this. Next time, perhaps."

And there *can* be a next time. Without the shadow of the past always over me, I can plan for things and truly look forward to them, even something as simple as pleasing a partner. We can have this life together and enjoy it.

Avitue turns softer, says, "You're adorable, you know that?"

"Why?"

"Because apparently, everything conjures up some wholesome desire on your part."

"I can't help it," I say, tracing her thigh with my unmarked hand. "Hopefully, it doesn't spoil your reputation to inspire wholesomeness."

Tension winds between us again. Avitue watches me, catlike in her study, as if she's waiting for any indication to pounce. I try to hold her gaze, my heart speeding in my chest. Can she hear it?

Eventually, she decides to stop holding me in suspense. I forget how to breathe as she positions herself above me, and I'm once more surprised by the evidence that *I* could excite her. I'm overwhelmed by the earthy damp heat of her, so close. She smiles down at me, and I rest my hands tentatively against her hips, as if touching her will disturb a pleasant dream. I don't know what I'm doing. I don't want to disappoint her.

"Cassiel." She says my name tenderly, threading her fingers through my hair. "I enjoy every moment with you."

Encouraged, I turn my head to kiss the inside of her thigh and taste her skin, closing my eyes to savor her as I work slowly toward my goal. Her contented hum becomes a sharp intake of breath at the barest tease of my lips against her clit, and I open my eyes in time to see the lavish arch of her back as she restrains herself from pressing into the touch. Witnessing her shiver of anticipation, I feel as if I'm adrift in her aura once more, though I know I'm not. This time, my own body compels me.

I'm vaguely aware of my fingers digging into her hips, of the desperate, hungry sound in the back of my throat as I explore the soft folds of her with my tongue, tasting the fullness of her arousal. I return to the sensitive point of her, alternating pressure and pace to find what startles a gasp or elicits a moan until she's no longer worried about me but bent on finding release. She rocks her hips into me, angling for greater sensation, and I take her swollen clit into my mouth, sucking until she cries out, bracing her hands against the headboard for support.

My name breaks in her mouth, the sound bitten off by a moan that urges me onward. She grinds into me, hungry, and I'm pinned by her weight in a new way. My tongue aches; the thought comes to me dimly, distantly. Avitue seems close, and it's all I care about.

"Cassiel," she gasps, pleading.

I continue to work at her with my tongue, finding a rhythm that makes her sigh, that has her punctuating all her praise with a gasp. I realize I want to feel her when she comes and bury two fingers inside her, three. She's so deliciously wet. If her body weren't pressing me into the bed, I might swoon at the realization that I did this, that I could please her this much. Avitue growls my name, says something that sounds like *more*, and I give her everything I can until I feel her clench around my fingers, a spasm of pleasure. I cling to her as she comes, and she utters my name once as a desperate cry, again as a satisfied exhalation.

No one's ever said my name this way, with so much focused attention, with all their breath. Avitue sinks into the pillows beside me, breathing hard though she doesn't need to. She kisses me with the evidence of her pleasure still on my lips, sighing against me.

"Was it everything you wanted?" she asks.

"Yes," I say, momentarily at a loss for words. Then, recalling what she once said to me, I repeat, "You wear desire beautifully."

She notices, laughs as she pulls me against her. The sheets are a shredded, bloodstained mess once more as I nestle my body into the warmth of Avitue's, seeking softness and comfort. She breathes a contented sigh against my neck, all the tension in her body gone.

"I've never taken several feedings from the same person," Avitue says. "Each time tastes better."

I hum thoughtfully. It's all I can manage through the postorgasm haze. I note the subtle shifts in the room's light as we laze in bed, late morning turning to early afternoon.

"Will you be okay?" Avitue asks.

Drifting contentedly at the edge of sleep, I don't immediately understand her question. "I feel better than okay," I mumble.

"I meant . . . Going home wasn't good for you."

I'm fine, an automatic reply, almost makes it to my lips. "I'll . . . be fine," I say instead. It's what I want to believe.

Avitue holds me tight, as if through touch alone we can merge into one body again.

"I should check the shop," I say sleepily. I don't move.

"I'll drive you," Avitue offers. She props herself up to get a better look at me and grins at what she sees. "You're an absolutely gorgeous mess."

It's flattering that Avitue thinks I'm gorgeous because, as I stand in her cavernous, sleek bathroom and find my reflection in the wide mirror, all I can focus on is the *mess* part of the description. By the amount of blood on my neck and shoulder, I look as if I've been gently mauled.

Her shower alone feels large enough to host a party in. Even though the space is done completely in dark-grey stone and tile, the placement of the lights and the spotless glass door make everything feel bright and open. I doubt Avitue has a reason to use this room at all. Like the empty refrigerator, it's all an act for no audience.

I'm trying to figure out how the fancy faucet works when a knock sounds at the door. "May I join you?" Avitue's voice follows.

I peer out of the shower. "Um, sure," I answer, expecting the door to open.

Instead, Avitue pops into the space in front of me, startling a squeak from my throat. I clap a hand over my chest and gulp down a breath.

She seems caught between apology and lust for a moment, eyeing me as if I've done something particularly attractive. "Your heart," she says, advancing until I feel the cold tiles against my back. "It sounds like a strong little bird with the most beautiful red wings." She seems to drink me in, the air between us somehow still charged even though I know she must be sated.

"Let me help you," she says, the array of showerheads springing on without so much as a glance on her part.

Resting her hands on my shoulders, she guides me into the spray. It's the perfect temperature and pressure, luxurious like everything else Avitue owns. I sigh, letting the warm water melt all the remaining tension in my shoulders. The water runs briefly red, and she watches the blood drain as if it's a regrettable waste, the first time she's taken her eyes off me. Steam fills the air, turning the glass doors opaque.

Avitue's voice is soft when she speaks. "What have I done to earn this? I thought I'd be alone forever. After a couple centuries, you start to think—" She suddenly won't meet my gaze. "I still can't believe you'd do all this for me."

"You defied Hell for me," I remind her.

"I'd do it again," she says, her eyes intense on me. "I'd do anything for you."

Avitue lathers soap in her hands and massages it into my skin, working her way down my body like a meditative exercise. She kisses a shoulder, a nipple, my belly, deadly serious the entire time. I keep respectfully quiet as if I've happened upon her amid a ritual only to realize that I'm its subject. When all the bubbles have drained, she kisses me, and I sigh into her, a release of breath to close the moment. She steps back, offering me the plush towel suddenly in her hands.

Without the blood on my neck, I find that where she bit me is already turning into what looks like the greatest love bite in the world. I lean toward the mirror and run my fingers along it gingerly, thrilled by the bold claim of it. Behind me, Avitue's wearing her satisfied smirk again.

"Do you want me to fix that?" she asks.

I cover the mark with my hand. "No. Although, if you have a scarf?"

I return to the bedroom, feeling refreshed both mentally and physically, and find that she's set out new clothes for me on the miraculously clean bed. They're not clothes I've ever worn before, but they're exactly my size in the colors I wear most often.

I plant a grateful kiss on her lips and say, "I don't know how I'm ever going to get used to this."

"Get used to what?" she asks, smiling against me.

"Everything. You," I say, overwhelmed again by the sense of possibility, of stepping into a new world and realizing it's mine.

FOURTEEN

I FIDGET WITH THE sword on my lap the entire drive to the bookshop. Avitue raised an eyebrow at me bringing it but didn't protest.

"They're not going to catch on to us," she says in an attempt to calm me.

"It's not demons I'm worried about," I say.

Avitue takes her eyes off the road for an uncomfortably long time to study me but doesn't say anything.

The door to the bookshop is unlocked when we arrive. Ana might have the keys, but I know she'd never forget to lock up. The lights are off. Avitue gives me a concerned glance.

"You can stay in the car," I say, my hand on the door.

"What's happening, Cassiel?" she finally asks.

I look through the dark glass, but I'm unable to see much inside. It's a beautifully sunny day. People push past us on the sidewalk, oblivious to the gathering tension.

"I think it's Gabriel," I say. "She wouldn't let this rest."

"I'm not leaving you with her alone. Not again."

"She could hurt you."

"I'm not leaving," she says, firm.

I consider arguing my point, but Avitue knows what we might be getting into. "Stay behind me. If she has her rapier, promise me you'll leave."

"But—"

"Promise."

Reluctantly, she nods.

We push into the gloom of the bookshop together.

My caution was for nothing. Gabriel wouldn't sneak around corners or crouch under counters. My mother isn't one to hide.

We find her sitting in my favorite chair in the reading nook at the back of the shop away from the windows. She's as relaxed as she'd be if this space were her office and she was expecting an appointment with us. She rises, a stiff smile the only change in her features. I hold out my arms, shielding Avitue behind me.

"I'm not here for your demon," she says, dismissing the assumption with a tired wave.

Gold wings gleam in her hand as she advances. I don't see any sign of her rapier, but there are a million other weapons she could be concealing. Again, I think of sparring. I force myself not to step back, not to give her ground.

She holds the emblem at eye level, her only threat. "Come home. Remember who you are."

I know she thinks she has me trapped. She's always had me trapped.

Avitue grabs for me as I step forward, but I give her a nod of reassurance and go to meet my mother for the last time. Shifting the sword to my left hand, I hold out my right to take the summons. Surprise flickers across Gabriel's face as she drops the emblem into my palm. She looks at me as if she doesn't know who I am, as if she can't recognize me when I'm not shrinking myself in her presence.

"I am home. And I know who I am," I say.

The angelic sigil on my palm glows, engulfing the token in radiance. Gabriel falls back, shielding her eyes from the burst of light. When the light dies, the token is gone, and I hold my palm out, the angelic sigil shining like a ward against her.

Only in rare moments have I seen Gabriel's impassive mask crumble. Even rarer for her to be at a loss for words.

This time, I don't even have to look at Avitue to find my wings. I feel loved. I feel cherished. My wings bloom into being even as tears sting my eyes.

"Mom," I try, the first time I've ever called her by that name.

She looks at me as if I've taken on some monstrous form, as if I'm exhibiting every telltale sign of possession and not shining with ethereal radiance.

"I tried to show you the right path. This isn't our way, Cassiel. These wings aren't proper," she says, a harsh whisper in the dark, and now I can identify that look.

Gabriel's not scared for me. She's scared of what this means for her. Anger seizes me.

"So you knew. You knew this entire time that there was another way to find our wings," I say, realizing that I punished myself for so long when there was always another known way.

In my entire life, Gabriel's never said she's sorry for anything, and I don't expect her to now, but the hurt on her face surprises me. "After your father's death, I just wanted to protect you girls. Especially you, Cassiel. You were so young."

"But—what does that have to do with my wings?"

Gabriel glances to Avitue as if loath to talk about our knowledge in her presence but then sighs, resigned. "You've told her too much, haven't you?"

I stand straighter, another act against regressing to my old self in her presence.

"I told you how my parents died," she says next, the words turning her cold again.

"You said they both died on a hunt."

"Do you know why the same thing didn't happen to you, why you weren't orphaned in one night?"

Ever since his death, the topic of that hunt has been strictly off-limits. Not through anything Gabriel explicitly said but implied through her overwhelming silence. Zuriel told me she removed all traces of our father from the house, as detached and efficient as going through the motions of a spring cleaning, and never showed her grief.

I tread carefully, worried she'll close up again. "I never thought about it that way."

"Of course not," she says, brushing me off as if I've always been a thoughtless, careless child. I bite my tongue. She continues, "My parents died on a hunt because they didn't follow our teachings, because like you, they found a way that seemed easier. Unlike drawing the strength of your light from your own inner discipline, relying on emotion opens you to unpredictability. As soon as anything disrupts your focus on the emotion you're drawing from—" She snaps her fingers, a grave look on her face. "Your wings are gone when you need them most."

Several tragic scenarios flash through my mind, each of them vivid and visceral despite Gabriel's lack of detail. I've witnessed enough death that it's not hard to imagine others, and the unexpected impact of it is enough to emotionally stagger me.

That's when Gabriel makes her move.

In a second, she has her wings—their span massive, the light overwhelming. I can't see her when she swats me aside with the tip of one wing, but I know instantly and with terrible clarity that she's going for Avitue. I collide with the edge of a shelf, its edge biting into my back and knocking the breath from my lungs. Catching my fall on my hands and knees sends a shock of pain through my joints that I can barely register. I need to rise, to fight. Tears blur the scene before me into the bright aura of Gabriel's wings.

Back on my feet, I raise the sword I've found still in my grasp. Hunter instincts don't fail. Even when stunned or surprised, you must hold to your weapon with everything you have.

Out of the brightness, the scene resolves. Gabriel. Rapier. Avitue, her head held back, the glint of the sword's edge at her throat.

"Gabriel," I say, the words too breathless and weak for what I feel.

I can't let her take more from me.

Fresh tears blur my sight, and I swipe them away, frustrated that my body's response to anger is crying. I've never been able to project the strength Gabriel wanted from me, and now I desperately wish that I could.

The threat's turned Avitue's appearance sharp again, her eyes wild gold when our gazes meet. My heart hammers. My throat constricts. My light surges even as my command over it falters. I'm suddenly too hot, too bright even for my own eyes, a star on the verge of supernova. Gabriel observes me, coolly disappointed, as if this is only another combat demonstration and she's proven her point again. I could never best her in a fight. How could I, feet away, while her sword is already at Avitue's throat, stop her now?

My light flickers down, wings dimming to an undefined haze before flashing back into form, two pairs, then one, then nothing, cycling as panic fully takes over.

"Return home where you belong," Gabriel says as if she's the one pleading with me. "I'll forget all this and spare the demon's soul."

"Don't," Avitue says immediately. "I'm not worth—"

"Please," I say, and I don't know who I'm saying it to—Gabriel to stop this or Avitue not to doubt her worth to me.

We've gotten this far.

Avitue witnesses the thought form, and she changes too.

"Cassiel," she says, the sound of her voice grounding. The startled fear in her eyes has gone, replaced by her confidence in me.

That's all I need. I find my breath. My light steadies. On instinct, I reach out with my marked hand again, find the line of the rapier's energy, and close my fist around its light.

Gabriel's eyes widen when she senses the energetic shift. I know I've done something, but I don't know what until Gabriel strains against the rapier's hilt as if attempting to tug it loose from thin air. Avitue takes the opportunity to gracefully sidestep Gabriel's reach like disentangling herself from an awkward dance partner.

"Go! I'll catch up," I tell her.

She hesitates for only the second it takes to make eye contact, but it's enough for Gabriel to recover from her surprise and consider alternative methods.

She reaches into her coat. Her wings stretch, readying for a charge. I feel my heartbeat in my chest and head, a single pulse that lasts forever.

My body thinks for me. *Stop her. Stop her.* I am only my intention.

I launch myself at Gabriel on the strength of my wings.

Avitue, freed from the immediate danger of the rapier's energy, vanishes. But I'm already on a collision course with Gabriel. Her initial target gone, she rounds on me, the dagger still pointed to kill. A reflex, an instinct. I snag the rapier from the air as I pass, use its edge to parry the dagger. Gabriel trips backward, and I, unused to the strength and speed of my wings, slam into her, sending us flying into a row of shelves.

Books rain down; wood creaks. We fall with the shelves as they domino into each other, heavy thud after heavy thud until they meet the wall with a final, ringing crash.

Under me, Gabriel hisses, and I can't tell whether it's in pain or anger. Her wings vanished on impact, but mine shine down on her.

"Are you okay?" I ask, realizing as I ask it that, even now, after all she's done, I don't want to hurt her.

She squints up at me. Freed from their bun, loosed strands of hair at her temples curl around her ears. At some point, I must've dropped the swords to avoid hurting her, but a clean cut on her cheek wells with blood.

Unbelievably, a grudging smile cracks her features. "Six wings. You'd never let me reveal your talents. And this is how you choose to use them." My time with Avitue has taught me how to see hunger, and I think I see it flash across Gabriel's face now—a possessive need that seeks control. "Six beautiful wings," she says, reaching to stroke my cheek.

I recoil. I don't feel any pride from her compliment, not after everything she's done. Almost thirty years for my own mother to say anything about me was beautiful. She suddenly looks at me as if I'm a marvel, an exquisitely crafted weapon. I'm still an object to her, but I've suddenly made myself into a desirable one.

My wings are only for me. I vanish them as I stand.

"Leave me and Zuriel to our lives. Please don't come back," I say, a gentle demand.

Gabriel stares, blinking as if still overcome by the light of my wings. I wish I could feel satisfaction at cutting myself off from her. It would be easier to feel smug at her disbelief, at the fact that I've accomplished things with my light she never has, but I'm surprised at how deep the loss cuts.

Gabriel stands and straightens her coat. "She'd smother your light. I'd nurture it," she says.

"You already had your chance," I say. "Please leave."

Her eyes dart to the rapier, abandoned on the floor. For a moment, I consider keeping it—out of spite, out of fear?—before retrieving it for her and handing it off. She holds it carefully as if seeing it for the first time, then sheathes it into an immaterial scabbard at her side. It vanishes, swallowed up by a spark of blue light, and with that, she turns on her heel and honors my request. The cheery front door chime sounds deeply out of place, and as it fades, I'm left standing alone in the dark mess of my shop.

She's gone, and I can breathe again.

Avitue appears at my side. "I'm sorry," she says eventually, clearly sensing that I feel no triumph here.

"I'm just glad it worked," I say, smiling through my tangle of emotions, through my tears.

Avitue's hands land on my shoulders, trace up my neck, and thumb away my tears. Her sharp hands are so soft. "You saved me," she says, her voice softened by awe.

"You saved me first," I say.

"I did *not*—"

"You did." I place my hands over hers and repeat, "You did."

The front door chimes again. We both pivot toward the sound, relaxing only when Zuriel calls my name. I go to her.

She's staring wide eyed at the mess but sighs in relief as soon as she sees me. "I felt Gabriel's light, then yours." She glances back at the mess. "You . . . fought her?"

Hearing Zuriel say it—I fought Gabriel!—grounds me. I fought our mother. Years ago, I could barely spar with her. Now, I can fight.

"She threatened Avitue," I say. "I had to."

Zuriel's gaze flicks to Avitue, and I know what she's thinking, an echo of Gabriel's own disbelief. I was a worthless hunter with no potential. I couldn't fight the demons, but I can fight *for* one.

"We're safe," I reassure Zuriel, raising my hand to my head as if I can measure weariness the same way I can take my temperature. I'm *tired*. I've never used so much of my light and never under such intense pressure. "I need to rest," I say.

Avitue pulls me against her. I gratefully accept the support as we walk out to the car. Tomorrow, I will fix the shop, process all the boxes that arrived in my absence, fill the online orders. Things will be the same but different. I'll have Avitue. I'll have my sister.

My hands shake too badly to fit the key in the lock. Too much energy too soon. The adrenaline, the light, all of it draining away at once and leaving my weary human body to stand on its own. But I can stand, and I do.

Zuriel takes the key from me, turns it in the lock, and pockets it.

"But I need . . ." I start, and then I see the shy smile on her face.

"I'll have to make a copy," she says. "One for me. If that's okay."

My throat is tight. I nod.

FIFTEEN

H ALLOWEEN NIGHT ARRIVES. ZURIEL mopes around Avitue's apartment, plucking at the ethereal string of her bow as if she's anticipating a fight will break out at any moment. Despite the halfhearted protests of Zuriel and me, Avitue drags us out to Ana's Halloween party, lecturing us on the sin of staying in on such a beautiful night.

Zuriel, still gravely serious, sets up her post for the night by an artful arrangement of pumpkins in the corner of Ana's suburban family home. Avitue tried to talk her into wearing something more appropriate to a casual party, but she's dressed herself in her usual clothes, leading people to guess at various high-powered businesswomen she must be dressed up as. When she didn't indulge them, it didn't take them long to give up. Glass of punch in hand, she takes in the rest of the room with a scientific interest, her stony expression warding off anyone with a goal of socializing. I stand at her side, using her presence as a shield. I'm very successful. No one tries to talk to me either.

We witness Avitue become the life of the party, drawing every normal human into her web of influence. She's innocent of any intention, the energy of the night catching her in its current. She's pure magnetism and charm. She's terrifying and beautiful and terrifyingly beautiful. This is her night, and she refuses to hide.

Someone asks where she got her fangs, and she beams and says she grew them herself. Another asks about her eyes—bright and raptor sharp. They've never seen such arresting contacts, they say. Avitue leans in to whisper something in their ear, and they look scared and aroused all at once. She spins tales about her life that sound ridiculous but are likely true. She asks invasive questions that people are all too willing to answer. When someone inquires about what she does for work, she says she's a contracted assassin and that she has, in fact, strangled a man to death in the grip of her thighs. Impossibly, everyone laughs.

"She's at the height of her power," Zuriel observes wryly.

"You're uncomfortable," I say.

"I'm—" Zuriel bites her lip. "I'm confused."

"You still don't trust her."

I'm hurt by the realization as I say it. Zuriel feels like the only family I have left, and I want her to at least trust Avitue. This time, when I start over, I want to keep my sister in my life.

"*You* trust her. I don't have a reason not to. She's not doing anything particularly *evil*."

Avitue's attention snaps to us from across the room. Waving off her new admirers, she saunters back over to us, an easy swing in her hips.

"I'm *very* evil, I'll have you know. Do not discredit me," she says to Zuriel as she drapes herself around my shoulders. She kisses the pulse at my throat, a move I'm sure serves only to fluster Zuriel, and bats her eyelashes innocently. "Do you feel the energy tonight? It's so good. I want blood. So much blood." Zuriel looks properly stricken now, and Avitue continues, "We could do it the humane way, even. Break into a blood bank or something."

"That's still illegal," Zuriel says, composing herself now that she's realized Avitue's only teasing.

"But you two are so *not evil* that maybe you could convince them to hand over the blood. Save me from a life of crime."

"Uh-huh," Zuriel says, unamused.

But Avitue doesn't register her long-suffering look. She's going for the table of food, leaping onto it, and rising with the bowl of punch in her hands. Everyone turns to look at her. Ana's mother covers her mouth with one hand.

"I'd like to propose a toast!" Avitue says.

Several people whistle and applaud. Ana shoots me a concerned look from across the room.

"Avi—" I start, taking one brave step away from my sister's side.

"I am ready to renounce my demonic ways," Avitue announces triumphantly. "I'm going to live an upstanding human life with my girlfriend, Cassiel, an absolute angel and a treasure!"

Cheers go up. People turn to find me in the crowd. Avitue chugs the entire bowl of punch.

Ana appears at my side just as I'm about to combust from embarrassment.

"I'm so sorry," I start rambling. "I know it's your special recipe and—"

But Ana seems unworried by that. Instead, she takes my hand and marches both of us over to the table where Avitue's hopping down. She's practically glowing, but her grin fractures when she sees Ana's downturned mouth.

"I get that you're in the throes of some kind of spiritual high right now, but you need to get it together," Ana says, poking a finger into Avitue's chest.

Avitue looks bewildered to have someone standing up to her, to find a *mere human* capable of being angry—and with *her*.

"I can replace your punch?" Avitue says, her eyes all wide innocence.

"It's not about the drinks! You're embarrassing Cass. Go spend time with her. Stop charming all my guests."

Avitue blinks. "I'm so sorry, Cassiel," she says, her party girl attitude instantly sobering to sincerity.

"I'm okay," I say automatically.

"You don't have to say you're okay when you're not okay," Ana says. She steps back, pointing from me to Avitue. "I support this unlikely union, but I love Cassiel. Be careful with her, okay?"

Avitue nods as if she's taking an oath.

"Good. Now I'm going to go talk your sister out of her corner," Ana says to me. Then, with a smile, she adds, "I should've known inviting angels and demons to my party would be high maintenance."

"We're not angels," I say meekly, but Ana's already turned away, and I'm drowned out by the conversation and music.

Avitue and I are left staring at each other, the empty punch bowl held between us.

"I'm sorry," she says again.

"Ana's protective of me," I say, staring down at my shoes like a shy girl at prom.

"I can understand that," Avitue says.

She returns the punch bowl to the table, freshly refilled in the blink of an eye. Inevitably, several people notice.

"Are you a magician too?" one of them asks.

Avitue wraps me in her arms. "No. Just a regular demon," she says with a wink.

She draws me away from everyone else and out into the crisp, quiet air of the garden. On the other side of the glass doors, the party goes on, sparkling and muted. I draw my coat tighter around me while Avitue is serene in only her tiny black dress.

"I can't believe we made it here," I say, looking up at the cold slice of moon. "We get to live now."

"We do," Avitue says. "How do you want to live?"

She asks it so casually, but it's such a huge and existential question. I grapple with it until I realize I don't have to know the answer now, that every moment I've been making that decision in big and small ways.

"I could always use another business partner," I say, glancing sidelong at her.

Avitue gasps excitedly, and I think she barely restrains herself from jumping up and down like a child. "I can go deep into my human persona. Become a book influencer for real. Carry all your boxes forever. Charm your landlord into zero rent." She gasps again. "Make them hand over the deed."

"That would be very devious."

"Oh no." She grins. "This is using my power for good."

I laugh. The future continues to open up before me. I can project into it and, for once, see myself happy.

Avitue offers her hand. "We can't leave a party without dancing."

"But I can't dance. And there's no music out here."

"We can do that thing where we hold each other and sway gently. Plus, there's the night energy. It's as good as any song."

I'm so swept up in the moment that I don't think when I reach for Avitue with my marked hand—and neither does she.

Our hands meet with the *pop* of electricity, and Avitue's taken with a violent full-body shiver that leaves her hair frizzy but nothing worse. She jerks her hand back from me, grimacing as she shakes it.

I rush to apologize. "Oh my god, I'm so sorry." I fist my hands in my hair, the reality of how bad that could've been thoroughly setting in. The mark's potential effect on Avitue was a huge unknown, something I was afraid could banish her or worse. Gifts from angels were never harmless to demons.

Yet when Avitue recovers and inspects her hand, she bears the same glimmering mark on her palm.

"Holy shit," she breathes, cradling one hand in the other as if her marked hand has become a foreign object to her. "What the hell? What the fuck?"

She goes on like that for a moment, cursing in soft wonder. Eventually, English seems unable to contain the depth of her feeling, and she resorts to the infernal tongue. Under her breath, it becomes sing-whispering. In time, the mark fades.

"What do you think this means?" she asks, meeting my eyes again.

I hover my hand close to hers, and the mark flares bright.

"It goes dormant, but it's still there," I say. "I don't know if it responds to me or to ethereal energy in general."

"We don't even know what the mark means for you yet," she says, watching the lines of white-blue light fade from her skin again.

I hum my agreement.

"At least I know your namesake doesn't hate me," she says. "Never thought I'd get the approval of anyone up there again."

"I told you you're very likable."

She hushes me playfully. "Not so loud. I need to be taken seriously." Folding me into her embrace, she whispers into my ear, "Do you feel the night music?"

"I swear you're making this up."

"I'm not," she says, giggling. "Ana knows about it. Just feel. It's mellowing out now."

I slip out of my physical awareness for a moment to find a thread running through the night like a pulse, a joyous heartbeat.

"I see," I say, leaning into her.

She moves, and I follow her lead.

<hr>

I return to Zuriel to find her with the same drink in her hand that she started the night with. She's moved from her initial corner into another, but at least Ana's with her this time. Whatever they were talking about, Zuriel breaks off when she sees Avitue. Ana turns to see us, smiling through the awkwardness as if she can smooth things over through sheer will. Avitue shrugs it off and reroutes herself toward the drinks, leaving us alone.

"What's wrong?" I ask Zuriel.

"Can I stay at your place tonight?" she asks.

"Sure," I say, a thousand questions brewing as I hand over my apartment key.

Ana makes an excuse about needing to tend to something in the kitchen, and we're back where we started, my sister and I huddled alone at our first party.

"It's the energy in Avitue's apartment," Zuriel starts. "Nothing about her seems grounded. Nothing feels *true*."

"But you said she's not lying. This morning, you didn't seem upset. You said you slept well."

"I don't mean that. I mean—" She sighs, switching her full drink to the other hand. It seems like a prop, an attempt to blend in. "I was way too tired to piece it all together the first night, but I was talking through my impressions just now with Ana. The apartment is nice, but I don't think it's real. I noticed it when I took a shower this morning. Like I was in some kind of demonic otherworld."

I think of the pocket dimension in the bookshop. Maybe the apartment isn't quite so unattached from reality but is still something she's fabricated, at least partially.

"She's so powerful," Zuriel says with an edge of frustration, as if she's run up against some unsolvable problem. "Imagine if she were interested in anything other than having a good time."

Across the room, Avitue's inevitably collected a new posse of admirers. Regardless of whether she intends to charm anyone, she does. Regaling them with another story, she dips into a mocking bow, playing out some interaction she had with a dead prince.

"And you," Zuriel adds. "It scares me that a demon with the kind of power I sense in her is interested in you."

"What are you saying?" I ask, my attention fully back on Zuriel now.

"She's lived for all of time following her whims. What if her thing with you is just—"

"Stop," I say, my heartbeat turning fierce.

As if attuned to the nuances of my pulse, Avitue stammers to a halt in her story, peering over her audience to me as if to check in, to make sure I'm okay.

"My namesake," I say, holding out my marked hand to show Zuriel. "Avitue carries the same mark now. That means something."

Zuriel studies the sigil on my palm, frowning. When she meets my eyes again, I curl my fingers over it protectively, holding it to my chest.

"She's angel-marked?" Zuriel asks.

I nod.

"That's never— Contact with an angelic sigil should at least maim her, maybe even kill her."

"I know."

Zuriel laughs, high and strained. She shakes her head, throws back her drink, and wanders off, saying that she needs a glass of water. I trail after her, worrying my hands.

"This is impossible. You're both impossible," Zuriel mutters under her breath between sips.

Someone ambles over to the table of food where bat-shaped cookies and cubed fruit are set out. We watch them refill their plate, oblivious to the unprecedented spiritual shift in the laws of the universe.

"Do you— Are you—" I try several questions and finish none of them.

Zuriel snatches a bat cookie and stuffs it whole into her mouth. She shakes a finger at me and downs another glass of water. I wait.

"Congrats on having your relationship blessed by an angel? What am I supposed to say?" She finds another cookie bat and bites off its wing. "You are truly terrifying."

"In a . . . good way?"

"Terrifying," Zuriel repeats, devouring the bat. "My own little sister."

Zuriel finds Ana to thank her and say goodbye, explaining that she's been "overwhelmed by insight" and needs time alone to think. Ana nods sagely and clasps Zuriel's hands in hers, thanking her for attending the party as if her presence was of great spiritual importance. Maybe it was.

Avitue's beginning to eye a man's throat a little too intensely from across the room. I wrangle her attention and return to Ana to say our own goodbyes. She calls tonight *auspicious* and offers a reading anytime we should need it.

Upon returning to Avitue's apartment, I pay closer attention when I cross the threshold. Just as I thought, it's not like the space in the store's back room, but there is *something*. Before I can puzzle through it, Avitue literally sweeps me off my feet. My startled yelp melts into laughter as she ferries me across the cold floor and into the soft warmth of the bed.

The city below is so bright that, even with the lights off, the bedroom is barely dark. I snuggle into Avitue, running my fingers through her hair, braiding by muscle memory and feel alone. I'm sure they'll be terrible braids. I'm sure I'm only distracting myself from the beauty of her, but she's happy to let me do it if it gives me something to do with my anxious hands.

We ruined and rebuilt my life in such little time, stronger and taller and brighter than it could have been without the destruction.

Avitue hums contentedly. "I love your hands in my hair."

She turns to kiss my knuckles, my palms, all the way up to my neck, my cheeks, my lips. She captures me in her embrace, and I think I could spend eternity lying in bed with her, safe in her arms. I say as much.

"When the time comes, I want to be like you," I say.

She moves back to hold my gaze. "It would hurt, Cassiel. And your light would become . . . something different."

"I want to stay with you. I don't want to give this up," I say. "I love you."

Avitue seems awestruck by my words. "You said I could love."

"If you want to, you can."

"Then I want to love you," she says.

Like a promise.

THE
BLOOD
THAT
BINDS
US

CASSIEL & AVITUE'S STORY
WILL CONTINUE

newsletter updates at tamarajeree.com

ACKNOWLEDGEMENTS

I began writing *The Fall* as an unemployed and depressed recent graduate struggling through the first year of the pandemic. I wanted to write a sapphic forbidden romance, something fun and escapist, hence the fairytale of the small bookstore and the cozy coffeeshop. But as with all my projects, I realized the true story was deeper.

Drafting and revising this book changed the course of my life and became an act of trusting myself.

I couldn't have done this without the kindness of those closest to me. Thank you to every friend who encouraged me, heard my anxious rambles, and provided a safe place for me to be myself. To my friends who read my drafts and provided feedback and encouragement: Devan Soyka and Carey Ford Compton, two great writers who I admire and trust with my work. To my writing mentors in the video games industry, Olivia Wood and Kait Tremblay, for cheering me on when things were hard and telling me it would get better. And again, to Olivia for providing the kinds of edits that made me a better writer overall. I edit with your voice in my head.

I wouldn't be the writer I am today without the time to flail and think and find my voice in my MFA program. Thank you to my instructors there: Terese Marie Mailhot, Brian Leung, and Sharon Solwitz. A huge thank you to Jeanne Cavelos and my Odyssey Writing Workshop peers for so sharply pointing out my strengths as well as places for growth.

Thank you to the amazing folks who turned this manuscript into a book. To Syd Mills for running with my wild idea for a riff on The Creation of Adam and amazing me at every phase. I couldn't imagine a better cover for my debut. To my designer Fay Lane for the amazing logo and perfect finishing touches. And finally, to my editor Maggie Morris. Thank you for your kind, insightful edits on my manuscript. You made my work truly shine.

And finally, thank you, reader, for holding this dream in your hands.

A Wolf Steps in Blood
An F/F Wolf Shifter Novella

UNDER THE FULL MOON, the wolf vomits ice cream, spring rolls, and chocolate almonds—the evidence of a binge from when she had fingers and walked upright. Though she's no stranger to the burn of stomach acid, it still sears her throat. Looming rain and blood dominate her senses. A few paces beyond where she shelters in the bushes, her pack feasts on a deer. She buries her purge and joins the others, their heads ducked down to rend flesh from bone. Nudging between two cousins, she noses the carcass enough to bloody her fur, taking small, dainty snatches of meat. She feels empty and light when the pack sends up a howl to honor the big sky. Her voice is the smallest of them all.

◆

After the hunt and the free air and the moon, all that's left of the night is the very human task of brushing my teeth. I watch my reflection and try not to think of statistics about stomach acid and enamel loss. We've lost so much that eroding the strongest, sharpest parts of myself makes a grim kind of sense. My ancestors didn't evolve for this. What use are teeth against the systems that haunt my family, my pack?

Even to my human nose, my room, my hair, my skin reek of processed meat and old fryer grease. No matter how regularly I wash my work uniform, no matter how often I shower, the smell infects everything. Only when I am a wolf can I shed its pervasive stench.

I let my hair down—long braids done by my cousin, always tied up under a visor for work—and collapse into bed. Tonight, I miss the rasp of the cicadas, that rural Alabama summer soundtrack. When winter arrives, I have trouble sleeping without them.

My cousin paces on the other side of the trailer's thin walls, the pattern of her steps suggesting that she's returned to her wolf. I sit up, think of checking in on her. Back when she had a bad boyfriend, the kind who blackened her eye, she'd spend more and more alone time as a wolf. I never asked whether she did it because she felt powerful that way or because she felt safe. In the end, they were the same. Power was safety.

One night, she came home rabid, howling, snarling. Half-wolf, half-woman. I'd never seen one of us that way, turned monstrous by grief or rage. Mom didn't help her or ask what was wrong. She calmly sent her away, telling her to come back after she'd had a run through the woods and gotten her head back on straight.

But Shiara returned manic, a spine clenched in her jaws. Wolves are no strangers to gore. I'd licked blood from thousands of bones. But unlike the hunt, this violence was different. Though she was a wolf, this violence was fully human. On the trailer steps, Mom held out her hands, and Shiara, like a pedigreed dog, obediently dropped the spine. I watched from behind the screen door as if the drama unfolding outside of it was on a television. Mom walked into the trees with the spine, and neither she nor Shiara ever spoke of the incident. I waited in fear for months thinking cops would show up to the trailer, but when the grisly story faded from the papers and no one came for us, my insomnia loosened its grip.

Shiara keeps one of his finger bones in her pocket, worrying it smooth like a river stone. Sometimes she sits on the back step and stares into the trees for hours. If I see the flash of white in her hand, I leave her be.

I try to roll over and ignore her pacing, but my worry only coils tighter. I knock on her door, my light tap rattling the thin wood in its frame. The pacing stops. I set my blunt nails against the door and scratch thrice. Our little sign, *Are you okay?*

The door swings open, revealing darkness beyond. She says nothing, only observes me, her wolf eyes glinting from the hall light. Half-wolf, half-woman. She's the only one of us who can maintain this partial shift so effortlessly, inhabiting the liminal as if born to it. Wolf eyes in a human face. Wolf teeth crowding a human mouth. Furred chest exposed by the deep cut of her camisole.

"Was the hunt good for you tonight?" I ask.

"*I* took down the deer," she says, voice low and raspy. "Javier's a fucking liar, and he knows it." She tilts her head, sizing me up. "You never try to take down the deer."

I fidget. "It's not really my thing."

Shiara steps closer. "Blood isn't your thing? Hunger isn't your thing? I want to tear out the throat of the world." She stabs a finger into my chest. "You do too." She smiles. Wolf teeth in a woman's face. "Goodnight, Yasmine."

The door shuts gently, soundlessly. On the other side a rending noise cuts the silence, as if Shiara's tearing up the carpet. I go to bed.

◦―◦◆◦―◦

Cleaning the restaurant bathrooms is one of my favorite tasks, and everyone is happy to let me volunteer each shift. Scrubbing toilets is the best way to exit the bustle of filling orders and putting on a customer service face. Sometimes, on the days when Mom has treated me to a cold silence, I use the time to cry into the soapy water. The witch blessing was too strong in her. She'd lost her wolf while the magic manifested as intended in me. I could return to the wilderness, and she resented me for it. Some days her jealousy was louder than others. I never reveled in the change and the hunt like my pack. The shift frightened me. My body changing frightened me. It was painful. I told Shiara this after a hunt once. She didn't understand. "Better than an orgasm," she'd said under a half moon.

Working at Tim's isn't too bad. I've managed an entire year here, one of three greasy restaurants in town. Mom complains of heartburn whenever I bring home the chicken left over after closing, so Shiara devours it all. The building is clearly an old Dairy Queen that closed decades ago, the chain's logo painted over in blue and the name *Tim's* hand lettered in white.

Ruthie, the owner—Tim was her grandfather—is one of few people outside the pack who I can feel comfortable with. She defends me against asshole customers who want to talk to the manager (joke's on them) and once, at closing, asked why I never had any cute boys come pick me up from work. I knew it was a well-meaning question she meant as a compliment. So many of my coworkers had husbands or boyfriends who were their rides home. Men were always trying to flirt with me as I rang out their orders. Ruthie, as I'd feared, observed it all. I fumbled for an excuse, certain that if she continued with her reasoning, I'd find myself fired over some little incident and never able to get a job in Pickens County again. People talk, and news spreads fast. These old white ladies would shut me out and turn nice-nasty.

Some of my panic must've shown through in my silence because guilt rearranged her features. "I'm sorry, hun," she said. "I wasn't trying to pry. You're good here." And she put her hand firmly down on the counter as if planting a shield between us and the rest of the world. "You understand me?" I surprised her and myself by bursting into tears on the spot, a fistful of bills I'd been counting clutched in my hand.

I'm dragging a bag of trash from the bathroom when the restaurant door swings open. This late, most locals prefer the drive-through, but travelers trying to eke out a few miles before turning in for the night like to come in as an excuse to stretch their legs. Pickens County scrapes by because of Highway 82 running through its heart. Our town boasts a total of two stoplights and three gas stations. Turn off the highway and onto Main Street and all you'll find are boarded-up shops. Keep exploring the county and you'll meet acres of farmland (corn, soy, grazing pastures) and dilapidated barns.

At first, I don't pay the customer much attention other than my automatic greeting. There's something about having a giant bag of literal garbage in hand that makes you avoid eye contact at all costs. But the autumn breeze that blows in with them hits me full in the face with bitter herbs, so acrid that they overwhelm the permanent grease and potatoes smell. My lips peel back from my teeth in disgust. Who would wear such a nasty perfume? I make the mistake of looking up.

Mistake because she's beautiful and very human and very much a witch. My gaze sweeps her up and down, frantic, but I can't see the herbs she carries. A length of tarnished silver chain disappears into the V of her shirt. The likely source, I think—a sachet of herbs securely held against the chest. But as my gaze flicks back to her eyes, I realize what this looks like.

"I'm sorry." I apologize because what is there to say during an unexpected standoff with a witch you've unintentionally ogled? I resume my shamed trash-carrying gaze when she stops me.

"I've never met a wolf before," she says, her voice and smile soft. Her hand is outstretched between us like she's caught herself in the human instinct of reaching out to pet a cute dog.

Despite the sting of the herbs, the wolf claws her way up my spine and stomps to the front of my brain, tail wagging, tongue lolling. Her excitement knocks me back. My wolf doesn't like strangers, and she likes surprises less. I once bit a man for trying to get too familiar with me in a dark parking lot. With the force of the wolf behind me, even my human teeth drew blood. He yanked back the offending hand, and suddenly I was a *crazy bitch*.

But this time, with this woman, the wolf wants to rub my face against her and mingle our scents. I'm dizzied by the passion behind it, the life-or-deathness of the desire, as if looking away from the witch will mean certain doom. My wolf has never been so irrational, and it scares me. Whatever she's feeling has brought down a sudden fever, and between the heat and the dizziness, I'm desperate to escape into cool, fresh air.

"I have to throw this away," I blurt, pushing for the door and the night.

By the time I cross the small parking lot to the dumpster, my thoughts are spinning. I haul the bag in and wander into the woods just behind. In the distance, a lumbering beast of a train rumbles along its tracks. Small animals scramble away from my clumsy steps. I walk and walk, muddying my shoes, snagging low branches in my hair. One catches my visor and knocks it to the ground. I can't find the blue of the fabric in the night's depths, and unlike Shiara, I can't shift only my eyes.

Light blooms a few paces away. The witch. She holds a glowing crystal aloft, and I immediately forget my visor. I want to run to her, wagging my tail. I want her to grasp my fur in her hands. I want to guard her with my life. The intensity of the thoughts turns me so dizzy I can barely take stock of her. She inches nearer as if I'm truly a wild animal who will dart again at a moment's notice. I hold my breath as she bends to retrieve my visor.

"I'm Kalta," she says, holding the visor out to me.

I don't take it. I stare at her, wonder and fear continuing to wage their war.

Her leather jacket is well worn and oversized as if she stole it from a brother. She's buzzed her natural hair close to the scalp and managed to bleach it an impressive platinum.

"Yasmine," I say, my name scraping out of my throat.

She echoes me, and that's when I see my own wonder reflected in her eyes.

"When's your shift over?" she asks, and my attention zeroes in on her full lips, stained a red so deep they're almost black.

My panicking heartbeat threatens to turn me ill.

"I'm done in an hour," I finally manage to answer, "but I wouldn't ask you to wait that long."

She closes the distance between us and resettles the visor on my head as if we're attending a private coronation in Alabama's backwoods.

"I'd wait for you," she says.

———◇———

An old blue Silverado is parked alone on one side of the lot. Abby, a young gossipy mom who usually gives me a ride home on the nights we close together, eyes me curiously as I turn down her offer and recite an excuse about a friend picking me up. I've never had a friend pick me up.

My heart races as I approach the truck, certain of Abby's gaze on my back. Through the truck window, I see Kalta slouched down in the driver's seat, her feet propped up on the peeling dash. I rap my knuckles on the window like a nervous fool. She startles as if I've jolted her from a daydream and dives across the bench seat to unlock the door. It squeals on its hinges as I pull it open, and despite Kalta being sprawled on her stomach, the truck is so high that we're nearly face-to-face again. She giggles and holds out her hand. I take it, bracing myself with her strength as I step up and pull the door closed behind me. We resume staring at each other until I blurt the most irrelevant thing.

"Nice truck," I say. I'm not sure whether I actually think it's nice, but it's the kind of short small talk my anxiety chooses. Not *Who are you?* or *Where are you going?* or *Did you also feel the stars realign?*

"Thanks," she answers easily. "It's seen more decades than me, but I get where I need to go, and that's what matters, right?" She opens her mouth to say more but stops herself.

The wolf in me takes note. I might not have the enhanced senses that come with a shift, but my nose has always been slightly better than the average person's. And we can tell when someone's nervous. Or lying. The cabin doesn't smell strongly of her, though the herbs are just beginning to settle into the upholstery. It smells like a man. And beneath his scent, the tang of old blood.

So—stolen jacket. I was right before, though not in the way I'd anticipated. I'd thought *stolen* lovably, affectionately. *Stolen* as in *I wore it so much it kinda just became mine.* *Stolen* as in *You can have this thing I love.* Stolen jacket. Stolen truck?

Did I just hop into a stolen truck for a pretty girl? Fuck. *Fuck.*

I glance over my shoulder and find Abby's car still idling in its spot. Her attention is down on her phone, but I know only a second ago she was probably staring at us.

"Kalta—" I start.

But my swift catalog isn't lost on her. "It's not what you think," she says.

My hand is back on the door. I'm already thinking of all the ways I can revise what I said and still get a ride home from Abby.

"It's my brother's truck," Kalta says. "He got into an accident, and I'm—" She cuts herself off again.

"What kind of accident?" I ask because clearly the truck is fine.

"Magic," she says, her eyes bright with tears.

The scent of blood. Magic that deals in blood is never safe, and if Kalta is involved in that magic, neither is she. The danger of what I nearly stepped into shocks me out of the fairytale cloud I lost my head in. I don't know Kalta. I don't know *who she is or where she's going*.

"I need to go," I say.

Kalta stares down at the cracked upholstery of the seat, resigned. I hoped she would explain, tell me something to make this all less alarming than it is, but her silence is damning. The truth is worse than whatever I could glean in a couple seconds.

The door practically shrieks when I open it.

"I'm sorry, Yasmine," she says, and it sounds like a plea.

Her fear and sadness tug on the fairytale, the wolf, the mystical *correctness* of us together. But wolves have enough problems as it is. I don't need to add more.

I hop out of the truck and slam the door. I feel dizzy, gutted. I fight for my breath as I walk, head down, to Abby. My steps are heavy as if I'm fighting against a current that's pushing me back to her, to Kalta.

Abby raises an eyebrow as I slump into her passenger seat. "Not your ride?" she asks.

"She was just bothering me for money," I say.

Abby sucks her teeth. "Honey, you don't need those type of friends."

She pats my knee in sympathy and turns us onto the highway. I glance up at the rearview mirror and watch until Kalta's blue truck melts into the dark.

Available in ebook and paperback

ABOUT THE AUTHOR

Tamara Jerée (they/them) is a Chicago-based bookseller. Sharp/soft sapphic pairings are their specialty; vampires and demons are their best friends. Their short stories have appeared in the Shirley Jackson Award-winning anthologies *Unfettered Hexes: Queer Tales of Insatiable Darkness* and *Professor Charlatan Bardot's Travel Anthology*. *The Fall That Saved Us* is their debut novel and a finalist for the Indie Ink Award.

instagram.com/tamarajeree

twitter.com/TamaraJeree

www.tamarajeree.com